NOTHING BUT THE TRUTH

Johnny Mack slammed his fist in the palm of his hand. "Why marry a man you'd refused to marry a dozen times over just to keep Sharon from aborting her baby?"

Lane swiped the tears from her cheeks. "He was your baby! All that I had left of you. I wouldn't allow anyone to harm him! Not then and not now."

Johnny Mack remained silent. His throat closed tightly. He'd known Lane had had a crush on him for years before he'd left town, but he'd had no idea the depth of her feelings for him. She was probably the only woman in his entire life who had ever loved him. And loved him so unselfishly.

He wanted to reach out and take her in his arms, but he could tell by her wary stance that she didn't want him to touch her. She had loved him fifteen years ago, but how did she feel about him now? How much had the passing of fifteen years, marriage to Kent and a lifetime of lies changed Lane?

"I was very foolish back then, wasn't I? I've grown up a lot since then. I've learned a great deal about love. What it is and what it isn't." Lane's voice softened and trailed off quietly. "I was so infatuated with you. Will is the only thing that matters to me now. I would do anything to protect him."

"Even murder Kent?"

"Yes," she said. "Even murder Kent."

Books by Beverly Barton

AFTER DARK

EVERY MOVE SHE MAKES

WHAT SHE DOESN'T KNOW

THE FIFTH VICTIM

THE LAST TO DIE

AS GOOD AS DEAD

KILLING HER SOFTLY

CLOSE ENOUGH TO KILL

MOST LIKELY TO DIE

THE DYING GAME

THE MURDER GAME

COLD HEARTED

SILENT KILLER

DEAD BY MIDNIGHT

DON'T CRY

Published by Zebra Books

After Dark

Beverly Barton

ZEBRA BOOKS
KENSINGTON PUBLISHING CORP.
http://www.kensingtonbooks.com

ZEBRA BOOKS are published by

Kensington Publishing Corp.
119 West 40th Street
New York, NY 10018

All Kensington titles, imprints, and distributed lines are available at special quantity discounts for bulk purchases for sales promotion, premiums, fund-raising, educational, or institutional use.

Special book excerpts or customized printings can also be created to fit specific needs. For details, write or phone the office of the Kensington Special Sales Manager: Attn. Special Sales Department. Kensington Publishing Corp., 119 West 40th Street, New York, NY 10018. Phone: 1-800-221-2647.

Zebra and the Z logo Reg. U.S. Pat. & TM Off.

ISBN-13: 978-1-4201-1893-3
ISBN-10: 1-4201-1893-5

First Printing: December 2000

10

Printed in the United States of America

To the important men in my life, from whom I've learned what intriguing, complicated, infuriating, incredible, fascinating and irresistible creatures the male of our species can be. Dee Inman, Sr., Houston Montgomery, Dee Inman, Jr., Billy Beaver, Brant Beaver, Roger Waldrep and Braden Waldrep.
And a special thank-you to my dear friend, Wendy Corsi Staub, for her support, encouragement and understanding.

Prologue

Your son needs you. Come home.

Johnny Mack Cahill read the note again. The damned thing didn't make a bit of sense. He didn't have a son, and his home had been here in the Houston area for the past fifteen years. He turned the hand-printed message over, noting the college-ruled notebook paper on which it had been written. Picking up the legal-size envelope he had tossed on the sofa along with his other mail, he tried to read the smeared postal service marking. All he could make out was "AL" and "35."

Alabama? Who from Alabama would be writing to him after all these years? Although he still sent Lillie Mae money from time to time, she never wrote to him. And he hadn't left behind anybody else who cared whether he lived or died. Or had he?

Who would be sending him such a cryptic message?

Come home. Home to Alabama? Home to Noble's Crossing? Hell would freeze over first!

Holding the envelope up to the light, Johnny Mack saw the shadow of something that hadn't fallen out along with the mysterious, succinct letter. He tapped the envelope. Two objects dropped to the open edge. He reached inside with the tips of his thumb and forefinger, then pulled out a folded newspaper clipping and a school photograph.

Shoving the remainder of his mail to the left sofa cushion, he sat down and looked at the color photo. The face of a handsome teenage boy stared up at him. A tight knot formed in the pit of Johnny Mack's stomach. There was something familiar about that young face, those sharp cheekbones, those dark eyes, that flirtatious smile. Looking at the picture was like looking into a mirror and seeing the reflection of the boy he had been twenty years ago.

Come home. Your son needs you. Quickly scanning the article, Johnny Mack discovered that a fourteen-year-old boy in Noble's Crossing, Alabama, had been suffering from amnesia since the day of his father's brutal murder. His mother, Lane Noble Graham, was considered the number one suspect, but as of yet had not been formally charged.

Johnny Mack stared at the newspaper photograph of *the suspect.* Lane. Dear God! Lane Noble. His gaze traveled back and forth from the school photograph of the boy, who someone claimed was his son, to the picture of Lane Noble, the boy's mother. Lane Noble *Graham.* Hell, had Lane actually married Kent Graham? He'd thought she was too smart to be taken in by that son of a bitch. Apparently not.

Come home. Your son needs you.

Whoever had sent him the message had made one crucial error—they assumed he and Lane had been lovers. They were wrong. Lane had been the one Magnolia Avenue debutante he'd never fucked. But she'd been the one he had wanted most.

Chapter 1

A loud clap of thunder momentarily drowned out the minister's words. Lillie Mae glanced at Miss Lane, standing so proudly at young Will's side, and noticed the way the boy held the huge, black umbrella over his mother's head. Protective. Caring. At fourteen, he was all long legs and arms. And piercing black eyes, so much like his father's.

"Ashes to ashes. Dust to dust." Reverend Colby ignored nature's comment on this event as he continued to spiel off the inane words that held little true comfort for anyone who had genuinely cared for the deceased.

A jagged bolt of lightning struck the earth nearby. Several ladies gasped loudly. Her body trembling, her face pale, Mary Martha Graham cried out and moved toward the open grave as if she intended to throw herself onto the coffin again.

Lord Almighty. Lillie Mae groaned silently. That was all this day needed—for crazy Mary Martha to put on another show for the townsfolk. Hadn't they all endured enough having to listen to her hysterical tirade at the funeral, without having to witness more of her insane grief?

"Oh, Kent, I loved you." Mary Martha hovered over the steel gray casket. "You know I did. Please, brother, please come back. Don't leave me."

James Ware stepped forward and slipped his arm around his stepdaughter's waist, then drew her backward to once again stand between her mother and him. She turned quickly and buried her face against his chest, weeping uncontrollably.

Lillie Mae noticed the look of pity on Miss Lane's face and knew how much she longed to comfort her former sister-in-law. But due to the circumstances, it wouldn't be proper for the suspected murderess to offer a loving embrace to the deceased's grieving sister. Poor Miss Lane. It just wasn't fair that she might be arrested, her a good woman who had never done an unkind thing in her life.

The downpour continued, growing heavier as the graveside service progressed. A tepid, humid wind blew the rain beneath the dark burgundy tent under which the family had congregated. Lillie Mae stood with Miss Lane and Will, just outside the protective covering. When Will had been asked to join the Graham family, he had declined and instead stayed loyally at his mother's side.

Lillie Mae knew that people would say it was a bad day for a funeral. Some might even imply that the heavens were weeping for Kent Graham. Not likely. She considered the nasty weather a statement on Kent's life—dark, dreary, cold and destructive. That sorry SOB didn't deserve to be put to rest on a bright, sunny day. Indeed, if the day and the service had been an honest tribute to Kent, the devil would have popped up from hell, bringing fire and brimstone with him to singe the hallowed ground. Then Old Scratch would have personally escorted Kent's twisted soul straight to Hades.

When the service ended and the gathering dispersed, Mary Martha's shrill scream stopped the crowd's quiet departure. Lillie Mae glanced over her shoulder in time to see James Ware and Police Chief Buddy Lawler physically restrain Kent's *little sister*. She struggled with them like a madwoman, her wide-eyed gaze darting in every direction.

Edith Graham Ware tilted her regal head, every strand of her perfectly coiffured red hair untouched by the moisture in the air. She glanced casually at her overwrought daughter, then stabbed Lane with her sharp glare. The accusatory look in her green eyes issued her former daughter-in-law a warning. Lillie Mae didn't think many folks noticed that look. They were too busy watching Mary Martha being dragged, kicking and screaming, from the graveside. A shudder of foreboding racked Lillie Mae's bone-thin body. She knew the power the grande dame of Noble's Crossing had—enough to counteract any power Lane's family name possessed.

Lane reached out, slid her arm through Lillie Mae's and gazed pleadingly into her eyes. Miss Lane was cautioning her, once again, that no matter what happened, no matter how difficult things became, nothing mattered except protecting Will.

"Let's go home," Lane said, then turned to her son. "Do you want to say goodbye to your grandmother before we leave?"

"I don't have anything to say to Grandmother as long as she keeps treating you this way."

Lillie Mae didn't think she had ever been prouder of Will than she had been today. A boy on the verge of young manhood, he was still part child, and yet his loving, caring attitude toward Miss Lane said a lot about the man he would one day become, the fine and honorable man his mother had raised him to be.

She closed her umbrella and slid into the backseat of Lane's white Mercedes. When they got home, she'd fix a pot of coffee for them and prepare a light lunch. Miss Lane hadn't eaten enough to keep a bird alive since Kent's death. And no wonder, considering how quickly she had become the number one murder suspect. And even Will's normally voracious appetite had lessened in the five days since life as they knew it had ceased to exist. The more she tried to blot out the memories of that horrible day, the more vivid they became—like a recurring nightmare over which she had no control.

They drove in silence, away from Oakwood Cemetery, down through Baptist Bottoms, past the old trailer park, over the Chickasaw Bridge and straight onto Sixth Street. Lillie Mae's gaze lingered on the rusted gates hanging open to where the trailer park had once existed. She had lived there in a small two-bedroom trailer for years, with her only child, Sharon. Every morning at five-thirty, she had driven her old Rambler from Myer's Trailer Park on the west side of the Chickasaw River all the way across town to Magnolia Avenue, to the Nobles' estate. And every evening at seven-thirty, she had driven home, back across the river that divided the town into the haves and have nots.

She and Sharon had belonged to the have nots, and to this day she blamed herself for the savage, raging hunger that had been inside Sharon—the need to escape from poverty any way she could.

Johnny Mack Cahill had been the most notorious

of the have nots. Local society hadn't just scorned the boy; they had hated him. He had shown no respect for their snobbish hierarchy, and he had thumbed his nose at them time and again. But when he'd entered their world, bedded their women and laughed in their faces, they had punished him severely.

He had sworn he would never return to Noble's Crossing, but Lillie Mae prayed that her unsigned note would bring him home again. If he did come back, all hell was bound to break loose since quite a few folks thought he was dead. But if ever Will needed his real father, he needed him now. And if it was ever the time for Johnny Mack to repay Miss Lane for having saved his life, now was that time.

Lane stood in the doorway of Will's room. Light from the hallway cast soft shadows over the bed and the long, slender form of her sleeping child. And despite the fact that he already stood six feet tall, John William Graham was still a child. A child approaching manhood—racing toward adulthood, bursting with the energy of raging male hormones.

He was in so many ways his father's son. Far too handsome for his own good. Black hair and eyes. Tall and lean. And possessing a killer smile that was already drawing the attention of all the teenage girls in Noble's Crossing. But Will was also her son, and she had raised him with the love, security and wealth his own father had never known. She had instilled in her precious Will a sense of honor and dignity and respect for others that Johnny Mack had lacked.

In her heart and mind, she never had been able to separate the father from the son, and now that Will was a young carbon copy of Johnny Mack, she realized how foolish she had been to think she could keep his parentage a secret forever. If Kent hadn't been tall and dark, too, someone would have figured out the truth long ago. Maybe, just maybe, they would have all been better off if that had happened.

But hindsight was twenty-twenty. If she had it to do over again, would she lie to Kent and allow him to believe that Will was his child? Even though Kent had been her boyfriend of sorts since they were little more than children, she had never been in love with him. Sometimes, she wasn't sure she'd ever even liked him. Their parents had been friends—social equals—and distantly related. Both families had delighted in the thought that someday the Grahams' only son and the Nobles' only daughter would unite the two oldest and wealthiest families in the county.

And despite his declarations to the contrary, she doubted that Kent had ever really loved her. Oh, he had wanted her, pursued her and scared away most of the other young men who had shown an interest in her. He had wanted to marry her, to possess her, to rule her, but he had never loved her. And when he'd realized that even as his wife, she would never truly belong to him, his desire for her had turned slowly to hatred.

Lane stood over Will's bed and watched him breathe, much as she had stood over his cradle when he had been an infant and stared at his little chest rising and falling in a reassuring rhythm. From the first moment she had held him in her arms, she had loved him and known that she would do anything—pay any price— to keep him safe, secure and happy. Not once in fourteen years had she ever looked at Will without thinking of Johnny Mack.

"Oh, you were good, lady," Kent had told her. *"You had me convinced Will was mine. But I should have known*

better. I should have guessed. I saw the way you were with him, how you adored him. You'd never have felt that way about a child of mine. My God, every time you looked at Will, you thought about Johnny Mack, didn't you?"

Lane brushed a stray lock of jet black hair off Will's forehead. "Sweet Jesus, don't ever let him remember what happened the day Kent died," she whispered. "Let the memories stay buried forever. Even if I have to spend the rest of my life in prison, so be it. Just take care of Will. He's all that's important."

The cemetery was shadowed and quiet. Moonlight spread across the large ornately carved monument and the new grave, mounted high with floral arrangements. John Kent Graham. His mother's only son. But not his father's only son.

Smart. Handsome. Charming. A man who had been loved and cherished and desired. He'd had the world at his feet, like a gift from the gods. And he had squandered that gift, as if it had been a meaningless trifle. He had taken everything and given nothing.

The dark figure knelt, and a gloved hand caressed the tombstone. Beautiful, yet cold and hard. Just as Kent had been.

Kent, who had known how to charm and connive, how to use and in turn be useless himself. Kent, who had possessed everything a man could want and hadn't been smart enough to appreciate it.

"You were a sorry son of a bitch! And I'm glad you're dead. Do you hear me? I'm glad you're dead!"

The figure rose from the ground and glanced around, wondering if by chance anyone else might be paying a nighttime visit to a departed loved one.

All would be well as long as Will didn't remember what had happened that day. If his memories returned, he would have to be dealt with, one way or another. For everyone's sake, maybe the boy would get lucky and never be able to recall the events of his father's murder.

Will's father. Ha! No one, least of all Kent, had ever suspected that Will was another man's son. And not just any man, but Johnny Mack Cahill's bastard progeny.

How had Kent felt, realizing the child he had raised as his own, the boy who bore his name and called him Dad, was in reality the son of the man he had hated most in this world?

Ironic. Poetic justice. What goes around comes around.

Had Johnny Mack, whose black soul was no doubt burning in hell, welcomed Kent when he arrived? Had he smiled that damn pussy-melting smile of his and had the last laugh on Kent?

A soft, muffled chuckle wafted through the silent night air. The lone figure spit on Kent Graham's grave, then turned and walked toward the wrought-iron entrance gates.

Chapter 2

Monica Robinson took a deep breath, ran a quick, caressing hand over her short brown hair and entered the fray. The place was crowded, filled with Houston's elite. She stopped a passing waiter, lifted a flute of champagne from the silver serving tray and took a sip. Nice. She liked the taste of champagne. Especially expensive champagne. After taking another sip, she allowed the liquid to linger in her mouth a few minutes before swallowing it.

She scanned the huge room, searching for her date. It was a damn shame they were both so busy that they seldom arrived at functions together. But she wouldn't change one single thing about her life, except maybe.... *No, don't go there. You can't change the fact that after the divorce, Eric chose to live with Herb instead of you.*

Other than the fact that her thirteen-year-old son lived in Dallas with his father, Monica's life was perfect. Perfect by her standards. She was Fairfield Realtors' top seller for the second year in a row. Her apartment was luxurious, her car a new Lexus, her friends smart, witty and well-connected, and her lover was one of the wealthiest men in Texas.

Where the hell *was* Johnny Mack? She didn't think he would be late for a charity function that could mean hundreds of thousands of dollars for his pet project, the Judge Harwood Brown Ranch. She supposed a man as rich as Johnny Mack could afford to be a philanthropist. But sometimes she wondered if his good deeds were prompted as much to appease a guilty conscience as they were acts of a kind heart. Of course, she didn't know exactly what Johnny Mack might be guilty of since their time together was seldom spent discussing the past—his or hers. But her instincts told her that a man such as he hadn't lived thirty-six years without committing some unforgivable sins.

She caught a glimpse of him in the crowd. As always, a group of ladies surrounded him. The damn man oozed sex appeal. All he had to do was walk into a room and every woman within a hundred-foot radius creamed her pants. And she should know. She was one of those ladies. God forbid he ever use that killer smile on a woman. There was something lethal about his cocky grin.

His six-foot, four-inch height made him highly visible in a congested area. As she approached him, Monica finished off her drink, set aside the glass and spoke hastily to a couple of acquaintances. The closer she got to him, the stronger her mating instincts. They hadn't had a night alone together in over a week, and she was so horny she felt like dragging him off to the nearest closet.

When she eased up beside him, he casually slipped his arm around her and introduced her to the women, whose strained smiles barely masked their jealousy of her.

"Monica, you remember Charlene McNair, don't you?" Johnny Mack lavished his smile on the horse-faced oil heiress, who was one of the ranch's biggest supporters.

"Nice to see you again, Mrs. McNair. Is your husband here tonight?"

Charlene's smile wavered slightly. "Denny's about somewhere."

Johnny Mack eased Monica around to face the other two women. "And these lovely ladies are Florence Barr and her daughter Ashley. They're planning a visit out to the Judge Harwood Brown Ranch this weekend."

Monica dutifully shook hands with both women, noting the striking resemblance between parent and child—two pink-faced, barrel-shaped females in designer dresses. "Y'all will be very impressed with the ranch and with the work being done there. All the boys at the ranch have been deserted by their families and by society." She knew the spiel by heart. She should. She had heard Johnny Mack spouting it off on numerous occasions.

"We can hardly wait," Ashley replied, but her gaze never left Johnny Mack's face.

"We'll be expecting you around ten next Saturday morning." Florence patted Johnny Mack's shoulder. "Your giving us a personal tour will be so much more meaningful."

Monica breathed a sigh of relief when, ten minutes later, she and Johnny Mack were able to escape the charity-minded threesome and make their way to the buffet table.

"God, I'm starved," Monica said. "I had to skip lunch today. I was showing the Wright house to a couple, which ran me over two hours, and I had to make a mad dash across town to show the Daily Towers penthouse.'' She piled her plate with an assortment of delicacies.

''What say we ditch this joint early and go to my place,'' he whispered in her ear.

''Can you do that? Leave this shindig early?''

''By my estimation, I've already schmoozed close to two hundred thousand out of folks tonight.''

''Yeah, well, the way Mrs. Barr and her daughter were looking at you, I'd say they may be expecting more from you than a tour of the ranch.''

''Tsk-tsk, what a cynic you are.'' Johnny Mack lifted a shrimp to his mouth.

''I thought that was one of the things you liked about me. My cynicism.''

''I like a lot of things about you, Monica.''

''And I like a lot of things about you, too,'' she told him.

''I guess that's the reason we're still together, isn't it?''

''Yeah, that and our mutual dislike of long-term commitments.''

''Eat up and let's get out of here.'' He downed several more shrimp, then leaned over and said in a low voice, ''Meet me at the front door in ten minutes. I see Malcolm Winters has just arrived. While you pacify your stomach, I'll go talk a little business.''

Business. Business. Business. Johnny Mack seemed to live to do *business*. By all reports, the man was a multimillionaire, who had the Midas touch. Any deal in which he was involved was considered a sure thing. Except for his charity work, especially his devotion to the Judge Harwood Brown Ranch, the only time the man spent away from business was when he took an occasional weekend off and went to his ranch in the Hill Country. He had never asked her to accompany him. And as far as she knew, no other woman had ever been invited into that private domain.

They had become lovers nearly a year ago, sometimes staying the night in her apartment, sometimes in his, and once or twice they had gotten away for a few days together. To New Orleans six months ago and to Jamaica last month. She knew how Johnny Mack liked his coffee, knew who his friends and enemies were in Houston, knew which side of the bed he preferred, and she trusted him implicitly. But she knew nothing about his past—nothing more than what the world at large knew. He had been a poor kid who had gotten in trouble when he first arrived in Houston fifteen years ago. A saintly old judge named Harwood Brown had taken Johnny Mack under his wing and saved him from a life of crime. He had sent the young man to college and had personally taught him what it meant to be an honorable man.

She often wondered where Johnny Mack had come from and why he never spoke about the years before he had come to Texas. Just what was there in his past that he didn't want anyone to know? It didn't really matter, of course. She was simply curious. It wasn't as if she planned a long-term future with him. Even if that was what she wanted, and it wasn't, she knew marriage was an alien concept to her lover.

He rode her like a wild man, pumping into her with a force that pinned her to the bed. She clawed at his shoulders as the pressure inside her built to the exploding point. There was an uncontrollable power to his lovemaking, a ravaging possession that set him apart from all her previous lovers. Johnny

Mack Cahill knew how to pleasure a woman and a the same time conquer her completely.

She cried out with the force of her climax. He thrust to the hilt one final time and groaned dee; in his throat.

She snuggled her head against the pillow an; sighed with satisfaction as the aftershocks of he: orgasm trembled through her body. She lay there and watched him rise from the bed, his naked bod: lean and sleek, his muscles superbly toned. Damn but he was good. The best she'd ever had. When thei: affair ended, as she knew it would, she'd miss him.

He returned from the bathroom wearing a blac! silk robe loosely tied at the waist. "Want a drink?" he asked.

"Some of that ancient brandy of yours would b: nice right about now," she told him.

"Stay put. I'll be right back." He winked an; grinned.

Something was up. Johnny Mack never offered he: a drink and conversation after lovemaking. Usuall; he held her for a while, and then they drifted off t: sleep. On a few occasions, when they stayed at he: apartment, she had awakened the next morning t: find him gone.

So, why had he changed the routine tonight? Wh: after-sex drinks and conversation?

He returned and handed her a snifter of golde: brown liquor, then sat on the edge of the bed besid: her. "You miss having Eric around, don't you?" Johnny Mack lifted his own crystal glass to his lip and sipped the brandy.

She was momentarily taken aback by his question Except in the most casual way, they never discusse: her son. The subject was painful for her and one sh: usually tried to avoid.

"Yes, I miss Eric. But you know that. Whose shoulder did I cry on when my son told me that he preferred to live with his father permanently?" Swirling the brandy around in the antique snifter, Monica stared into the glass, as if she could foresee the future in its depths. Glancing up, she narrowed her gaze and asked, "What's this really about? Why the sudden interest in my relationship with my son?"

Johnny Mack downed the contents of his glass, set the snifter on the bedside table and stood. With his back to Monica, he said, "I just found out that I may have one."

"One what?" she asked, but her accelerated heartbeat and the sinking feeling in her stomach told her that she already knew the answer to her question. Was it possible that he had accidentally gotten some other woman pregnant? Surely not. Johnny Mack Cahill never—ever—had unprotected sex.

"A kid," he replied. "A son. A fourteen-year-old son."

Monica let out the breath she had been holding, and instant relief spread through her body. Fourteen. That meant a child from his distant past. A child from the life he'd had before he came to Texas.

She slipped out of bed, picked up her black-and-red-striped robe lying on the floor and eased into it. "Come on. I'll make us some strong coffee and then we can talk."

Johnny Mack rubbed his neck as he paced back and forth along the foot of the king-size bed. "What I'm going to tell you isn't something I want known. I expect you to keep it in strict confidence."

She laid her hand on his back. "You trust me, don't you?"

"Yeah."

"Then, come on. Coffee first, then conversation."

Ten minutes later, they sat in the living room—a large, professionally decorated area that epitomized a modern contemporary style. Two china cups rested, untouched, on the silver tray Monica had placed on the coffee table.

"So tell me," she said. "Why do you think you may have a fourteen-year-old son?"

Johnny Mack got up, walked over to the glass and metal desk in the corner, pulled out an envelope from beneath the desk blotter and brought it back with him. He handed the envelope to Monica, then sat down beside her.

"Go ahead," he said. "Take a look."

Monica shook out the contents. A note written on lined paper. A newspaper clipping. And a wallet-size photograph. She scanned the letter and the article quickly, then looked at the picture. A handsome, dark-haired boy, with a sharply chiseled face, almond-shaped black eyes and a breathtaking smile. Johnny Mack's smile.

"Whoa!" The one word escaped her lips on a released breath.

"So, you think he could be mine?"

She glanced from the school picture to the black-and-white photograph in the newspaper clipping. "Do you know her? The boy's mother?"

Johnny Mack avoided Monica's direct gaze. He stared past her, toward the glass doors leading to the balcony, which overlooked Houston. "Yeah, I know her. Or I did know her. Fifteen years ago."

"How well did you know her?"

"Lane and I were never lovers, if that's what you're asking."

Monica noticed a pained expression in his eyes. Barely discernible. But it had been there. She knew him too well not to be aware of something so powerful, no matter how fleeting. This woman—Monica read the name from the paper—this Lane Noble Graham had meant something to Johnny Mack. And whether he wanted to admit it or not, she apparently still did.

"The boy looks like you," Monica said. "Any chance he's a relative's kid?"

"Anything's possible." Johnny Mack spread his long legs, dropped his hands between his knees and interlocked his fingers. "What I want to know is why someone sent me this message. Hell, who sent it? And if this boy, Will Graham, is my son, why wait all these years to tell me?" He maneuvered his fingers back and forth, locking and unlocking them as he stared down at the carpeted floor. "If the kid is Lane's child, then he can't be mine."

"Are you sure?" Monica asked. "Couldn't there have been a night when you'd had too much to drink or one time you just forgot or—"

"I'd never have forgotten making love to Lane."

His voice froze Monica, inside and out, as though an Arctic blast had instantly reduced the temperature to subzero. It wasn't just what he had said that affected her so profoundly, but the way he had said it. Johnny Mack had been in love with this woman. And that fact surprised Monica. She had thought Johnny Mack incapable of falling in love.

"If she is his mother, and this newspaper article"— Monica shook the clipping she held in her hand— "states that she is, then he can't be yours."

Johnny Mack rubbed his hands up and down his thighs, then slapped his knees and shot straight up onto his feet. "I phoned Benton Pike first thing this morning, and he called in a private detective to find out everything he can about the boy."

"Then, you've done all you can do. You've contacted your lawyer, and he's having the matter investigated. It could be that whoever sent you the message wants something from you. Perhaps some sort of reward money."

"Yeah, that's what Benton said, but my gut instincts tell me that this note is on the level, that Will Graham is my son."

"If you feel that strongly about it, why don't you go to . . . to"—she checked the name of the newspaper—"to Noble's Crossing yourself and—"

"I once swore hell would freeze over before I'd ever return to Noble's Crossing."

"That was before you found out that you might have left behind some unfinished business."

"I left behind a lot of unfinished business." Johnny Mack opened the balcony doors, stepped outside and gripped the railing with white-knuckled fierceness.

Monica eased up behind him, slipped her arms around his waist and laid her head on his back. "Why can't you go home to Noble's Crossing? What are you so afraid of?"

"I'm afraid to face the ghost," he admitted.

"Whose ghost?"

"My own."

Chapter 3

Johnny Mack parked his rental car in front of the brick pillars. The rusted iron pins that held the dilapidated open gates in place hung precariously in their holes. A soft August breeze flitted across the weed-infested landscape, fluttering the tall grass without disturbing the hardy bushes and trees. Fifteen years ago these five acres of land on the outskirts of Noble's Crossing had been the site of a mobile home park. Now only the remnants of the gravel drives remained.

He had shared a one-bedroom, ten-year-old trailer with Wiley Peters, an alcoholic Vietnam veteran who had lost his left eye and half his left arm in the war. Wiley, one of Faith Cahill's many lovers, had been the only soul in town willing to take in a rebellious thirteen-year-old, after his mother's death had left him without any kin. Wiley hadn't been much of a guardian, but nobody in Noble's Crossing had given a damn. Johnny Mack Cahill had been a bad seed from the day he was born. Wild and surly, filled with anger and bitterness, he'd been nothing but white trash. Wiley had put a roof over Johnny Mack's head, and when he occasionally won big at cards, he had provided a few groceries and a new pair of jeans. Most of the time, Johnny Mack had been on his own, picking up odd jobs in order to survive.

It had been in that trailer park on a blistering summer evening that Johnny Mack had discovered sex. He had been fourteen, big, rowdy and eager to get laid. His first lover had been thirty, a trailer trash whore with a husband doing ten-to-fifteen in the state pen for armed robbery. They had fucked themselves silly that summer. Then when fall came, she'd moved her trailer and left town with a former boyfriend who had a good-paying job in Mobile.

Laura. No, Lorrie. Or was it Lorna? Hell, he couldn't remember. And why should he? That had been twenty-two years ago. Back then sometimes he didn't even ask a girl's name before or after. The young Johnny Mack Cahill had been a real hard-ass and had deserved his bad boy reputation.

Opening the door of the blue Escort, he got out and stood beside the leased vehicle. He could have driven his Jaguar up from Houston instead of flying in and renting a car, but when he made his first appearance in town, he didn't want anyone speculating about his success. He wanted that bit of news to come as a surprise to everyone. Their not knowing right away that he was a multimillionaire would make this damned trip a lot more interesting. That and the fact a few people still thought he was dead.

He walked down the dirt and gravel trail, wondering if he could find the spot where Wiley's trailer had been parked. So long ago. A million years. He stopped beside a towering cottonwood tree, its branches reaching into the clouds like a New York skyscraper. The

Hickmans' trailer had sat beside the cottonwood. The first time he had screwed Sharon, he'd braced her against that tree. They had been a couple of horny kids, both experienced beyond their years, friends through common backgrounds. Love had never entered into their relationship, but they had shared a lot of hot sex on and off from the age of sixteen until he'd left town.

If John William Graham turned out to be his son, was it possible Sharon was his mother? From the private investigator's initial findings, Johnny Mack had learned that Lane and Kent Graham had adopted Will shortly after his birth on April 20, fourteen years ago. That meant he had probably been conceived in late July. Pike had said the investigator would do his best to discover the name of the boy's birth mother. He had told Pike he wanted that information—whatever it cost and no matter what had to be done to get it.

Johnny Mack lifted his tan Stetson off his head and held it against his leg as he ran his hand through his hair. On the flight in from Houston, he had sorted through the limited knowledge he had about the boy who might be his son. Fourteen. Straight-A student. Played baseball and football. Adopted as an infant by newlyweds Kent and Lane Graham. Parents divorced four years ago. By his own choice, Will lived with his mother.

Of all the men on earth to have raised a boy who might be his son—why Kent Graham! From first grade on, they had been rivals, Kent the golden boy, always winning, always superior. Until they'd grown up. Johnny Mack had had either the respect or the fear of all his male peers, and the undying adoration of just about every female in town. Kent had both envied and hated him.

Then Kent had heard the ugly rumors that had

been floating around Noble's Crossing for years. The whispered innuendoes, the murmured gossip about John Graham having fathered Faith Cahill's son. The thought that they might be half brothers had amused Johnny Mack and enraged Kent.

But the death knell had sounded for Johnny Mack when Kent found out that Lane Noble, the girl he had chosen for himself, had a crush on his despised enemy. Their boyhood rivalry had burst into an unquenchable flame of warfare. And that flame had been kindled to a white-hot intensity the night Kent had found Johnny Mack with his mother. Edith Graham had been out for revenge against her womanizing husband. And what better way to get it than to bed his illegitimate son?

After what this town did to him, Johnny Mack had sworn he would never return to Noble's Crossing. He had known then as he knew now that if he had returned, he would have killed Kent Graham.

Had Kent suspected Johnny Mack was his adopted son's natural father? Obviously not. Kent never would have accepted a child of his into the prestigious Graham family. And Miss Edith would have drowned the boy at birth if she had known Johnny Mack had sired him. Unless. . . . Was it possible that Edith was Will's natural mother? She had been in her early forties fifteen years ago, not young, but young enough to have gotten pregnant.

Edith Graham Ware, her slender hand gripping the portable phone, gazed through the French doors leading to the patio and gardens. Mary Martha sat beneath the shade of a willow tree, silent and unmoving, as traumatized today as she had been since the day after Kent's funeral. Jackie Cummings, the private

nurse they had recently hired, sat across from Mary
Martha, reading to her from one of her favorite books.
Despite the warmth of the summer day, Edith thought
an hour outside might do her daughter some good.
At least it had put a little color in the girl's pale
cheeks.

Edith hated waiting on anything or anyone, and
being put on "hold" by her husband's secretary did
little to soothe her irritation. How dare James call
and leave her such an outrageous message on the
answering machine!

*Someone using the name Johnny Mack Cahill phoned our
new district attorney to ask questions about Kent's murder
and Lane's part in the crime. And he asked about Will,
too.*

"I'm so sorry, Mrs. Ware, but the mayor went out
for a bite of lunch and I'm afraid he didn't mention
exactly where he was going," Penny Walsh said. "Perhaps you can catch him later."

Without so much as a thank-you, Edith punched
the Off button and flung the telephone down on the
seat of the Chippendale arm chair to her left. Johnny
Mack Cahill, indeed! It wasn't possible that Johnny
Mack was still alive, was it? Kent had been so sure his
half brother was dead. Even Buddy Lawler agreed
that there was no way the man could have survived.
But what if he had? And what if he had found out
about Will? What if he wanted revenge?

Other than the fact that the young man had possessed a certain charm—in bed—Johnny Mack never
had been anything but trouble. And if, by some miracle, he was still alive, he would be even more trouble
now. In fact, he would be downright dangerous.

If he was alive and if he came home and tried to
help Lane, Edith would have to put a stop to him.
And she could do it. After all, she was Edith Noble

Graham Ware and this was Noble's Crossing. Her town. She still possessed enough power to have the likes of Johnny Mack put six feet under, if she had a mind to. The movers and shakers in Noble's Crossing were either relatives or people who owed her favors.

If Johnny Mack wasn't dead and he decided to come back to town and stir up a stink, he'd be sorry. She would see to it personally.

"Harder, baby, harder," Arlene panted, her long red nails biting into her lover's fleshy buttocks. "Give it to me, Jimmy boy!"

With his round belly slapping against Arlene's flat, stretch-mark-scarred stomach, Mayor James Ware thrust into the luscious woman lying beneath him. God, how he loved to fuck Arlene. She was all woman, and made him feel like a real man.

"You've got the sweetest pussy in the state and you know it."

Arlene lifted herself up, wrapping her long, slim legs around James's waist. With one final plunge, he spilled himself into her. She scored his buttocks with her nails. He groaned as he shook in the aftermath, then smiled when he felt her trembling and heard her cry out as she climaxed.

When he lowered himself to her side on the small cot in the back of her beauty parlor, half his butt hung off the edge. Scooting closer, he pulled her into his arms and kissed her shoulder. "I can't get enough of you, sugar," James whispered in her ear, then nipped the lobe.

Arlene shivered. "You're going to have to get your clothes on and get out of here, Jimmy boy. I have customers coming in right after my lunch break."

"I can slip out the back way, into the alley." James licked the moisture from Arlene's left breast.

"One of these days, somebody's going to see you sneaking out of here and tell Miss Edith." Arlene traced the curve of James's spine with the tip of her sharp fingernail.

"Nobody's going to see me. Besides, I could think up some excuse to tell Edith. Right now, she's so wrapped up in Kent's murder that she hasn't got time to be bothered with anything else."

"If I was Lane, I'd be throwing myself a party to celebrate that bastard's death. If she did kill him, I can't say I blame her."

"What did Kent ever do to you?" James jerked Arlene up against him so hard she gasped.

"Not a damned thing. I never had anything to do with Kent Graham, but everybody in town knows why Lane left him."

"Didn't your mama ever teach you that it wasn't polite to speak ill of the dead?" James grinned.

"All my mama ever taught me was that the way to a man's heart wasn't through his stomach." Slipping her hand between their damp bodies, Arlene fondled James's limp penis.

"I never knew a gal who enjoyed sex as much as you do, except maybe Sharon Hickman."

"Yeah, I suppose Sharon spread her legs for just about all you Magnolia Avenue boys, didn't she?"

James chuckled, remembering the stunned look on Edith's face when Kent told the family about the letter Sharon Hickman had sent him. A letter written on her deathbed.

"What are you thinking about, Jimmy boy, screwing Sharon?"

"No, ma'am, I was thinking about the next time you and I can get together," James lied.

He wasn't fool enough to tell her that he had been thinking about Sharon, nor did he dare mention what weighed most heavily on his mind—the call he had received from the district attorney this morning. Wes Stevens had said that someone claiming to be Johnny Mack Cahill had phoned him and asked a lot of questions about Kent Graham's death and what the odds were that Lane would be arrested for the crime. He had asked about Will, too. And this man had implied he was returning to Noble's Crossing.

But how was that possible? Johnny Mack Cahill was dead, wasn't he? He'd died the night Buddy Lawler had dumped his body into the Chickasaw River.

"Why don't you figure out a way for us to go off on another weekend trip the way we did in March," Arlene said. "I like it when we don't have to sneak around."

"I'll see what I can do, sugar." James stood, picked up his boxer shorts from the floor and slipped into them.

While he finished dressing, he glanced over at Arlene, and his sex grew hard again. Damn, what he would give to have her in his bed every night. He had been married to Edith for ten years, and for the first four he'd wondered if she had emasculated him completely with her position of power in their marriage. Then he had renewed his affair with Arlene, right after her second divorce. It had started out as nothing but a good time for both of them. Somewhere along the way, they had gotten serious.

They'd been secret lovers when they were teenagers, but he had known he could never marry her. They were from different sides of the Chickasaw River. His parents would never have accepted a girl like Arlene. Now he wished he had told his parents and the whole town to go to hell. He wished that he'd had the balls to defy his family. If they had married and left Noble's Crossing twenty years ago, Arlene's two kids would be his, and they wouldn't have to sneak around to be together.

There were times when he thought he really had the guts to ask Edith for a divorce, but then he would remember all her beautiful money. The old bat would chew him up and spit him out in little pieces if he ever left her, especially for someone like Arlene Vickery Cash Motes Dothan, a three-time divorcee who came from the other side of the river.

For now, he was trapped in a loveless, childless marriage. He would have to wait a little longer, until he had enough money stashed away so he, Arlene and her two kids could leave Noble's Crossing and never look back. By the time Edith found out about what he had done, it would be too late for her to do anything about it.

Driving along Magnolia Avenue in broad daylight for the whole world to see, Johnny Mack wondered if he was a fool. His last memory of Rich Man's Land, as the locals often called this area, had stuck in his mind for fifteen years. As much as he had tried to forget everything and everyone associated with Noble's Crossing, *she* had been the one and only thing he'd never been able to forget. She had saved his life that night—the night some good ole boys, headed by Buddy Lawler, had beaten him senseless behind the Nobles' house, tossed him into the Chickasaw River and left him for dead.

He wondered if she still lived on Magnolia Avenue. Had she gone home to her mother after the divorce? Of all the women he had known in Noble's Crossing, of all the women who had played a part in his life back then, it never ceased to amaze him that Lane Noble was the one who haunted him to this day.

Not Sharon Hickman, despite the friendship and hot sex they had shared. Not grande dame Edith Graham, who had bedded him as an act of revenge against her husband. And not even Mary Martha Graham, with all her pale strawberry blond beauty and her heartbreaking sadness.

Why Lane Noble? Lane Noble *Graham*. The mother of a boy who might be his son.

She had been a smart, quiet girl with the kind of looks a guy wouldn't notice. But he *had* noticed her. He'd noticed how different she was from her friends, those snobby little blue-blooded debutantes. When around their social set, the others never had acknowledged their acquaintance with him, although sooner or later he had fucked them all. But Lane, whom he'd never touched, always had a shy smile and a warm hello for him.

The night Kent Graham had stood on the sidelines, watching while Buddy Lawler and his cohorts beat the hell out of him, Johnny Mack had known in his gut that they meant to kill him. And he would have died that rainy September night if shy, sweet little Lane Noble hadn't found him on the riverbank, after he had dragged himself out of the cold, deadly water.

Johnny Mack slowed briefly in front of the Noble home, a house built before the Civil War and occupied by the Noble family for six generations. He had spent three days and nights in that house, fifteen years ago. Lane had hidden him away, nursed him back from near death and given him the only good memories he had of Noble's Crossing.

One by one, the stately mansions along Magnolia Avenue came into view as Johnny Mack eased the rental car down the street. Even if other things in this one-horse town had changed, been improved and modernized, nothing—absolutely nothing—had changed on Magnolia Avenue. Same fine homes, neatly manicured lawns and an invisible sign telling the rest of the world, "Private Property, Keep Out."

That was where he had made his mistake all those years ago. He had trespassed. And no one, especially Kent Graham, had ever forgiven him. Hell, nobody had cared what he did or who he screwed as long as he stayed on the other side of the river, with the likes of Sharon Hickman. But once he had set his sights a little higher, all hell had broken loose, and his flirtations with the Noble's Crossing debutantes had nearly cost him his life.

Fifteen years ago he had sworn he would never come back to this goddamn town. But that had been before he found out he might have left behind a child.

Chapter 4

"They say his head was smashed in so bad his own mama wouldn't have recognized his face." Arlene Dothan lifted Jackie Cummings's silver blond hair and twisted it into a neat French twist. "Lord knows Kent Graham wasn't one of my favorite people, but it gives me shivers thinking about how he died."

"If you ask me, the boy was somehow at the root of all Lane and Kent's problems. People are saying that Kent and Will fought like cats and dogs. That's what comes of adopting a child." Jackie preened in the wall-wide mirror over the beauticians' work stations. "No telling what sort of people that boy came from."

"I never could figure out why Lane and Kent rushed into adopting a child so soon after they married." Arlene slipped in the hairpins to secure Jackie's French twist. "I've heard folks say they thought Kent was probably sterile. What do you think, Jackie? You're bound to have heard something, now that you're living there on Magnolia Avenue and working as a nurse to poor little ole Mary Martha."

"I have no earthly idea whether Kent Graham was sterile or not," Jackie said. "I do know Miss Edith doesn't want to believe that boy isn't her grandson. Seems she thought he was Kent's child by one of his old girlfriends. But right now her main concern seems to be Mary Martha. You know that woman hasn't said a sensible word since the day after Kent's funeral. Of course, she's been unstable for years, and we all know she doted on that brother of hers. No wonder she went off her rocker completely."

"I used to think what a lucky little boy Will Graham was to have been adopted by Lane and Kent, to be a member of those families," Arlene said. "You know a lot of folks in Noble's Crossing are of the opinion that Will could have been one of John Graham's bastards, and he got his own son to adopt the boy to keep him in the family."

"I've never believed that tale," Jackie said. "It's true that John Graham couldn't keep his pants zipped, and he probably left a few bastards spread out over the state; but he never bothered bringing any of them into the family."

Arlene picked up the bottle of salon hair spray. "You know, I've seen Will now and again over the years. He's a handsome boy and quite a young gentleman."

"He's awfully close to Lane," Jackie said. "She made him a good mother. Of course, that didn't surprise anybody, did it? But Kent surprised us all, the way he turned out. He sure had us fooled, didn't he?"

"Some people blame Lane. They say when she left him four years ago, his drinking got worse. But I think they're wrong to blame her. Those folks don't know beans about what Lane might have put up with for those ten years she was married to him." Arlene shook her head, lamenting Lane's fate. She knew what it was like living with a bad man, a man who didn't mind using his wife's face for a punching bag.

"Anyone who knows Lane knows she didn't kill Kent. She's just not the type to murder somebody."

"I understand she's holding up real well, all things considered," Arlene said. "Guess you've heard what some folks are saying—that the boy killed Kent and she's just covering for him."

"She's spoiled him rotten, that's for sure. And it doesn't help people's opinion of him that he's so good-looking and such a charmer, even at fourteen. Folks are bound to be jealous of a boy like that who seems to have everything."

Biting softly into her bottom lip, Arlene looked down at Jackie. The woman was a loyal customer and an acquaintance of long-standing, and for those reasons, she wouldn't correct her misconception of Lane's son being *spoiled rotten*. "Will Graham is a good-looking boy, now that's for sure. And the last time I saw him, he put me in mind of somebody. There's something awfully familiar about him. I can't quite place who he reminds me of, but sooner or later, it'll come to me."

The entrance door opened. A rush of hot air swept into the cool comfort of Arlene Dothan's Kut and Kurl beauty salon.

"Glenn! You're early," Jackie whined. "Arlene hasn't finished making me beautiful for tonight."

Glenn Manis, short, stocky and sweating profusely, wiped his face with a white handkerchief and flopped his wide butt down on the K-Mart wicker sofa in the waiting area.

Arlene had known Glenn since they were kids. He

was a nice guy, with a good job as a maintenance man for the city of Noble's Crossing. He seemed to be hog-wild crazy over Jackie. The two had been dating nearly a year now.

"I'm in no hurry." Glenn smiled at his girlfriend, the action adding a few character lines to his amazingly youthful face. At forty, Glenn didn't have any noticeable wrinkles, and his once blond hair had darkened to a light brown. "As far as I'm concerned, you're already beautiful enough for any occasion."

"How come you're early?" Jackie asked.

"I walked over straight from the mayor's office, with a bit of news I thought you and Arlene might find interesting."

Arlene sprayed Jackie's hair until not even a hurricane force wind could have mussed it. "Wouldn't be something about Kent Graham's murder, would it? I swear, it's the only thing this town is talking about."

"I can't reveal any privileged information without endangering my job with the city, but since Penny Walsh overheard it, too, then the news is bound to be all over town before sundown." Glenn crossed his hefty right leg over his left knee. "I could be persuaded to share my news if you'd get me a Coke."

Arlene patted Jackie on the shoulders. "Sit still. I'll do your nails as soon as I get Glenn his Coke."

While Arlene raided the cola machine, Jackie whirled around in the swivel chair and gave her boyfriend a hard stare. "Is it something deliciously juicy?"

Arlene popped the lid on the can and handed Glenn his cola. "Here's your bribe. Now tell us."

Glenn's face flushed slightly. "Y'all never will guess who might be coming back to town." Tilting the cola to his lips, Glenn gulped down the refreshing drink.

"What sort of news is that?" Standing, Jackie unsnapped her plastic cape and tossed it onto a nearby chair. Snips of shimmering platinum hair dropped to the floor. "Come on, Arlene, do my nails."

"So, who's coming back to town?" Arlene followed Jackie to the manicurist's table.

"Don't you girls want to guess?"

"Lord, what is this, twenty questions?" Arlene sat across from Jackie, then lifted the woman's hand into a dish of warm, soapy water. "Are we playing a game?"

"The news is very interesting," Glenn said. "Come on. I'll give y'all a few clues."

"You're acting totally ridiculous." Jackie puckered her plump, pink lips into a pout.

"It's a man who left town fifteen years ago." Glenn sipped from the cola can. "He lived over in Myer's Trailer Park. You dated him a time or two, Arlene. And so did you, Jackie."

"You can't mean Johnny Mack!" Arlene's big hazel eyes widened; her mouth gaped open.

"Johnny Mack is coming back to town?" Jackie asked, her voice quivering slightly. "But why would he come back, after all these years?"

"Yeah, I wondered the same thing," Glenn said. "While I was changing out the light fixture in Penny's office, I heard Mayor Ware talking to the DA on the phone. Seems some guy claiming to be Johnny Mack Cahill had called the DA's office and was asking some questions about Kent Graham's murder." Glenn finished off his cola and tossed the empty can into a nearby wicker wastebasket. "That phone call sure as hell upset James Ware. He called Miss Edith right away. Me and Penny heard every word."

"Wonder how Johnny Mack turned out?" Arlene smiled, then sighed. "Now there was a man for you. Even at twenty, he was a force to be reckoned with,

wasn't he? Folks used to say the likes of him would
wind up in jail for sure.''

"I still say, why would he come back to Noble's
Crossing after all this time?'' Jackie repeated her question. "He hated this town as much as it hated him.''

"Well, it seems Kent Graham's murder isn't all
Johnny Mack was interested in,'' Glenn told them.
"I heard James Ware ask the DA what possible interest
the man claiming to be Johnny Mack Cahill could
have in Will Graham.''

"A very good question. Why *would* he be interested
in Will Graham?'' Arlene asked.

"Are you saying that Johnny Mack Cahill is coming
back to Noble's Crossing because of that boy?'' Jackie
lifted her hand out of the water. "But why?''

"Weren't you listening, honey pie? That's what the
mayor wanted to know.'' Crossing his big arms over
his rotund chest, Glenn leaned back on the sofa.

"Why would Johnny Mack give a hoot about Kent
Graham's kid?'' Arlene asked. "Those two despised
each other.'' Arlene reached for Jackie's hand, but
she jerked it away.

Jackie turned around to face Glenn. "That boy isn't
anybody to Johnny Mack. Doesn't make any sense
why he'd be interested.''

"Could be the old rumors are true about Johnny
Mack and Kent being half brothers,'' Arlene speculated. "If that's so, then Will would be Johnny Mack's
nephew.''

"Could be,'' Glenn said. "But I got my own notion
about why he'd come back to town, if he thought
that Will and Lane needed him.'' Glenn glanced from
his girlfriend to Arlene and then back to his girlfriend. "We all know Will's adopted, so that means,
somewhere, Will has a real mama and daddy. Right?''

"Right,'' Arlene said. "Lord have mercy! Now I

know who Will reminds me of. He looks like Johnny Mack did when he was a kid. Why didn't we see it before now, Jackie? You and I were as close to Johnny Mack as anybody in this town."

"Speak for yourself," Jackie said.

"Excuse me, *Ms. Cummings*, but the truth is that you and I both dated Johnny Mack."

"Everyone knows that you dated him on and off for years, whenever a certain someone else wasn't available, but I never really dated him. He pursued me . . . and I shunned him."

"Lightning's going to strike you dead, Jackie Jo Cummings." Arlene laughed, a hoarse, throaty, lifetime smoker's rumbling chuckle. "You were as hot for Johnny Mack as every other girl in town."

"I was not! I found him uncouth and crude and—"

"And exciting," Arlene said. "We all did. He was the boy even the Magnolia Avenue girls fantasized about."

Glenn cleared his throat. "Well, explain this to me, ladies, if Johnny Mack is Will's natural father, why on earth would Kent and Lane have adopted him?" Glenn shook his head and grunted. "Johnny Mack and Kent sure weren't friends, and they certainly didn't run with the same crowd."

"Nobody ran with Johnny Mack," Jackie said. "He was a loner."

"So maybe the answer doesn't lie with Johnny Mack. Maybe it lies with whoever Will's real mother is," Glenn said. "Could be that Lane and Kent knew when they married they could never have a child of their own and someone in town told them about a girl with a child she wanted to give away. Nobody knows where they got that boy."

Arlene tapped her long fake nails atop the manicurist's desk. "I feel sorry for Will, and sorry for Johnny Mack if Will really is his son."

"And for the poor girl who had to give away her lover's baby?" Glenn asked as he exchanged a pensive glance with Arlene.

"I think y'all are assuming an awful lot." Jackie laid both of her hands flat atop the desk. "Do my nails! Glenn and I are supposed to be at Heartbreakers by seven, and I still have to go home and change. This is my one night off this week, and I want to make the most of it."

"I guess we could narrow down the possibilities," Arlene said. "Every girl in town didn't sleep with Johnny Mack that last summer before he left town. He was mostly fooling around with the Magnolia Avenue girls."

"Any smart girl from Magnolia Avenue could have gotten an abortion." Jackie snatched her hand out of Arlene's grasp, inspecting the beginnings of her manicure. "So that means Will's mama was probably trash just like Johnny Mack. Now, wouldn't that be something? The bastard son of white trash being raised in the lap of luxury as the child of Lane Noble Graham. If Miss Edith suspected such a thing, she'd have a heart attack and keel over dead. Can you imagine her having Johnny Mack Cahill's child as her heir?"

"Well, my money's on Johnny Mack being the father," Glenn said. "But who could the mother have been? There weren't many women between the age of sixteen and sixty who would have said no to Johnny Mack."

"I think there's one possibility that we've all overlooked," Jackie said.

"What's that?" Arlene asked.

"That Lane Noble is Will's natural mother."

* * *

Johnny Mack checked into the Four Way, a clean but inexpensive motel on the other side of the river. The place hadn't changed much over the years. Some new furniture. A fresh coat of paint. A bigger neon sign.

Johnny Mack glanced at his watch. Nearly six-thirty. He wanted to shower and change before he called on anyone here in Noble's Crossing. For the time being, he didn't want anyone to suspect just how successful he was. How rich and powerful. Later, when it served his purposes to reveal the truth, he would let everyone know just who they were dealing with.

Picking up his suitcase, he tossed it on the bed, snapped open the lid and reached inside for his favorite pair of faded black jeans. Even though he was accustomed to tailor-made suits, linen shirts and silk ties, he was still more comfortable in jeans and boots. Despite his innate ability to wheel and deal with the best of them, he found the most pleasure in the days he spent at the ranch. Although the Hill Country was peaceful and serene, somehow he never felt quite as lonesome there as he did surrounded by people in Houston.

He had spent fifteen years trying to escape from his past, trying to become someone other than the town bad boy. And he had spent the past ten years trying to atone for the mistakes he had made when he'd been too young and stupid to realize that actions had consequences.

God in heaven, had he gotten some girl pregnant that last summer here in Noble's Crossing? Had he really left behind a child?

Just as he stripped out of his clothes, the cellular phone in his jacket rang. He reached down on the bed, slipped his hand inside the pocket, lifted the phone and flipped it open.

"Cahill."

"Johnny Mack, I've got a report sitting on my desk that I think will interest you," Benton Pike said.

"An update from the PI?"

"Yep."

"Did he get the information I wanted?"

"He sure did. We know who John William Graham's natural mother is."

Chapter 5

"He's registered at the Four Way," Police Chief Buddy Lawler said. "From the description the desk clerk gave me, it could be Johnny Mack."

"He registered under the name Johnny Mack Cahill, right?" James Ware merely wanted to confirm what his old friend had already told him. "And he paid for a week in advance?"

"What are the odds it could be Johnny Mack?" Buddy paced the polished oak floor in the paneled study of the Graham mansion. "We both know that he was fish food fifteen years ago. How could he have survived that beating, let alone had the strength to swim ashore?"

"He was as tough as they come." James poured himself a drink from the bottle of Scotch he kept on his desk. Nodding toward the liquor, he asked, "Care for some?"

"No. I'm keeping a clear head until I find out for sure who our visitor is."

"And what are we going to do if it turns out to be Johnny Mack?" James lifted the glass to his lips, took a sip and swallowed.

"Let's say it is him," Buddy suggested. "He's stayed away for fifteen years. Why would he return now?"

"Wes Stevens said that this man—whoever the hell he is—called his office and inquired about Kent's murder and about Lane and Will. It's possible that he's found out the truth about Will."

"How the hell would he have found out?" Buddy removed his tie, undid the top button on his shirt and loosened the collar. "Unless he's kept in touch with someone here in Noble's Crossing all these years."

"The same someone who might have helped him fifteen years ago," James said. "Someone who knows what we did to him."

"Don't jump to conclusions. We don't know anything for sure. We don't even know if this man really is Johnny Mack Cahill."

"Sure we do." James downed the remainder of his Scotch, set the glass aside and wiped the perspiration from his forehead with the back of his hand. "He was the kind of guy you couldn't kill. We should have known he wasn't dead. If he made it to shore, just about any woman in this town would have helped him."

"I know one woman who wouldn't have helped him," a distinctly feminine voice said.

Both men turned toward the door which had just opened. Edith Ware's red lips curved into a closed-mouth smile as she walked into the room. Thin and petite, with her cinnamon hair cut in a stylish chin-length bob, Edith did not look like a woman nearly sixty.

"How much did you overhear?" James asked.

"Oh, don't fret, my love. I've known your dirty little secret for quite some time. You men were all too adamant about Johnny Mack being dead. I finally confronted Kent with my suspicions one night when he'd had a little too much bourbon."

"Why didn't you say—" James glared at his wife.

"Miss Edith, I promise that whoever this man is— Johnny Mack Cahill or somebody just using his name—he's not going to cause any problems for this family as long as I'm police chief."

Edith clasped Buddy's shoulder, her perfect, sculptured red nails biting into the material of his jacket. "I know I can count on you to keep things under control. But if this man is Johnny Mack returned from the dead, then I suggest we bide our time and see exactly what he's up to. Could be he's come back for revenge."

When James groaned and Buddy slapped his right fist against the open palm of his left hand, Edith narrowed her gaze on the portrait hanging over the ornate Jacobean desk. John Graham posed with his arm around his son. Their son. John Kent Graham. "Or perhaps Johnny Mack has come back for Will," Edith speculated.

"Or to help Lane," Buddy said. "If he knows about Will, he might know what Lane did for that boy."

Edith slid her hand down Buddy's arm and ran her fingertips over the bulge in his jacket created by the shoulder holster he always wore. "Someone in this town has known all along where Johnny Mack was, and that person is the one who summoned him back to Noble's Crossing. We want to make sure he doesn't stay long enough to make waves. It shouldn't be too difficult for you to find a way to make him disappear again. Give him fair warning that he isn't wanted in

Noble's Crossing now any more than he was wanted fifteen years ago.''

"And if he doesn't heed the warning?" Buddy asked.

"Let's take this one step at a time," Edith said. "First let's find out who this man is and proceed from there."

"It's going to rain." Lillie Mae cleared the dishes from the kitchen table. "I feel it in my bones."

"I wish it would rain," Lane said. "It's so hot and humid I can hardly breathe when I go outside."

"I don't see how you two can discuss the weather as if everything's all right!" Will shoved back his chair, shot straight up and stomped out of the room.

"Go see about him." Lillie Mae nodded toward the den. "God only knows why Sharon wrote that letter to Kent. If she'd had any idea what her confession would do to Will and to you and—"

Lane placed her arm around her housekeeper's shoulders. For many years, she and Lillie Mae had shared a special relationship, closer than many mothers and daughters. For fifteen years they had been bound together by two secrets, one that had been revealed a few months ago when Lillie Mae's only child, Sharon, had died.

"Maybe what she did was wrong, but I think she did it for the right reason." Lane hugged Lillie Mae, then turned and headed toward the den.

Lane found her son standing by the row of windows overlooking Magnolia Avenue. She walked up to him, but didn't touch him. Knowing him so well, she gave him enough time for his quick temper to cool.

The street outside lay in early evening shadows. A hot breeze shimmied through the trees that lined the enormous brick walkway outside their antebellum home. The home her ancestors had built before the Civil War. The home that had been part of her parents' legacy.

"The only way to stay sane when the whole world's gone crazy is by keeping things around you normal, by going on with life's little mundane matters." Lane glanced at her son, the child to whom she had devoted her life. Not a boy any longer and yet not quite a man. Fourteen and fragile and vulnerable as only the very young and innocent can be. Her poor, sweet baby. Innocent no longer. Kent had taken that away from him, too, when he had heartlessly ripped Will's heritage from him and unmercifully shattered his sense of identity.

"Whose child am I?" he had asked her as he lay in her arms and cried the day of Kent's death.

"You're mine," she had said. *"Mine."*

"Our lives won't ever be normal again, will they?" Will's voice caught with emotion. A voice already as deep and husky as his father's had been.

When he laced his long fingers together and moved them back and forth, Lane watched her son's nervous habit and remembered another young man who used to lock and unlock his fingers whenever he felt agitated or uncomfortable.

"You're right. Our lives won't ever be the same," she said. "But someday we'll put all of this behind us and—"

"Why won't you let me tell them the truth about what happened that day?" Will faced his mother, his gaze colliding with hers.

"You don't know what happened that day. The police understand that the shock of Kent's death has caused your partial amnesia."

"I know you didn't kill Da—Kent. We both know

you weren't even here when I found his body." Moisture glimmered on the surface of Will's black eyes. "If you'd just let me tell Chief Lawler what I do remember."

"No!" She reached out for him, took his big hand into her small one and gave it a reassuring squeeze. "We've been over this time and time again, Will. If you tell Chief Lawler what you remember, it will look as if you might have killed Kent. And we know that's impossible, don't we?"

"Do we, Mama? Do we really know it's impossible? If I can't remember anything that happened after I hit him, then how—"

"You hit Kent once," she reminded Will. "Once. You do remember tossing the bat aside after you hit him that one time. And the autopsy plainly stated that Kent was hit repeatedly. Someone else picked up your baseball bat and killed him." She grabbed Will's shoulders and gave him a stern shake. "Do you hear me? You did not kill him!"

"Then, who did?"

Standing on tiptoe to reach her six-foot teenager, Lane wrapped her arms around him. "I don't know. But I know that you didn't."

"And I know you didn't." He hugged his mother fiercely, holding on to her for dear life.

She stroked the dark, straight hair that hung to his collar. Like silk in her fingers. Shiny and soft and almost blue-black in the evening sunlight spilling through the windowpanes.

Lane pushed him away gently. "Why don't you go help Lillie Mae finish cleaning up in the kitchen? I bet she'd like the company."

"I'll apologize to her. She's put up with a lot from me lately, and she doesn't deserve my anger." Will's lips curved into a smile. Lane caressed his cheek, then gave him a little shove toward the door.

"No, she doesn't," Lane agreed. "Lillie Mae has suffered as much as any of us. And she loves you more than anything in this world."

"Yeah, I know. I—I—"

"Go help her. You don't have to say anything. She'll understand."

When Will joined Lillie Mae in the kitchen, Lane slumped down in the enormous leather chair that had been her father's favorite seat. She still missed her parents and probably always would. Her father's death in a needless accident, caused by a reckless drunk driver, had reminded her how very brief life is and how very, very precious. When she had come out of the foggy, grief-induced haze following Bill Noble's death, she realized two things. One being that her mother, whose injuries in the accident had left her little more than a vegetable, would require constant care. For eighteen months, she, Lillie Mae and several private nurses had seen to Celeste Noble's every need. She had died peacefully in her sleep, with her daughter at her side. And Lane's second realization was that she couldn't continue in her marriage to Kent. They had both been miserable, and with each passing year, Kent had become more and more abusive. He had never struck her, but he had verbally tormented her, making their lives unbearable. And a part of her had lived in fear of him, never forgetting what he had once done to her

Even though Kent hadn't been the best of fathers, he had loved Will, and Will had adored Kent, the way little boys so often hero worship their fathers. Will's adoration of Kent had ended the first time he overheard Kent berating her. And Kent's love for Will had ended the day he received Sharon Hickman's letter.

Why couldn't Sharon have taken their secret to her grave? Why had she felt twangs of conscience when she was dying? She might have eased her own burden of guilt by her deathbed confession, but in freeing herself, she had damned the rest of them to hell. Will. Kent. Lillie Mae. Her. And even Kent's family.

Lane had been taught that lying was a sin. And sins required punishment and atonement. She had never realized just how terrible the punishment would be for their lie. Or how costly the atonement.

Will was an innocent child. The one person who shouldn't have to suffer for the adults' sins. But he was the one suffering the most. He was the one who stood to lose everything. He had already lost the only father he had ever known. And now, if she was arrested, put on trial for Kent's murder and was found guilty, he would lose his mother, too.

The distinct chime of the doorbell echoed through the quiet house. Lane rose to her feet and walked into the hallway.

"I'll see who it is," Will called out as he emerged from the kitchen.

She nodded agreement and turned to go back into the den. But something stopped her. A tightening in her stomach. A gut reaction warning her that something was wrong. She glanced over her shoulder as Will opened the front door.

"Hello," the deep, husky male voice said. "Does Lane Noble still live here?"

"Yeah, but she's Lane Graham now," Will said. "Who are you?"

"Will!" Lane screamed his name.

When her son turned around, obviously startled by her outburst, he moved a fraction to the right, giving

Lane a better view of the front porch. The tall, broad-shouldered man wearing a tan Stetson filled the doorway. He had changed. Grown older. Tiny age lines surrounded his mouth and eyes.

"What's wrong, Mama?" Will asked.

"Nothing," she replied. "This man is here to see me. You go in the kitchen and tell Lillie Mae to put on a fresh pot of coffee."

Hesitantly, Will obeyed her, leaving her alone to face a ghost from her past.

"Hello, Lane," the man said.

"Hello, Johnny Mack."

Chapter 6

"Who was that at the front door?" Lillie Mae asked.

"I don't know. Some tall guy wearing a Stetson," Will replied. "Mama said he was here to see her and for me to come tell you to put on a fresh pot of coffee. Wonder who he is?"

"Tall man? Wearing a Stetson?" Lillie Mae's heart beat in an erratic rat-a-tat-tat rhythm. Had her prayers been answered? "Black hair, dark complexion? About thirty-six?"

"Yeah, I guess that describes him. I didn't get that good a look at him before Mama ran me off."

With his message delivered, Will turned to exit the kitchen. As his hand reached the doorknob, Lillie Mae rushed across the room and grabbed his arm. A startled gasp rounded his mouth as his gaze questioned her.

"What's wrong?" he asked.

"Don't go in there and disturb your mama. Her business with that man is private."

"You know who he is, don't you?"

She tightened her hold on the boy's arm—the boy who meant more to her than life itself. He was all she had in this old world. Lane's son. Oh, she knew that Miss Lane hadn't nurtured him in her body, that she hadn't given birth to him, but he was her child all the same. Will belonged to Lane as surely as if he had grown inside her. Together she and Lane had loved Will, sacrificed for him and protected him at all costs. But in the end, they hadn't been able to protect him from the truth. Or from Kent's vindictive rage!

"I think I know who he is," Lillie Mae admitted, as she released her tenacious hold on Will's arm. "I sent for him, to help your mama."

"Is he a lawyer? Somebody you think can do a better job for Mama than James can?"

"We'd best wait and let your mama answer your questions."

Will narrowed his eyes, squinting them so that the expression on his face was identical to the look she had seen on Johnny Mack's face a hundred times in the years she'd known him as a boy and a young man. Such an angry, embittered young man. But then he'd had a right to be all that and more. Life had dealt him a pretty sorry hand, and he had played it the best way he'd known how.

"I hate this!" Will gritted the words through clenched teeth. "More secrets! That's all my life has been—ugly, dirty secrets."

"Now, you stop that!" Lillie Mae shook her bony index finger in Will's face. "There's nothing ugly or dirty about your life. You're a good boy. Not one thing that has happened is your fault. Do you hear me? Just like your mama has told you, you're the only innocent one in all of this mess."

Will's face flushed crimson. "Maybe I'm not so innocent. Maybe I'm the one who . . . who—"

She grabbed his shoulders and shook him. "I don't want to ever hear you talking such nonsense. Let your mama and me and . . . and that man out there"— she inclined her head in the direction of the foyer— "handle everything. We're not going to let anything bad happen to you. Not ever again."

"That man out there—" Will mimicked her head nod. "What's he got to do with us? Why would he help you and Mama *handle* things?"

"Because he owes your mama his life." Lillie Mae released her tight grip on Will, then lifted her chin and squared her shoulders. "He's come back to Noble's Crossing to pay a long overdue debt."

"How'd Mama save his life?"

Lillie Mae saw the curiosity in Will's eyes. What would it hurt if she told him about Johnny Mack, about what happened that long-ago September night, without revealing the man's relationship to Will? Sooner or later, Will would have to be told, but it would be up to Lane to decide when to tell Will who the stranger was and to introduce father and son.

"Come on back in here and sit down while I put on that fresh pot of coffee." Lillie Mae motioned for him to sit at the kitchen table. "You stay in here with me and I'll tell you about how your mama brought home a half-drowned man who'd been badly beaten and dumped in the Chickasaw River."

With his attention focused solely on the tale yet to be told, Will pulled out a Windsor oak chair from the round table and sat.

"When did this happen? How old was Mama?"

Lillie Mae grinned. She could kill two birds with one stone—keep Will occupied so Lane could talk to Johnny Mack and at the same time give Will some insight into Lane's past relationship with his biological father.

While busying herself with preparations for the coffee machine, Lillie Mae let her mind drift back to that night nearly fifteen years ago when Miss Lane had dragged a half-dead Johnny Mack through the back door. She had never seen a sorrier sight. His face had been so bruised and bloodied, she hadn't recognized him at first. Them that had done the deed had meant to kill Johnny Mack. But they had miscalculated the boy's strength, determination and sheer survival instincts. He'd grown up hard and tough and wild. It took a lot to kill a man like that.

"This man . . . well, he wasn't much more than a boy back then, but he was a tough kid . . . he had done things that got some of the menfolk here in Noble's Crossing all riled up."

"What had he done?"

"Don't interrupt me. Besides, some of this story is X-rated, and you'll have to wait until you're twenty-one to hear it."

That comment gained Lillie Mae one of Will's beautiful smiles. Those smiles had warmed her heart for fourteen years and would continue to do so until the day she died. There was absolutely nothing she wouldn't do for this boy.

"Go on," Will said. "But don't leave out the X-rated parts, even if you have to sanitize them for me. Okay?"

"Sanitize them, huh?" Lillie Mae grinned. "Well, this young man had romanced a few ladies who belonged to other men. He was a regular heartbreaker, and your mama'd had a crush on him since she was fourteen. Just the age you are now."

"Then, why didn't she marry this man instead of marrying Kent?" Will's smile vanished, erased by memories of the man who had so cruelly disowned him.

"That's another story, but mainly because this other man left town a long time ago—before Miss Lane married Kent." Lillie Mae paused, took a deep breath and then continued her tale. "Your mama used to spend a lot of time down by the river. Thinking. Daydreaming." Using her thumb, Lillie Mae motioned toward the back of the house. "Her favorite sanctuary was the old boathouse. Anyway, that night she went down there and guess what she found lying on the riverbank, half-drowned and beaten so bad he couldn't even stand up?"

"This man—the one she'd had a crush on since she was fourteen?"

"Right. So, she helped him get on his feet, and halfway dragging him, she got him to the back door of this house. That's when she started hollering for me. We took him to my room because it was the only bedroom on the ground floor. Miss Lane wanted to call a doctor, but he said no, not to call anybody. That's when he told us that they had tried to kill him."

"Who had tried to kill him?" Will sat perched on the edge of his seat, his eyes wide with speculation.

"He didn't tell me who, but I suspect he told your mama. And I got my suspicions."

"How'd he get better without seeing a doctor?" Will asked. "And what did Grandfather and Grandmother Noble think about him staying here in their house?"

"Your grandparents were out of town, so they never knew about Miss Lane rescuing him. Your mama and me took care of him, the best we could. He was tough as they come and he was determined not to die. I think plotting revenge is what kept him alive. That and . . . and your mama.''

"Who is he?" Will looked Lillie Mae square in the eye.

"Best your mama tells you."

Will snapped his head around and glared at the closed kitchen door. "He's Johnny Mack Cahill, isn't he? He's the lowlife, son of a bitch bastard that Kent told me was my real father!"

For years after he had left town, Lane had dreamed of this moment. Johnny Mack Cahill coming home— home to her. But as time went by and she never heard from him, she had given up her dream. And somewhere along the way, the love she had once felt for Johnny Mack had slowly turned to hatred. It had been apparent that wherever he'd gone and whatever he'd done with his life, he had forgotten about her. So with each passing year, it had become easier and easier to blame him for her unhappiness.

But now, suddenly, after fifteen years, he was back— big as life and twice as deadly. What once would have been a dream come true was now a nightmare realized. The devil incarnate stood in front of her. Temptation personified. Every woman's fantasy. And every woman's downfall.

Why now, dear God? Why now?

"It's been a long time," Johnny Mack said in that deep, sexy Southern drawl, as he removed his Stetson and held it in his hand. "You're even prettier than I remember."

Heat rose inside Lane, warming her as it flushed her skin. A compliment from Johnny Mack had always set off a flood of butterflies in her stomach. If all else about their relationship had changed, that one aspect hadn't. *Don't believe a word he says,* an inner voice cautioned. *He's a charmer. A seducer. A heartbreaker.*

"I don't mean to be rude," Lane said, ever the polite, mannerly Southern belle her mother had raised her to be. "But why are you here? What are you doing in Noble's Crossing?"

You swore you'd never come back—that hell would freeze over first. What changed your mind?

She tried not to stare at him, not to take inventory of his physical assets. But with a man as devastatingly male as Johnny Mack Cahill, she found it impossible not to visually appreciate his long, lean body and his ruggedly handsome face. Dressed casually in jeans and a dark cotton shirt, he looked like a working man all cleaned up for a night on the town.

Just where had he been all these years and what had he been doing? And why, after fifteen years, had he shown up on her doorstep tonight?

"Aren't you even going to ask me to sit down?" He eyed the living room from his position in the foyer.

"Is this a social call?" she asked, her stomach churning, her nerves rioting.

"I'm not sure what kind of visit this is," he admitted. "A search for the truth, maybe."

Lane willed herself not to gasp aloud. Did he know? Had he somehow found out about Will? But how, after all these years? Was it possible that the story of Kent's murder had reached him wherever he lived now? Maybe he wasn't here because of Will. Maybe he didn't know he had a son. Perhaps he had come back to Noble's Crossing to help her. If that were true, then he was, as the old adage said, a day late and a dollar short. If she had ever meant anything to him, he would have come back for her long before now.

"And just what truth are you seeking?" She stuck out her chin defiantly, as if daring him to mention Will. At the thought of her son, she glanced toward the closed kitchen door and prayed that Lillie Mae could keep Will occupied until she could get rid of her uninvited company.

"Worried about the boy overhearing our conversation?"

Johnny Mack's lips curved into the turn-a-woman's-knees-to-jello smile that Lane remembered only too well. So, he knew she had a child, but just how much did he really know about Will?

"Yes," she admitted. "Until I know why you're back in town, after an absence of fifteen years, I'd prefer my son not meet you."

"Fair enough." Without another word, Johnny Mack reached inside his back pocket and pulled his wallet from his jeans. After retrieving a folded piece of paper, he spread it apart to reveal a newspaper clipping and a small photograph. He held the items out to Lane. Their gazes met and locked. A hard knot of apprehension formed in the pit of her stomach. With trembling fingers, she reached out and accepted his offering.

The photograph was of Will. Last year's school picture. The knot in her stomach tightened. He looked just like Johnny Mack, feature for feature, right down to the devastating smile. How could Johnny Mack have seen this picture and not realized that the boy was his?

Hurriedly Lane glanced at the newspaper clipping and recognized it as being the front-page story about Kent's murder that had run in the local paper. The *Herald,* which she co-owned with Miss Edith. Lane turned her attention to the last item in her hand. A sheet of lined notebook paper on which two succinct sentences had been written. *Come home. Your son needs you.*

Bile rose into her throat. Her knees weakened. She closed her eyes, momentarily shutting out the truth. Johnny Mack knew that Will was his son!

"We can't talk here," she told him, then neatly folded the items and handed them back to him. "We need to talk privately, where there's no chance of our being overheard."

Johnny Mack glanced past her toward the hallway leading to the kitchen. "All right. Where and when? The sooner the better."

"Yes, I agree. The sooner the better." Lane's mind splintered into fragments, each flying off in a different direction. Without even thinking she blurted out, "Tomorrow. I'll meet you, wherever you say."

"I'm staying at the Four Way," he told her. "What time?"

Only people who couldn't afford better stayed at the Four Way. It was one step above a rat hole. Clean, but shabby. Lane supposed that Johnny Mack's finances hadn't improved much over the years.

"Ten o'clock in the morning," she said.

He nodded agreement, but his gaze remained riveted to her face. She sensed that he wanted to say more, that he wanted to touch her. To shake her hand. To squeeze her shoulder. Something. Anything. To make a personal contact. She couldn't let that happen. She didn't dare.

Lane took an uncertain step backward, away from him. Johnny Mack had been the most dangerous young man she had ever known, and her instincts told her that he was far more dangerous now. There was something about him, an air of confidence that had been lacking fifteen years ago. What had given him the aura of self-assurance that had replaced the mask of cocky bravado he had worn as a youth?

"Ten o'clock tomorrow at the Four Way. Room seventeen," he said. "And don't be afraid of me, Lane. You're the last person on earth I'd ever hurt."

Before she could respond, he turned away. She caught up with him just after he opened the front door and stepped out onto the porch. She hung back, hesitant to move too close. Lingering in the doorway, she called his name.

"Johnny Mack?"

His body stiffened. But when he glanced back over his shoulder, his seductive smile was in place. "Yeah?"

"I didn't send the note." She swallowed hard. "I had no idea where—" She stopped abruptly when she heard footsteps behind her. She eased back inside and slammed the door in Johnny Mack's face.

She knew before she turned around that Will had come out of the kitchen. He stood in front of her, his eyes filled with questions.

"Is he gone?"

"Yes, he's gone," she said.

"He's Johnny Mack Cahill, isn't he?"

"Yes." *Heaven help us all, yes, he's Johnny Mack Cahill. Your father. And my destroyer.*

"I'm glad you made him leave. I don't want to ever see him again!"

Will rushed past her, his long legs taking him quickly up the spiral staircase to the second level of the house. Lane hurried after him, but halted halfway up the stairs.

"Will!"

The sound of his door slamming reverberated in her ears. She sank down on the steps, a feeling of hopelessness encompassing her. How much more could her son endure? What was his final breaking point? She had to keep him safe from anything and anyone who might harm him. And that included Johnny Mack.

"Has Johnny Mack gone?" Lillie Mae stood at the bottom of the staircase.

Lane glanced at the rail-thin old woman who had been her only confidante and dearest friend for the past fifteen years. "Did you send that note to Johnny Mack?"

Standing at attention, like a proud soldier, Lillie Mae said, "Yes, I sent the note. Even if he doesn't realize it right now, Will needs his father—his real father. And whether you'll admit it or not, you need Johnny Mack, too. You need a strong man at your side if you're going to fight and win this battle. And it's way past time for Johnny Mack to pay the piper."

Edith Ware opened the door to Mary Martha's room. Jackie Cummings jumped up out of the chair in front of the television in the sitting area and smiled a warm greeting to her employer.

"Come on in, Miss Edith."

Jackie all but bowed to her. Edith liked subservience in her employees. Actually, she appreciated subservience in all her relationships, even in her marriage. There had been only two people she had never been able to bend to her will. Her first husband, John Graham. And his bastard son, Johnny Mack Cahill.

Edith motioned for Buddy Lawler to follow her as she entered her daughter's sanctuary, a room that had changed little since Mary Martha was twelve. Pastels and lace and girlish frills. French Provincial furniture and a wall curio filled with dolls.

"How is Miss Mary Martha doing tonight?" Edith asked.

"She ate a few bites of supper," Jackie reported. "She's been sitting peacefully over there in her rocker for the past hour."

Edith turned her attention to her child. Her thirty-three-year-old child. Her only child, now that Kent was dead. Mary Martha possessed an innocent beauty that was deceptive. Flawless pale skin. Waist-length strawberry blond hair. And pale brown eyes that seemed incapable of seeing into the real world.

"What's that she's holding?" Edith took a step closer and barely stifled the gasp that came immediately to her lips.

"It's just a baby doll," Jackie said. "She's been toting it around all day. And tonight she's been rocking it and singing to it. I hope that's all right. I didn't see any harm in her playing with her doll."

"No, of course not." Edith bit down on her bottom lip. No harm at all for her mentally unstable daughter of thirty-three to play with a doll as if she were a six-year-old. Without glancing back at the hired nurse, Edith said, "Why don't you take a break, Ms. Cummings. Buddy and I will sit with Mary Martha awhile."

"Yes, ma'am. Thank you. I wouldn't mind a smoke."

"Remember to go outside for that," Edith said. "No one has smoked in this house since Mr. Graham died. The day he died, I burned every damn box of cigars he had."

"I'll go on the back porch." Jackie nodded hello to the police chief as she excused herself.

Edith moved slowly toward her daughter, halting as she came up behind the rocking chair. "She's been like this since the afternoon after Kent's funeral. I thought surely by now she would have improved."

Mary Martha rocked back and forth in the white wooden rocker. Holding the life-size baby doll in her arms, she crooned to it as a mother would to a child.

Edith caressed the top of Mary Martha's head. "I'm afraid to let a psychiatrist examine her. There's no telling what she might say."

"Then, we'll make sure she's taken care of until she's ready to come back to us on her own terms." Buddy Lawler knelt in front of Mary Martha and spoke to her in a soft, caring voice. "How are you tonight, sweetheart? I hear you ate a little bit of supper. That's good. You gotta eat more. Gotta keep up your strength. As soon as you get well, I'm going to take you down to the Gulf, and we'll gather seashells on the beach the way we did the last time we were there."

Ignoring him, Mary Martha continued humming, continued rocking, apparently oblivious to all that was around her. Buddy reached out and caressed the doll's cheek. Mary Martha gathered the doll close to her chest and held it there as if she thought Buddy was going to snatch it away.

"Don't take my baby! Don't you take my baby!"

Mary Martha's pathetic cry pierced her mother's heart. This tragedy was her fault. Everything was her fault. But it was too late to do anything that could help Mary Martha. And too late for recompense on her part. Nothing could change the past. The most she could do now was protect her child.

"No, no, sweetheart," Buddy said. "It's all right. I'm not going to take your baby away from you."

He rose to his feet and turned his back, but not before Edith saw the sheen of tears in his eyes. If anyone on earth loved Mary Martha, Buddy did. He had been in love with her since they were children, and his devotion to her was touching. There was nothing Buddy wouldn't do for Mary Martha. She envied her daughter on that count.

Edith clasped the top round on the rocker with white-knuckled ferocity. Taking a deep, calming breath, she nodded toward the settee by the fireplace and said, "Why don't you sit down, Buddy? We'll stay a few more minutes. Our just being here with her will somehow reassure her, don't you think?"

Buddy nodded, then sat on the settee. His gaze rested sorrowfully on Mary Martha. "Do you think it's all right to talk in front of her? I mean, you don't think she'd get upset, that she'd actually understand what we're saying?"

"Just what did you want to talk to me about?" Edith asked.

"Well, we haven't had much chance to discuss the current situation, not with Kent's funeral and then Mary Martha going to pieces the way she did."

"And what is the current situation?" Edith walked over to the vanity, picked up a silver brush and returned to stand behind her daughter's chair.

"For one thing Lane is the main suspect in Kent's murder. How do you want us to handle that? Do you want to see her arrested or not?"

"Oh, yes, that situation." Edith ran the brush through Mary Martha's fiery gold hair and wished that she had taken the time to do this when her daughter was a child. "Lane deceived Kent. She made his life miserable and all for what? For a baby she knew had been fathered by Johnny Mack Cahill. Even if she didn't strike the blows that actually killed Kent, her part in the deception helped to kill him long before he died."

"You know what the local gossip is, don't you?"

"Tell me."

"I hear folks are saying they think Will killed Kent, and Lane is just taking the rap for him."

Edith had loved her grandson—the boy she had thought was her grandson. Even now, knowing Will wasn't her own flesh and blood, she still cared for him. But she couldn't—wouldn't—allow Johnny Mack's son to inherit anything from John Graham's estate.

"Hmm . . . Interesting. But we know that poor boy is as innocent of any wrongdoing as . . . as my Mary Martha," Edith said. "He's a good boy, even if he is the spawn of the devil."

"Yes, of course." Buddy stared directly at Edith and nodded agreement. "And speaking of the devil—I plan to call on our visitor and find out just who he is and what he wants." Buddy rubbed his hands nervously up and down the front of his thighs. "If by some chance he really is Johnny Mack, then we don't want him hanging around and muddying the water, do we?"

"By all means, pay this man calling himself Johnny Mack Cahill a visit. Tonight. If he is who he says he is, give him fair warning that he's not wanted here now any more than he was fifteen years ago."

"I don't see how it can be Johnny Mack. Not after the beating we gave him." Sweat dotted Buddy's forehead and upper lip. "My guess is that what's left of him is at the bottom of the Chickasaw River."

"Then, if this man isn't who he says he is, find out who he is and what he wants. And get rid of him!"

"Eavesdropping, Ms. Cummings?" James Ware asked as he came up behind his stepdaughter's private duty nurse.

Jackie gasped and jumped, then turned to face her

accuser. "Mercy, Mr. Ware, you scared the bejesus out of me!"

"What's going on in Mary Martha's room?"

"Oh, Miss Edith and Buddy Lawler are visiting with her." Jackie gave James a provocative, come-hither smile. "I've just come upstairs after taking a smoke on the back porch. I wasn't eavesdropping. I was waiting. Didn't want to disturb their visit."

"Hmm . . . I see."

James would bet his bankroll that Jackie would be more than willing to scratch any itch he had. She had had that kind of reputation as far back as he could remember. But he wasn't interested in her. The only woman for him was Arlene. He had loved her since they were teenagers, but had been a gutless coward back then. He'd allowed his family to keep them apart. However, after all these years, finally, if his plans worked out, they would have the rest of their lives together. With Edith consumed by Kent's murder, now was the perfect time to tie up all the loose ends.

"You're in kinda late, aren't you, Mr. Ware? Business in town?"

James searched Jackie's eyes for any hint that she knew about his affair with Arlene, but her expression revealed nothing.

"A mayor's work is never done," he replied, hoping he had infused his words with just the right amount of humor.

"Is that so? Would you believe my beautician says the same thing—that her work is never done? You know my beautician, Arlene Dothan, don't you?"

Jackie's tittering laughter sliced like a razor blade along James's nerve endings.

"Yes, of course I know Ms. Dothan."

"I thought you did." Jackie snuggled up to James's side. "I'll make you a deal, *Mayor*—you don't mention anything about my eavesdropping to Miss Edith, and I won't mention anything to her about how well you know my beautician."

Chapter 7

Light from a full moon bathed the old boathouse with a soft, creamy wash and danced across the river in shimmering ripples. A fresh coat of white paint on the aged wood and new hinges on the side door told Johnny Mack that Lane had kept the structure in tiptop shape. He wondered if William Noble's boat still resided inside or if it had been sold years ago. Since leaving Noble's Crossing, he had often thought about this place, about the times he and Lane had met here. She had been so young. So naive. So innocent. God, how he had wanted her. And he could have had her. She would have given herself to him without reservations.

Johnny Mack tried the door. Locked. In the old days, Lane had always left the door unlocked for him. This had been their place, a sanctuary from the real world. Here, he hadn't been a trailer trash bastard, and she hadn't been the princess of Noble's Crossing.

Lane sure had been in a hurry to get rid of him

tonight. He'd seen the fear in her eyes. Had she been afraid that he would ask to be introduced to her son? Surely she knew that he'd never do anything to hurt her or the boy. Even if Will turned out to be Kent's son, he would never hurt him. Because he was Lane's child, too.

Johnny Mack strolled by the river's edge, the ground soft beneath his feet, the heels of his boots branding the damp soil. Ancient willow trees dripped their long, feathery branches into the thick green grass, creating secluded little tents around their trunks. The one and only time he had ever kissed Lane had been beneath one of these willows.

Nighttime insects chortled late summertime choruses, the sound blending with the gentle rush of the river. Southern humidity seeped into the skin of man and beast alike, creating a heat within and perspiration on the flesh. Even the buildings weren't spared the effects of the weather, sweating and moaning and waiting for the relief of autumn.

As a young man, he had loved summertime. Swimming in the river. Drinking cold beer over at Goodloe's Tavern. Watching the girls walk by in their short-shorts. Getting all hot and sweaty by heating up the sheets with a willing woman. And watching Lane Noble watching him while he mowed their grass and pruned their hedges. He had usually worked in cutoff jeans and without a shirt, getting himself a dark tan and giving the ladies an eyeful.

Johnny Mack chuckled. He had been such a cocky SOB. A white trash rounder who hadn't had sense enough to stay where he belonged. The ladies on Magnolia Avenue had been Off Limits to him, but he hadn't let that stop him. He had sampled the delights of the rich, pampered, spoiled debutantes— and a few of their mamas, too. But he had drawn the line at bedding Mary Martha because he'd known she might be his half sister. Even a bad boy like him had had his principles, few that they were. And even a guy who had prided himself on screwing his way through the country club set had known true quality when he had seen it, when he'd touched it, when he'd loved it. And in his way, he had loved Lane. God, he had worshiped Lane!

She had represented everything he had wanted, everything that was good and kind and genteel. Breeding and character and a gentle heart. He had known that she was far too good for the likes of him. But hell, she had been way too good for Kent Graham, too. So why had she married the sorry son of a bitch? The thought of Kent even touching Lane made him sick.

With her mind a jumbled mass of confusion, Lane escaped to the rose garden behind the house. She gazed up at the night sky as memories long buried deep in her heart resurfaced. Johnny Mack was back in town! Dear Lord, what was she going to do? She had truly believed that she would never see him again, that he would never return to Noble's Crossing.

Will hated Johnny Mack. Kent had seen to that with his vile, vindictive ranting, giving her son the worst possible scenario of Johnny Mack's life from birth to twenty-one. She had known Kent could be cruel, but until he had tried to destroy Will with his bitter hatred, she hadn't realized just how cruel her ex-husband could be.

God forgive her, she had wanted Kent dead. And thoughts of killing him had crossed her mind. But except to protect herself or Will, she never could have taken Kent's worthless life. But someone else had done the deed for her. Someone who hated Kent even more than she did. Someone who had been pushed over the edge.

Her greatest fear was that Will had murdered Kent. When she had found her son, dazed and confused, standing over Kent's body, she had decided then and there that she would protect her child, no matter what the cost to herself. She was as much at fault as Kent or Sharon or Lillie Mae. She had been a perpetrator in the great hoax. Every day of her married life, she had lied to her husband.

I did it for Will.

And for yourself, her conscience reminded her. *You wanted Johnny Mack's child. You would have done anything to have prevented Sharon from aborting his baby.*

If only she could go back fifteen years. No, she would have to go back farther than that. Back nineteen years. Back to when she was fourteen. Back to the first moment she laid eyes on Johnny Mack Cahill.

But what good would going back in time do? Would it change the fact that she had fallen head over heels in love, the way only a young girl can? No, of course it wouldn't change the inevitable. Nothing short of an act of God could have prevented her from loving Johnny Mack. She hadn't chosen to love the town bad boy, the womanizing hell-raiser to whom she had been nothing more than a friend.

"You're the only girl I've ever been just friends with," he had told her. And that admission had broken her young heart. She had wanted to be so much more than his friend. She had foolishly longed to be the love of his life.

Without even realizing what she had done, Lane found herself moving along the path that led from her mother's flower garden down to the old boathouse and pier on the river. How many hours had she spent in that boathouse, sitting on the deck of her daddy's small yacht with Johnny Mack? Alone. Secluded from the outside world. Talking, laughing and falling more and more in love with him.

She could not—would not!—allow those old feelings to rise from the ashes. She had burned her bridges years ago, when she'd finally realized that the price she had paid for loving Johnny Mack had been too high. In the beginning, every time Kent touched her, she had tried to pretend he was Johnny Mack. The fantasy had been a dismal failure. Eventually she had grown to hate Johnny Mack even more than she despised Kent.

The moment he saw the shadowy figure moving toward the boathouse, he knew who it was. She hadn't been able to stay away any more than he had. They had both been drawn back to the place where they'd spent so many happy hours. By the river. Fishing from the pier. Private moments inside the boathouse.

"I thought you'd come here," he said.

"Johnny Mack?"

The voice of the past. The voice he had never been able to get out of his head. Lane's sweet, rich, honey-coated Alabama drawl.

"Over here." He stepped out from beneath a sheltering willow and allowed the moon's glow to spotlight him.

"What are you doing here?" she asked.

"I could ask you the same question."

"I had to get out of the house," she admitted. "Your showing up out of the blue the way you did . . . Why didn't you just stay away? The last thing my son needs right now is to have to deal with you."

"Somebody thought *your* son needed me."

Lane hesitated on the pier at the edge of the boat-house, half in shadows. "Lillie Mae sent you the note."

"Ah . . . makes sense." He walked toward Lane slowly, giving her time to meet him halfway.

He could sense her uncertainty, could feel her fear. What was she afraid of? Surely not of him. He paused and waited, allowing her to step out of the murky, blue-black shadows. When she did, he sucked in a deep breath. Up at the house an hour ago, he had realized that Lane had grown up to be a beautiful woman. But in the brightly lit foyer, with Lillie Mae and the boy close by, he hadn't allowed himself to appreciate that loveliness. But now, alone together, with only the sticky summer breeze and the swaying willows as witnesses, he drank his fill of her.

He remembered her curly brown hair being waist-length and how sometimes when he had thought of her, he fantasied about that glorious mane of hair. But she had not only cut her hair so that the tips barely touched her shoulders, but she had lightened it to a dark blond. The slight plumpness which had plagued her from childhood through adolescence had melted away into mature, feminine curves. And those luminous blue eyes, which had once been so filled with life and love, were now hooded and wary and staring at him pleadingly.

"I told you that you didn't have to be afraid of me," he said. "I didn't come back to Noble's Crossing to hurt you, to cause problems for you."

She took another tentative step toward him. "Why did you come back? Why after all these years would you care about . . . about me or anyone else in Noble's Crossing?"

"I owe you my life. Of course I care about you, about the fact that you're the prime suspect in Kent's murder.'' Raking his hand across his mouth as if to wipe away a bitter taste, Johnny Mack glared at Lane. ''Why the hell did you marry Kent Graham?''

Lane's chest rose and fell with each labored breath she took. Thrusting out her chin, she looked directly at Johnny Mack. ''I married him so that I could adopt Will.''

Anger and pain blended with love and strength, wrapping the combined emotions around her words. She had made a declaration, her statement seeming to dare him to question her motivation. But it was more what she had not said than what she had that ripped at Johnny Mack's guts. Although she hadn't spoken the accusation aloud, he had heard it in the tone of her voice. *If you had taken me with you, I never would have married Kent.* Or was he wrong? Had he heard what he wanted to hear, assumed what he wanted to believe?

''I hired a private investigator to dig up information on Will,'' Johnny Mack told her. ''I know that his birth certificate—his original birth certificate—states that Sharon Hickman was his mother and Kent Graham was his father.''

Lane's eyes opened wide. Her lips parted slightly on an indrawn breath. ''How is it possible that your investigator got hold of a copy of Will's original birth certificate?''

''Don't you know by now that if you've got enough money, you can buy just about anything you want?'' Enjoying the shocked look on Lane's face made him feel like a real bastard. But he couldn't help wondering just how much more pleasure he would feel when he saw the reaction of people he hated—people like Miss Edith!

''And do you have a great deal of money?'' Lane asked.

"Enough to get whatever I want." That was a laugh. Yeah, he could have anything money could buy. And there had been a time when that would have been enough for him, when it had been all he wanted. But in the past few years, he had come to realize there were a few things all the money in the world couldn't buy.

"And just what *do* you want, Johnny Mack?"

"The truth," he said. "Is Will Kent's son or is he mine?"

Lane lowered her lashes and averted her gaze. "Will is my son! He's been mine since the first moment I held him."

She was like a tigress, claws extended, teeth bared, ready to strike out at any threat to her cub. Johnny Mack had never known a mother's love, never felt sheltered and protected by the woman who had given birth to him. In an odd sort of way, he envied Will Graham. What would he give to have a woman like Lane love him half that much?

"I know he's yours. I'm not disputing your claim on him. I just want to know—no, I need to know— the truth. Is Will my son?"

Lane wrapped her arms around her body, clasping her elbows. "What possible difference could it make to you after all this time? For all you knew, you could have left behind half a dozen women pregnant with your baby. You didn't care then. Why should you care now?"

This wasn't the Lane he had known. Sweet. Gentle. Innocent. There had been no anger, no hatred in that girl. But hatred radiated from this woman. A hatred focused directly at him.

Damn but the truth hurt. Hurt like hell. Lane was right. Despite using condoms as a general rule, he still could have left behind more than one pregnant woman that summer. And even if he had known he'd gotten some girl pregnant, he would have left Noble's Crossing anyway. He had been running for his life back then. Staying in this town would have meant signing his own death warrant.

"Even if I'd cared, I could hardly have stayed on," he said. "You know as well as I do that when I high-tailed it out of town, quite a few people thought I was dead."

"In all the years since you left, you never wrote. You never called. When you said goodbye to me at the bus station in Decatur, you cut all your ties to me and to Noble's Crossing."

"And if I had called?" he asked.

"You didn't."

"But if I had, would you have told me about marrying Kent? About adopting Will?"

"There is no point in playing 'what if,' is there? Lillie Mae thought she was doing the right thing by sending you that note, but she was wrong. There's nothing you can do for me. And if you think I'll let you hurt Will any more than he's already been hurt, then you'd better—"

"I'm not here to hurt Will." Johnny Mack grabbed Lane's hands, which she had knotted into tight fists. Her arms went stiff, her body rigid at the touch of his flesh against hers. "Why do you hate me so much?"

He stroked the underside of her wrist with his thumb. She shivered. He released her immediately, realizing she was not only completely aware of him as a man, but that she was also just a little bit afraid of him, too. God, she was the one person in this town he didn't want to fear him!

"Tell me the truth," he said. "Don't I deserve even that much?"

She turned her back on him, as if looking at him

was too painful. In a quiet, but amazingly strong voice, she said, "Sharon came to me after you'd left town. She told me she was pregnant and that you were the father."

Johnny Mack felt as if a hard fist had just punched him in the gut and knocked all the air out of him. Will *was* his son. Sometime during that long, hot summer fifteen years ago, he had gotten Sharon pregnant. Maybe a condom had leaked. Maybe he had forgotten to use one. Damn, he couldn't remember every time he'd screwed Sharon that July. Back then, he had spent more time humping every willing female than he had doing anything else. But he'd always kept a pack of condoms handy.

"Why did she come to you? You two weren't exactly best friends." Johnny Mack shifted his weight from one foot to the other as he tried to rein in the anger boiling inside him.

"She wanted to borrow money from me for an abortion."

"Hmph! Sounds like Sharon. She wouldn't have wanted to be saddled with a kid. So, why didn't you loan her the money? It doesn't make any sense to me why you'd ruin your life by marrying Kent and raising Sharon's child."

Lane closed her eyes as if trying to blot out some horrible memory. Reflected moonlight caught in the teardrops trickling down her cheeks.

"Lane?"

He closed the distance between them, but when he reached for her, she sidestepped him and stood rigidly at his side, her stance daring him to touch her. Lane possessed a solitary strength, as if during the past fifteen years, she had learned that she could rely on no one except herself. He could see that strength in her cold eyes, in her tightly coiled body, in the aura of self-assurance that surrounded her. This woman wasn't the girl he had known. She was as much a stranger to him as he was to her.

"I made a deal with Sharon." Lane swallowed, clearing her throat. "If she wouldn't get an abortion, I'd adopt her baby."

"And she agreed, knowing you were just a nineteen-year-old kid yourself?"

"We—we concocted a plan," Lane explained. "Sharon had been sleeping with Kent, after you left town, after she suspected she was already pregnant. We thought that if she told him the child was his, he might believe her. And if I agreed to marry him and adopt his child, then—"

"Then he'd want the kid for sure, if you were part of the bargain!" Johnny Mack slammed one big fist in the palm of his other hand. The slap reverberated in the nighttime stillness. "Damn! But why? Why marry a man you'd refused to marry a dozen times over just to keep Sharon from aborting her baby?"

Lane swiped the tears from her cheeks. "He was your baby. All that I had left of you. I wouldn't allow anyone to harm him! Not then and not now."

Figuratively brought to his knees by her admission, humbled to the point of wanting to prostrate himself in front of her, Johnny Mack remained silent. His throat closed tightly. He'd known Lane had had a crush on him for years before he'd left town, but he'd had no idea the depth of her feelings for him. She was probably the only woman in his entire life who had ever loved him. And loved him so unselfishly.

He wanted to reach out and take her into his arms, to hold and comfort her, to thank her for such a precious gift. But he could tell by her wary stance that she didn't want him to touch her. She had loved him fifteen years ago, loved him enough to make a tremendous sacrifice for his child, but how did she feel about him now? How much had the passing of fifteen years, marriage to Kent and a lifetime of lies changed Lane? She probably hated him now. If she did, he couldn't blame her.

"I was very foolish back then, wasn't I? I've grown up a lot since then. I've learned a great deal about love. What it is and what it isn't." Her voice softened and trailed off quietly. "I was so infatuated with you." Sucking in air, she tilted back her head and stared up at the starry sky. "Will is the only thing that matters to me now. I would do anything to protect him."

"Even murder Kent?"

The moment he saw the hurt look in her eyes, the silent gasp form on her lips, he wished back the words. But it was too late. Just as it was too late to go back fifteen years and change the past. All he could do now was accept the blame for what he had done— for all the harm he had caused. He had known, somewhere in the darkest, most private recesses of his soul, that the day of reckoning would come. Sooner or later, a man always paid for his sins.

"Yes, even murder Kent," she admitted.

Her voice was so whispery quiet that he barely heard her over the drumming roar of his own heartbeat.

"Do you have a good lawyer?" He broke off a willow limb and began stripping the leaves, avoiding eye contact with Lane.

"James Ware has been handling everything for me."

"Kent's stepfather?"

"After James Ware, Sr.'s, death, James, Jr., became my father's lawyer as well as the Graham family lawyer," Lane said. "He doesn't think there's enough evidence for a grand jury to indict me, but then James isn't a criminal lawyer. If I'm indicted, I'll hire someone else. An expert."

Johnny Mack tossed the bare willow branch into the Chickasaw River and watched it float away downstream. "I can afford to hire you the best criminal defense attorney in the South. One phone call from me and Quinn Cortez will be on the next plane to Alabama."

"You must be very, very rich, Johnny Mack, if you can pay Mr. Cortez's fees." Lane nodded toward the path that spiraled along the riverbank. "Let's walk. I'm too jittery to just stand here."

He fell into step beside her and noticed that their bodies formed a connected shadow. One tall. One short. Side by side, joined together without physically touching.

"Want to tell me what happened?" he asked. "I'm here, Lane, because I want to help you. I want to try to make things right, if I can."

Her brittle laughter tore at his gut, like the talons of a falcon ripping apart its prey. Without saying a word, she had told him that he was offering too little, too late.

"Will hiring Quinn Cortez to defend me ease your conscience?"

She knew him too well. Even after all these years, she could still see inside his soul. Lane had been the only person who had ever been able to see past his cocky, bad boy exterior. The only woman who had ever cared enough to search for the good in him.

"Yeah, it would be a start. After all, you know better than anyone that I did a lot of damage before I left this town. I have to start somewhere to make it up to you . . . and to Will for—"

"He doesn't want to have anything to do with you."

"What?" Johnny Mack stopped dead still. "Are you saying he knows that I'm his father?"

Lane halted and turned to face Johnny Mack. "Yes, he knows. And I'm afraid that, right now, he hates you."

"Did you tell him about me?"

"No, but I wish I had." She keened softly, as if trying to ward off some impending disaster. "Kent told him. And he didn't do it kindly. He took out all his anger and hate on Will."

"That bastard!"

"Kent was a bastard all right. He enjoyed hurting Will because he was yours. And he enjoyed hurting me because . . . Kent Graham wasn't a very nice man."

Saying that Kent wasn't a very nice man was a gross understatement. It was like saying Alaska was cool in the winter. "How did Kent find out I was Will's father?" He grabbed Lane's shoulders, but stopped himself just short of shaking her.

"Sharon wrote a deathbed confession." Lane's forced smile hardened her face. "She told Kent everything. How we had duped him, making him believe Will was his. Sharon was doing some conscience easing of her own." Lane pummeled her fists against Johnny Mack's chest. "That stupid, stupid woman! All she'd cared about was money. But when she found out she was dying, her conscience started bothering her. She never thought about what the truth would do to Will. Not once did she put her child's welfare first."

He manacled Lane's wrists in one hand, halting her pounding assault. She glared at him with pure loathing. Like a blinding flash, a cold, bitter truth hit Johnny Mack. "How much did you pay Sharon?"

"What?"

Gripping one shoulder, he shook Lane. Gently but

forcefully. "Tell me the truth. How much did you pay Sharon for my son?"

"Oh!" Her mouth formed an astonished oval. Tears glistened in her eyes. "Fifty thousand dollars. I asked Daddy to give it to me for a wedding present."

"She sold you her baby." Johnny Mack released Lane. Anger exploded inside him like bottle rockets on the Fourth of July. He needed something to hit. A punching bag. Kent Graham. Buddy Lawler. "Why didn't Lillie Mae tell me about Will? She's known where I was for nearly ten years now."

"I have no idea why she didn't tell you about Will or why she never told me that she knew where you were. But I assume Lillie Mae did what she thought was best for Will, just as I did. When you left, you swore you'd never come back. You washed your hands of Noble's Crossing and everyone in it. We got along just fine without you. We didn't need you."

"But you need me now, don't you? At least Lillie Mae thinks so."

"She's afraid that I might be indicted for Kent's murder, and if I'm—"

"You will not be convicted of killing Kent, even if you did murder the son of a bitch." Johnny Mack gripped Lane's chin between his thumb and forefinger. "Do you hear me? Quinn Cortez has never lost a case. And I'm calling him tonight."

Lane stood on the porch and watched Johnny Mack get in his car and back out of the driveway. He was coming to lunch tomorrow to meet his son. He had invited himself, showing her that a part of the brash, unmannerly boy he had once been still existed somewhere inside him. All her protests had fallen on deaf ears. Short of calling the police when he showed up tomorrow, she didn't know how to stop him. And at this point, involving the local authorities wasn't an option.

Like a hurricane wind, Johnny Mack had stormed back into her life, wanting, needing and demanding. And making promises. In the past he had never made promises to her, and yet he had broken her heart all the same.

I want to meet Will. . . . I'll call Quinn Cortez and have him on standby, ready to take the next plane to Alabama when we need him. . . . You won't be convicted of Kent's murder, even if you did murder the son of a bitch. . . . I'd never hurt you, Lane. I'd never hurt you. . . .

He would never hurt her again and not because he had said he wouldn't, but because she would not let him. Kent had destroyed her naivete, her ability to easily trust in the goodness of others. And Johnny Mack had taught her the foolishness of loving with blind devotion. She had once loved with all her heart, completely, holding back nothing. But now she loved no one, except Will and Lillie Mae. Trusted no one, except Will and Lillie Mae. Johnny Mack couldn't hurt her—not any longer. But he could hurt Will.

Lane glanced up at the second story of the house and noted the light shining in the windows of Will's room. She had to talk to him, explain about Johnny Mack, make him understand that he wasn't the horrible human being Kent had said he was.

But just how much about Kent and about Kent's death did she dare discuss with Will? How much could she dredge up without renewing Will's nightmares? She had believed it was a blessing that he couldn't remember Kent's murder, whether he committed the crime himself or had simply been a witness to it. If Will had killed Kent, if he had taken his baseball bat and bludgeoned Kent to death, wouldn't it be better if he never remembered?

If only she had been there. If only she could have stopped Kent from spewing his putrid hatred and torturing Will with a distorted version of the truth. But Lillie Mae had been there and hadn't been able to prevent disaster. Or had she? Was it possible that Lillie Mae. . . . No! She had to stop speculating about what happened the day Kent was murdered. It didn't really matter who killed him. All that truly mattered was keeping Will safe.

Lane took one step at a time, preparing herself for the confrontation with her son. What could she say to him? How could she make him understand that regardless of what Kent had said about Johnny Mack, the man wasn't a monster. He was simply a guy who had made some bad choices, a man who had made up his own rules as he went along and had been hell-bent to snub his nose at local society. She couldn't defend most of the things Johnny Mack had done, but she could paint a more honest picture of Will's biological father. Even if she hated Johnny Mack, she didn't want Will to hate him.

Chapter 8

Lillie Mae met Lane the moment she entered the house. A frown marred her wrinkled face. Lane had known Lillie Mae long enough to recognize the look as one of agitated concern. *Is she worried that I'm angry with her because she sent for Johnny Mack?*

"You and I need to talk," Lane said. "But first I'm going upstairs to see to Will. I have to explain some things to him about Johnny Mack and make him understand—"

"Will's gone."

"What?"

"Miss Edith called right after you went out." Lillie Mae grimaced as if the mention of Kent's mother left a bitter taste in her mouth. "She asked Will to come over there and see Miss Mary Martha. Seems she's been calling for Will."

"Calling for him by name or just calling for her baby?"

Lane hated the way Mary Martha often referred to

Will as *my baby*. Since the first time her sister-in-law held Will, Lane had felt a certain uneasiness every time Kent's sister had lavished attention on him. Mary Martha had an almost unhealthy attachment to Will, but whenever she had mentioned that fact to Kent, he had dismissed it as foolishness.

"You aren't jealous of Mary Martha are you, sweetheart?" Kent had said. *"She's just being a devoted aunt. No need for you to concern yourself."*

"I don't know if she asked for him by name. Will didn't say. Just told me that his aunt was calling for him." Lillie Mae nodded to the door. "Did Johnny Mack leave?"

"Yes."

"Will he be back?"

"Yes. Tomorrow. He invited himself to lunch."

"Sounds like Johnny Mack." The corners of Lillie Mae's mouth lifted slightly, with just a hint of a smile. "Why don't you go in the den? I'll make us some herbal tea, and we can have that talk."

Lane nodded. "Tea sounds good about now."

As Lane made her way to the den, she wondered if she should go over to the Graham house next door and check on Will. No, she shouldn't. Her son considered himself a capable young man. At fourteen, he often resented Lane's smothering motherly attention. It had been difficult enough before Kent's murder to allow Will breathing space, but now—dear God, now!—she couldn't bear for her son to be out of her sight for more than a few minutes. What if his memory returned when she wasn't with him? What if he remembered that he *had* killed Kent?

Easing down into the tan leather chair near the windows overlooking the west side of the house, Lane sighed. Mentally and emotionally weary, tired from carrying heavy burdens in her heart, she lifted her feet to rest them on the huge leather ottoman.

Her gaze scanned the room, which she had left unchanged since her parents' deaths. This den had been her father's sanctuary, a place to escape from his busy work schedule as the owner of Noble's Crossing's only daily newspaper—the *Herald*—begun by William Alexander Noble in 1839 and co-owned today by Lane and Edith Graham Ware.

Shortly after her marriage to Kent, her father's newspaper had been on the brink of being gobbled up by a New York conglomerate, but Edith had come to the rescue, saving the paper from Yankee invasion. Now Lane depended on the revenue from the paper to support herself and Will and to keep up the Noble estate. No matter what happened, she would never touch the trust fund her father and Edith had jointly set up for Will.

Lately Lane found herself gravitating toward this room, this small, cozy haven nestled away from the activity of the rest of the house. Dark paneled walls and wide crown molding in rich wood tones recalled the elegance of a bygone era, as did the heavily carved desk and the antique Persian rug. A portrait painted by renowned Atlanta artist Gower Mayfield hung over the fireplace—a portrait of a young, beautiful Celeste Noble and her only child, Lane, at the age of five.

She missed her parents terribly and probably always would. Although she and her mother had seldom seen eye-to-eye on anything, she had adored Celeste, the royal social butterfly of Noble's Crossing. No one could give a party the way Mrs. William Noble had. Her lavish soirees had been the talk of Alabama in the late sixties and early seventies. Perhaps if her mother hadn't spent so extravagantly, her father might not have found himself between the proverbial rock and hard place when the family's ownership of the *Herald* had become endangered.

She had not only loved her father, but she had admired him greatly. Bill Noble had been a gentle man who had possessed a strong moral character and a charitable soul. He had known almost everyone in town by name and treated rich and poor with the same respect. He had been the one who had first hired Johnny Mack Cahill to do yard work on Magnolia Avenue.

When Celeste had protested about Johnny Mack's presence, Lane's father had said, in his calm, yet authoritarian voice, "The poor boy needs someone to give him a chance. He has no one, except that drunken Wiley Peters, to see after him. I don't like the idea of anyone going hungry, and I have an idea that Johnny Mack has gone to bed hungry more than once in his life."

"Mark my word, Bill Noble, we will all rue the day you brought that young hellion into our lives!" Celeste had said. In retrospect, her statement had been eerily prophetic.

After having overheard that conversation between her parents, Lane had made a point of checking out this dangerous boy. Sitting in the window seat in her upstairs bedroom, she had watched him as he mowed the grass and pruned the shrubs. She had been all of fourteen and filled with sexual urges she simply hadn't understood. All she had known was that every time she looked at Johnny Mack Cahill, her body tingled and her mind created images of his muscular brown arms holding her close as he gave her her very first kiss.

"Tea's ready." Lillie Mae stood in the doorway, a silver tray in her hands. She smiled tentatively at Lane. A peace offering? *Are you upset with me?* Lillie Mae was asking silently. *And if you are angry, will you forgive me for summoning Johnny Mack?*

"Put the tray over there." Lane inclined her head toward the large mahogany desk with elaborate ribbon detailing on the drawers. "Please, pour us both a cup. Then come sit over here by me and we'll talk."

Lillie Mae's hesitant smile broadened, creasing lines into her pale cheeks. "We need him, Miss Lane. We need him bad. Otherwise, I never would have sent for him."

Lane only nodded, uncertain how she should or could react. She didn't doubt for one minute that Lillie Mae had acted out of love and concern for Will and her. But she couldn't share Lillie Mae's certainty that Johnny Mack would be their savior. How could a man who had once wreaked so much havoc on this town, whose irresponsible acts had damaged so many lives, suddenly become the solution to their problems? If trouble possessed a name, that name was Johnny Mack Cahill.

Lillie Mae handed Lane a Royal Doulton china cup filled with hot Earl Grey tea. No lemon. No sugar. No cream. "I figure that with him being fifteen years older, he's not the same boy who left Noble's Crossing in the dark of night, letting a lot of folks think he was dead. He's thirty-six. Older and maybe a lot wiser. And I know for a fact that he's got money. He's been sending me a check every month for years now, and I've been putting it in a savings account in case you and Will ever needed it. If Johnny Mack don't offer to pay for you a good out-of-town lawyer, we'll use that money to do it."

Lane accepted the cup, then set it aside on the small table to her right and grasped Lillie Mae's hand. "I love you dearly and I understand why you wrote to Johnny Mack, but . . . what makes you think he can help us?''

Lillie Mae squeezed Lane's hand as she looked into her eyes, her expression one of devotion and love. ''Johnny Mack never took advantage of you, of your innocence, and we both know he could have. And when he left this town, he refused to take you with him. You're the only woman I know he ever treated special. And I figure after you saved his life, he knew he owed you. All I did was call in your marker.''

Lane released Lillie Mae's hand, leaned back in the chair and closed her eyes. ''He told me that he's very rich.''

Lillie Mae eased her thin body down into the wing chair across from Lane. ''I figured as much. He could hardly afford to send me so much money every month if he wasn't.''

''He hired a private investigator who somehow got hold of Will's original birth certificate.'' Lane massaged her temples with circular swirls of her index fingers.

''Did he think Kent was Will's father just because that's what Sharon put on the birth certificate?''

''He asked me if he or Kent was Will's father.''

''What did you tell him?''

''The truth.''

Lillie Mae released a long, relieved sigh. ''Did you tell him everything? I mean about how Sharon came to you wanting money for an abortion and how y'all tricked Kent into adopting Will?''

Lane picked up the cup of tea. ''Yes. I explained how and why Kent and I married and adopted Will and that until Sharon's deathbed confession, Kent believed Will was his son.''

''Why that girl of mine had to get religion before she died and confess her sins is beyond me.'' Tears gathered in the corners of Lillie Mae's faded gray eyes. "I loved her, my Sharon. But Lord knows she wasn't worth shootin'. I guess folks thought that her dying the way she did, from AIDS, was punishment for her sins. But it wasn't God's punishment. It was her own doing. If she hadn't been hooked on them drugs, she'd never have come down with that horrible disease."

Lane kept silent. She agreed with Lillie Mae's assessment of Sharon's wasted life, but where Lillie Mae had a right to malign Will's biological mother, Lane didn't. After all, Sharon had given her something she otherwise would never have had—Johnny Mack's baby.

"So, Johnny Mack knows the truth." Lillie Mae glanced at Lane, her gaze speculative. "But you didn't tell him any details about your marriage to Kent, did you? You didn't tell him what a high price you paid for Will's life."

"No, I didn't tell him. And I don't want you sharing my secrets with him, either. Do you understand?"

"Yes, I understand. I understand only too well."

The fact that his grandmother met him at the door instead of one of the servants told Will how eager she was to see him. Maybe he shouldn't think of Edith Ware as his grandmother anymore, now that he knew Kent wasn't his father. But how could he turn off his emotions? Miss Edith, as everyone referred to her out of respect for her position in the community, had always been his doting grandmother, someone who had lavished attention and money on him all his life.

Edith reached over and squeezed his arm, a sad, uncertain look in her eyes. "Thank you for coming,

Will. I know that things have been strained between us since your father's—since Kent's death.''

"Yes, ma'am. I suppose, since you believed Kent was my real father, finding out that he wasn't came as a big shock to you.''

"Yes, of course. It was a major shock to all of us, except Lane, who had known all along that—''

"I don't want you to say anything against my mother,'' Will said. His stomach knotted painfully. He wasn't going to listen to Miss Edith making accusations against his mother. Not now or ever. He might be only fourteen, and others might consider him just a kid, but he knew things. He knew that his mother had suffered more than anyone else. He had heard the things Kent had said to her before their divorce. He knew the way Kent had treated her. And now, with Kent dead, people thought she had murdered him. But he knew better. His mother couldn't kill anyone. Not unless it was in self-defense or to protect someone she loved.

"As you wish,'' Edith replied. "We won't discuss Lane. Not tonight. At the moment I have a more urgent problem.'' Edith ushered Will into the marble-floored foyer and closed the door behind him. "Mary Martha is quite agitated and we can't calm her. Jackie has suggested giving her a sedative, but my poor girl has been overmedicated since Kent's death. And sometimes the medication has an adverse effect on her. I was hoping that you could calm her. All your life, you've been able to work wonders with Mary Martha.''

"You know that I'll do what I can, but if she's still in as bad a shape as she was the day of Dad . . . Kent's funeral, then I doubt she'll even know who I am.''

"She hasn't spoken a word to anyone since the day after the funeral,'' Edith said. "Not until tonight.

She'd been rocking one of her dolls for several hours and she kept calling it her baby. Then suddenly she flung the doll aside and said it wasn't her baby, that her baby was a big boy now. That's when she started calling for you."

Tears pooled in Edith's eyes. When she closed them, droplets glistened on her eyelashes, and moisture trickled onto her cheekbones. "You've always played that little game with her. You know, where you pretend that you really are her child. I was hoping that you'd play along with her tonight." Edith opened her eyes and looked squarely at Will. "And if she says anything . . . you know, about Kent—"

"Don't you think you should call the doctor?" Will asked. "Not just old Doc Morgan, but a real psychiatrist. Someone who might be able to help her."

"If she doesn't improve, then of course we'll have to seek psychiatric help. You know we've taken her to numerous doctors in the past, and she's even stayed at several private clinics; but no one's ever been able to help her."

Will started up the stairs, then halted when he noticed that his grandmother remained in the foyer. "Aren't you coming up with me?"

"No." She shook her head. "I think it's best that you see her alone. She always preferred to have you all to herself. But after your visit, please . . . Just let me know how things went."

Will nodded agreement. "Sure."

Mary Martha's room was at the end of the hall. He stood outside the closed door for a couple of minutes, took several deep breaths and mentally prepared himself for whatever he found when he walked into his aunt's bedroom. When he knocked, Jackie Cummings opened the door immediately.

"Well, hello, Will." Jackie stepped back just enough

to allow him entrance. "Miss Edith said you were on your way over. I sure hope you can calm your aunt down. As you can see, she's made a mess of this room, but Miss Edith wouldn't let me give her another sedative. And I guess she's right. We've kept Mary Martha pretty doped up ever since your daddy's . . . er, Kent's funeral."

Will glanced past his aunt's nurse and quickly scanned the room. A child's room. A little girl's haven. With dolls tossed hither and yon, the bed linens ripped from the mattress and pillows and books scattered about over the floor, it appeared that the *little girl* who lived here had thrown quite a temper tantrum.

Mary Martha stood huddled in a far corner, her eyes glazed, as she systematically ripped pages from a book. The paper floated to the floor like autumn leaves drifting off tree branches.

"No bedtime story. No bedtime story," she repeated again and again as she continued destroying the book.

Will took several hesitant steps in his aunt's direction. He wasn't sure why, but there had always been a unique connection between Mary Martha and him. For as long as he could remember. In retrospect, he now assumed that he had connected well with his childlike aunt because he had been a child himself. But even as he grew older, the ties that bound them had not been severed. She had often called him *my baby,* and when she had been *in one of her moods,* his parents had allowed her to enjoy the fantasy that she and not Lane was his mother.

"Aunt Mary Martha?"

She stopped her repetitive page ripping the moment she heard his voice. "Will?" Her gaze searched the room. When her vision focused on him, she smiled. A weak, delicate smile. As delicate and frail as the willowy woman who held out her hand to him. "Will, is that you?"

"Yes, ma'am. It's me. Grandmother said you weren't feeling well, so I came over to see about you."

"Oh, my sweet baby." Mary Martha dropped the partially destroyed book and glided across the room like a spirit floating on air.

He had always thought his aunt looked like an angel. Tall, slender and small-boned. Pale skin, strawberry blond hair and light brown eyes. Tonight she looked especially pale and thin. And the flowing white gown she wore added to the seraphic illusion.

Will met her halfway in the middle of the huge room. Lifting her trembling hand, she placed her fingers on his cheek and stroked with the utmost gentleness. "They took you away from me and told me you were dead. But I knew it wasn't true. You're my own sweet baby, all grown up."

"Yes, ma'am."

She continued caressing his face. "I've been sick. That's why I couldn't take care of you. That's why you live with Lane, you know."

"Yes, ma'am." He was hearing the same old story. Whenever she was in one of her delusional states, Mary Martha thought he was her child. Why, he didn't know. And if anyone else in the family knew, they had never explained it to him. Indeed, everyone had denied having a clue as to why his aunt seemed haunted by the loss of a nonexistent child.

She grabbed his hand and tugged in a gesture requesting he follow her. "They say that Kent is dead. But I don't believe them. He would never go away and leave me. He promised me that he would never ever leave me."

How did he reply to that? What could he say that

wasn't an out-and-out lie and yet still not upset her? "Aren't you tired, Aunt Mary Martha? Wouldn't you like to lie down? I could stay and read to you until you fall asleep. You always liked for me to read to you."

"Kent used to read to me, when I was just a little girl."

Mary Martha led Will to the row of bookshelves across the back wall. At least a third of the books lay scattered on the floor. She stepped over some of the volumes and walked on others as she made her way to the shelves.

"Read *Hansel and Gretel* to me." She searched the row of books for the specific fairy tale. When she couldn't find it immediately, she turned to Will. "It isn't here. Kent hid it from me, didn't he? He hides my book from me sometimes, until I . . . until I . . ." As if suddenly realizing that the floor was littered with reading material, Mary Martha fell to her knees and rummaged through the volumes. "I like it better when you read to me, Will." She snatched up a thin hardback, its spine broken and pages loose. "Here it is. This is Kent's favorite, too."

Will helped his aunt to her feet. The moment he placed his arm around her waist, he realized she had lost weight and was now even thinner than she had been a month ago. Lillie Mae would say that his aunt was nothing but skin and bones. He led Mary Martha to the bed. His gaze met Jackie Cummings's inquisitive stare; then she glanced down at the unmade bed and nodded.

"Give me a couple of minutes to put the sheets and blanket back on." Jackie scurried about picking up the discarded bed linens.

Mary Martha gave Jackie a disapproving glare, then shook her head sadly. "Mama says it's getting more and more difficult to find good help these days," she told Will in a hushed tone. "We mustn't tell Mama that the bed was unmade. She'd be frightfully upset. Kent says we mustn't bother Mama and Daddy. They're both very busy. They don't have time for us. He says we have to depend on each other. Kent loves me best. More than anyone else. And I love him best, too."

Jackie cleared her throat. Will saw that she had made the bed, except for adding the spread, which still lay on the floor in a rumpled heap.

"Come along." Will walked his aunt to her bed. She sat on the edge and smiled at him. "Go ahead," he told her. "I'll tuck you in."

"And then read to me." The corners of her small, pale lips curved upward in a sad little smile.

When she stretched out in the canopied twin bed, Will lifted the pink top sheet and matching blanket up to her waist. Leaning over, he kissed her forehead and then reached for the book she held in her hands. When he started across the room to bring the white wooden rocker closer to the bed, Mary Martha cried out to him.

"Don't leave me!"

"I'm not leaving," Will reassured her. "I was just—"

Jackie quickly scooted the rocker into place in front of the nightstand.

"Thank you," Will said. "I think I can handle things here. Would you mind going downstairs and telling Grandmother that Aunt Mary Martha is doing much better."

"All right. But I won't be long. Just in case you need me."

Will sat in the rocker, opened the tattered volume of *Hansel and Gretel* and began reading. As was their usual routine, he stopped occasionally so that she could look at the illustrations. By the time he had finished the story, his aunt was asleep, a look of angelic peace on her beautiful face.

All his life he had wondered why his aunt was the way she was. Why did her mind so often wander off into a fantasy world? Why, when she wasn't *at herself*, did she think he was her baby? No one in the family seemed to know. Lane had tried to explain to him, years ago, that some people are so delicate and sensitive that they can't cope with reality.

He laid the book on the nightstand, stood and turned to leave. His grandmother waited in the doorway, Jackie Cummings hovering behind her.

"She's asleep," Will told them.

"Thank you," Edith said.

When Will reached the threshold, both women stepped back enough to allow him to exit. Jackie hurried past them into the bedroom, made a big to-do over checking on Mary Martha, then picked up the spread off the floor, folded it neatly and laid it across the foot of the bed.

Standing in the hallway with Edith, Will questioned her. "What happened tonight to make Aunt Mary Martha tear her room apart?"

A pained expression crossed Edith's face. "I'm afraid it was my fault."

"How was it your fault?"

"Buddy Lawler had paid us a visit tonight. You know how devoted he is to Mary Martha. Well, after he left, I stayed with her awhile. I've been so worried about her ever since Kent's funeral. I made the mistake of mentioning Kent. The poor child adored her brother so, and she's been distraught ever since . . . ever since he was murdered."

"My mother didn't kill Kent," Will said. "If Aunt

Mary Martha were at herself, she'd be on Mama's side in all this. You know she would.''

"Don't upset yourself, Will. No one in this family is blaming Lane for Kent's murder. It's just that all the evidence . . . well, things don't look good for her. She is the prime suspect and—''

"You could tell Buddy Lawler not to arrest Mama. You could tell him to find the real murderer. Buddy would listen to you.''

"Yes, of course. And that's exactly what he's going to do. Find Kent's murderer,'' Edith said. "But Will''—when she reached out to touch him, he side-stepped her—''you must prepare yourself for the worst. If Lane is arrested, you know that you have a home here with James and me . . . and Mary Martha.''

"If you let them arrest Mama, I'll never forgive you. I wouldn't come here to live with you. I don't know why you'd want me. You're not even my real grand-mother.''

"If you didn't come here, dear, where would you go? Who would take care of you?''

"I'd stay with Lillie Mae. She is my real grand-mother, you know.'' When Edith pursed her lips and frowned, her expression one of intense disapproval, Will grinned. "Or maybe I'd live with my father. My real father. You know, Johnny Mack Cahill.''

Johnny Mack's gut instincts warned him, even before he opened the door to his motel room, that something wasn't right. Past experience told him that danger lurked just around the corner. Or in this case, just beyond the closed door.

He inserted the key. The lock clicked. His hand covered the knob and turned it until the door swung halfway open. The interior lay in total darkness. He knew he had left a lamp burning. Hesitating in the doorway, he considered his options.

"Come on in and close the door behind you," a male voice said.

Johnny Mack would have recognized that voice anywhere, anytime. For years after he had left Noble's Crossing, he'd heard that voice inside his head. Taunting him. Laughing at him. Damning him.

"I could have you arrested for breaking and entering, Chief," Johnny Mack said, as he flipped the wall switch to illuminate the room and reveal the identity of his uninvited guest.

"God Almighty, it is you, isn't it!" Dressed in his official police uniform, Buddy Lawler stood on the far side of the room. His hand hovered over his gun belt. Sweat dotted his forehead and moistened his upper lip.

"Yep, I'm Johnny Mack Cahill, in the flesh." He spread his arms wide in a take-a-good-look gesture. "I'm back from the dead and looking damn good for a corpse, don't you think?"

Chapter 9

He had often wondered what he would say and what he would do if he ever saw Buddy Lawler again. That cocky little bantam rooster had always been a thorn in his side, an irritating echo of Kent Graham's hostility. On his own, Lawler never would have made a move. But with Kent's backing and the aid of half a dozen friends, Buddy had beaten the hell out of him and dumped him into the Chickasaw River, leaving him for dead. For all intents and purposes, the police chief of Noble's Crossing was a murderer. Or if you wanted to be completely accurate, just a would-be murderer.

"How the hell did you . . ." With nervous fingers, Buddy unsnapped the flap on his holster and rubbed his thumb across the butt of his Magnum.

"What are you planning to do, shoot me?" Johnny Mack grinned. He was about as afraid of Buddy as he would be of a piss ant. Funny thing how a man who had once nearly killed him could now seem so insignificant and oddly pathetic.

"I would have bet my life that you were dead, Cahill. I even told Miss Edith that I was sure of it."

"And what did she say?" Johnny Mack held up a restraining hand. "No, don't tell. Let me guess. She wasn't as sure as you were that I was dead. What did Miss Edith do, put out a death warrant on me the way Kent did fifteen years ago?"

"Miss Edith doesn't want you here, that's for sure." Buddy's voice quivered ever so slightly. "I came here to see for myself if it was really you."

"It's really me."

"Yeah, well, you're not wanted in Noble's Crossing any more now than you were fifteen years ago." Buddy surveyed Johnny Mack from head to toe, his gaze searching, as if looking for any sign of a weapon. "If you know what's good for you, you'll leave town. Tonight."

"Ah, but that's the problem. I never did know what was good for me, did I?"

"You don't want to wind up the way you did back then, do you? Only this time, we'd finish the job." Buddy stuck out his chest and tilted up his chin with false bravado.

"Are you threatening me?" Johnny Mack's smile widened.

"Just giving you a friendly warning." Buddy rubbed his sweating palms up and down on either side of his hips, one hand never far from his holster.

Oh, how he loved watching Buddy sweat. Large circles of moisture spread out under his arms and stained his immaculate tan shirt. A crimson flush tinted his cheeks. Perspiration dampened his entire face and trickled down his neck and beneath his collar. Johnny Mack smelled fear. It was a scent he recognized easily. Men who knew they were going to lose—and lose big—always had that odor about them. In his business dealings over the past ten years, he had put that kind of fear into many a man. And now, his presence—his very existence—had scared the shit out of Buddy Lawler.

"I'm not leaving," Johnny Mack said.

The throbbing pulse in Buddy's neck protruded. "I'm going to be honest with you, *boy*. If you haven't hightailed it out of here by tomorrow morning, I'm going to find some excuse to put your sorry ass in jail. And I can arrange for an accident to happen while you're incarcerated. Do I make myself clear?" Keeping one hand near his pistol, he balled the other into a tight fist.

Nobody had called Johnny Mack *boy* in that condescending tone since he'd left Noble's Crossing. The use of the word as an insult brought back unpleasant memories. He had been the boy from the wrong side of the tracks. The bad boy who couldn't be trusted. The white trash boy who did yard work for the rich and wasn't good enough to speak to their womenfolk. The boy who wouldn't bow and scrape and be grateful for the crumbs his betters had tossed him.

When Buddy moved cautiously toward the door, Johnny Mack blocked his path. The scent of fear intensified. His expression one of sheer terror, Buddy, who wasn't more than five-feet-nine, looked up at Johnny Mack, who stood a good seven inches taller.

When Johnny Mack slapped his big hand down on Buddy's shoulder, Buddy shuddered and swallowed hard. Their gazes met and locked. Fear collided head-on with fearlessness.

"Let me make myself perfectly clear to you," Johnny Mack said. "Nobody's running me out of

Noble's Crossing. I'll stay as long as I want to stay. I'm not the white trash poor boy I used to be. Y'all will find it a lot harder to get rid of me now."

"You're making a big mistake going up against Miss Edith."

"She's the one who'll be making a mistake, if she goes up against me. I want you to give her a message. Tell her that trouble's back in town and there's a bad moon rising, so she'd better watch out."

The back door opened and closed. Lane rose from the chair in the den where she had been sitting waiting for her son to return home. She caught him just as he reached the staircase. The moment he saw her, he stopped dead in his tracks.

"How's Mary Martha?" Lane asked.

"She's sleeping now. I read her a bedtime story."

"What was wrong? Why did your grandmother . . . why did Miss Edith think you were needed?"

"Did you know that Aunt Mary Martha hadn't spoken a word since the day after Kent's funeral?"

"No, I had no idea. There hasn't been any communication between Miss Edith and me since the funeral."

"Aunt Mary Martha needs help, Mama. She needs it bad. She'd ransacked her room before I got there, and Grandmother wouldn't let Jackie give her another sedative." Will shrugged. "All I could do was calm her down. Temporarily. She thinks Kent is still alive. And she was doing that thing again. You know, when she calls me her baby and says crazy things about her being my mother. She isn't . . . I mean, there's no way she could be my mother, is there?" He gazed at Lane, his dark eyes filled with questions and accusations.

Will sighed loudly, then dropped down to sit on the third step from the bottom. When he looked up at Lane, she thought her heart would break. His expression said it all. Her son was lost and confused and hurting. And she wasn't sure there was anything she could do to help him.

Lane sat beside him and placed her arm around his slumped shoulders. "Mary Martha isn't your birth mother. I realize you have no reason to believe me since I've lied to you your whole life, but I'm telling you the truth now. Johnny Mack Cahill is your biological father and Sharon Hickman was your biological mother. DNA tests would prove those facts. I explained all of this to you after Kent . . . after Kent found out the truth."

"Yeah, I know." Will speared his fingers together, locking them crossways and rubbing the heels of his palms with his thumbs. "You let me read the letter Sharon wrote Kent. It's just that Aunt Mary Martha—"

"Mary Martha has severe mental problems. She's been unbalanced all her life, even as a young girl. And she has been fixated on you ever since the first time Kent placed you in her arms. I can't explain it. I'm not sure anyone can."

Will stared down at his feet, his clasped hands dangling between his spread knees. "You know, I'm glad that Kent wasn't my father. He was a terrible man. A drunk. A real loser. And he treated you like . . ." Will lifted his head and looked at Lane. "I wish you were my birth mother. I don't give a damn who my real father is, but I wish . . ."

Lane tightened her hold about his shoulders, then leaned her head against his and placed her hand on his knee. "I know, my darling, I wish I were your birth mother, too, but you couldn't be more mine if I had given birth to you."

"Mama." He turned and went into her arms, then laid his head on her shoulder and wrapped his arms around her. Lane wasn't sure whether she was comforting Will or he was comforting her. Perhaps both. Each wishing for the impossible.

"Everything will be all right." Lane caressed his head as if he were a toddler, her fingers stroking the soft silkiness of his black hair.

"Why did you marry Kent and adopt me?" Will lifted his head enough to make direct eye contact with Lane. "You never loved Kent and you knew I wasn't really his baby, so. . . . Sharon Hickman wrote in the letter she sent Kent that you wanted me because I was Johnny Mack Cahill's son. Is that true? Is that the reason you wanted me?"

Lane took Will's hands into hers and stared deeply into his eyes, praying that she would choose the right words. "Yes, that's the reason I wanted Sharon's baby. I was nineteen at the time and had fancied myself madly in love with Johnny Mack since I was fourteen. We were never lovers. Only friends. His choice, not mine. But I was so in love with him that I would have done anything to save his baby."

"I can't believe someone like you could have loved a man like Johnny Mack Cahill." Will pulled his hands from her grasp. "Kent told me what kind of man Johnny Mack was. He was nothing but white trash. A high school dropout who made a living doing yard work and got his kicks by screwing every woman in town."

"John William Graham!"

"I want to know the truth about my real father. My mother was trash and so was my father, wasn't he? Kent didn't lie about that, did he?"

"No, Kent wasn't lying. But his rendition of the truth was slightly prejudiced. Kent had despised

Johnny Mack since they were kids, and the two were always competing. You see, honey, the reason you look a little bit like Kent is because he and Johnny Mack were half brothers. Your grandfather Graham was a womanizer and—''

"Then, Johnny Mack is a bastard, just like me."

Lane gritted her teeth in an effort to stop herself from loudly and vehemently correcting Will. Calmly, she said, "Don't use that word to describe yourself. Not ever."

"Sorry, Mama. Does illegitimate sound better?" he asked sarcastically.

"You have every right to be angry and confused, and if I could spare you from the ugly truth, I would. God knows, I've spent fourteen years trying to protect you."

"So, my father really was a white trash, high school dropout bastard who did yard work for a living and screwed around?"

"If you're trying to upset me by using foul language, then you've succeeded," Lane told him. "If you need to lash out at me, then go ahead. I think I'm strong enough to take it."

"I don't want to hurt you, Mama. I just want you to level with me about my real father."

"All right. Johnny Mack was everything Kent told you he was, but . . . there was a lot more to Johnny Mack, too. He was a very handsome young man, and practically every female in the county found him fascinating. He'd grown up the hard way. Without a father. With a mother who neglected him. And with no money. He wasn't a nice boy from a good family. But he wasn't all bad either, despite what Kent would have had you believe."

"What kind of guy gets a girl pregnant and walks

out on her?'' Will asked, his jaw tense, his dark eyes narrowed as he sought an answer from his mother.

"He never knew Sharon was pregnant, and by the time she told me, none of us had any idea where he was." There was no point in telling Will that several people—including Miss Edith—had believed Johnny Mack dead.

"So what's he doing back here now?"

"Lillie Mae has known for the past ten years where he was. She sent for him. She thinks that you and I need him."

Will shot up off the stairs and bounded down into the foyer. "Why would she think we need him? We don't want him here, do we? If he'd wanted to help you, to repay you for saving his life, why wasn't he around when Kent was treating you like dirt?"

"What do you know about my saving Johnny Mack's life?"

"Lillie Mae told me about some men beating him up and dumping him into the river and your bringing him home and the two of you taking care of him. She told me tonight, when you were in the living room talking to him."

"I see."

"You told him to go back to wherever he came from, didn't you? You told him we didn't want him in our lives. Lillie Mae was wrong. We've got each other. We don't need him."

"Johnny Mack won't leave just because you want him to. He's determined to help me, if I'm arrested for Kent's murder. And he wants to meet you."

"Well, I don't want to meet him."

"He invited himself for lunch tomorrow."

"And you told him it was all right?"

Lane shook her head. "No, of course not. I didn't say it was all right. But you have to understand that

Johnny Mack isn't the type of man to take no for an answer. He never was. If he wants something, he goes after it."

"And what does he want, Mama? Does he want you?"

"He wants you, Will. He wants his son."

"He's a little late, don't you think? I don't want him. And I will not sit down and share a meal with him. Do you hear me? If he shows up here tomorrow, you tell him that I said as far as I'm concerned, he can go straight to hell."

James prepared his wife a whiskey on the rocks and handed it to her. Edith stopped pacing the floor to accept the liquor.

"You saw him. You talked to him. And you're sure he's really Johnny Mack Cahill?" Edith glared at Buddy Lawler, who stood, hat in hand, in the center of the Persian rug in the library.

"Yes, ma'am, it's Johnny Mack all right. He's the same—swaggering, cocky, belligerent—but he's different, too. After what happened fifteen years ago, you'd think when I gave him a warning, it would have at least scared him a little. But it didn't. He's not scared."

"What did you find out about him?"

"Not a damn thing from him, but I'm having a check run on him, and we should have some answers by tomorrow, if not sooner," Buddy said.

"He's come back because of Lane," Edith said, then sipped on her drink. "There's no way he could have found out about Will, not unless. . . . Maybe he and Lane have kept in touch all these years."

"Well, whatever his reasons for being here are, he told me he was staying until he got good and ready to leave. And he gave me a message to deliver to you, Miss Edith.''

"Why that cocky young son of a bitch!" Edith downed the remainder of her drink, coughing when the strong liquor burned a hot trail down her throat. "What was the message?"

"Tell Miss Edith that trouble is back in town and there's a bad moon rising, so she'd better watch out."

"He's threatening me! I want you to arrest him and—"

"You can't arrest the man for sending you an unpleasant message," James said.

Edith snapped her head around and glowered at her husband. Her pipsqueak of a husband. What had she ever seen in James Ware? "Of course Johnny Mack is going to be trouble. That's all he ever was. If we don't find a way to get rid of him—"

"Perhaps you'd better find out more about exactly who Johnny Mack Cahill is now, my dear, before you make plans for Buddy to eliminate him," James suggested. "Besides, he didn't do such a good job of it the first time, did he?"

"Damn it, I thought he was dead," Buddy said. "Kent thought he was dead. Hell, we all did. Me and the boys had beaten the crap out of him before we tossed him into the river. No normal, ordinary man could have survived."

Edith clutched the empty glass in her hand. "Yes, well, we all know that Johnny Mack wasn't and no doubt still isn't just an ordinary man."

There had never been anything ordinary about her first husband's bastard son. From childhood, the boy had been extraordinarily good looking. But then John Graham had been a handsome man. And despite the fact she had been a trailer trash whore, Faith Cahill had been strikingly beautiful. Edith had always known about her husband's philandering ways and had heard rumors about Faith's child, that he hadn't belonged to Faith's husband, who had been killed in a barroom brawl when her child was an infant. Then the first time she had seen the boy, when he was six, on the street in town with his mother, she had known Johnny Mack was John's son. As much his son as Kent had been. Except that Kent bore the Graham name and was the heir apparent to the Graham fortune.

"Should I be jealous, my dear?" James asked, a smirking grin on his round, ruddy face. "A man doesn't like to know his wife considers another man extraordinary."

Edith whirled around, rage in her eyes, and threw her empty glass straight at her husband. He ducked just in time to prevent contact with his head. The crystal tumbler hit the edge of the marble hearth behind him and shattered into jagged shards.

"You're a stupid fool, James." Edith gave him a murderous glare, then turned back to Buddy. "Find out everything you can about Johnny Mack and call me, even if it's at two in the morning. I'm not going to allow that piece of trash to come back into my town and threaten me. And if he thinks he's going to claim Will as his son, then he'd better think again. He doesn't deserve to be a father to that boy."

"I'll go down to the station right now," Buddy said. "And I won't leave until I get some information about Johnny Mack."

"Yes. Fine." Edith dismissed him with a wave of her hand. "See yourself out."

When Buddy left the room, James turned to go, but before he reached the door, Edith called after him. "Where are you going?"

"I'm going upstairs, to my room," he replied. "I'll see you in the morning, my dear."

Edith watched her husband walk away from her. Groaning, she ran a nervous hand over her sleek, short hair. After John's death, James had been attentive and caring, and before they had married the sex had been rather exciting. James had been, if nothing else, an eager lover. The fact that he was nearly twenty years younger than she and far from rich hadn't bothered her then. He had agreed to sign a prenuptial agreement that protected her assets. As far as the age difference was concerned, even her worst enemies would have to admit that Edith Graham Ware didn't look her age.

But if she had it to do over again, she wouldn't have married James. She would have enjoyed an affair with him and then moved on. Her husband was attentive, agreeable and often reminded her of a lapdog. He tried his best to please her, but the subservience which she demanded from him was the very thing that she hated most about him. Although she had grown to hate John Graham, the man had never bored her. In or out of the bedroom. And truth be told, she had found the fact that she couldn't dominate him highly stimulating. They had been two strong-willed people who, when they came together, exploded into flames.

And it had been the same with his son. Only more so. What Johnny Mack had lacked in skill as a young lover, he had more than made up for in stamina and lustiness. A quiver of sexual longing spiraled up inside Edith at the thought of Johnny Mack. What would he be like now, as a man and as a lover?

"You called James a fool," Edith said aloud, then huffed softly. "But you're the fool, Edith, for entertaining thoughts about that man."

Johnny Mack hadn't come back to Noble's Crossing to renew his affair with her, of that she was certain. If he had returned for any woman, it was Lane.

Smiling softly, Edith glided across the room, removed the lid from the whiskey and poured the liquor into a glass. She lifted the tumbler to her mouth and took a sip.

But Lane would soon be unavailable. She was going to be arrested, tried and convicted of Kent's murder. It was only a matter of time. A matter of giving Buddy and DA Wes Stevens their orders. A matter of calling in a few favors. She wanted Lane punished. She wanted Will and Mary Martha protected. And she wanted Johnny Mack to learn that around here, she still ruled the roost.

Chapter 10

James Ware made kissing sounds into the telephone and sighed contentedly when he heard Arlene's throaty giggles. More than anything, he wished he were with her tonight. In her bed, in her arms. Hell, just in her!

"I miss you, Jimmy boy. I miss you every minute we're apart."

"I miss you, too, sugar. You know how bad I want you right now, don't you?"

"Not bad enough to leave that big old mansion and come across the Chickasaw River to my house."

"Now, you know I can't sneak out at night. I can't take a chance that one of the servants might see me and tell Edith. I know for a fact that your friend Jackie already suspects something's going on between us."

"She's just guessing. I haven't told her a thing. I promise I haven't. I wouldn't do anything to make problems for you. For us. It's just I'm so tired of waiting. I want us to get married and have a real life together.''

"Try to be patient just a little while longer, sugar. Just a few more transactions and I'll have enough money for us to get away from Noble's Crossing forever.''

"You aren't doing anything awfully illegal, are you?'' There was genuine concern in Arlene's voice. "You've told me that you're ciphering money out of Miss Edith's accounts, but I don't understand how—''

"Don't you worry your pretty head about it,'' James assured her.

Hell, yes, there was something illegal about what he was doing, but he was counting on Edith being too damned embarrassed, when she found out, to actually have him hunted down and prosecuted. Besides, he planned to change his name. He had already arranged for phony birth certificates and social security cards for himself, Arlene and her kids. Those alone had cost him a pretty penny. He had a tidy little sum in his Swiss bank account, but not quite enough.

As long as Edith never learned that her precious Kent had discovered the discrepancies in her accounts and confronted him, then he was safe. How the hell that drunken lout's brain had functioned well enough for him to have figured out what was going on, James would never know. But Kent sure wasn't going to tell anybody. Not now.

James smiled. Nope. Kent Graham wasn't ever going to cause anybody trouble again. Not him. Not Lane. Not Will. Not poor Mary Martha.

"I can't help worrying about you,'' Arlene said. "You know how much I love you, how much I've always loved you.''

"Not as much as I love you.''

He grew hard and aching just talking to Arlene. She had always had that effect on him. When they'd first gotten back together, he had thought it was only lust, that he could have an affair with his teenage sweetheart and remain unhappily married to his rich wife. But eventually he had realized just how much he enjoyed being with a woman who made him feel like a real man. And Arlene had that knack—making him feel ten feet tall. For that alone, he loved her.

"Give me some more kisses," she said.

He puckered his lips and smacked a second series of silly kisses into the telephone. "I'll see you tomorrow. Close up the shop early for lunch."

"Dream about me tonight?"

"I have wet dreams about you every night, sugar." She giggled again. "Bye now, lover boy."

"Bye."

James hung up the receiver and rolled over onto his back, stretching out in the walnut antique bed that was at least a hundred years older than he was. No telling how many generations of Grahams had slept in this bed. He eased his hand inside his pajamas, slid his fingers down over his belly and encircled his erect penis. He wondered how many men had lain in this bed, an unwelcoming wife sleeping across the hall, and jerked off while they were thinking about another woman.

Johnny Mack checked the digital clock on the nightstand. Eleven-fifteen. He sat in the armchair, the only chair in his motel room, propped his sock feet up on the bed and leaned back his head. Stretching his arms, he groaned. Who had said, "the more things change, the more they stay the same"?

Noble's Crossing and its inhabitants were not the

same as they had been fifteen years ago, and yet Johnny Mack Cahill was still *persona non grata*, as much now as in the past. He laughed at the irony. His chuckles sounded to him more like self-pitying groans. The funny thing was that fifteen years ago he wouldn't have known what *persona non grata* meant. Now the phrase and similar ones immediately came to mind and easily rolled off his tongue. Four years of college and eight years of sharing a home with Judge Harwood Brown had polished his rough edges and given him the ability to pass himself off as a gentleman.

But nothing and no one had ever been able to eradicate his survival instincts, those screw-them-first-before-they-screw-you principles he had learned the hard way and at a very young age. Actually those savage instincts were what had helped him become the entrepreneurial wonder of Houston during the past ten years. A man with nothing to lose and no one to fear took chances others wouldn't.

When he'd told Lane he was a rich man, she had seemed unimpressed. But then, Lane and her father had been the only ones in town who hadn't judged others by the size of their bank accounts or the prestige of their family lineage. She had been his friend when none of the other Magnolia Avenue ladies would acknowledge his presence in public. Like old Bill Noble, she had given him a chance and had actually thought he was worth the effort.

Of course, he hadn't been worth their efforts. Not then. But now, maybe he was. God knew he had tried to become a better man. Someone Lane would be proud of.

Once, Lane had not only believed in him, trusted him, cared about him, but she had saved his life. That night when she'd found him beaten and half-dead, she had practically dragged him from the riverbank to her backdoor. Then she had hidden him away for three days, until he could stand on his own two legs and walk out on her. He had been tempted to take her with him, to show Kent Graham and everyone else in Noble's Crossing that their sweet, little princess had given up everything just to be with him. But he had cared too much for Lane, respected her too much, to drag her down to his level. He'd thought that taking her with him would ruin her life. Now he wondered if leaving her behind had achieved the same result.

Reaching behind him to where his jacket hung on the back of the chair, he felt around inside the pocket, removed his cellular phone and dialed the unlisted number of an old friend. A fellow beneficiary of Judge Harwood Brown's generosity and unique style of reforming bad boys.

"This had better be important," Quinn Cortez said, when he answered the phone.

"Hello to you, too."

"Do you know what time it is?"

"Not midnight yet," Johnny Mack said. "And if I remember correctly, you're a night owl and seldom go to sleep before twelve."

"Yeah, well, a man goes to bed for other reasons than to sleep."

"Sorry." Johnny Mack chuckled. Quinn's reputation with the ladies was more than gossip. He didn't think he had ever seen his friend with the same woman twice. "I wouldn't be calling if it weren't important. So, tell whoever you've got there in bed with you that I won't keep you long."

"Get to the damn point, Cahill."

"I need you to be ready to take a plane out of Houston at a moment's notice. You'll fly into Huntsville, Alabama, then rent a car and drive over to Noble's Crossing."

"Want to tell me why I'm going to do this?"

"Because there's a good chance that my son's mother will be arrested for her ex-husband's murder and she'll need the best criminal lawyer money can buy."

"That would be me, old friend. So, how about filling me in on some details? I had no idea you had a kid."

"Neither did I," Johnny Mack admitted. "I'll fill you in on the details later. By the way, when you do come to Noble's Crossing, you'll find me at the Four Way. It's a cheap motel, but it serves my purposes for the time being."

"Traveling incognito?"

"Yeah, something like that."

Buddy stretched out on the cot in the back of his office at the police station and laid the computer printout on his chest. He had removed his holster and loosened the top buttons on his shirt hours ago, after he'd read over the printout of Johnny Mack Cahill's police record from fifteen years ago, when he had been arrested for vagrancy in Houston, Texas. September 30. Less than two weeks after Buddy and his friends had beaten Johnny Mack and dumped him into the river.

That night had haunted Buddy for years. He had never killed anyone before that night—and he'd been sure he had killed Johnny Mack. He hadn't liked the guy, although at one time he'd had a grudging respect for him and had even envied his success with women. But their paths had seldom crossed. It wasn't that Buddy had been one of the Magnolia

Avenue boys; but he had lived on the right side of the Chickasaw River, and his old man had been the county sheriff and one of John Graham's hunting and fishing buddies.

Everybody in town had heard the rumors about Johnny Mack being John Graham's illegitimate son, and it was a known fact that Kent hated his half brother with a passion equaled only by his determination to woo and wed Lane Noble. When Kent had found out about Lane's crush on Johnny Mack, he'd gone into a rage. Buddy had seen Kent in dark moods before, but nothing like the uncontrollable fury that had driven Kent to ask him to kill Johnny Mack.

"I know how you feel about the guy," Buddy had said. "But you can't mean you actually want to see him dead. We could just run him out of town."

"If you ran him out of town, he'd come back. That son of a bitch won't be satisfied until he's fucked every woman on Magnolia Avenue. He's already had my mama. Did you know that? Yeah, I saw them with my own two eyes. In the summer house, both of them naked and going at it like a couple of animals."

"Damn, man, you actually caught Miss Edith with Johnny Mack?"

"Mama doesn't know I saw them, but Johnny Mack knows. I told him that he was going to be sorry, that I'd make him pay." Kent had grabbed Buddy's shirtfront and glared wild-eyed at him. "Now he's after Lane. I won't let him have her. She's mine. She's always been mine. Our families have all but had us engaged since we were babies."

"Lane isn't the sort of girl who'd—"

"He's been sniffing around Mary Martha, too," Kent had said, knowing full well how Buddy felt about his sister. "You want Johnny Mack getting in Mary Martha's pants before you do?"

The very thought that anyone would take advantage of his precious Mary Martha had outraged Buddy, just as Kent had known it would. Two days later, he had rounded up six friends, and while Kent watched, they had cornered Johnny Mack by the Nobles' boat-house. It had taken all six of them to subdue him. He had fought like the devil, but even Johnny Mack hadn't been able to overcome six-to-one odds.

Buddy realized if he had known then what he knew now—that he had beaten the hell out of the wrong brother—he would have strangled Kent with his bare hands.

The telephone rang. Buddy jumped. As he rose from the cot, the printout fell off his chest and onto the floor. In two strides, he made it to his desk and lifted the receiver.

"Chief Lawler."

"This is Lieutenant Mills from HPD. I got a message that you wanted some information on Johnny Mack Cahill."

"Yeah. Sure do. It seems the only thing y'all have on him is a conviction for vagrancy fifteen years ago," Buddy said. "The guy's here in my town, making some threats, and I want to head off any trouble. Have you got anything, any information, on or off the record, that could help me find a reason to get him out of Noble's Crossing?"

The laughter on the other end of the phone chilled Buddy to the marrow in his bones.

"Look, Chief Lawler, I don't know what sort of threats Mr. Cahill is making, but if I were you, I'd take him seriously. As far as giving you any sort of damning report on the man, that I can't do. You see, Johnny Mack Cahill is one of the big dogs here in Houston. The pack he runs with is comprised of multi-millionaires. You know, the movers and shakers.

Cahill's got a reputation for being the shrewdest, deadliest shark of them all."

Buddy swallowed the surprise and sudden fear clogging his throat. "Are you telling me that Johnny Mack Cahill is a multimillionaire?"

"Yeah, that's exactly what I'm telling you."

"And he has no criminal record other than the vagrancy conviction fifteen years ago?"

"That's it."

"Yeah, well, thanks, Lieutenant."

"Sure thing." The lieutenant hesitated, cleared his throat and said, "By the way, Chief, y'all might want to lock up your women while Cahill's in town."

Long after Buddy had hung up the receiver, he could hear Lieutenant Mills's laughter ringing in his ears.

Lane changed clothes for the third time since breakfast. *This is ridiculous,* she thought. *What difference does it make what I'm wearing when Johnny Mack comes for lunch?* But, heaven help her, it did matter. She had been a plump young girl whose greatest asset had been her parents' social position back when she'd lusted after Johnny Mack from afar. She had always been the moon to her mother's sun, a pale reflection of Celeste's striking beauty. She hadn't truly come into her own until she had reached her mid-twenties, and with maturity, her curves had slimmed. Regardless of her feelings for Johnny Mack, she couldn't deny her purely feminine need for him to see her as the woman she was today.

Lane stripped out of the red dress, which always gained her compliments when she wore it. Red was too flashy. Too bold. Too self-confident. But the jeans and T-shirt she had put on before she had gone down to breakfast had been far too casual. Even Lillie Mae had suggested she might want to dress up a bit more.

After rummaging through her wardrobe, she chose black slacks, a sleeveless black shell and a crisp white shirt, which she left hanging loose and unbuttoned. She added silver jewelry. Hoop earrings. Several bangle bracelets. And a Celtic cross that hung on a sterling silver chain and rested between her breasts.

"Why are you so nervous?" Will asked from where he stood just outside Lane's open bedroom door.

Lane gasped. "Oh, my goodness, honey, I didn't know you were there."

"Lillie Mae sent me up here to tell you that she and I have had another talk and . . . well . . . I'm going to stay for lunch and meet Johnny Mack Cahill."

Lane smiled. "Oh, Will, that's—"

"I'll stay, but don't expect me to be nice to this guy."

"You'll be courteous, won't you, honey?"

"Yeah." Will shuffled his feet. "But only for your sake."

"Thank you."

"I won't like him."

"No one is asking you to like him," Lane said. "All you have to do is meet him and judge for yourself. My guess is that Johnny Mack is as nervous as we are."

"I'm not nervous," Will corrected her.

"Well, I am. I want you and Johnny Mack to like each other. He is your father and, despite my reservations about him, if I am arrested for Kent's murder—"

"That won't happen!"

"But if we have to deal with the worst case scenario and I am arrested, tried and convicted, then at least you'll have a father to take care of you."

"You think a guy like that would want a teenager

messing up his life? My guess is that once his curiosity is satisfied, he'll be long gone.''

"He didn't have to come back to Noble's Crossing," Lane said. "When Lillie Mae sent him a message, he could have ignored it, but he didn't. He came back to find out if you were his son and . . . and to see if he could help me."

"You and Lillie Mae are singing the same song," Will told her. "What is it about this guy that makes both of you defend him? He got Lillie Mae's daughter pregnant and deserted her, but she tells me he's not a bad man. And he strung you along and had you madly in love with him, so in love with him that you ruined your whole life by marrying Kent just so you could adopt me. But you tell me you want me to like him. Do *you* like him, Mama? Is that what this is all about? Are you still in love with him?"

Lane picked up a brush from her vanity, gave her hair a few strokes and tossed the brush aside. "For your information, Will Graham, you're the best thing that ever happened to me. And as for liking Johnny Mack . . . I don't know him. Not now. He's a stranger. Did I like the Johnny Mack I knew fifteen years ago? Yes, I liked him, despite his less than sterling reputation. And as for loving him now. . . . No, Will, I don't love him. But to be totally honest, I'm not absolutely sure that I hate him either."

There were fresh flowers on Kent Graham's grave. Every day the florist delivered blood red roses. Half a dozen. Per Edith Graham's instructions. Damn shame. Waste of good money.

In the distance, the mowers had begun their day's work at the other side of the cemetery. But they were too far away to notice, to see who was paying an early morning visit to a man who should have been put six feet under years ago.

Kent had been a monster. He had preyed on the weak. He had used and abused those who had loved him. He had destroyed everything he had touched. His life had been like an insidious cancer that wound its malignant evil around healthy minds and bodies and slowly but surely devoured them.

He hadn't deserved to live. It was a pity that a man could die only once. If only Kent could have suffered more. Suffered for days. For weeks. For years. Suffered the way his victims had suffered.

Chapter 11

Johnny Mack Cahill sat in the upholstered chair at the banquet-size, eighteenth century pedestal table in the dining room of the Noble mansion on Magnolia Avenue. An impressive breakfront china cabinet, filled with heirloom treasures, soared from floor to ceiling and spanned half a wall behind him. He had never been in this room before today. Actually, until his brief recuperative period of three days and nights, fifteen years ago, he had never set foot in any room other than the kitchen. And even during that brief stay, he had gone no farther than Lillie Mae's bedroom and bath.

In Houston, he was welcome in the homes of the wealthiest, most privileged citizens and had dined at finer tables than this. So why the hell did he feel like an intruder, someone who had forgotten to wipe the mud off his feet before he walked on the polished parquet floors and the priceless Persian rugs?

Because this was Noble's Crossing, and in this town

he was and always would be the bastard son of a trailer trash whore.

"Don't you like your salad?" Lane asked.

"No. I mean yes. The salad is fine. Thanks." What was wrong with him? He was stammering around like some insecure teenager who had no idea which fork to use. But he was no teenager. He sure as hell wasn't insecure. And Judge Brown had drilled table manners into him the first month he had lived on the old man's ranch.

He forced himself to take a bite of the salad. Usually he enjoyed a good meal. But at this precise moment, he wished he hadn't invited himself to lunch. Why hadn't he told Lane that he would just stop by today? If he had, he could have spared all three of them this nerve-wracking experience. Sitting here with Lane, who obviously was forcing herself to be pleasant to him, and with Will Graham, who had neither spoken to nor looked at him, was absolute torture.

But what had he expected? That Will would call him Dad and welcome him into his life with open arms?

Moments ticked by in which no one spoke, then Lane commented on the weather and how hot it had been this summer. Lillie Mae removed their salad plates and served the main course. She hesitated in the doorway, then huffed loudly, the disgust evident in her expression.

"Will, why don't you ask Johnny Mack to play a game of chess with you after lunch?" Lillie Mae suggested. "You know, your mama taught him how to play a long time ago."

Johnny Mack glanced at the boy, who kept his head bowed over his plate, but suddenly shot Johnny Mack a sharp, quick look of pure anger. His son hated him, that was plain to see.

"Actually, you turned out to be a much better player than I ever was," Lane said, stepping in to fill the void that her son's silence created. "Daddy taught me when I was a little girl, but I was no match for him."

"Actually, I haven't played chess in years." Johnny Mack lifted his glass of iced tea. "I used to play with Judge Brown. But I never could beat that wily old fox."

"Who was Judge Brown?" Lillie Mae asked.

"He was the man who plucked me out of jail fifteen years ago and gave me a chance to prove that I was more than a worthless, white trash bastard."

Lane's mouth formed a silent gasp. Lillie Mae cleared her throat. When Johnny Mack glanced at her, she nodded toward Will, who for the first time since Johnny Mack's arrival met his gaze head-on.

"They think I'm a kid," Will said. "They don't talk vulgar around me, even though I've told them a hundred times that I hear a lot worse every day at school and all the kids use language that would make their hair stand on end."

"Regardless of those facts, I'd rather you didn't hear such language from me or Lillie Mae." Lane looked directly at Johnny Mack. "Please, tell us more about Judge Brown, but I'd appreciate it if you'd use less colorful language."

"Sorry. I'm not used to being around a ... an impressionable young man." Johnny Mack grinned at his son, who simply continued staring at him. "But I want to be honest with Will about who I was and who I am."

"You were explaining who Judge Brown was," Lane said, her gaze quickly darting back and forth from Will to Johnny Mack.

"Yeah, so I was. Judge Brown was an old man when

I knew him, and he retired from the bench a couple of years after I met him. He'd made it his mission in life to try to save as many young men as he could from *a life of crime*."

"What were you in jail for?" Will asked.

"Will, that isn't polite," Lane said.

"Ah, Mama."

"It's all right, Lane. Will has a right to ask me why I was in jail." Johnny Mack would rather not have to tell his son about his sordid past, but he figured the boy had already heard an earful about him. About what a hell-raiser he had been when he was growing up in Noble's Crossing. And if Will deserved anything from him, he deserved the truth. The boy's life had been built on lies, one stacked on top of another.

Lane nodded. Lillie Mae crossed her arms over her waist as she stood in the doorway.

"When I left Noble's Crossing, Lane and Lillie Mae gave me two hundred dollars, but by the time I'd been in Texas a couple of weeks, I didn't have a dime in my pocket. I'd picked up an odd job here and there, enough to eat on, but one night when I didn't have the money for a place to stay, I got picked up for vagrancy and thrown in jail. That's the only crime I've ever been convicted of. Vagrancy."

"But you committed a lot of crimes that you've never been convicted of, haven't you?" Will smirked, like someone who knew he had inflicted a wound and was damn proud of his accomplishment.

"John William Graham!" Lane scolded.

"No, don't be upset with him." Johnny Mack lifted his napkin from his lap and tossed it on the table. "He's right and we all know it." Johnny Mack scooted back his chair and rose to his feet. "I don't know where you got your information, Will, but somebody obviously has filled you in on what a rounder I was back in the old days." He glanced at Lane's house-keeper. "I wasn't worth a damn, was I, Lillie Mae?"

"You were always worth something. At least Miss Lane thought so," Lillie Mae said, then turned and walked out of the dining room.

Johnny Mack focused his attention on Will. "You don't like me very much, do you, son?"

"Don't call me son. You don't have the right. And as for not liking you—I hate your guts." Will jumped up out of his chair so quickly that he knocked it over onto the floor. "We don't want you here. We don't need you. Not now." Will's eyes narrowed to slits. His nostrils flared. Color stained his high, sharply chiseled cheekbones. "Where were you when we really needed you? Tell me that! When Kent was making life hell for Mama. And where were you the day Kent told me who my real daddy was and what a sorry, no good son of a bitch you were?"

Will ran from the dining room, like an animal being chased by hunters. Lane rose slowly, her napkin falling from her lap onto the floor as she stood. She looked at Johnny Mack, and the pain and sorrow he saw in her eyes tortured him far more than the angry words Will had hurled at him.

"Should you go after him?" Johnny Mack asked.

"No," Lane replied. "Lillie Mae twisted his arm to get him to agree to have lunch with you today. She told him to do it for me." Lane lifted her head, tilting it upward just slightly in a show of strength and determination. "You see, my son is very protective of me. The first time he heard Kent demeaning me, degrading me, Will lashed out at Kent. And each time Kent got drunk and took his frustration out on me, Will came to my defense. Finally, I realized that, for Will's sake as much as my own, I had to divorce Kent. By that time, Will's feelings for his father—for the man he thought of as his father—had changed drastically. He still loved Kent, but he no longer respected him."

"I'm sorry that I pushed my way in here today. I should have waited until you were ready. Until Will was ready. I have a tendency to be too aggressive. But in my own defense, I should tell you that all I want is to find a way to make things right. For you. For Will. Whatever you want . . . whatever you need, is yours for the asking. Please, Lane, let me help you."

"Will was right. You really are too late to help us. Perhaps, before Kent was murdered—"

Johnny Mack slammed his fist down on the antique table, the jarring effect clanging china against crystal and bouncing the pieces of silverware together. "Damn Kent! I should have stayed here fifteen years ago and gotten rid of him myself. If a man ever deserved killing, it was Kent Graham. And if I'd known you were married to him and he was abusing you, I'd have ripped him apart with my bare hands. God, why didn't Lillie Mae send for me sooner?"

"She was helping me perpetuate the lie that Kent was Will's father. She and I both did what we thought was best for Will. And I'm sure Lillie Mae wasn't certain that you would come to our rescue. After all, you'd never exactly been the reliable type, had you?"

"Hmph. Maybe y'all thought it preferable for Will to be Kent's son rather than mine. After all, Kent was the heir to the Graham fortune and his place in local society was far superior to mine. Y'all probably thought that I didn't have anything to offer a child. Absolutely nothing. No money. No prestigious name. No family lineage."

Lane glowered at Johnny Mack, her expression one of angry disbelief. "Do you honestly believe that's the reason Lillie Mae didn't contact you?"

"I don't know, but it makes sense." It made too much sense. And the truth hurt like hell. "Kent Graham was your kind, wasn't he? You were both Alabama blue bloods with pedigrees back to Adam. Maybe you thought Will deserved to be a part of all that—to truly belong to the Graham family."

Lane rushed him, her eyes wild with pain and rage. Skidding to a halt a foot in front of him, she jabbed her index finger on his chest. "I thought Will deserved a chance to live, instead of being aborted by the girl you'd gotten pregnant. If I'd known where you were and if for one minute I'd thought you would've wanted Will and me, I'd have paid off Sharon and come running to you with your baby. *You* were the one I loved." She stabbed his chest with her finger. "You were the one I wanted. Not Kent. But you were too blind, too stupid, to realize that I would have given up everything to have been with you."

"Lane . . ." When he reached for her, she side-stepped him, the look in her eyes daring him to touch her.

Dear God, she was right. He had been too blind to see the truth. He had thought her feelings ran no deeper than a teenage crush on the town bad boy. How wrong he had been! A girl with a silly crush didn't throw away her own life in order to save a man's baby. But a woman who truly loved a man might. If that woman was Lane Noble.

But it was apparent that the love she had once felt for him had died long ago. He saw no evidence of it now. If Lane felt anything for him, it was contempt.

"I got over my girlish infatuation years ago, so don't think that . . ." Turning her back on him, Lane took a deep breath. "Your presence here isn't helping me, and it certainly isn't helping Will. Why don't you just go back to Texas and leave us alone?"

"I can't do that."

Johnny Mack came up behind her, a hairbreadth between his chest and her back. He ached to reach out and place his arms around her, to draw her close within his embrace. He felt the tension in her body as she stood there rigid as a statue. He suspected that she was holding her breath, waiting to see if he would touch her. He wanted to. God, how he wanted to.

"You told me yourself that you might need a good lawyer," he said. "If the evidence against you warrants a grand jury hearing, then it's possible you'll be arrested for Kent's murder."

"I can hire my own lawyer."

"I've already hired one for you."

She spun around and glared at him. "You've already contacted Quinn Cortez?"

"Last night. One phone call from me and he'll fly to Noble's Crossing at a minute's notice."

"Then, you two really must be good friends if he's willing to stay *on hold* until we see what the district attorney is going to do."

"Quinn has been my best friend for over fourteen years. When we were both going through Judge Brown's retraining program, we were a couple of young hoodlums. No one who knew Quinn back then would have thought that one day he'd become a renowned trial lawyer."

"He has quite a reputation. And I'm sure his fees are astronomical. I take it that you're paying his retainer."

"I know your financial situation, Lane, or least enough that I realize all your money is tied up in the *Herald* and that Edith owns fifty-one percent of the newspaper." He glanced around the room. "It must take a small fortune to keep up this place."

"If you feel that hiring Quinn Cortez as my lawyer

repays me for saving your life, then consider me repaid. You can go back to Texas with a clear conscience. If I am arrested—"

"Quinn doesn't lose cases. Even if you killed Kent, he can get you off."

"Then, I don't have anything to worry about, do I?"

Jackie removed Mary Martha's lunch tray from the table and set it outside the bedroom door. The housekeeper would pick it up later, and when evening came, she would deliver the next meal. Sometime during the afternoon, Jackie would have to take Mary Martha down into the garden for her daily hour in the sun. Miss Edith was convinced that a daily outing was essential to her daughter's recovery.

Glancing down at the sleeping, childlike woman curled into a fetal position, Jackie shook her head. What a shame that a woman with everything going for her—money, social position and beauty—would turn out to be a mental case. Such a waste.

Why couldn't I have been born with a silver spoon in my mouth? Jackie wondered.

She had been raised on the other side of the Chickasaw River, a block away from Arlene's family and three blocks away from Myer's Trailer Park. All her life she had wanted what the folks in Rich Man's Land had. For as long as she could remember, she had envied girls like Mary Martha Graham and Lane Noble.

The only thing that had separated them—other than the river—had been money. Lots of money.

Grinning like the proverbial Cheshire Cat, Jackie shoved open the bathroom door, sat on the closed commode lid and pulled a pack of cigarettes and a lighter from the pocket of her uniform. After lighting up, she took a deep draw and closed her eyes. Savoring the smoke. And daydreaming about her good fortune. She had known that taking this job as Mary Martha's nurse would pay off for her, one way or another. She had figured ingratiating herself to the Queen Bee of Noble's Crossing was a smart move.

Ever since she'd found out that James Ware was bonking Arlene, she had considered blackmailing the mayor. But Arlene was her friend. Besides, James Ware didn't have a dime of his own money. Miss Edith held the purse strings, and from what she had heard, she was downright stingy when it came to doling out cash to her hubby.

She had hoped something would pan out, that somehow living here on Magnolia Avenue, even as one of the hired hands, would open some doors for her. But she had never dreamed what a goldmine she would discover or just how profitable learning certain damning information would be. She'd get paid a bundle to keep quiet. Enough so that she would never have to work again. If she were to tell what she knew, heads would roll. Important heads.

She wouldn't act too soon. This situation needed some consideration. When would be the best time to spring the trap? And just how much was the information really worth? All she had to do was mention going to the DA and she would get whatever she wanted. *Think, Jackie, think. How much? A million? Two million? More? Mustn't be greedy. Two million should do nicely.*

"I should have known he wouldn't come back to Noble's Crossing unless he had enough power to hurt us." Edith tapped her manicured nails against her cheek in an unconscious gesture. "So he's rich now. A multimillionaire."

"From what I can find out, he's one of the most powerful men in Texas," Buddy Lawler said. "Seems Johnny Mack's a genius at wheeling and dealing."

"Just like his father and grandfather before him." A tentative smile curved Edith's red lips. "Blood will tell."

The smile vanished as memories of her mother flashed through her mind. Her weak, fragile, little mother, who had committed suicide when Edith was ten. Thank God, she hadn't been her mother's daughter in any way. She was made of stronger stuff. But unfortunately, she had passed on her mother's weak genes to Mary Martha. *Yes, blood will tell.*

"If Johnny Mack is here to help Lane, then he has the money to do it," Buddy said. "And if he wants Will—"

"He may be top dog in Houston, but around here, I'm in charge. I'm the one who pulls the strings and makes the puppets dance to my tune."

"Meaning?" Buddy lifted his eyebrows as his gaze settled inquisitively on Edith.

"Meaning that with Johnny Mack now rich and powerful, the playing field is almost equal. And fighting an equal is so much more fun, especially when you win."

"And just what will you win?" Buddy asked.

"What do you think I'm fighting for? The safety of my family, that's what. Johnny Mack Cahill has been, since the day he was born, a threat to me and my children."

"Are you sure protecting your family is the only thing you hope to accomplish?"

"What are you implying?"

"I know you, Miss Edith." Buddy cleared his throat.

"You're the type of woman who likes revenge. Why else would you have had an affair with Johnny Mack if you hadn't done it to get revenge against Mr. John? And why now would you be so insistent that Lane is guilty of murdering Kent, unless it was to take revenge against her for lying to Kent and to you about Will's paternity?"

"Why you . . ." How dare he speak to her in such a manner! Buddy Lawler was an underling. A loyal, obedient underling. So why, now, was he acting so boldly, questioning her authority? "What do you think gives you the right to say such a thing to me? You forget your place. You forget to whom you're speaking."

"No, ma'am, I know who you are and I didn't mean any disrespect." Buddy lowered his head in a subservient manner. Embarrassment stained his cheeks. "But you know why I'm involved, why I've always been involved." He lifted his gaze just a fraction, enough to make eye contact with Edith. "Fifteen years ago I followed Kent's orders to get rid of Johnny Mack, but you know why I did it. And I'm knee-deep into things now for the same reason. All I'm asking is for you to assure me that no matter what happens, your first priority is taking care of Mary Martha."

"Yes, of course that's my first priority." Edith laid her hand on Buddy's arm and patted him in what she hoped was a reassuring manner. After all, Buddy was the last person she wanted to offend. She needed him. Mary Martha needed him. "But there's no law against my getting a little sweet revenge while I'm keeping my daughter safe."

"No, I don't suppose so," Buddy agreed, somewhat reluctantly. "But if I see that you're putting her at risk in any way, I'll remind you."

Damn him! He was much too sure of himself. "There

will be no need to remind me. And you hear this, Buddy Lawler, if I didn't know that everything you've said to me came out of your devotion to Mary Martha, I'd make you very sorry that you ever took that corrective tone with me." Edith drew back her hand and slapped Buddy's face. "Do you understand?"

His face crimson, except where the white imprint of Edith's hand marked his cheek, Buddy clenched his jaw and spit out a brusque, "Yes, ma'am."

Johnny Mack parked his rental car on the side of the road and walked through the open black wrought-iron gates that separated the driveway of the Graham mansion from Magnolia Avenue. Only twice before today had he set foot on the Graham estate. The first time had been when he had screwed Edith Graham in the summer house. And the other time had been the night he had brought a slightly tipsy and very distraught Mary Martha home when he'd found her wandering along the road near the country club. She had probably been the prettiest girl in Noble's Crossing—delicate and fragile like a porcelain doll. Any man would have wanted her. Most probably had. But he wouldn't have—couldn't have—had sex with her. Even then, he hadn't been an amoral man. His feelings for Mary Martha hadn't been sexual, not even when she had thrown her arms around him and tried to kiss him. What he'd felt for her had been pity and concern.

She had begged him to make love to her, but he had declined her offer as gently as he'd known how. That was when she had broken down and cried. And told him she was pregnant. He had held her, comforted her and had listened to a sordid tale that had turned his stomach. Part of him had believed her, and yet another part of him had refused to accept the truth of her scandalous story. Everybody in town knew that John and Edith Graham's only daughter was *touched in the head*.

Johnny Mack hesitated when he reached the front portico. He wouldn't be any more welcome here now than he would have been fifteen years ago. Here in his father's ancestral home.

But it was time that he and Miss Edith met again, face-to-face. Time for him to prove to her that he was a man to be reckoned with. Time for him to warn her—in person—that he was back in town. He had returned to *the scene of the crime*—to the town where he had almost been murdered—because of Lane and Will. Now he was staying in order to protect them from injustice. And the fact that there wasn't a damn thing Miss Edith could do to force him out of Noble's Crossing gave him great satisfaction.

Without another moment's hesitation, Johnny Mack rang the doorbell. The thunder of his own heartbeat roared in his ears.

Simultaneously as the doorbell rang, Edith caressed Buddy's stinging cheek, and Jackie Cummings led a serene Mary Martha into the room.

Buddy jerked away from Edith and rushed to Mary Martha's side. "You look mighty pretty today, honey. How are you feeling?"

Such devotion. Such mindless devotion. Poor Buddy. He had never loved anyone except Mary Martha, and her daughter wasn't capable of appreciating all that young, tempting virility. At thirty-eight, Buddy was in his prime. Not a big man, but ruggedly built, with broad shoulders and a narrow waist. He looked quite appealing in his police uniform. And as much as she had tried to deny it, Edith found him attractive. Whenever he gazed at her with those intense blue eyes, she couldn't help wondering how he would react if she made the first move.

"Miss Mary Martha ate a good lunch today," Jackie said. "And when she woke from her nap, she was all ready for a little walk in the garden, weren't you, dear?" Jackie, whose arm was laced through her patient's, smiled warmly.

"She chills easily, even on warm summer days," Edith said. "Perhaps you'd better run back upstairs and get Mary Martha a shawl."

"Of course." Jackie helped Mary Martha to the sofa, seated her and continued smiling as she nodded to Edith and hurried out of the living room.

There was something about Jackie that bothered Edith. Oh, she was all smiles and sweetness and was totally obedient. But there was an odd look in her eyes, as if she were assessing the net worth of everyone and everything in the house.

Edith sat beside her daughter. "Would you like for me to join you on your walk today?"

"Where's Kent?" Mary Martha asked. "I want Kent to take a walk with me."

Edith closed her eyes momentarily, then leaned over to clasp her daughter's hand. She sighed deeply and said, "Kent's not here, dear. Don't you remember?"

Mary Martha shook her head. "Where is he?"

The housekeeper, Mrs. Russell, knocked on the door, then entered. "I'm sorry to bother you, Mrs. Ware, but there's a gentleman here to see you."

Edith released Mary Martha's hand, then sat up straight as she glanced at Mrs. Russell. "What gentleman?"

Before the housekeeper could reply, the dark devil burst into the room. As rude and crude and devastat-

ingly handsome as he'd ever been. A man like no
other. Now in his prime at thirty-six. And sexier than
any man had a right to be.

"Your housekeeper is mistaken," Johnny Mack
Cahill said. "We both know that I'm no gentleman."

"What are you doing here, Cahill?" Buddy demanded.

"I've come to pay a visit on old friends."

Johnny Mack grinned, and for a split second Edith
felt that odd tug in the pit of her stomach. What
was it about this man's smile that made women—all
women—go weak in the knees?

"Johnny Mack?" Mary Martha rose from the sofa,
her lips curving into a smile as she gazed at their
uninvited guest.

"Hello, Miss Mary Martha." He removed his tan
Stetson and nodded.

"It's so good to see you." Mary Martha took a
tentative step in Johnny Mack's direction. "I haven't
seen you in quite a while."

Edith snapped to her feet and reached for her
daughter, who shrugged off her mother's grasping
hand and walked straight to Johnny Mack.

"Kent says I shouldn't be nice to you." She gazed
up at Johnny Mack as if she were utterly delighted.
"But I told him that I liked you and I could be nice
to you if I wanted to." Mary Martha laid her hand
on Johnny Mack's arm. "I told him that you were so
good to me that night . . . that night . . . I'm not
supposed to remember, am I? Kent said not to tell
anyone, but I told you. And you believed me, didn't
you?"

"Mary Martha, dear, please don't upset yourself,"
Edith said.

Dear God, she had to find a way to make her daughter keep quiet. The more she talked, the more she

might remember. And Edith couldn't allow that to happen. If Mary Martha started remembering the ancient past, she might remember more recent events.

She might remember what had happened the day Kent died.

Chapter 12

"Buddy, will you be a dear and take Mary Martha for her afternoon stroll?" Edith glanced at Mrs. Russell, who waited in the doorway. "Go upstairs and tell Jackie to hurry up with Miss Mary Martha's sweater."

Mary Martha squeezed Johnny Mack's arm. "You will excuse me, won't you? Mother insists I get some sunshine every day."

"Of course."

What the hell had happened to Mary Martha? Johnny Mack wondered. She had always been emotionally fragile, and for good reason if what she'd told him fifteen years ago was true. But even that night, when she had been drunk and hysterical and begged him to make love to her, she'd still had a precarious hold on reality. But now . . . dear God, now she was completely lost.

Had Kent's death affected her so severely? Had the love/hate relationship she had shared with her brother finally destroyed her?

As she accepted Buddy's arm and he guided her toward the French doors leading out onto the side veranda, Mary Martha paused. Glancing over her shoulder, she smiled at Johnny Mack, a bittersweet expression on her face.

"You will come back again, won't you? You've been ever so kind to me. But you mustn't come when Kent's here. I'm afraid he's terribly jealous of you."

Johnny Mack exchanged a knowing glance with Buddy, and for a split second he almost felt sorry for the guy. They both knew that Mary Martha's mind was gone, that she had finally been pushed off the emotional high wire on which she'd been walking most of her life. Just how much did Buddy really know about the woman he loved? Had she ever told Buddy the same fantastic tale she had once told him? And if she had shared her secret with him, had Buddy believed her?

Breaking eye contact with Johnny Mack, Buddy hastily led Mary Martha outside, leaving Edith with the task of handling her unwanted guest.

Deadly silence. The soft sound of Edith Ware breathing. The clatter of footsteps in the foyer. The respectful reentrance of the housekeeper.

"Jackie's on her way down now," Mrs. Russell said.

"Yes, thank you." With only a nod of her head, Edith dismissed the servant.

Planting her hands on her slender hips, jeweled rings sparkling on almost every finger, Edith tossed back her head and stared him up and down, from head to toe. "You look more like John now than you did when you were twenty."

"Is that a compliment or a—"

"It's a compliment and you damn well know it. John was a handsome devil. So are you." She looked him square in the eye. "So was my Kent."

"I suppose I should say that I'm sorry about Kent's death and offer you my condolences, but it's difficult to work up any sympathy for a man who ordered my murder." He noted the slight flinch, the practically indiscernible change in Edith's expression, but he knew his comment had, despite her calm demeanor, struck a nerve.

"I hope you don't intend to spout off that nonsense around Noble's Crossing." Smoothing across the soft wool of her gray slacks, Edith slid her left hand down her slender hip. "There's no one who will collaborate your story."

"Are you worried that I've returned for revenge, Miss Edith?"

She did flinch then, and gave him an eat-dirt-and-die glare. "Why else would you have returned? Buddy delivered your succinct message. I took it as a threat. Are you telling me that it wasn't a warning?"

"Succinct. Short and sweet. No wasted words." He liked the surprised expression on Edith's face. "The high school dropout learned a thing or two in college. Like the meaning of simple little words that used to stump me when you and others used them."

"You went to college?"

"I'm sure that by now you know I did. I assume you had Buddy run a check on me. I'm surprised you haven't hired a private detective."

"That's still a distinct possibility."

"As for the message I sent by your lackey—" Johnny Mack chuckled. "Was it a threat or a warning or . . . hmm . . . If revenge was high on my list of priorities, I'd have come back before now. Five years ago, I already had enough money to buy Noble's Crossing, lock, stock and barrel." How he wished that he had come back five years ago. If only he had known. . . . But once he'd left this damn little town and time had passed, his thirst for revenge had been partly quenched. Eventually, he had realized that he hadn't been an innocent bystander in the events leading up to the night Buddy and his cohorts had dumped him into the river.

"If you're that wealthy, I'm surprised you didn't come back and try to prove your allegations. You certainly never struck me as the noble type. Certainly not the forgiving type."

Noble? Only once in his life. When he had left town and refused to take Lane with him. Forgiving? "I'm about as forgiving as you are, Miss Edith."

Someone cleared their throat. Edith tensed. Johnny Mack turned and saw Jackie Cummings as she entered the living room. Jackie was someone else who had changed and yet had remained the same. Same bleached white-blond hair. Same skinny body. Glancing at the way her uniform fit snugly across her nicely rounded breasts, he wondered if she still wore a padded bra as she had done in high school or if she'd had breast augmentation. On their first date, he had slipped his hand inside her bra and discovered a lemon instead of the ripe orange she falsely advertised.

But the years hadn't been kind to Jackie, nor, he suspected, had the two-pack a day smoking habit she had started in her teens. She was thirty-five, but looked ten years older. And there was a used, weary look about her that told him she hadn't lived an easy life.

"Well, hello there, stranger." Jackie slinked over to him, giving him a come-hither smile. "Where have you been so long? This town has been dull as dishwater without you."

"Jackie, please take Miss Mary Martha her sweater."

Edith glowered at her daughter's nurse. "Buddy has taken her for a stroll in the garden."

"Sure thing, Miss Edith." Jackie gave Johnny Mack a lingering smile, then scurried across the room and exited through the French doors.

"One of your old lovers?" Edith asked.

"I'm not the type to kiss and tell," he replied. "You should know that."

Despite her iron-willed control, Edith blushed. He could tell by the way her breathing had accelerated slightly that she was remembering. That last summer. When she had seduced her husband's bastard son. He had enjoyed the irony almost as much as Edith had, but their revenge against John Graham had come at a high price. Kent had seen them together in the summer house. That had been the beginning of the end for Johnny Mack. And he suspected that it had changed Kent's relationship with his mother forever. No doubt Kent had used that knowledge against Miss Edith. He had been the type of man who would have had no qualms about blackmailing his own mother.

"Why are you in Noble's Crossing?" Edith asked again.

"Two reasons." He paused, forcing her to wait, something he knew Edith hated to do. "First reason—I came back to claim my son."

Edith gasped silently, then bit down on her bottom lip as if in an effort to keep from blurting out, *How do you know about Will?*

"So, you didn't realize I knew about Will. Sorry to disappoint you, but I know the whole story."

"Then, you know that Lane duped Kent. She lied to him for years, and then when the truth finally came out, he was devastated. And now, unfortunately, Lane is the prime suspect in Kent's murder."

"That brings me to the second reason I'm back in town—to make sure Lane doesn't get railroaded."

"Are you implying—"

"I'm not implying anything," Johnny Mack said. "I'm stating a fact. Take it as a threat or a warning or whatever the hell way you want to take it. But mark my word, anybody who goes after Lane will have to come through me to get to her." He moved closer, until only inches separated him from Edith. He cupped her chin between his thumb and forefinger. "I can't be scared off. I can't be run off. And I can't be bought off."

When he released her, Edith rubbed her chin and all but hissed at him. "This is still my town. My county. My state. You may be a big shot out in Texas, but around here you're just white trash with money."

Slapping his Stetson on his head, Johnny Mack let out a loud belly laugh. "Yes, ma'am, Miss Edith, you're exactly right. But you might want to remember this—I still don't play by the rules. And these days, I'm the one who always wins."

With that said, he nodded, turned and walked off, leaving Edith to digest his comments. He hoped the bitch choked on them.

Buddy walked upstairs with Mary Martha and waited around until Jackie settled her into her rocking chair and handed her her baby doll. Immediately she began rocking and singing to the life-size doll. After giving Mary Martha an affectionate kiss on the forehead, he nodded to Jackie and left the room. Pausing on the landing, he allowed himself a few minutes before going downstairs to face Miss Edith.

He supposed he fell in love with Mary Martha when she was only twelve. She had been the sweetest, prettiest thing he'd ever seen. Like a storybook princess. And she had liked him. For a friend. Then when she was sixteen, he had asked her for a date and couldn't believe his good fortune when she had accepted. She had later explained to him that Kent had told her she should date Buddy, that he was a good ole boy and she would be safe with him. And she had been safe with him. Oh, he had wanted her. Wanted her so bad that he'd gone around with a hard-on just thinking about her. But whenever he'd tried more than kissing her, she had pushed him away.

He had been stupid enough to think that she was saving herself. Saving herself for when they got married. He had been wrong on both counts. She had never had any intention of marrying him. And she hadn't saved herself for him.

So over the years, while he had never stopped loving Mary Martha, he had married and divorced once and had a couple of long-term affairs. But when his last relationship ended over a year ago, he had, as he'd always done, come flying back to this house like a homing pigeon.

He loved Mary Martha and probably always would. God knew he would do anything for her, even lie down and die, if necessary. But he could never have her, in the way a man wants a woman, needs a woman. She had been ruined long ago, physically and mentally. There was nothing left of Mary Martha Graham except a pathetic little girl who pretended that all was right in her world. And if he could do nothing else for her, he could keep that world bright and shiny and safe.

Balling his trembling hands into fists to steady them, Buddy took a deep breath and marched down the stairs. From the foyer he heard the hum of Miss

Edith's distinct voice. Who was she talking to? Johnny Mack had left over an hour ago.

When Buddy entered the library, he paused just as he stepped over the threshold and, realizing she wasn't aware of his presence, listened to her telephone conversation.

"You heard me, Wes," Edith said. "It's time to send whatever evidence you have against Lane to a grand jury. We've waited long enough. Nothing else is going to show up now. Kent's been dead for over two weeks. I want formal charges brought against Lane. And one more thing—do your best to get a capital murder indictment!" She slammed down the receiver.

Goose bumps broke out on Buddy's arms. She was actually going through with it—forcing Wes Stevens to move forward in Kent's case, when the police had nothing but circumstantial evidence against Lane. No fingerprints had been found on the baseball bat used to perpetrate the crime. He and his investigators had come to the conclusion that whoever had beaten Kent to death had done it fast and quick. In the heat of passion. And the coroner's findings had substantiated theirs. He doubted that Wes could make a case for capital murder. Only the fact that Lane had found the body and called the police and the possible motive of her having killed Kent to, in some way, protect Will made her the prime suspect. A lot of people had disliked Kent. In the past few years, he hadn't ingratiated himself to anyone with his drunken binges that often resulted in Miss Edith calling the police to pick him up for his own safety. Buddy had lost count of the times he had personally locked Kent up for the night. And each time he had been tempted to take the law into his own hands.

At least half a dozen people, including him, had as much or more motive than Lane. But she was the only suspect without an alibi and the only one found with the body. Lillie Mae had been with Will, giving them both an alibi. Miss Edith had been with Mary Martha. James Ware had been with Arlene Dothan, a fact James had admitted only under great duress. And he himself had been at the police station. And yes, he, as much as anyone else, had wanted to see Kent Graham dead.

"Wes will never get a capital murder indictment," Buddy said, then smiled when Miss Edith jumped and gasped aloud.

"Mercy, Buddy, you scared me to death." She lifted her hand and fluttered it over her bosom. Her ample bosom. It amazed him that a sixty-year-old woman could be so attractive, so downright sexy. But Edith took full advantage of being wealthy, getting a nip here and a tuck there from time to time. The last thing he wanted was for Mary Martha's mother to turn him on. But he hadn't been with a woman in months, and Miss Edith had been flirting with him lately. It didn't take a genius to figure out that she was on the prowl. And the strong resemblance between mother and daughter only added to Miss Edith's appeal.

"The most he can hope for is felony murder, and my guess is, if the grand jury hands down an indictment, it could be for nothing more than manslaughter," Buddy said. "If Lane was protecting Will, as some folks are speculating, and she didn't mean to kill Kent, only stop him from tormenting the boy, then—"

"I'll take what I can get," Edith said, her mouth curved into a snarl. "Lane deserves to be punished and so does Johnny Mack."

"And just how will convicting Lane of Kent's murder punish Johnny Mack?"

"Because Johnny Mack has sworn to be her protector, her savior, her knight in shining armor." Edith sauntered over to Buddy and laid her hand on his chest. "That means he cares about her, perhaps more than anyone ever suspected. And when a man like Johnny Mack cares . . . ah, my dear Buddy, that means we have a weapon to use against him."

"You aren't willing to accept the fact that Kent brought his brutal death on himself, are you?" Buddy captured Edith's hand as it strayed down his chest, her fingertips edging beneath his belt buckle. "You need someone other than yourself to blame for the way your children turned out, don't you? If you'd been paying attention to what was going on in your own house, instead of trying to out-fuck your whore-hopping husband—"

"No one speaks to me that way." Edith drew back her hand and prepared to strike, but Buddy manacled her wrist and stopped her blow in midair.

"How dare you! Release me this instant!" Edith tried to jerk free, but Buddy increased the pressure until she cried out. "Damn it, you're hurting me."

Buddy yanked her forward until her breasts pressed against his chest. Twisting her arms behind her, he held her in place and lowered his head. His lips hovered over hers. She stared at him, wild-eyed and breathless.

"This is what you want, isn't it, Miss Edith?" Buddy ground his erection against her mound. "This is what you liked about Mr. John and Johnny Mack. And what you can't get with James. You like it a little bit rough, don't you? You want a man to dominate you."

"You son of a bitch, let go of me or I'll scratch your eyes out." As if to demonstrate her threat, she bared her teeth and snarled.

He brought his mouth down on hers with forceful

intent. Crushing. Bruising. Invading, when she tried to protest verbally. The moment his tongue touched hers, she moaned and suddenly ceased struggling. When she melted against him, he deepened the kiss.

Not here. Not now. What little part of his mind that still worked cautioned him. He couldn't screw Miss Edith in this house. Not with Mary Martha upstairs.

Abruptly, Buddy ended the kiss and gave Edith a gentle backward shove. She stood there glaring at him, her breasts rising and falling with each labored breath.

"You know where I live, if you're interested in finishing what we started," he told her.

"Don't you feel the least bit disloyal to Mary Martha?" Edith asked. "After all, you profess to love my daughter more than life itself."

"I do love Mary Martha, but you and I both know that she and I have no future together. I can never take her in my arms and carry her to bed and make love to her the way I want to do." Buddy swiped his mouth with the back of his hand, wiping the taste of Miss Edith from his lips. "I'm a man and I have needs. But don't kid yourself into thinking I care about you. If I could have Mary Martha instead, then—"

"Shut up! Just shut up!"

"What's wrong? Haven't you ever been any man's first choice, Miss Edith, or have you always been an also ran? Mr. John preferred any pretty woman in town over you, didn't he? And James . . . well, just because you aren't warming his bed doesn't mean he's doing without. And what about Johnny Mack? Do you honestly think you meant anything to him?" When Edith gasped, Buddy chuckled. "Yeah, Kent told me all about catching you two. Ever wonder how many other people he told?"

"Shut up! I could ruin you and have you run out of town for treating me like this. But you know I won't, because I need you. Because Mary Martha needs you."

For the first time in all the years he had been associated with the Graham family, Buddy felt a sense of power. And he liked it. He liked it a lot. But he didn't dare push Miss Edith too far. He knew just exactly what she was capable of doing.

"If Wes has enough evidence to take to a grand jury, then I could go ahead and arrest Lane, today," Buddy said. "Is that what you want?"

"Trying to placate me?"

"Trying to cooperate," he said. "We both want the same ending to this story, and that means pinning Kent's death on Lane. So, I ask you again, do you want me to arrest her today?"

"No. Not today. Wait for the indictment. Then I want her arrest to make the front page of the *Herald*."

"You'll try and convict her in her own newspaper. You are a devious bitch."

"Yes, I am. And don't you ever forget it."

Lane rested on her antique Louis XVI style bed. With her arms folded behind her, her fingers entwined and her head braced against her open palms, she stared up at the ceiling. After her divorce from Kent, she had returned home and immediately redecorated her old bedroom. She had brought down some of her maternal grandmother's antiques that her mother had stored in the attic during the late sixties. More than anything, Lane had wanted her bedroom to be a sanctuary from the world, a welcoming, feminine abode to which she could retreat.

Glancing around the room, she smiled as her gaze

scanned the off-white walls, the poppy red drapes and matching Roman shades that graced the three windows overlooking the back of the house. Then her gaze lingered to appreciate the eighteenth century Italian commode over which she had hung an assortment of photographs of Will, from infancy to the present day. The summer cotton gown she had worn last night lay across the back of the Italian fauteuil, which she'd had reupholstered in a muted red-and-gold-striped silk brocade.

She loved this room. She felt safe here, in a space she had never shared with Kent. There were no bad memories haunting these four walls.

How had she reached such a low point? How had Bill and Celeste Noble's spoiled little darling become the prime suspect in a murder case? All her life, she had been a good girl, obeying orders, following the rules. Pleasing her parents had been so important to her. As her mother had pointed out to her quite often—she was all they had, and because they gave her only the best, they expected nothing less than the very best from her.

Falling in love with Johnny Mack Cahill had been a major faux pas, a secret act of defiance that her mother had only suspected and her father had quietly ignored. Her parents had never known the truth about Will's paternity, and now that they were gone, she was glad that they had died not knowing. Her father would have understood and even stood by her, but her mother would have disowned her.

Closing her eyes, she sighed and tried to relax. She had come upstairs to take a nap because she hadn't had a good night's sleep since Kent's murder. She had intended talking to Will when he came home, but he had phoned Lillie Mae to tell her that he was going to a matinee movie with a couple of his school buddies and he wouldn't be home until dinnertime. He was avoiding her as well as avoiding the situation. But sooner or later Will would have to deal with the fact that Johnny Mack was his father and the man wasn't going to go away just because Will wanted him to.

And you're going to have to deal with the fact that Johnny Mack is back in town and you can't stop those old feelings from resurfacing. You thought Kent had destroyed your ability to feel any kind of sexual urges, that his cruelty forever vanquished your desires, your sexual hungers. You thought you'd never again want a man, need a man. But after all these years, you've discovered that what you thought was dead was only traumatized and waiting to be healed.

But Johnny Mack is no healer, she reminded herself. He wasn't a destroyer the way Kent had been, but he was a user. She didn't dare trust him. Not with her life. Not with Will's life. Not yet. And most certainly not with her heart. Not ever.

The insistent ring of the telephone on her bedside table brought her abruptly back to the present moment. She rolled over, reached out and grabbed the receiver.

"Hello."

"Lane?"

"James, is that you?"

"Yes."

"You're talking so low, I can barely hear you."

"Listen, Lane, as your lawyer . . . and as your friend, I'm advising you that Wes Stevens is taking what evidence he has against you to a grand jury, and my guess is that within a week, maybe less, you'll be indicted for Kent's murder."

"Oh, God!" She sucked in several huge breaths of air. "I knew it was bound to happen, but I had hoped . . ."

"You're going to need a better lawyer than I am," James said. "If I held the purse strings, I'd offer to hire someone for you, but I doubt Edith—"

"I appreciate the thought," Lane told him. "But you needn't worry about me."

"But I do. I know you don't have the cash—"

"I have a friend who has offered to hire one of the best criminal lawyers in the country for me."

"If I were you, Lane, I'd take him up on that offer."

Johnny Mack pondered his options. He could stay put at the Four Way or he could leave in the morning and move to either a Holiday Inn or a Ramada Inn, the only two other choices in Noble's Crossing, unless he wanted to stay at Miss Charlotte's Bed & Breakfast. Or he could rent an apartment, maybe even a house. Although he might have to make a few short business trips back to Houston from time to time, he had no intention of leaving town until he had made every effort to connect with his son. And he certainly wasn't going to desert Lane, as long as the possibility that she would be indicted for Kent's murder hung over her head.

Restless, unaccustomed to having this much idle time on his hands, Johnny Mack paced the floor. Maybe he should take in a movie tonight, after he had dined alone at the restaurant next door to the motel. Or he could hit one of the bars. He wondered if the Boogie Barracks was still the hottest spot in town or if that old honky-tonk had been closed down years ago. Years before he was legal drinking age, he'd gone there with Wiley Peters. The proprietor had been an old war buddy of Wiley's and hadn't worried much about checking his clienteles' IDs.

Sharon had liked the Boogie Barracks. They had

done their share of drinking and dancing in that place. And once they had even gotten it on in the men's bathroom, when Sharon had followed him inside a stall. Heaven help Will, having inherited his genes from Sharon and the son of Satan himself, Johnny Mack Cahill. The boy was predisposed to be a hellion. But he wasn't. Not yet. And both of his biological parents had been well on their way to hell when they were fourteen.

If he could do anything for Will, he would spare him from making the kinds of mistakes he had made. Back then, he hadn't cared what he'd done or who he had hurt. All that had mattered was surviving and finding a way to ease the loneliness and the pain of being unloved and unwanted.

No one had given a shit about him, and he had felt the same about everyone else. *Don't care and you can't get hurt. Don't want what you can't have and you won't be disappointed.*

But Will wasn't him. And although Sharon had given birth to Will, he was far more Lane's child than Sharon's. From the report the PI had compiled on Will, Johnny Mack could see—in print—that Will Graham was no bad seed. He was the young man Lane had raised him to be—smart, studious, athletic and, as a general rule, courteous and considerate. Will had been given every possible advantage as the son of Kent and Lane Graham. He had known his place in this one-horse town, and that place had been as the young *king of the hill.* Even though he had known he was adopted, he had probably never questioned his right to one day take his place as the heir apparent, just as Kent had done.

But how did Will feel now? Now that he knew the truth? Would that inherited wild streak break free and lead him into trouble?

"Not if I can help it!"

A loud knock on his motel room door gained Johnny Mack's attention. He wasn't expecting anyone. He grabbed his shirt off the bed where he had thrown it when he'd gone into the bathroom to shave for the second time that day. Thrusting his arms into the sleeves of his black western shirt, he headed for the door. The undone pearl snaps on his shirt glimmered in the muted light from the two bedside lamps. After glancing through the viewfinder, he immediately opened the door.

"Lane?"

"May I come in?"

With the late afternoon sun at her back, the light painted her with transparent gold, from head to toe. She looked like a golden goddess, a vision from the dreams he had tried so hard to forget.

"Something's wrong," he said, then stepped aside to allow her entrance.

She waited until he closed the door behind her before she replied. "James telephoned to tell me that Wes Stevens is taking the evidence he has in Kent's murder case to a grand jury as soon as possible. I think now is the time for you to call Quinn Cortez. It's probably only a matter of days before I'll be indicted for Kent's murder."

Chapter 13

"Come over and sit down." When Johnny Mack reached out to take Lane's hand, she deliberately withdrew toward the closed door.

She didn't think she could bear for him to touch her. If he did, she might fall apart in his arms. She had been holding herself together since Kent's death by sheer willpower alone. And although she desperately needed someone to lean on, that person couldn't be Johnny Mack. For so many years, she had had no one to count on but herself. She had been the one to take charge, make all the decisions and carry life's burdens alone. For her sake and for Will's sake, she had needed to be strong even in her weakest moments. Lillie Mae had always done what she could, but it wasn't the same as having a strong man to stand by her in times of trouble. And to complicate matters, Lane wasn't sure she could trust Johnny Mack, or any other man—not after what Kent had done to her.

"You can't know for sure that you'll be indicted,"

Johnny Mack said. "There had to be dozens of people who wanted to see Kent dead. Surely the police— Scratch that! I forgot for a minute that I'm in Noble's Crossing and that the police chief is in Miss Edith's hip pocket."

Lane nervously twisted the straps on her shoulder bag. "The police have been gathering evidence for two weeks now, and I honestly don't think they've checked out the possibility that anyone else could have committed the crime."

"That tells me that Edith doesn't want another suspect. Why do you suppose that is?"

"Maybe she honestly thinks I killed Kent."

"Or maybe she knows who did and would rather see you take the rap."

"I can't believe that Miss Edith would protect Kent's murderer," Lane said. "After all, she was his mother."

"Edith doesn't have any maternal instincts. She tried to rule her children the way she tried to rule Noble's Crossing. Miss Edith always did what was best for Miss Edith. I don't think that's changed."

Lane nodded agreement, then let her gaze travel slowly over Johnny Mack. She couldn't help noticing that his shirt was undone enough to reveal the hard, dark flesh of his naked chest. He was bigger and broader than he had been at twenty-one, but still muscular and sleek. Even as a fourteen-year-old, she had sat in the window and watched him while he mowed their grass and pruned their shrubbery. And during the hot summer months, he had worn nothing but a pair of cut-off jeans. Like every other female in town, she had lusted after the baddest bad boy Noble's Crossing had ever spawned.

Heat rose within her. Sensual heat. She didn't want this. Not now. Not ever. She had enough problems in her life without adding an affair with Johnny Mack to the mix. An affair that could end only in more heartbreak for her.

Think business, she told herself. *You're here to accept an offer. A repayment for an old debt. As Lillie Mae had said, to call in your marker. Concentrate on that and nothing more.* Allowing herself to think of Johnny Mack as a desirable man would be like playing with fire. She had already had her heart singed by that particular blaze and didn't relish letting it happen a second time.

Their gazes met and held again for only a brief moment. An intense awareness passed between them. Feeling as if he had somehow touched her, Lane shivered, but realized the intimacy had been only in her mind.

"Won't you sit down?" He gestured toward the lone chair in the room.

Lane sat in the chair, while Johnny Mack eased down on the edge of the bed. She crossed her legs at the ankles, placed her bag in her lap, folded her hands together and laid them atop her bag.

"I'll call Quinn and tell him what's happened."

"Thank you. I hope you know that I wouldn't be here ... that I wouldn't accept your offer to pay for an attorney if I could afford Quinn Cortez's fee myself."

How ironic that the man who had once done yard work for her family now had more money than she did. If things were different, she would be extremely pleased for Johnny Mack, pleased that he had done so well. It had to be very satisfying for him to return to his hometown, where he'd been labeled a worthless bad boy, as a wealthy and powerful man.

"You don't have to explain anything to me," he told her. "And you certainly don't have to thank me. I owe you my life." He leaned over, placed his hands between his spread knees and twined his fingers together. "And I owe you my son's life, too. Don't you think that picking up the tab for your legal fees is a small repayment for your having saved two lives?"

She couldn't take credit for what she had done instinctively, for the things she'd done for love. She had saved him and saved his son because, for her, there had been no other choices.

"There's one other thing I want from you," Lane told him.

He lifted his gaze to search her eyes. "Anything. Just name it."

"I don't want Will involved in this case," Lane said. "I do not want Mr. Cortez asking him a lot of questions and upsetting him. Buddy went very easy on Will the day Kent was murdered. Even though Edith knows Will isn't Kent's son, she's still very fond of him, and I'm sure she'll persuade Buddy and Wes Stevens to protect Will in this situation."

"What exactly does Will need protection from?"

"From having to relive that day." Lane came forward so that she sat perched on the edge of her seat. "I'd rather confess to killing Kent than to have Will destroyed by . . ." Did she dare trust Johnny Mack? No, not yet.

"Destroyed by what? The truth? It's been my experience that the lies are what hurt us."

"I have to go. Please, let me know when you've contacted Mr. Cortez."

Lane sprang up out of the chair. Her shoulder bag dropped to the floor. When she reached down to pick it up, her hand encountered Johnny Mack's. He lifted the bag; then together they rose and stood facing each other. Without saying a word, he stationed the straps of her expensive leather purse on her shoulder. But his hand lingered, hovering close to her neck.

Her heartbeat accelerated. The drone of her blood rushing through her body hummed in her head. He was so close she could feel the warmth of his breath, could smell the faint hint of aftershave he used, could sense the tension in his muscles.

Unable to move, to run, as her common sense told her to, Lane glanced down and suddenly realized that their bodies were almost touching. She had been this close to Johnny Mack only once before, and that was a moment she would remember to her dying day. That last summer before he'd left town. Down by the boathouse. Under the willow trees that lined the riverbank. He had kissed her the way she'd always dreamed he would. And when he'd pulled her close, she had felt the hard, pulsing throb of his sex against her belly. She would have lain down on the ground and given herself to him, but he had released her and, without explanation, walked away.

If only he had made love to her that night, maybe she and not Sharon Hickman would have gotten pregnant with his child.

Johnny Mack cupped and lifted her chin, forcing her to face him. *Don't do this to me,* she silently pleaded. *It has taken me fifteen years to stop loving you. Don't make me care. Don't make me love you all over again.*

As mesmerized by his lethal masculine charm as she had been when she was a teenager, Lane made no protest when he slipped one arm around her waist. As he eased his other hand around to clutch the back of her neck, he brought her forward just enough so that her breasts rubbed against his chest. Of its own accord, her right hand lifted and laid her open palm on his naked flesh. How could this be happening?

She had thought she was incapable of responding this way to a man's touch.

A sense of unreality claimed her. This was a dream. One she had had more times than she could count. Years ago, when she had been young and naive and trusting. When she had been eager to experience the pleasures of sex with the man she loved.

But this dream had died a brutal death, as so many of her dreams had. Killed by reality. Destroyed by Johnny Mack's departure from her life. Bludgeoned by Kent's insensitivity that had eventually turned to cruelty.

"Lane." He whispered her name. Soft, low and deep.

A quivering sensation spiraled through her body, from the very depths of her feminine soul. Was he asking permission? her hazy mind wondered. Or was he giving her fair warning?

The moment his lips touched hers, she braced herself for the bruising crush that she had come to expect whenever Kent kissed her. But there was no demanding lunge, no hard, grinding pressure.

Remember, her mind murmured, *remember how it was with Johnny Mack.* She sighed, as much from the memory as from the present pleasure. His lips were warm and wet and captured hers with a languid, sensual expertise that took her breath away. He tasted and tempted, licked and nipped. Tenderly. Patiently. But only when she opened her mouth with a gratified sigh did he ease his tongue inside and explore her more intimately.

Rational thought ceased to exit as a longing that would not be denied took control of Lane. She wanted more. Oh, God, she needed so much more.

The feel of his hard, hot flesh beneath her hands excited her in a way she had never dreamed possible—not after Kent brutalized and humiliated her. When Johnny Mack lowered his hands to grasp her buttocks and fit her tightly against his erection, she couldn't control her body's instinctive preparation. The gush of moisture. The clenching and unclenching. The ache that only sex could ease.

"I want to make love to you," he told her, his lips against her ear. "I denied us both what we wanted fifteen years ago, but we aren't the same two people we were then. If this is what you want—"

Why had he said anything? Why hadn't he just taken her to bed and made love to her? He was asking her to make the decision. If she let things go any farther, it would be her choice.

"You're very good at this," Lane said, as she wriggled in an effort to free herself from his hold. "Comes from a great deal of experience, no doubt."

He released her immediately, but made no move to separate his body from the nearness of hers. When he looked her square in the eye, she saw anger and something more. Regret?

"When it's right between a man and a woman, it doesn't matter who or how many have come before. Or at least it shouldn't," he said.

She knew he hadn't been pining away for her all these years and certainly hadn't lived a celibate life. But she *had* pined for him, year after year, until she had grown to hate him. And since the day she'd asked Kent for a divorce, she hadn't been with a man; hadn't wanted an intimate relationship ever again. Knowing that she would never have to let Kent or any other man touch her had been such a great relief.

"And how many times has it been right between you and some woman?" Lane asked.

He stared at her as if the answer to her question should be obvious. "It's been good. It's been fun. It's been exciting. And it's been satisfying. Every time I've taken a woman, I've enjoyed it.''

Just as she had thought. Once a stud, always a stud. If she gave herself to him, she would risk everything because she would fall in love with him again. But for him, she would be just another easy lay. The thought of being one more notch on Johnny Mack Cahill's bedpost didn't appeal to her in the least.

"I should go," she said, but her feet wouldn't cooperate, leaving her planted directly in front of the man from whom she wanted to escape.

"Mm-mm." He nodded.

"Please, call me after you've spoken to Mr. Cortez." He nodded again.

She finally forced her legs into motion and headed for the exit. After opening the door, she halted, pivoted halfway around and said, "If you really want to be a father to Will, I'll help you. It won't be easy, and I can't guarantee that he'll ever accept you into his life; but he needs to know that a better man than Kent Graham is his father."

"Thanks, Lane."

"Don't thank me. Not yet." She managed to plaster a weak smile on her face. "And I'll warn you now. If you ever hurt that boy, I'll make you sorry you came back to Noble's Crossing."

"Always the mama tiger protecting her cub," Johnny Mack said.

"Yes, I am. And if you're thinking I killed Kent to protect Will, then you're right to think that way. I would have killed Kent, but someone else beat me to it."

"I wish I had been the one. I wish I'd broken his damn neck a long time ago. Before he ever laid a hand on you."

She could no longer sustain the quavering smile

or the false bravado. If she didn't leave now, she would probably fall into a million shattered pieces right here in front of Johnny Mack. And like Humpty Dumpty, all the king's horses and all the king's men couldn't put her back together again.

"Call before you come by the house," Lane said. "And I'll make sure Will's there."

Rushing outside, she didn't realize Johnny Mack had followed her, not until she heard his footsteps. When she paused and glanced over her shoulder, he stopped and looked at her as if he had something to say.

"What is it?" she asked.

"Sex has been a lot of things for me, but it's never been perfect. I've never thought to myself that this time she's the right woman, the perfect woman for me."

"Oh."

"I just wanted you to know." He turned and walked back into his motel room.

When he closed the door, Lane took a deep breath and ran to her car. *Don't think about what he said,* she warned herself. *If you think you're the woman with whom it could be perfect, that you're that one and only right woman for him, you're fooling yourself. Having sex with Johnny Mack would be wrong. For you and for him.*

But, dear God, it would be good. So good.

Johnny Mack eased back in the cushioned, wrought-iron chaise longue and looked over the rim of his sunglasses at his son horsing around on the far end of the pool with a couple of his buddies. George Markham III and Theodore "Ted" Upton IV. Both boys were sons of Magnolia Avenue parents. And Will was one of them, a blue blood through and through, despite his questionable lineage. Perhaps all that was required to be a blue blood was being raised as one of the privileged few.

Back in the good old days when he had been the gardener's assistant, he had listened to the squeals and giggles and hardy laughter coming from behind the fence that enclosed the pool area on the Noble estate. And he had wondered what it would be like to belong to Lane's circle of friends, to have nothing more to do on a summer day than play around the pool.

When he had first gone to work for Bill Noble, he'd been sixteen and seldom had more than pocket change, except when Wiley won big at cards, which wasn't often. During that first summer, late in the day, when all the kids had gone home and the Nobles were eating dinner in their elegant dining room, he had slipped into the pool area and hoped Lillie Mae hadn't gotten around to cleaning up yet. Sometimes he had found half a slice of a sandwich or an untouched cookie or some chips just lying on a plate. And there had usually been tea or cola in a glass, diluted in strength by melted ice cubes. He hadn't considered it stealing to eat the leftovers that would have otherwise ended up in the trash. And he suspected that Lillie Mae had deliberately left the cleanup until after dark because she had known that without those meager crumbs, he would often as not have gone to bed hungry. And she had known just as surely that he would never have taken a handout from her.

That had been twenty years and a lifetime of regrets ago. He reminded himself that he had left behind that wild, angry, young hellion the day he'd left Noble's Crossing. The day he had told Lane that he couldn't take her with him. But no matter how successful, how rich he became, a part of that hungry teenager still lived within him. A part of him was still hungry, still angry and still knew that he wasn't good enough to kiss Lane Noble's pretty little feet.

Glancing down at the patio floor beside the chaise, he saw ten red toenails. Ten toes. Two size-six plastic pool sandals. As he lifted his gaze, a pair of shapely calves came into view. A red fishnet robe hit her mid-thigh, its open cutwork leaving little to the imagination. A form-fitting red swimsuit, with high-cut legs and low-cut back accentuated every curve of a well-proportioned hour-glass shape. Everything male within him reacted to the sight of delicious female flesh.

Lane stood over him, a glass of iced tea in each hand. "I thought you might be thirsty. Lillie Mae made up a fresh pitcher of tea."

After pulling himself up into a sitting position, Johnny Mack straddled the middle of the chaise and reached out to take one of the glasses Lane held. "Thanks."

She nodded to the threesome frolicking in the pool. "Will seems to be enjoying himself. It's the first time since Kent's death that I've seen him genuinely smile." Lane seated herself in a padded, wrought-iron chair stationed at the matching table over which a huge umbrella shaded a wide circle from the afternoon sun. "Is he still avoiding you?"

"What do you think?"

"I'm sorry. I'd thought by now he would at least be speaking to you without my instigating the conversation." Lane lifted the glass to her lips and sipped the cold tea.

"He's been doing a very good job of avoiding me, despite the fact that I've been around every day for nearly a week now. He's damned determined to pretend I don't exist."

"I warned you that winning him over wouldn't be easy."

Lane set her glass on the table and picked up a bottle of sun block. After squirting a small amount into her hand, she dotted some on her nose and rubbed it in. Johnny Mack noticed that her nose and her shoulders still freckled when the rest of her tanned nicely. In so many ways she was still that sweet little girl who, like her father, had been kind to him. But in other ways, she had become a woman he didn't know. Was that how she thought of him, as an old friend who had become a stranger?

"After this coming weekend, he'll be back in school," Lane said. "I dread to think about what some of the kids might say to him. After all, his father was murdered three weeks ago and there's a good chance his mother may be arrested for the crime."

"He's tough. He can handle a few smart-ass remarks." Johnny Mack gulped down half a glass of tea, then placed his glass beside Lane's on the table.

"I'm worried that he might handle himself the way you used to do and wind up getting into fights." Lane sighed. "I've even thought about sending him away to school, but I honestly don't think he'd go. He wouldn't want to leave me. And to be honest, I can't bear the thought of being separated from him. If I'm convicted of killing Kent and am sent to prison, I don't—"

"Quinn has told you that even if you're indicted, it's highly unlikely you'll be convicted of anything, not even manslaughter." Johnny Mack leaned back in the chaise and stretched out his legs. "The police don't have enough evidence. And what they do have is circumstantial. Besides, if the grand jury is fool enough to indict you, we'll just follow through and find out who really killed Kent. The PI I have on retainer arrived in Noble's Crossing four days ago, and he's doing the police's job by searching for other suspects. If there's anyone with a motive, who had the opportunity to kill Kent, Wyatt Foster will unearth them.''

"You're spending a fortune on trying to prove my innocence.''

He could tell, even though sunshades protected her eyes, that she was looking directly at him. Her body leaned, ever so slightly, in his direction.

"I have a fortune to spend,'' he said.

"So you do.'' Lane sighed deeply. "I don't think either of us ever thought the day would come when I'd be a charity case and you'd be my benefactor.''

Before he could reply, she got up, shed her see-through robe and ran to the edge of the pool. Just watching the way she moved—the sway of her round hips, the fullness of her bouncing breasts, the curve of her slender waist—aroused him painfully. Spending hours each day with her had become torture. She was the only woman in his entire life he had ever wanted desperately and not had. In his youth, he had appeased his desire with other women. With lots of other women. But even then, sex with another woman hadn't diminished his desire for Lane. And now, when he hadn't been with another woman since arriving in Noble's Crossing, finding a way to persuade Lane to become his lover had reached the point of obsession.

Were her breasts as round and full as they appeared to be? Would her nipples be large and dark or small and pink? Was the hair between her legs thick? Curly? Would he be able to bring her to a climax with the touch of his fingers, the attention of his mouth? When she came, would she scream or whimper? Would she cry out his name or moan softly?

"Miss Lane, there's a call for you." Lillie Mae entered the patio through the kitchen door, halting Lane just as she started to dive into the pool.

"Who is it?"

Lillie Mae handed Lane the portable phone and waited, a worried look in her weary gray eyes. "It's James Ware."

Johnny Mack shot up off the chaise, and by the time Lane held the phone to her ear, he stood behind her, his hand on her shoulder. She quivered, a barely discernible shudder rippling through her body.

"Hello, James."

Johnny Mack leaned closer, inclining his head so that when she held the telephone a fraction away from her ear, he was able to hear James's part of the conversation.

"Lane, I wanted to warn you," James said. "The grand jury's handed down an indictment against you for felony murder. Now's the time for that damn good lawyer your friend hired to take over from me. Buddy will be there to arrest you this afternoon."

"Yes, I understand. Thank you, James."

"I'm as sorry as I can be about this. I don't think you killed Kent, but . . . as you well know, nobody around here listens to me. I wish I could do something to help you. I wish . . . hell, I wish I wasn't scared shitless of my wife."

"It's all right. I appreciate your forewarning me."

Johnny Mack took the phone from her and tossed it onto the chaise longue. Lane swayed ever so slightly. Without a moment's hesitation, he wrapped his arm around her waist to lend her support.

"What was he forewarning you about?" Lillie Mae asked.

"The grand jury has indicted me for Kent's murder."

Will pulled himself out of the pool and wrapped a towel around his shoulders. "What's going on?"

Lane clung to Johnny Mack. "Will's going to be so upset by this."

"Dammit, woman, for once, think of yourself," Johnny Mack told her.

"Mama?" Will halted several feet away, his gaze riveted to Johnny Mack's arm around Lane's waist.

"The grand jury has indicted your mother," Johnny Mack said. "She needs all of us to stay calm and focused on getting her out of this mess. She needs you to act like a man now, Will, and not some whiny kid. Can you do that? Can you be the man your mother has raised you to be?"

Chapter 14

Glenn Manis swigged on a can of Miller Lite as he ground his wide behind into the old recliner. Grabbing the TV remote control, he belched loudly. While he flipped through the stations, searching for an interesting sporting event or a show about hunting or fishing, he occasionally glanced back over his shoulder to see if Jackie had finished up in the bathroom. She had left the door partially open, so he could see a glimpse of the shower. Jackie liked to pretend she was sexy and that giving him a peek at her naked body emerging from her bath drove him wild. Her skinny body didn't exactly drive him crazy, but what she could do with her talented mouth sure as hell did.

He had been dating Jackie for a year now, and sometimes he thought about asking her to marry him. After all, neither of them were getting any younger, and if he hadn't done any better than Jackie by now, the odds were that he never would. Besides, he'd rather have a skinny, ugly wife who was good in bed than a better looking one who was as cold as ice.

Jackie was no prize. But then neither was he. In school he had been the dumpy, goofy geek who couldn't get a date. And Jackie had been the bug-eyed, bean pole white trash girl who no man would look at twice. But by the time she was sixteen, she had figured out a way to gain male attention. She bleached her hair, started stuffing her bra, stopped wearing panties and started putting out. And every guy in town soon learned where to go to get a top-notch blow job.

Back then, he hadn't been romantically interested in Jackie. The girl he had tried his damnedest to make notice him had been Sharon Hickman. Now, there had been a looker, with big tits, a sweet ass and a face like a movie star's. And he had heard there wasn't nothing Sharon wouldn't do in the sack. But except for Johnny Mack Cahill, who had dipped his quill in just about every ink well in town, the only guys Sharon paid attention to were the boys from Rich Man's Land.

Of course, the girl he had dreamed about, fantasied about throughout his teenage years, had been one of the most unattainable girls in town. Mary Martha Graham. The angel. He didn't think he'd ever seen a more beautiful girl in his life. Not even Sharon Hickman. But as far as he knew, the only guy Mary Martha had ever dated was Buddy Lawler.

Suddenly the words of a TV news reporter brought Glenn back into the present. He jerked straight up and turned up the sound. Had he heard right? Good God almighty! The whole town had been waiting for the news and now it was official.

"This afternoon Police Chief Buddy Lawler arrested Lane Noble Graham for the murder of her ex-husband, local businessman Kent Graham.'' The reporter continued speaking while the station played a videotape showing Lane, shackled in handcuffs, being brought into the police station. Buddy had his hand on her arm, guiding her through the crowd. Behind her, two tall, dark-haired men kept pace, as if they were guarding Lane.

"Well, I'll be damned,'' Glenn said. "That there's Johnny Mack Cahill himself. Looks like what folks have been saying is true. He's back in Noble's Crossing to stay.''

When the videotape ended as Lane disappeared inside the police station, the reporter continued his coverage of the biggest scandal to hit Noble's Crossing in the past fifty years.

"Representing Ms. Graham is renowned trial lawyer, Quinn Cortez, whom our sources say flew in from Houston, via private plane, this afternoon. As most of you will recall, Mr. Cortez made a name for himself six years ago, when as a young lawyer only a year out of law school, he was chosen by the Latin singer, Paco Urbano, to defend him in the sensational murder trial of his live-in girlfriend. Despite all the evidence against Urbano, Cortez was able to persuade the jury that the Hispanic heartthrob was innocent. Mr. Cortez has become famous—or in some opinions, infamous—for having never lost a case.

"And as to the other man seen with Ms. Graham— that's former Noble's Crossing resident Johnny Mack Cahill. Our sister CBS station in Houston tells us that Cahill is now a multimillionaire entrepreneur, well known in Houston's social circles as a generous philanthropist as well as a business shark, who possesses the Midas touch.

"What is Cahill's connection to the Graham murder case, you might ask? Noble's Crossing residents who knew Cahill as a young man say a better question to ask is what is Cahill's connection to Ms. Graham and just how personal is their relationship?''

"Well, I'll be damned,'' Glenn repeated. "Ain't this a kick in the butt. The press is gonna have a field day with this one.''

"What are you mumbling about out there?'' Jackie, wearing nothing but a towel, stood in the bathroom doorway, one hand on the door facing and the other on her scrawny hip.

"Come here, honey pie.'' Glenn motioned with his flabby arm. "You're not gonna believe this. They just arrested Lane for Kent's murder and—''

"That's not news. The whole town's been expecting as much ever since Wes Stevens sent the evidence to a grand jury.'' Jackie sashayed into the living room, a come-hither smile on her face. "Folks are laying odds against her, you know. They think that whether or not she killed Kent, she'll be convicted. Seems Miss Edith wants to see her go down.''

"Well, Miss Edith just might not get what she wants this time.''

"What makes you say that?'' Jackie plopped down in Glenn's lap and wrapped her arm around his thick neck.

Glenn readjusted his body in the brown vinyl chair, enough so that he could place Jackie's ass directly over his dick. Maybe if she would squirm around a bit, he'd get hard. And if that didn't work, he would just let her talented fingers put him in the mood.

"Seems Lane's done gone and got herself a high-priced lawyer.''

"Who's that?'' Jackie loosened the towel she had draped around her and let it fall to her waist.

He wouldn't hurt Jackie's feelings for nothing in

this world, so there was no way he could tell her that the sight of her fried egg tits didn't do a damn thing for him. "Quinn Cortez, that's who."

"Quinn Cortez? He's sure going to cost her a pretty penny. That guy's fee must be at least a million for a murder case."

"Well, Lane's rich, ain't she? And if she runs out of cash, Johnny Mack shouldn't have no trouble picking up the tab. That reporter says our Noble's Crossing's bad boy done made himself a fortune out in Texas."

"Good for Johnny Mack. Good for all of us nobodies from this side of the Chickasaw River if we can find a way to get rich." She licked a circle around Glenn's ear. "Let me tell you a little secret. I've got a way of making us a small fortune." Jackie lifted her hips enough to whip the towel off and toss it onto the floor. "How'd you like for us to honeymoon in Vegas with two million bucks?"

Glenn unzipped his pants, grasped Jackie's hand and slid it inside his briefs. "What are you talking about? How do you think you can get your hands on two million dollars?"

She circled his penis and began a slow, practiced motion that soon elicited a groan from Glenn. "That's for me to know and you to find out. I just happened upon some information that certain people are going to want kept quiet, and I know for a fact those people are going to be willing to pay me to keep my mouth shut."

"You're talking about blackmail, Jackie Jo."

"I sure am, sweetie. Blackmail that's going to make me rich."

*   *   *

"Why can't you get Mama out of jail tonight?" Will glared at his father. "I thought you were going to help her."

Johnny Mack felt as helpless as Will did. The thought of Lane spending even one night in jail enraged him. Damn, was there no justice in this world? A woman like Lane didn't belong behind bars. Hell, even if she had actually murdered Kent—and he now believed she hadn't—she shouldn't be treated like a criminal. Fingerprinted. Photographed. Interrogated. Instead, she should be given a medal for ridding this world of vermin like Kent Graham.

"I'm willing to do anything to help your mother."

"It doesn't look like it from where I stand," Will accused.

"Then, you're wrong," Quinn Cortez said. "Your father hired me to defend Lane and—"

"He's not my father! He hasn't earned the right to be a part of my life or Mama's life."

Will's cheeks flamed. Moisture shimmered in his eyes. Johnny Mack sensed that the boy was close to tears and was trying valiantly not to cry in front of Quinn and him. Johnny Mack hadn't ever thought of himself as paternal, but every instinct within him wanted to grab Will, hold him tight and find a way to make him believe that everything was going to be all right.

"Your problems with Johnny Mack are none of my concern. That's something the two of you will have to work out," Quinn said. "But the two points I wanted to make in order to explain that your . . . that Johnny Mack is helping Lane are these: Number one, he's paying my fee, and believe me, I don't come cheap. And number two, I'm the best at what I do, and if anyone can gain your mother an acquittal, I can, and Johnny Mack knows it."

"Just because you've got an ego the size of Texas doesn't mean you can keep Mama from being convicted." Holding his tightly balled fists close to his hips, Will glowered at Quinn as if daring him to disagree.

Quinn's lips twitched in a hint of a smile as he glanced at Johnny Mack. "This kid's yours alright. Not only does he look just like you, but he's got your kick-ass attitude, too."

Avoiding glancing directly at his son, Johnny Mack nodded, agreeing with Quinn's statement. Without commenting, Will stormed out of the room, into the foyer and up the stairs. Quinn shrugged.

Lillie Mae brought in a silver coffeepot and two china cups. Surveying the room, she asked, "Where's Will?"

"He went upstairs," Johnny Mack said.

"Did you two get into another argument?" She placed the tray on the desk in the den.

"Nothing serious." Johnny Mack walked over, poured coffee into the two cups and picked up one. "Will's upset about Lane's arrest. He wants somebody to blame for the fact she's in jail, and I just happen to be a convenient target."

Lillie Mae picked up the second cup and carried it over to Quinn. "Are you going to be able to get Lane out of jail in the morning?"

"As soon as the judge sets bail, she'll be free to go. But it seems the judge couldn't be reached tonight, so we have no choice but to wait."

"Judge Harper is an old friend of Edith's." Lillie Mae spat out the other woman's name.

"So are Judge Gillis and Judge Welch." Johnny Mack knew how things worked in this county. It would take a miracle for Lane to get a fair trial, but there was no way to prove that Edith Ware was calling in favors and using whatever means at her disposal to make sure Lane didn't get an even break.

"I've had to deal with situations like this before," Quinn told them. "With no more evidence than Wes Stevens has against Lane, I can make a jury see that she isn't guilty beyond a reasonable doubt."

"I won't let that girl go to prison." Lillie Mae shot a quick glance in Johnny Mack's direction. "Before I see that happen, I'll confess to murdering Kent myself."

"Did you kill him, Mrs. Hickman?" Quinn asked.

"What?" Lillie Mae swirled around, her eyes wide, her hands trembling as she faced Quinn.

"You had almost as much reason to hate Kent as Lane did." Quinn lifted the cup to his lips and sipped the rich, black coffee. "Will's your grandson. You would have done anything to protect him, just as Lane would have. Am I right?"

"You're right. I would have done anything . . . and I still would." Lillie Mae stuck out her chin and looked Quinn square in the eye. "If it'll help Miss Lane's case, you put me on the stand and show that jury that it could just as easily have been me who took that baseball bat and beat the living daylights out of Kent."

Johnny Mack placed his hand on Lillie Mae's shoulder. "I know Lane would appreciate what you're trying to do, but you didn't kill Kent and—"

"How do you know I didn't?" With that said, Lillie Mae turned and walked out of the den.

"What do you make of that?" Quinn asked.

"I'm not sure."

"Do you think the old woman could have done it?"

"At this point, I'm not sure of anything much," Johnny Mack admitted. "Except that upstairs"—he inclined his head toward the ceiling—"I have a son who hates me. And across town in the city jail, I have a woman who's depending on me.''

Buddy peeled off his sweat-stained shirt and tossed it on the floor, then unsnapped his pants. Damn, it was a hot night. Humid and sultry. Good sign that it would rain by morning. Rain was exactly what they needed to lower the temperature and ease the humidity.

What he personally needed was a cold beer and then a good night's sleep. Today had been one hell of a day. He had been preparing himself for over a week now, steeling his nerves for the moment he would have to read Lane her rights and take her into custody. For a couple of minutes there this afternoon at the Nobles' house, he had thought Johnny Mack was going to jump him. If looks could kill, he would be a dead man now. The thought that someone he had once tried to kill was now rich and powerful sure had a way of putting the fear of God into him. And arresting Lane only added to his crimes against Johnny Mack.

But a man did what a man had to do. Arresting Lane was part of his job. Sure, he could have sent someone else to actually do the deed, but he thought he owed Lane that much—to arrest her himself.

Scratching his hairy chest, Buddy sauntered out of the bedroom, down the hall and into the kitchen. Since light from the living room partially illuminated the kitchen, he didn't bother turning on the overhead fluorescent fixture. He opened the refrigerator, grabbed a bottle of Budweiser and popped the lid. After taking a long, refreshing swig, he searched the cabinets for a can of something he could empty onto a plate and stick in the microwave. He lifted a can of spaghetti and meatballs from the cupboard, then rummaged through a bottom drawer for a can opener.

He liked Lane. He always had. Even when they'd been kids. What wasn't there to like? Lane was a good person who had married a very bad person and ruined her life. He felt sorry for her, but what could he do? He couldn't go against Miss Edith. He couldn't jeopardize all that he had built in this community. If Edith Ware wanted Lane tried for Kent's murder, then that's the way it would be.

Buddy just hoped that Quinn Cortez was as good as his reputation. That being the case, then Lane would go free, and most of Noble's Crossing would still think she was guilty. After that, he could issue a statement that the police department would continue the investigation, searching for other suspects, but eventually he would see to it that Kent's murder became another unsolved crime.

Just as Buddy found the can opener and removed it from the drawer, he heard a series of soft, rapid knocks at his back door. Who the hell? It was nearly eleven-thirty.

He went to the door, looked through the glass panes and saw the shadowy figure of a woman. What the hell was she doing here? He unlocked and then opened the door. Edith Ware rushed inside and slammed the door behind her.

"You said that I knew where you lived when I was interested in finishing what we started." She slithered her bejeweled fingers from his collarbone to his belly button. "Well, I've had a very good day today, and I want to celebrate." Her hand sneaked beneath his boxer shorts and dove straight to his penis. "I'm ready to finish what we started."

When her small, warm hand circled him, Buddy grew hard as a rock in five seconds flat. He hated

Miss Edith. Hated her for being partly responsible for Mary Martha's pitiful condition. Hated her for having protected a lying, miserable son of a bitch like Kent. Hated her for trying to crucify a good woman like Lane.

And he hated her for making him want her.

He felt like a damn fool. Miss Edith was old enough to be his mama. But there was nothing motherly about Edith Ware. Even at sixty, she wasn't anything more than a rich bitch in heat.

Buddy grabbed Edith by the hair of her head, dragged her over to the kitchen table and lifted her up and on top of the vinyl table cloth. He forced her legs apart, hiked up her white linen skirt and wasn't surprised to find that she wore neither stockings nor panties. Still gripping her head with one hand, he slipped his hand between her legs. When his fingers covered her mound, he encountered smooth flesh. She shaved her pubic hair.

"Bitch!" He freed his sex from his briefs, then took a good look at the woman spread out before him. In the shadowy dimness of the kitchen, it would be easy enough to pretend that she was Mary Martha.

She shuddered as if just the contemplation of what he was about to do excited her. When he rammed himself to the hilt within her, she grabbed his buttocks and issued a demand.

"Fuck me good and hard!"

Chapter 15

A horde of reporters awaited them when they emerged from the county courthouse where Judge Harper had apprised Lane of the formal charges against her—felony murder. Bail was set at a hundred and fifty thousand dollars, and the trial was slated to begin on October 2. This was a high-profile case, with both the victim and the defendant well-known in the community. Quinn had made it clear to Wes Stevens that there would be no plea bargaining because his client was innocent. And Quinn had assured Lane that in a case such as hers, involving circumstantial evidence, the burden of proof would most definitely be on the state.

"And they can't prove, beyond a reasonable doubt, that you murdered your ex-husband," he had told her.

The morning rain had left the streets and sidewalks wet, with iridescent puddles of water and oil glistening on the concrete. Gray clouds obscured the afternoon

sun, casting a gloominess over the town that matched
Johnny Mack's deadly mood. He understood exactly
why Lillie Mae was considering confessing to Kent's
murder. Hell, if he'd been in town when it happened,
he would confess himself, to spare Lane the misery
she was enduring.

Although she was beautiful in her simple tan slacks
and white cotton shirt, she wore no makeup, which
brought attention to the dark circles under her eyes.
She looked so tired. So fragile. So in need of a strong
shoulder to lean on. And he was determined that no
matter how much she protested, he was going to be
that strong shoulder.

Quinn warded off the press, answering some questions with a smile and others with a growl, while
Johnny Mack protected Lane. Holding her around
the waist, he lifted his other hand in a warning signal
to Back Off and blasted the crowd with his killer stare.
As if understanding they were in danger of being
annihilated, the reporters allowed Johnny Mack to
lead Lane through their clamoring crowd and out to
his waiting Lincoln Continental, which he had rented
earlier today. No need to hide his wealth at this point,
since everyone in town knew he was worth millions.

Once inside the vehicle, Johnny Mack leaned over
and fastened Lane's safety belt. Without conscious
thought, he brushed the loose strands of blond hair
off her cheek and tugged them behind her ear. Any
excuse to touch her. If he did what he really wanted
to do, he would lift her onto his lap and wrap his
arms around her. Then he would take a M-16 and
blow the reporters to smithereens. Outside the safety
of his car, news-hungry vultures from local, state and
national television and newspapers surrounded them.
Even reporters and photographers from the local *Herald*. Miss Edith's doing. He would bet his life on it. As

co-owner of the town's newspaper, she had probably cracked the whip, issuing orders to cover the news, regardless of the fact Lane's arrest *was* that news.

Johnny Mack watched Lane as she gazed at the marauders shouting questions at her, while the force of their combined bodies actually swayed the big car. Damn fools!

"Please, get me out of here." Lane's voice held a hint of hysteria. Her large blue eyes pleaded.

Johnny Mack inserted the key, started the motor and shifted into Reverse. When he revved the engine, the reporters backed away a couple of feet. Before they had a chance to regroup and swarm forward again, he pressed down on the accelerator and whipped the car out of the parking lot adjacent to the courthouse. Within minutes they were flying up Riverton Street, heading away from downtown.

"Did Will go to school today?" Lane asked.

Johnny Mack remained focused on the road, but he caught a glimpse of Lane in his peripheral vision. He could almost feel the tension in her body as she sat there, ramrod straight, a doomed expression on her face.

"He didn't want to go, but Lillie Mae convinced him that it was what you'd want him to do."

"Bless Lillie Mae. She seems to know exactly how to handle Will."

"She uses guilt to make him tow the line," Johnny Mack said. "All she has to do is mention to him that she knows he doesn't want to disappoint you. I can see how important it is to him to please you. That boy loves you, Lane. He'd do just about anything for you."

"Yes, he probably would. Just as I'd do anything for him."

"Is there any chance that Will might have killed Kent . . . killed him for you?"

Lane gasped. Johnny Mack stole a quick glance at her. What little color she'd had in her cheeks disappeared.

"I don't ever want to hear you say such a thing again." Lane reached over, laid her hand on Johnny Mack's arm and manacled his biceps. "If there's ever the slightest suggestion that Will might have killed Kent, I'll confess and put an end to it immediately."

Johnny Mack slowed the car's speed from forty-five to thirty and began looking for a place where he could pull off the road. If he remembered these streets correctly, he wasn't far from the turnoff to the town's Spring Park.

"What are you doing?" Lane asked. "I thought you were taking me home."

"I am," he said. "But I think we need to take a short detour for a few minutes and discuss Will. In private. There's something you haven't told me about my son, isn't there?"

Johnny Mack slowed to fifteen miles an hour as he circled the nearly empty park. A couple of joggers and three elderly walkers made use of the dirt track, while geese and ducks swam in the pond and waddled about near the road. After easing the Lincoln into one of the gravel drives, he killed the motor and turned to Lane.

"Did Will kill Kent?"

When Lane avoided making eye contact, he knew for certain that this was a subject she did not want to discuss. Her continued silence seemed like an admission of the boy's guilt. Had Will bludgeoned Kent to death with his baseball bat? Was Lane protecting her son, at the cost of her own freedom?

"Answer me, Lane." Twisting sideways in his seat,

he reached over and grabbed her chin, forcing her face up, but still she refused to look at him. "Dammit, woman, your silence is more damning than words."

Her hot gaze flashed a warning that he'd have to be a fool not to recognize. A sign of maternal protection. "Drop it. Now. Will didn't kill Kent. He was with Lillie Mae when it happened. She wasn't feeling well and—"

"That's what y'all told the police, but is that the way it really happened?"

Lane undid her seat belt, unlocked the car door and shoved it open. Johnny Mack reached out to restrain her, touching her hip, but she slipped through his fingers and ran from the car. Dammit! What was wrong with her? Why was she running from him? Him of all people. Didn't she realize that she could tell him the truth, share the deepest, darkest secrets, and he would keep her trust? She would always be safe with him.

He had come home to help her. To help her and Will. If *their* son had killed Kent, he couldn't help the boy unless he knew the truth.

After disengaging himself from his seat belt, he opened the door and quickly followed her. Taking rapid strides, he caught up with her on the small bridge that separated the north side of the park from the south side. She stopped running, leaned over the railing and stared into the algae-thick pond, which was fed by an underground spring. He didn't have to see her eyes to know she was crying. Her slender shoulders trembled. Silent tears.

He came up behind her and engulfed her in his arms, holding her there, her back to his chest. She shuddered and released a long, loud sigh. Mournful. Agonized. Desperate.

"It's all right, babe," he whispered in her ear as

he nuzzled her neck. "We don't have to talk about it now. But soon. When you're ready. No matter how bad it is, I'll move heaven and earth to help you and Will."

She swallowed the lump of emotion lodged in her throat. "You—you really mean that, don't you?" She draped her arms over his where they crisscrossed at her waist.

"I know my past record isn't very good, but I'm not the same selfish, cocky boy who left town fifteen years ago. I've matured and hopefully gained a little wisdom along the way." With the utmost gentleness, he turned her in his arms until she faced him. "The way I see it, you and Will are my family. And a man— a real man—protects what's his. He keeps them safe, at any cost."

"Will is your son . . . your family. But I'm only Will's adoptive mother, not—"

"Shush."

Her bright blue eyes looked up at him, and for a split second he saw the same expression he had seen when she'd been nineteen and had begged him to take her with him when he left town. Hope. Love. Those sentiments shined in her eyes. But within an instant, those beautiful emotions disappeared, replaced with uncertainty and sadness.

How could he even begin to tell her what he felt when he didn't know himself? He could admit that of all the women who had been a part of his life, she was the only one he'd been unable to forget. He could thank her for Will, for giving the boy life when Sharon would have destroyed him. He could beg her to forgive him for not taking her with him, for not saving her from Kent.

And he could tell her that he wanted her more than he had ever wanted anyone or anything. That a raging hunger rode him hard and it was all he could do not to act on his baser instincts.

He could have had her years ago. She had been more than willing. But she had been so sweet and innocent. And so trusting. He had been so damn proud of himself for letting one naive little rabbit free from the trap that had caught so many others. But how could he have known that by releasing her, he had in turn trapped himself? Always wondering. Always thinking of what might have been. Never knowing.

Each woman was a mystery, waiting to be solved. But more often than not the solution held no reward beyond solving the riddle itself. Would it be that way with Lane? Once he'd had her, would she become just one more woman in a long line of women?

He wrapped her securely in his embrace, keeping her close. She relaxed against him, as if she could no longer bear her own weight. Her arms encircled him and held tight.

"Lane, I—"

A car horn blew. Someone yelled out a greeting. Lane lifted her head off his chest and searched for the source of the sounds. On the paved drive that circled the outer edges of the park, a young woman in an SUV had stopped to talk to one of the elderly walkers.

Lane disengaged herself from Johnny Mack's arms. "Take me home." She glanced down at her wristwatch. "Will should be there by now. He'll worry if we don't show up soon."

As she turned to go back over the bridge, he grabbed her arm. She halted and stared at him, wariness in her eyes.

"Whatever the truth is, you need to share it with

me," he told her. "You're not helping Will by lying for him."

Lane jerked free. "Don't you dare presume to tell me what's best for *my* son."

Damn! Somehow, no matter what he said, it turned out to be the wrong thing. Lane was hiding something. Will was more involved in Kent's murder than anyone knew. She was covering up for the boy. And he would bet his last dime that Lillie Mae was helping her.

What if Will *had* killed Kent! Would he actually allow his mother to go to prison for a crime he had committed? If so, what kind of young man did that make Will? A spoiled, selfish. . . .

"You're right," Johnny Mack said, his voice terse. "It's apparent that even though I'm Will's father, you still don't trust me enough to be honest with me. Maybe I haven't earned the right to make a judgment call when it comes to Will. But dammit, Lane, no matter what you think of me or how you feel about me, you've got to know"—he laid his fist over his belly—"in your gut, that I'd never do anything to hurt Will."

"You wouldn't mean to hurt him," she said.

Johnny Mack's cellular telephone rang. Lane jumped. He pulled the phone from the inside pocket of his sport coat, flipped it open and growled his name. "Cahill here."

"Where the hell are you two?" Quinn demanded. "I've been at Lane's house for the past ten minutes. Lillie Mae and Will are climbing the walls worrying that something has happened to Lane."

"Lane's fine. We got sidetracked. We're on our way."

When Lane's gaze questioned him, Johnny Mack

said, "That was Quinn. Your presence is required at home."

"Johnny Mack?"

"Yeah?"

"Don't say anything to Will about . . . please, don't ask him anything about the day Kent died."

"I won't ask him anything if that's what you want. Not now. But you'd better have a damn good excuse to give Quinn, because he's going to want to ask Will and Lillie Mae a lot of questions."

"Lillie Mae, yes. Will, no."

If he thought it would do any good, he would shake her until her teeth rattled. But she had made up her mind to protect Will, no matter what. It would prove an impossible task to convince her that lying for Will would, in the long run, only harm him. But sooner or later, he would have to find a way to unearth the truth, even if it meant alienating Lane.

Will met them at the door. The moment Lane stepped over the threshold, she opened her arms and Will walked into her maternal embrace. His son had neither a glance nor a word of greeting for him. What had he expected? Thanks, Dad, for guaranteeing a hundred and fifty thousand dollars bail to get my mother out of jail. Thanks for getting her safely away from a vicious group of reporters. Thanks for bringing in one of the best criminal lawyers in the country to defend her.

When he entered the living room, Lillie Mae came to his side and whispered, "You got a phone call about an hour ago. Some woman. Said her name was Monica Robinson. Said you had her number."

"Thank you." He could tell by the frown on Lillie

Mae's face that she disapproved of him receiving a call at Lane's house from another woman.

"Who is she?" Lillie Mae asked.

"Monica?"

"Yes. Who is she?"

"A friend."

"A lover?"

"Why the third degree?" he asked.

"I hoped you'd changed." Lillie Mae glanced around the room as if to make sure no one overheard her. "Like always, one woman isn't enough for you. You're still tomcatting around, aren't you?"

"My love life is none of your damn business," he told her, his voice low and controlled. "But since you're so determined to believe the worst of me and your opinion of me actually matters, I'll explain. I've been in a monogamous relationship with Monica for a year now."

"Are you going to marry her?" Lillie Mae asked.

They had been so engrossed in their conversation that neither Johnny Mack nor Lillie Mae had realized that Will had approached them. Not until he spoke.

"Are you getting married?" Will asked. "To the woman who called here earlier?"

"What?" From across the room, Lane gasped the question.

Quinn, who was standing next to Lane, a glass in his hand, gave Johnny Mack a raised eyebrow. He figured Quinn was drinking Jack Daniels, the only whiskey Lane's father had ever kept in the house. Despite his wealth and sophistication, Bill Noble's taste in liquor had been plebeian.

"I'm not getting married," Johnny Mack said. "The woman who called here is a good friend. Nothing more."

As much as she tried to hide her emotions, Lane

could not disguise the expression on her face. She looked as if he had slapped her. The last thing he wanted was to inflict more pain, but he seemed to have a knack for doing just that, especially where Lane was concerned.

Shit! Why the hell had Monica called and opened up this hornet's nest? *Because you haven't bothered to call her since you left Houston, you idiot!*

"If y'all will excuse me, I'll return Monica's call." He glanced across the room at Quinn. "When you finish up here with Lane, we can head back to the motel. I want to check out of that dump and find a better motel, until I can rent a condo or an apartment for us."

"There's no need for you to rent a place," Lane said, only a hint of a quiver in her voice. "This house is huge, and we have rooms we never use. You and Quinn are welcome to stay here until the trial is over."

"That's very hospitable of you, Lane," Quinn said. "We'd be delighted to take you up on such a generous offer."

"Y'all living here will be convenient for all of us. I'll have my lawyer within arm's reach twenty-four hours a day, and if Johnny Mack stays here, it'll give Will and him a chance to become better acquainted."

"I don't want him here!" Will skewered Johnny Mack with a drop-dead glare.

Ignoring his son's outburst, Johnny Mack focused on Lane. "Thank you for the invitation, but are you sure?"

"Yes, I'm sure. And you're quite welcome." Lane nodded to Johnny Mack, then smiled at Quinn. "You're both welcome." She glided across the living room and slipped her arm through Quinn's. "While Lillie Mae prepares dinner and Johnny Mack makes his phone call, why don't I show you around the

house and you can choose which bedroom you'd
like." She glanced at Will. "Do you have any home-
work you should be doing?"

"Yeah, sure." Will shrugged. "I'll be in my room.
Call me when dinner's ready."

Johnny Mack could have strangled Quinn for
responding so enthusiastically to Lane's invitation.
When they disappeared upstairs, he had to force himself not to follow them. Quinn Cortez was a lady-
killer, and Lane was very vulnerable right now. Later,
he would have a talk with his old friend—and warn
Quinn to keep his hands off personal property. And
God help him, that was how he thought of Lane. She
was his. First. Last. Always.

If the lady was in the market for a lover, then she
had damn well better choose him.

They sat around the large glass and wrought-iron
table on the patio as the sun set and splashed the
western horizon with vivid hues of pink, crimson and
lavender. The lulling cadence of the river's flow
added to the summertime music of the cicadas singing nearby. Lillie Mae had served barbeque ribs,
which were Johnny Mack's favorite. But he hadn't
known, until tonight, that they were Will's favorite,
too.

Except for an occasional question to Quinn about
Lane's case, Will had remained quiet and sullen, not
once speaking to or looking at Johnny Mack. But
there had been no lulls in conversation, no periods
of awkward silence, thanks to Quinn. That half-breed
Mexican- Irishman had certainly inherited the gift of
gab from his mother's Celtic ancestors. He could
relate a tall tale with the best of them. But from his
father, Quinn had inherited his Latin charm, which

he lavished on Lane tonight. And Lane seemed to be absorbing Quinn's attention like a dry sponge soaking up water. Was she that needy, Johnny Mack wondered, that she would fall for Quinn's flattery?

When he caught Lane's eye, she smiled, but there was no warmth in her eyes, no genuine congeniality to her expression.

"Did you make that call to your friend?" Lane asked.

"Yes," he replied.

"I suppose she misses you and wants you to come home soon."

"Not really. Monica has a busy life and many other friends." Johnny Mack didn't want to discuss Monica with Lane. He didn't want to discuss any of the other women in his life—past or present—with her. Monica had mentioned missing him, and had asked how much longer he would be gone, but she hadn't seemed disappointed when he'd told her he was staying in Noble's Crossing for the duration of Lane's trial. Monica was a good friend and an enjoyable lover, but he suspected that she knew their time together was over.

"Excuse me." Will jumped up abruptly. "I'm going to go shoot a few hoops."

"Want some company?" Quinn asked.

"Nah. I'd rather have some time alone. Thanks anyway."

The minute Will disappeared around the corner of the house, Lillie Mae suggested that everyone go inside for after-dinner coffee. Before Johnny Mack even got out of his chair, Quinn was up and assisting Lane.

Just as the couple started to go through the French doors leading off the patio into the house, Johnny

Mack grabbed Quinn's arm. "Could I talk to you for a few minutes, old pal?"

Lane gave Johnny Mack an inquisitive stare, but saved her gracious smile for Quinn. "We'll have coffee waiting when y'all finish your private conversation." She followed Lillie Mae, leaving the two men alone.

"What's up?" Quinn asked.

"That's what I want to know." Johnny Mack released his friend's arm, but stood eye to eye, command and determination in his stance.

"I'm clueless, *amigo*." Quinn shrugged.

"Clueless my ass. And don't you *amigo* me. What the hell do you think you're doing with Lane?"

"What am I doing? I'm being charming and attentive to a very lovely lady who is in great need of male appreciation."

"Well, you don't have to be so damn charming. There's no law that says you have to be a Latin lover all the time. Besides, Lane is off limits to you."

"And why is that? I find her an incredibly desirable woman."

Johnny Mack's black eyes narrowed to angry slits. "Lane isn't the type for a one-night stand or even a brief affair. She's vulnerable and lonely and she could be easily hurt. So stay the hell away from her."

"I agree. And I have no problem with drawing the line at being Lane's attorney and her friend. What I want to know, Johnny Mack, is will you be able to take your own advice?"

"What the hell do you mean by that?"

Quinn laid his hand on Johnny Mack's shoulder. "This is Quinn you're talking to. We've been best friends for nearly fifteen years. I know you better than you know yourself. You've got the hots for that woman. And maybe there's something more to the

way you feel about her. More than the fact that she
saved your life and has raised your son. Man, if you
could see your face when you look at her, you'd know
what I mean."

Was Quinn right? Did his feelings show on his face?
In his eyes? If so, could Lane read him as clearly as
Quinn did? And just what could others see that he
couldn't?

"Lane's special to me," Johnny Mack admitted.
"She's always been. . . . What I feel for her is different
from what I've felt for other women."

"Then, why not follow through and give the lady
what she needs?"

"I'm not going to hurt her. She's been hurt
enough."

"And would becoming her lover harm her?" Quinn
asked as he squeezed Johnny Mack's shoulder. "She
is hungry for you, my friend. I see the desire in her
eyes, too."

"Go inside and have your coffee. And while I'm
gone, don't flirt with Lane anymore," Johnny Mack
said, deliberately avoiding the subject of Lane's passion for him. "I'm going to find Will and see if he'll
talk to me."

"That boy is very hostile toward you. Don't be surprised if he tells you to take his basketball and put it
where the sun don't shine."

"Tell Lane I've taken a walk. She doesn't need to
know that I'm—"

"Giving her son the third degree?"

"You know, without my saying so, that Will could
be the one who killed Kent. Lane could be protecting
him."

Quinn nodded. "Don't push the boy too hard."

"You just keep Lane entertained. But keep your
hands off her."

"I will try my best to accommodate you on both counts."

The sound of Quinn's deep-throated laughter drifted on the twilight breeze as he saluted Johnny Mack with a mock bow, then turned and went into the house.

He stood at the side of the house and watched Will as he made hoop after hoop. The boy was a natural. Tall. Lean. Athletic. With an amazing power of concentration. But the most amazing thing about this smart, handsome, fantastic boy was the undeniable fact that he, Johnny Mack Cahill, was his father. A reckless act of sex, one long-ago summer night, had created this perfect child. No love. No commitment. No thought beyond the pleasure of the moment. How was it possible? Nature sure as hell had things screwed up. All a guy had to do to become a father was have a climax. Without a thought of the consequences. Without any plans for the future. Without wanting to reproduce.

Johnny Mack studied his son, searching for any resemblance to Sharon. The shape of his face, a little rounder than his own, with a softer, less square jaw. And his nose was Sharon's. Smaller, with a slight tilt at the end. But the eyes, the mouth and even the sulking expression were pure Johnny Mack. The height and build, as well as the black hair and dark eyes, were gifts passed down from John Graham, may the frigging old bastard rot in hell. Traits that he, and now Will, had shared with the old man and with Kent.

If he never did anything else right in his entire life, he had to make it right with Will. He owed this boy something more than money, which he now had in abundance. Will might have killed Kent. Lane could be covering for the boy, willing to go to jail to protect her son. But what would it do to Will if he let his mother take the rap for him?

"Are you going to shoot hoops with me or are you going to stand back there and watch me all night?" With the basketball held high, Will turned his gaze on Johnny Mack.

Barely able to halt the smile forming on his lips, Johnny Mack stepped out of the shadows and held out his hands. Will tossed him the ball. And the game was on. For a good thirty minutes, father and son ran, dribbled, blocked and scored. In the end, Will won by making the final hoop with a jump shot.

Johnny Mack, sweat glistening on his forehead and dampening his cotton knit shirt, laid a hesitant hand on his son's damp back. Will grinned, then tossed the ball through the hoop one final time. When it slipped through the net and bounced off the driveway, Will let the ball roll off into the yard.

"You play in school, don't you?" Johnny Mack commented.

"Yep. Football, baseball and basketball. Kent . . ." He balked after mentioning his adoptive father's name. "Kent wanted me to play all the sports, just like he did. There was a time when his approval was very important to me."

"Before he found out that you weren't his biological son."

"No, before that even," Will said. "My feelings for Kent started changing right before he and Mama got a divorce. By then, I was ten and old enough to understand that he wasn't good to her. He never hit her—except that once, after he got the letter from Sharon Hickman. But he talked awful to her all the time, and he treated her like dirt. He treated just about everybody like dirt when he was drinking. And the past few years, he drank all the time.''

"Kent wasn't a very nice man," Johnny Mack said. "When your mother married him, I don't think she realized what a bad person he was or how much damage he could inflict on her. And on you."

"He used to think I was the greatest thing in the world. His son. But when he found out that you were my real father, he hated me. He did a hundred-and-eighty-degree turn. You can't imagine the things he said to me.''

"Do you want to tell me what he said that day? Want to tell me what happened?''

Will looked Johnny Mack square in the eye. "What you're really asking me is did I kill him? Did I pick up my baseball bat and beat him to death when he was too drunk to fight back?''

Chapter 16

"No one could blame you if you did kill Kent," Johnny Mack said. "If he attacked you, it was self-defense."

"He didn't attack me," Will said. "Not physically. Just verbally. He told me all about you or at least his version of who and what you were. And he said I'd turn out to be a no-good, sorry bastard just like you. Guess he didn't know you were a fucking multimillionaire, did he?"

"Do you want to tell me what happened that day?" Johnny Mack asked.

Will shrugged. "Mama told me not to say anything to anyone about what really happened, and I agreed. But that was before she was arrested. I can't let her take the blame for something I probably did."

"What do you mean something you probably did?"

"I don't remember everything that happened that afternoon. I remember that Kent came by the house. Mama wasn't home. She was down at the *Herald* checking on something or other. Lillie Mae was home, and she tried to stop Kent from coming into the backyard; but she couldn't stop him. He was drunk and angry. When Kent got drunk, he got mean.''

"If Lillie Mae was there, then she knows what happened.''

"She wasn't outside the house when Mama came home and found me with Kent's body. You see, when Lillie Mae begged Kent not to say all those horrible things to me, he slapped her. He slapped her so hard that she fell to the ground.'' Will swallowed. His breathing deepened and quickened. "When he did that to Lillie Mae, I took my baseball bat and hit him to make him stop, so he wouldn't slap her again. I hit him once and knocked him on his ass. Then I helped Lillie Mae up and took her to her room.

"That's all I remember, until Mama came home and found me in the backyard, standing beside Kent's body and the baseball bat lying on the ground. She cleaned the bat and put it back where it had been; then she told me that I was to say that Lillie Mae and I were together the whole time and that I came outside just as she was coming in to call the police. She said that Lillie Mae would back up my story. I didn't realize then that Mama knew by eliminating me as the chief suspect, she'd put herself in that spot.''

"Has your mother contacted a psychiatrist to help you try to remember what happened?''

"No!'' Lane screamed as she ran forward, past Will and straight to Johnny Mack. Her eyes wide, her nostrils flared, her hands curved into talons, she screeched, "Damn you! I warned you not to ask Will anything about Kent's murder. He doesn't know what happened. He's confused about the events of that day. Whatever he's told you—''

Johnny Mack grabbed Lane's shoulders. Her breathing accelerated. Every muscle in her body tensed as she glared at him, pure unadulterated rage pulsating within her.

"I understand that you're trying to protect Will," Johnny Mack said. "But, my God, Lane, you don't have to protect him from me. He's my son. All I want to do is help him. Help both of you."

"Mama, it's all right," Will said. "It's time I told the truth."

"See what you've done!" Lane jerked free of Johnny Mack's hold. "You come back here after fifteen years and think you have a right to interfere in our lives. Well, you don't have a right! Accidentally getting someone pregnant doesn't make you a father. You had no problem leaving us behind fifteen years ago. Sharon or me. I wish you had never come back to Noble's Crossing. I wish Lillie Mae had never written you that damn note."

"Mama, this isn't Johnny Mack's fault," Will said. "I've been wanting to tell the truth to somebody. Why not to him? He is my father, and I'm beginning to believe him when he says he wants to help us."

Lane glared at Johnny Mack. Then when she looked at Will, her expression softened. "Please, trust me to do what's best for you."

"I do, Mama, but we can't keep on lying. We can't keep pretending that I wasn't in the backyard when Kent was murdered. I know that I hit him once with my baseball bat. What if . . . what if, after I helped Lillie Mae to her room, I went back out in the garden and killed him?" The tears gathered in the corners of Will's eyes threatened to overflow.

A tight fist of pain clenched Johnny Mack's stomach.

Lane reached out, grasped Will's hands and held

them securely. "Oh, sweetheart, stop torturing yourself trying to remember."

"Johnny Mack asked if I'd seen a psychiatrist. Do
you think a psychiatrist could help me remember?"

"I heard what Johnny Mack said." Lane released
one of Will's hands so that she could caress his cheek.
"Maybe a psychiatrist could help you. I don't know.
But is that what you want? Do you really want to
remember what happened that day?"

Will nodded. "You didn't kill Kent, but you're
being accused because you tried to cover up the
truth—that I probably did it. I don't want you taking
the blame for something I did." Will wrapped his
arms around Lane and laid his head on her shoulder.

"Oh, Will, my sweet darling. Don't you know that
what happened with Kent is my fault? I'm the one
who lied to him. Not you. I'm the one who married
him when I was in love with someone else. I'm the
one he really hated."

In his peripheral vision, Johnny Mack noticed Lillie
Mae and Quinn standing hesitantly, side by side, on
the patio, but well within earshot. He held up a hand
in a restraining signal, and Quinn nodded.

"Let's clear this up once and for all." Johnny Mack
approached mother and son. "I'm the one Kent Graham hated. Any fault in this matter is mine. If I had
known what was happening, that Kent took his frustration out on the two of you, I would have killed him."

"But you didn't kill him," Will said. "I did."

"We don't know that for a fact." Lane hugged her
son tightly.

Despite the overwhelming desire to wrap Lane and
Will in his arms, Johnny Mack made no move to touch
either of them. He watched. An outsider. A father by
biological accident only. But he intended to change
that fact. If ever Will needed a father, now was that

time. Especially if the boy really had bludgeoned Kent to death with his baseball bat.

God in heaven, this was his fault. All of it. Every miserable moment Lane and Will had spent at the mercy of Kent Graham. What was that old saying? Oh, yeah. All his chickens had come home to roost. As a teenager, he had been a hell-raiser, with no thought beyond getting some pussy and irritating the hell out of the snobs who lived in Rich Man's Land. He had sowed more than his share of wild oats and in the process had damaged so many lives, including his own. But by the grace of God, via Judge Harwood Brown, he had been given a chance to reinvent himself. For years it seemed that he had gotten off scot-free.

Others had paid for his sins. The most innocent of all. His son. And Lane, who had saved two lives and been rewarded with a double portion of misery.

"Why don't we pick up this discussion in the morning?" Johnny Mack suggested. "We all need some breathing space and a chance to let our emotions cool off a bit. Tomorrow, if you both agree, I'll make some phone calls and have the best qualified psychiatrist in the U.S. come to Noble's Crossing. Once we get to the bottom of what really happened that day, then we can decide where to go from there."

Johnny Mack's gaze connected with Lane's.

"Don't overstep the boundaries," she told him. "You aren't making the decisions for Will or for me."

"How about if the three of us make the decisions together?" Johnny Mack asked.

"Like a family?" Will lifted his head from Lane's shoulder and gazed at his father.

"No," Lane said.

"Yes," Johnny Mack countered.

"I think you're right; we should pick this up in the morning, when we're all thinking more clearly." Lane tugged on Will's hand. "Let's go in."

Johnny Mack waited until Lane and Will had walked past Quinn and Lillie Mae and into the house before he even so much as took a deep breath. When Johnny Mack joined the others on the patio, Quinn laid his hand on Johnny Mack's shoulder.

"In the morning, let me talk to Lane," Quinn said. "If it turns out that Will killed Kent in self-defense or if he had some sort of mental breakdown, then there's no way the boy will serve time for the crime. Six months or a year in a private hospital and—"

"Miss Lane or I would rather go to prison than see that child suffer any more than he already has," Lillie Mae said.

Johnny Mack's gaze settled on the housekeeper. "If I didn't know you so well, I'd think you might have killed Kent. But you wouldn't let Lane and Will go through this torment if you'd committed the crime."

"Just because I didn't do it, doesn't mean I couldn't convince the police and a jury that I did."

"My son's a lucky boy to have a mother and a grandmother who love him so much."

"Yeah, well, all our maternal love can only do so much for him, protect him only so far. I think what happened tonight proves how much our boy needs his father. We all need a strong man to help us through what lies ahead. And for all your faults, past and present, you, Johnny Mack, are the strongest man I've ever known."

"You can count on me, Lillie Mae. My days of running away are over. I'm back in Noble's Crossing to stay for as long as Will and Lane need me."

* * *

No one had seen. No one had heard. Slipping up the stairs while everyone was asleep had been easy. Having a key to the back door. Knowing the code for the alarm system. Being familiar with all the rooms in the house. Everything had come together just right.

Do what has to be done before daylight. Leave no clues. Make the death appear to be a suicide. The handwriting in the note wasn't a perfect match, but close enough. Pray that no one questions its authenticity.

The door creaked slightly. The nightlight in Mary Martha's bedroom cast a soft, pale glow over the frilly decor. Move quietly. Don't wake her.

Jackie was snoring. Good. A deep sleep. She would never know what hit her. No pain. No suffering. She had made a big mistake. Blackmailed the wrong person. If she told what she knew, the results would be devastating. Couldn't let her live. Couldn't allow her to cause harm to someone so dear.

Killing a person like this was wrong. But the only other choice was unthinkable. Kent's murder had been justified. He had been an evil son of a bitch. A monster who had inflicted pain and suffering on others. But Jackie's only crime was greed. Poor, stupid bitch.

Don't think about it. Just do it. And be careful not to wake Mary Martha. But what if, even with the silencer on the gun, the sound of the muffled shot woke her? No, it won't wake her. Jackie had been instructed to give her a sedative before bedtime so they both could rest during the night.

Carefully creeping closer and closer to Jackie's bed. Ever watchful. Mindful that discovery was possible, though highly improbable. The grandfather clock in the hallway struck the half hour. Damn unnerving racket!

Adjusting the silencer. Listening. Waiting. Warming the cold steel with the heat of a hand. Leaning over Jackie's body. Placing the gun to her forehead at just the right angle. Her eyes flashing open. Shock. Fear.

Pulling the trigger. Bile rising from the stomach, the taste lingering in the mouth.

Glancing across the room to where Mary Martha lay undisturbed. Thank God. Poor, sweet Mary Martha.

Blood oozing from the wound, creating a large red blot on the pristine white pillowcase.

Lifting her lifeless hand. Placing the gun. Readjusting the arm to a position in which it would have been had Jackie actually fired the weapon and ended her own life.

Laying the forged note on the desk. Propping it up so it wouldn't be missed by the servant who brought up the breakfast tray.

One more problem solved. One less thing to worry about. Now, to find a way to eliminate an even more deadly enemy. Johnny Mack Cahill had to be dealt with—and soon. He and that damn lawyer he had hired would keep digging until they unearthed the truth. That mustn't happen. Even if it meant committing another murder.

Mary Martha woke, got out of bed and went to the bathroom. It was still dark outside. *Wonder what time it is? Wonder if Mother and Kent are already downstairs eating breakfast?* Sometimes they liked to eat early. But not this early.

She could go to Kent's room and wake him. He had told her that she could come to his room any

time she wanted and he didn't mind if she woke him.
He was always so good to her. Her brother. Her dear
brother.

Kent loved her. Loved her more than Mother or
Father ever had. He told her so and she believed him.
Kent wouldn't lie to her.

But he had lied about her baby. He had told her
it was dead. But it wasn't. Kent and Lane had adopted
her little boy and named him Will. Why had Kent
lied about her baby? Why had he given her baby to
Lane?

Wandering around in a haze, searching for something, but she wasn't sure what, Mary Martha saw the
bed on the opposite side of her bedroom. Why was
there another bed in her room? Had someone spent
the night with her?

She tiptoed closer and closer until she saw that
someone indeed was asleep in the other bed. *But I
don't know who she is.*

"Hello, there," Mary Martha said. "Who are you?"

When the person didn't respond, Mary Martha
reached out and shook the still body. That was when
she noticed the big, wet, red spot on the pillow and
the wide-open eyes of the woman in the bed.

Something was wrong. The woman wouldn't speak.
She wouldn't move. Was she dead? Dead like Kent!

Kent was dead. Dead and buried. Tears filled Mary
Martha's eyes. How could she live without Kent? He
loved her more than anyone else. Without him, her
life was meaningless. Kent had wanted a little sister,
so Mother had given him one. He had told her so.
They were soul mates. Always and forever. If Kent
had gone to heaven, then she should be there with
him. Why had he gone there without her?

Floating across the room, leaving behind the lifeless
body of the woman she didn't know, Mary Martha

made her way back into the bathroom. With a weak, shaky hand, she searched through the row of medicine bottles on the shelf inside the linen closet until she found the one containing her sleeping pills. She read the label to make sure, then emptied the pills into the palm of her hand. After dumping the sleeping tablets into her mouth, she ran water into a glass and washed the medicine down her throat.

All I have to do now is go to sleep, and when I wake up, I'll be in heaven with Kent. He'll be so glad to see me. I know he's been lonely without me. Lane will take care of my baby, the way she always has. Will doesn't need me as much as Kent does.

After hours of restless sleep, Johnny Mack woke with a start. Sitting straight up in bed, he listened, thinking a noise might have awakened him. But he heard only the breathing of an old house in the wee hours of the morning. After lifting his wristwatch from the nightstand, he noted it was fifteen till five.

He crawled out of bed and padded barefoot across the room. Glancing out the window, he saw no hint of the approaching dawn. Still dark. Quietly, serenely dark. Mysteriously, deadly dark.

Yawning, he scratched his bare chest. Maybe he should go down to the kitchen and fix himself some coffee. In a couple of hours, he would have to face his son again. And face the boy's possessive, protective mother. He had to find a way to convince them both that before they could help Will, the boy would first have to remember what had happened the day Kent was murdered.

Suddenly Johnny Mack noticed movement below in the garden. From the pale illumination of light coming from inside the house, he saw the shadow of a woman moving across the patio and through the garden. Lane? What was she doing awake this early? And where was she going? *Or where had she been?*

Picking up his discarded jeans from where he had tossed them on a nearby chair the night before, Johnny Mack removed his pajama bottoms and replaced them with his pants, then put on his wrinkled shirt. Quickly slipping into his leather house shoes, he made an instant decision. He was going after her. Obviously she'd had as bad a night as he had. If she needed him, he wanted to be there for her. Besides, maybe it was better if they spoke privately, before they met with Will.

Moving as quietly as he could, Johnny Mack made his way down the back stairs, through the kitchen and out onto the patio. Lane was nowhere in sight. But he knew, instinctively, where she had gone.

The Nobles' garden remained as well-manicured as it had been in the past, covering over two acres that led from the back of the house, down three separate rows of concrete steps within the verdant garden enclosure. A stepping-stone path led from the garden to the river and the old boathouse.

At one time the Noble mansion had stood alone, the center of a huge plantation. But eventually the town had built up around the estate, and over the years, one by one, the other fine homes had been erected on what had once been Noble land.

What did it cost Lane to maintain the house and grounds in the same manner her family had been doing for generations? The upkeep on this place must be bleeding her meager resources dry. Her father had left her his forty-nine percent of the *Herald,* but what little money he'd had left was in a trust fund for Will and any future children Lane might have. Smart man that he was, Bill Noble had made sure that Kent Graham couldn't get his hands on a dime.

Johnny Mack knew for a fact that the *Herald*'s profits had been declining each year. He also knew that Lane had secretly sold off some of her mother's jewelry. If she hadn't needed the money so badly, she would never have parted with any of Celeste Noble's jewels. After all, some of the items had been in the Noble family since before the Civil War.

When he had found out about the sale of the jewels, he had asked Wyatt Foster to locate the items and buy them back for Lane. When the time was right, he would return them to her.

As he drew nearer the banks of the Chickasaw, he wondered if he would find Lane on the riverbank or inside the boathouse, sitting on the deck of her father's boat. When they used to meet to talk—only to talk—they had often sought privacy inside, on Bill Noble's boat, but on warm nights they had usually sat on the riverbank.

And that was where he found her. Sitting in the grass, her knees bent, her arms draped around her legs. The moonlight washed her with fluid gold. Pale. Shimmery. Sheer. Her hair hung loosely over her bare shoulders.

What had driven Lane out of her house before daylight? Why had she been unable to sleep? If he called her name, would she rise and come to him? Or would she run?

When he approached, she sat there unaware of his presence as she stared up at the dark sky. She wore nothing but her yellow cotton gown, the material thin and filmy, plainly revealing the curves of her body. Everything male within him reacted to all that was female within her. And he understood, as if God had written the message in stone and handed the tablet to him, that he had been waiting for this moment all his life. He had denied his feelings as a teenager. He had told himself that he respected Bill Noble and Lane herself far too much to violate Lane, to take her innocence. But she was no longer an innocent. And he had waited a lifetime to take what he knew in his gut had always belonged to him. Did she understand as he did that the time for them to become lovers was long overdue?

Only two things could stop him from taking what he wanted. An act of God. Or Lane saying no.

Chapter 17

Lane wrapped her arms around herself and rubbed her hands up and down her bare arms. Even in August it was cool late at night and early in the morning down by the river. Why hadn't she thought to wear her robe? Better yet, what was she doing here? *You're running scared.* Trying to escape from the dream. But that's all it was, just a dream. Not reality, and only reality could truly harm her.

But she could easily turn the dream into reality. One word from her and Johnny Mack would become her lover. She wasn't blind to the way he had been looking at her. He wanted her. Wanted her as he had wanted countless other women over the years. If she went to him, gave herself to him, could she accept the fact that she wasn't special, that she wasn't the one woman on earth destined to tame the beast within him? Those had been a young girl's foolish fantasies. She was older and wiser now. She had once loved him with all her heart, and he had respected her and appreciated her friendship. But that had been years ago. What was there between them now? Distrust. Suspicion. A child they both wanted desperately to help. And a primitive lust that infected every other aspect of their relationship.

She had never known passion, never experienced a desire so great that it tormented her day and night. In the beginning of her marriage, she had tried to love Kent, had tried to enjoy the physical part of their marriage, but his selfishness and jealous need to erase Johnny Mack from her heart had created a barrier between them. And later on, Kent's cruelty had destroyed what little affection she'd ever had for him.

What would it be like to be with a man she truly wanted? Even knowing that she could expect nothing more than a brief affair with him, wouldn't it be worth the risk of losing her heart all over again just to— finally—have the one man she had always wanted?

The eastern sky quivered with a predawn softness, the labor pains that would soon bring forth the birth of a new day. The half-moon paled in the darkness as if preparing to take a final bow before exiting. While the river hummed with a repetitive, seductive motion, a morning breeze rippled over the dark surface.

Lane rose to her feet, bare and damp on the cool, dew-laden grass. And that was when she saw him. The outline of a tall man. She gasped, then relaxed when she realized it was Johnny Mack. But that relief was short-lived. Even in the semidarkness she could see the look of longing and determination in his black eyes, and she knew that he had followed her. Not to talk about Kent's murder. Not to discuss Will. Not to remind her that he had returned to Noble's Crossing to help her.

The closer he came, the more of his large, wide-shouldered body the fading moonlight revealed. He appeared to have gotten out of bed hastily. His hair was mussed and his shirt unbuttoned. An air of raw, masculine energy permeated every inch of his big body.

She stood frozen, like a deer trapped in the head-lights of an oncoming car, knowing what lay ahead and yet unable to flee from danger. Fear combined with desire, creating conflict within her. The rational part of her mind warned her to run, but her body begged her to remain, to open herself up and accept the inevitable.

"Lane." He spoke her name as if it were an endearment.

"No, we can't." She took a tentative, backward step.

"Yes, we can." He moved toward her, but stopped abruptly when she continued backing away from him, her silhouette quickly disappearing behind the curtain of drooping willow limbs.

"You don't understand." When her behind encountered the trunk of the willow tree, which blocked her escape route, Lane waited, her breathing ragged and quick. She was trapped. Trapped by the tree at her back. Trapped by Johnny Mack towering over her as he closed the gap between them. And trapped by her own desperate desire.

"Make me understand." He laid one hand on the tree trunk, his fingers spread out above her head.

He was close. Too close. She shut her eyes to avoid looking directly at him. How could she face him with the truth about her marriage to Kent? *Coward,* she chided herself. *Sooner or later you'll have to tell him what a stupid, naive fool you were. And how pitifully weak and helpless you allowed yourself to become before you broke free.*

"I was a virgin when I married Kent." She opened

her eyes and watched the expression on Johnny Mack's face. He grimaced as if he were in pain, and then he swallowed hard. "I had dreamed that my first sexual experience would be with you."

"It should have been." He lifted his other hand and touched her face. Tenderly. Hesitantly. As if he were afraid she would bolt and run. "You can't imagine how much I wanted to be the one to initiate you."

"It was never right between Kent and me. Not from the very beginning. And later on . . ." Lane breathed deeply, garnering strength from an inner reserve that was almost depleted. "By the time Will was a toddler, I had stopped sharing a bed with Kent. The only time we were ever . . . ever intimate was when he forced the issue."

"Are you saying that he raped you?" Johnny Mack's caressing hand knotted into a tight fist as he jerked it away from Lane's face.

"Yes, he forced me. More than once. And each time, he told me to just pretend it was you, that he knew I'd been doing that all along. I've never told anyone about Kent's brutal attacks. No one knew except Lillie Mae, and I didn't tell her. She guessed the truth. And she swore she'd stop him permanently if he ever touched me again." Lane slid away from the tree, away from Johnny Mack, and ran to the edge of the water.

"Lane!" Johnny Mack followed her, but when she stopped and turned to face him, he made no move to touch her.

A multicolored pastel dawn light spread across the eastern horizon, hinting that morning was approaching. The nighttime's soft warmth had yet to be replaced by the onset of August sizzle, the smoldering, humid heat only a matter of hours away. The cool breeze coming off the water kept the temperatures several degrees lower here by the river, day and night.

Lane stared at Johnny Mack, but she felt as if she were looking straight through him, looking back in time to when she had been Kent Graham's wife. Back to when she had been at his mercy and too ashamed to even tell her parents about the nightmare her marriage had become.

"After the third time he forced me, I told him that if he ever came near me again, I'd kill him." Lane heaved a deep sigh. "I bought a gun. And you know that I've always hated guns. Then I threatened him with a divorce. I honestly intended to go through with it. But then Daddy was killed in the car crash, and I had to deal with taking care of Mother for nearly two years. And Will still loved Kent. So we simply lived separate lives most of the time. It seemed easier that way for both of us."

"How could you have stayed married to him, after what he'd done to you?"

Had that been censure in Johnny Mack's voice? Was he condemning her for not divorcing Kent sooner? In retrospect she realized that she should have ended the marriage long before she did. But at the time, she had thought she was doing the right thing.

"I remained Kent's wife until Will was nearly ten and I finally understood that staying with Kent was hurting Will far more than getting a divorce would. By that time Kent's drinking had gotten so bad that even Miss Edith agreed that Will was better off with me. And it was Miss Edith who paid Kent's child support payments for him."

"Everything you've done for the past fifteen years has been for Will, hasn't it?" Johnny Mack shook his head, as if trying to deny the obvious. "Because he was mine."

"Yes, before he was born I loved him because he was yours. But the moment I lifted him into my arms for the very first time, he became mine, too."

"He should have been ours."

Lane nodded. "Yes, he should have been. But in a strange sort of a way, he is ours."

"Don't you see, Lane, that you and I should have been together back then. We should be together now."

When he reached for her, she held up her hands in a Stop gesture. "I dreamed of your making love to me for so many years. Since I was fourteen. Even after you left town and I married Kent, you were the only man in my heart."

"I should have taken you with me."

"But you didn't. And every time Kent touched me, I wished it was you. And eventually all the love I'd felt for you turned into hatred."

He stared at her, his eyes wide with disbelief. "You don't hate me, Lane. God, honey, you can't really hate me."

"I hated you because you left me. I hated you because you'd gotten Sharon pregnant. I hated you because I blamed you for my having to marry Kent. And I hated you because you never called, you never wrote." Lane lifted her loosely curled fists and slapped at Johnny Mack, her hands haphazardly striking his chest. Tears streamed down her face, over her nose and into her mouth. "I hated you because . . ." She gulped down her sobs and continued the half-hearted flogging, her arms moving slower and slower as she cried harder and harder. ". . . because I loved you so much and you never came back for me."

Lane shivered when Johnny Mack's arms wrapped around her. He pulled her closer, slowly, carefully, with the utmost tenderness. When he lowered his head to press his lips against her temple, she crumbled, allowing her body to collapse into his. Longing for comfort, she gave in to the weakness of being a woman in need of a man. Her man. And even if it would be only this once, for now, for this predawn moment, he was hers. Completely.

Later she might regret her compliance. But despite her doubts and fears, she was willing to risk everything just to belong to Johnny Mack. When his lips caressed the side of her face, sweetly, gently, she felt the heat rise within her. Warmth spread through her like a hot summer sun. And moisture coated her feminine folds as her body prepared itself. A clenching sensation tightened and released between her legs, and she ached with a need like none she had ever known.

Johnny Mack kissed her eyelids, her nose, her cheeks, her chin and finally touched her lips with his. Like the flutter of a butterfly, so soft, his tender touch erased her tears.

"I would never force you," he whispered against her mouth. "I want to make love to you. More than I've ever wanted anything in my life. Will you let me, Lane? Will you let me love you?" His big fingers speared through her hair as he grasped the back of her head, claiming her with a certainty that mocked his plea for permission.

"I might disappoint you," she admitted. She had never truly enjoyed sex with Kent, and often she had wondered if that fact had been as much her fault as Kent's. Perhaps she was one of those women who couldn't. . . . But with Johnny Mack it would be different, wouldn't it?

Cupping her face with his hands, he gazed deeply into her eyes. "Will you trust me not to hurt you? Will you give yourself to me and allow me to love you the way I want to do?"

She sucked in a deep breath. "Yes." Her voice trembled.

"Then, don't worry, honey. You won't disappoint me. You couldn't."

His kiss began with seductive little licks and nips. When she responded, he progressed to the next level and took her mouth with his. Wet. Warm. Possessive. And when she sighed, he slipped his tongue inside, and she gloried in the mating dance he initiated. While she still quivered from the heated kiss, his lips moved down her throat and over her chest. His mouth covered one nipple through the thin barrier of her cotton gown. Lane's knees buckled.

"I want to see you," he said, his voice a husky growl.

And without waiting for her response, he tucked his index fingers under the narrow straps and eased them down her arms and bunched her gown at her waist. He looked at her boldly. She blushed. Would he think she was beautiful? Or would he be disappointed?

After an indrawn breath, he groaned. "I used to wonder about your breasts. When we were together, I tried not to look at them, but they were so full and round that it was all I could do not to touch them."

He lifted her breasts in his hands, as if weighing them, then flicked both nipples with the pads of his thumbs. Lane keened when a sensation of pure lust shot through her. She didn't know how much more she could take. He had done nothing but kiss her and rub her nipples, and already she ached with longing.

While he lowered his head to take one tight peak into his mouth and suckle, he ran his hand up under her gown and traced a path from thigh to hip. When Lane tossed back her head and moaned her pleasure as his lips tormented one breast and then the other, he clasped her buttocks in both hands and dragged her up against his swollen sex. The thin barrier of her gown was no protection from the strength of the coarse denim or his iron-hard erection.

Before she realized what he was doing, he slid her gown down her hips. It fell to the ground, circling her ankles like melted lemon sherbet. After encouraging her to step forward, he slid one hand between them and splayed it over her flat belly. She grabbed his shoulders to steady herself and was glad she had when his hand moved lower. His fingers forked through her pubic hair and delved farther, seeking entrance. When he pushed two fingers inside and used his thumb to massage her intimately, her thighs closed around him, holding his hand in place. Tension spiraled tighter and tighter inside her.

"You have no idea how much I wanted to do this back when you were sixteen and I first noticed that you weren't a kid anymore," he told her. "It was always you, Lane. You were the one I wanted. The one I knew I could never have. The one I wasn't good enough for."

"Oh, Johnny Mack, if only I'd known how you felt. I thought you didn't want me."

"I wanted you the most. Always."

As if he had come to the end of his patience, he lifted her off her feet. "Is your father's cruiser still in the boathouse?"

"No, I sold the boat," she said breathlessly. "Over a year ago."

Holding her securely in his arms, he took her lips in a ravaging kiss. When he allowed her to breathe again, he said, "I can't tell you how many times over the past fifteen years I've dreamed about making love to you in that boat. That was my fantasy back when we used to spend so much time down here by the river."

"You've actually thought about me?" Was he lying, simply telling her what he thought she wanted to hear? Or had he actually dreamed of her, as she had of him?

"Lady, you honestly don't know, do you?"

"What do you mean?"

Without responding to her question, he carried Lane beneath the nearest willow tree and laid her on the ground. The grass-cushioned earth beneath her was dew-laden, but she barely noticed. Not when Johnny Mack straddled her. His open shirt skimmed over her hips, and the coarse denim of his jeans scraped along the outer sides of her thighs. It was in that moment she realized that she was totally naked. And he wasn't.

"You were my fantasy," he admitted, his eyes hot with desire as they raked over her face and breasts. "You were everything I wanted and the one woman I knew I could never have. You were way too good for me and I knew it. But I wanted to be good enough, to be worthy of you."

"I can't believe you ever felt that way about me." Her heart beat erratically. Joy overladen with regret and fear burst inside her, like fireworks exploding into the sky.

"When I got rich and started living the good life in Houston, I thought about you. I pictured you happily married to some great guy, and I figured you'd have two or three kids. Not once did it ever cross my mind that you would have married Kent." Johnny Mack gazed into her eyes. "I never came back because I thought you were better off without me."

Lane stroked his stubble-rough cheek. "You were my fantasy, too. I knew you were fooling around with a lot of women, and I was so jealous of them. I desperately wanted to know what it would be like to be one of your women.'' Lifting herself up just enough to bring her breasts into contact with his hairy chest, she wrapped her arms around his neck and brought him down to her. "I dreamed that I would be the one you'd truly love. I wanted you to be mine forever.''

He grabbed her hand, jerked it away from his face and dragged it down his body. She knew his destination, even before he laid her hand over his sex.

"If you want me, Lane, then take me.''

His eyes glittered like black diamonds, the need that rode him hard showing plainly in his expression. Big, dark and dangerously male, he waited. Despite how much he wanted her, he was giving her the power to make the next move.

With unsteady fingers, she unzipped his jeans and gasped when his large, erect penis surged toward her. Without hesitation, she caressed him, her fingers wrapping around the long, hard length of him.

"I want you, Johnny Mack. I've always wanted you.''

His smile created havoc inside her, like the aftereffects of a bomb blast. A lethal combination of masculinity and sensuality made him irresistible. He smelled of sleep and body musk and night air. He looked like a dark angel come to earth to entrap her and capture her soul. And he felt like molten steel beneath her fingers.

Without saying a word, he forcefully loosened her grip around his penis, lifted her hand and laid her arm across the cool, thick blanket of grass on which she lay. His fingers skimmed her body, paraded over her breasts, down her belly and to the apex between her thighs. He spread her legs apart and lifted her hips just enough to allow him a full view of his objective. Unsure and suddenly nervous, Lane squirmed when he lowered his mouth to her mound.

"Easy, baby. Easy." He kissed a spot just above her pubic hair and nuzzled her belly with his head.

Giving herself over to him completely, trusting him to take care of her, Lane surrendered. She was his in every way a woman could belong to a man.

With her body open to his pillage, he spread kisses along one inner thigh and then the other. Sensation after sensation of pure, undiluted passion rippled through her. And when his tongue touched her intimately, she lifted her hips and dug her heels into the moist soil at her feet. For one brief moment she wondered what he thought of her, naked, aroused and abandoning herself to sexual pleasures. But then his lips sucked and his tongue laved and all coherent thought left her mind.

His fingers reached upward and found her tight nipples. She moaned deep and loud as he plucked and caressed. The tension built higher and higher until she flew apart, into a million shards, shaking with an orgasm unlike anything she had ever experienced. As the aftershocks of release tingled through her body, Lane opened her eyes and looked up into Johnny Mack's smiling face. And she realized that he knew the truth.

"You never climaxed when Kent made love to you, did you?"

Unable to speak, she simply shook her head.

"Then, I'm the first man who's ever made you come." He spoke the words triumphantly, inordinately, masculinely pleased with himself. "I want you to come for me again."

"What?"

She tried to rise from the ground, but before she did more than lift her head, Johnny Mack attacked, zeroing in on the flesh that seemed too oversensitized to react. But within minutes, he had brought that numb flesh back to life, and Lane wholeheartedly accepted the pleasure that was forthcoming.

As she climaxed for the second time, Johnny Mack lifted his head, shrugged out of his jeans and brought his big body up and over hers.

"I don't have a condom," he moaned into her ear.

"I don't care."

"Do you know what you're saying, what we're risking?"

"Yes."

He lifted her hips and surged into her. His shaft thrust deep and wide and filled her to the hilt. The mating began in a frenzy of need beyond enduring, of a hunger born from starvation. He rode her fast and hard. She responded with equal fury. And when he came, jetting his release into her receptive body, he growled with animalistic pleasure, and she held on to him while her body shook with fulfillment.

He rolled over onto the ground beside her, his breathing ragged, and then pulled her up and on top of him. For one long, endless moment they stared at each other, but neither spoke. She laid her head in the crook of his shoulder and curved her back, snuggling against him. He draped her in his embrace, holding her securely against his damp body.

She wanted to tell him that she loved him. That she had never really stopped loving him, not even when she had hated him. But instead she said, "Was it . . . was it. . . ?"

He kissed her temple and caressed her naked hip. "My fantasy come true."

"Mine, too." She sighed and cuddled close, refusing to think about anything, except this one glorious moment.

Chapter 18

Lillie Mae watched them as they came through the garden. Miss Lane in her gown and Johnny Mack with his shirt undone. They had been down by the river, down by the old boathouse. Alone at dawn. With a wispy breeze still stirring and the softness of night barely dissolved into the harsh light of day, they stood at the far edge of the patio, arms wrapped around each other, and kissed. Lillie Mae glanced away, down into the kitchen sink, not wanting to intrude on their private moment.

She had known this would happen, sooner or later. Once Johnny Mack returned to Noble's Crossing, there had been no denying that the old attraction was still there between Lane and him. Lillie Mae sighed. Only now, he and Lane were adults, not kids, and what happened between them would be all the more powerful, especially since they were dealing with fulfilling the fantasies of first love. Even if Johnny Mack still might be unable to properly label what he had felt for Lane fifteen years ago, Lillie Mae knew. That boy had loved Lane.

Without glancing back out the window, she prepared the coffee machine, then opened the pantry door and walked inside to get a new bag of flour for her homemade biscuits. When she heard the back door open, she peeped out into the kitchen and saw Lane heading up the back stairs. Before Johnny Mack could follow, Lillie Mae scurried across the kitchen and grabbed his arm.

"Wait up a minute," she told him.

He whipped around to face her. "Damn! Scare the daylights out of a man, would you?"

"I want to talk to you."

"You're up awfully early, aren't you?"

"Not as early as some folks," she replied.

"Meaning?"

"Meaning I saw you and Miss Lane walking up from the river."

"Never thought you were the nosy type, Lillie Mae."

"I'm not," she replied. "And under normal circumstances whatever went on between you and Miss Lane would be none of my business, but these aren't normal circumstances, are they?"

"What are you trying to tell me?"

"I'm giving you a warning," she said. "That gal has gone through more than anybody should have to go through and her not even thirty-five yet. If you hurt her, you'll have to answer to me. Don't make her no promises you don't intend to keep."

Johnny Mack buttoned his wrinkled shirt and stuffed the ends into his damp jeans, then ran a hand through his disheveled hair. "Lane told me that you'd once issued Kent a warning. Want to tell me about it?"

Lillie Mae lifted her eyebrows in a speculative glare. "So, she told you about what Kent did to her."

"Yeah, she told me that when she refused to sleep with him, he raped her. And she also told me that you threatened to kill Kent if he ever touched Lane again."

"He never raped her again," Lillie Mae said. "But I sure didn't ever forgive him for the misery he put that gal through. He was a mean, hate-filled drunk, and he deserved to die. And I would have killed him. Gladly. But I didn't. And neither did Miss Lane."

"But she would have, if she'd had to, to protect Will, just as you would have and just as Will would have in order to protect Lane."

"You've got that right. It's been just the three of us against the world for a long time. And now, you're here. Finally. Where you belong. With Lane and Will."

Lillie Mae broke eye contact, then turned and walked across the kitchen and into the pantry. After retrieving a sack of flour, she came out to find Johnny Mack waiting for her at the door.

"Breakfast won't be ready for another hour," she said.

"Why didn't you send for me sooner?"

She sidestepped him and carried the flour sack over to the counter, where she opened it and dumped its contents into a large cannister. "I was tempted. More than once," she admitted. "But of course those first five years, I didn't know where you were. After that, when you started sending me those money orders and I saw the envelopes were marked Houston, I asked Miss Lane if she would want to know where you were and if she did, would she ask you to come back to Noble's Crossing."

"And what did she say?"

"She said no. By that time, she'd started hating you. And she was convinced that you'd never come back. I guess I figured she was right." Lillie Mae opened a top cupboard and brought out a large mixing bowl. "Besides, I knew that if you came back, you and Kent would have wound up trying to kill each other." Using a cup nestled inside the bowl, she measured out flour from the cannister. "I had no way of knowing that you had enough power to fight Miss Edith's rule over Noble's Crossing. And to be honest, I thought I was protecting Will from the ugly truth. I knew how Kent would react if he ever found out Will wasn't really his child."

"I didn't do much to earn your trust or Lane's, did I?" Johnny Mack pulled out a chair from the kitchen table, turned it backward and sat, his legs straddling the seat. He crossed his arms over the back of the chair and rested his chin on his arms.

"I don't blame you for the kind of boy you were." Lillie Mae retrieved milk from the refrigerator and shortening from a cabinet under the counter. "What chance did you have to become a decent human being, with no father and Faith Cahill for a mother? You and my Sharon were a lot alike, both growing up with no fathers, both of you wild and dirt poor and hungry for what you couldn't have. God knows I tried to be a good mama, but I couldn't give Sharon nothing she wanted and very little of what she needed."

"Sharon was damn lucky to have had you, to have had someone in her life who loved her, who cared what happened to her."

"She was a lot like her father, that gal of mine." Lillie Mae's chest heaved with the deep breath she took. Thinking about the life Sharon had chosen, about the depths to which she had sunk, broke Lillie

Mae's heart. If only Sharon had taken the fifty thousand dollars Miss Lane had given her and done something worthwhile with her life, she might still be alive. But no, she had blown that money, used it up quick as a wink on a car and clothes and drugs. The drugs were what killed her, long before the HIV ever entered her body.

"Didn't you ever worry about Will?" Johnny Mack asked. "I mean with Sharon for a mother and me for a father—"

"Didn't worry much. Most of what was wrong with you and with Sharon was being poor nobodies from the wrong side of the Chickasaw River. If you two had been raised by two loving parents, with a little money and a lot of discipline, y'all would have turned out all right."

"And that's what you wanted for Will, wasn't it?"

"I don't deny it." Lillie Mae cut the shortening into the flour and added a little milk. "Sharon didn't want her baby, and you were long gone. Of course I wanted my grandchild to be raised in the lap of luxury, for his daddy to be a Graham and his mama a Noble."

"Didn't it ever bother you not being able to tell Will that you were his grandmother?"

"Maybe it did. Sometimes. But mostly I was just grateful that Miss Lane loved Will so much. And in the beginning, Kent was different. He adored Will, and in his way, I think he loved Lane. I had no idea what a cruel, hurtful man he could be."

"If you had it to do over again, would you? Would you help Lane perpetuate a lie?"

Lillie Mae began working the dough with her hands. "If I didn't know what I know now, I suppose I would have. But if I'd realized . . ." How could she even begin to tell Johnny Mack about how difficult Lane's life had been, how much sorrow and pain she had endured? But he should know. The only way he could ever truly know Lane, the woman she was today, was to understand what she had lived through. "These past fifteen years haven't been easy for Miss Lane."

"Because she married Kent." Anger tinged his voice.

"Yes, in great part because she married Kent." Lillie Mae sprinkled flour on a wooden board and up and down the rolling pin. "But there were other things. Her father's sudden death in that car accident. And nearly two years of watching her mother die slowly." She dumped the dough onto the board and patted it out until the entire surface rose to about half an inch high. "And realizing how little money her father had left took Lane by surprise. With only the income from the *Herald,* she had to figure out ways to keep up this big old house and the grounds and to pay for nurses for Miss Celeste."

"Why didn't Kent help her financially?" Johnny Mack lifted his chin from his arms and ran a hand over the beard stubble covering his jaw.

"Kent didn't have any money. It hadn't taken him long to go through the trust fund Mr. John left him. And you might recall just how tight Miss Edith is with the purse strings. She's known for her stinginess."

"And naturally, Miss Edith refused to help Lane."

"Miss Lane never asked her mother-in-law for help. I reckon she knew Witch Edith wouldn't part with any of her money, except the child support for Will." Using a round cutter, Lillie Mae formed the biscuits and laid them out on a greased pan. "For a girl who grew up without a care in the world, Miss Lane wasn't prepared for reality. Marrying a man she didn't love. Raising a child, while protecting the truth about his true identity. Dealing with an abusive husband, a crazy sister-in-law, a bitch mother-in-law and an invalid mother. And growing to hate the man she had once loved. Hard days. Sad days. More than most could have endured. Many a time I thought that girl would come unraveled, but somehow she kept it all together.''

"For Will.''

"Yes, mostly for Will.'' Lillie Mae placed the pan of uncooked biscuits into the oven.

"You truly love Lane, don't you?'' Johnny Mack stood, walked across the room and placed his hand on Lillie Mae's shoulder.

She looked him square in the eye. "I sure do love her. And I admire her. And I want to see her happy. Can you do that for her? Can you make that girl happy?''

"I don't know,'' Johnny Mack admitted. "But I promise you that I'm going to try.''

Lillie Mae smiled, a sense of relief washing over her. She had done the right thing sending for Johnny Mack. She wiped her hands off on her apron and patted him on the cheek. "You'd better go upstairs and get a shower and shave before breakfast. You don't want Will coming down and seeing you looking like a bum who's been out tomcatting all night.''

Lillie Mae winked at him. He winked back at her before he kissed her on the cheek and then headed up the back stairs.

Lillie Mae laid the silverware at each place setting on the kitchen table just as Will bounded downstairs.

"Good morning. Am I the first one up?''

"Looks that way.''

"I'm starving,'' he said. "I think I'll go ahead and eat and not wait on Mama and our guests.''

"Mind if I join you for that early breakfast?" Quinn Cortez halted halfway down the stairs.

Will watched as his mother's lawyer entered the room.

"Come on in, Mr. Cortez," Lillie Mae said.

Will glowered at the man who smiled cordially at his grandmother. What did Cortez think of him? After his confession to Johnny Mack and his mother's hysterical reaction last night, he had escaped to his room and shut himself off from the world. But a guy could hide out only so long before he had to face his accusers, before he had to face himself and admit the truth. But what was the truth? Had he really murdered Kent? Was he capable of brutally bludgeoning to death the man he had once believed was his father?

He knew that his mother feared the worst. And so did Lillie Mae. They had lied to protect him, but now what would happen since Johnny Mack knew the truth? He wasn't sure why he'd told Johnny Mack what had happened the day of Kent's death, why he'd been honest with him. Maybe it was because the man was his father. Or maybe it was because he had finally begun to trust him a little bit. He sure seemed sincere when he said all he wanted to do was help them.

What about Quinn Cortez? Did this man think he had killed Kent? The last thing he wanted right now was to be given the third degree, without his mother and Johnny Mack around for support. Maybe he should act like a man, confess the truth to the police and accept the consequences. But God help him, right now he didn't feel much like a man. He felt like a kid. A kid who was scared to death and wanted his mama.

"I'm not going to cross-examine you, Will, if that's the reason you're looking at me that way," Quinn said.

"Sorry." Will took a seat at the table, and within seconds, Lillie Mae placed a plate of bacon, eggs and hash browns in front of him.

Quinn helped himself to a cup of coffee and sat down at the table across from Will. "Did you get any sleep last night?"

"Not much," Will admitted as he speared a bite of scrambled eggs with his fork. "I guess you think I'm a pretty rotten kid for keeping quiet and letting my mother take the rap for something I probably did."

"Hush up, Will," Lillie Mae scolded. "You didn't kill Kent, so stop saying you did."

"You think I killed him, don't you, Mr. Cortez?" Will glared at the lawyer.

Quinn took a sip of coffee, then set the cup down in front of him. "I don't know, Will. I think it's possible that if Kent Graham pushed you too hard, you might have snapped and beaten him to death. But it's just as possible that you simply witnessed the murder, and the shock of it caused your partial amnesia."

"Do you think Johnny Mack is right about me seeing a psychiatrist?" Did seeing a psychiatrist mean he was nuts, crazy, the way Aunt Mary Martha was?

"I think we need to do whatever is necessary to help you remember what happened the day Kent was killed. Your mother hasn't helped the situation by lying to the police."

"Mama did what she did to protect me." Will lifted the egg on his fork, stared at the food for a second, then shoved it into his mouth and followed it with half a strip of bacon.

"I understand your mother's reasoning," Quinn said. "But now that we know the truth, the best thing we can do for you and for Lane is help you recall everything that happened that day. You and your mama"—he glanced over his shoulder—"and Lillie Mae aren't fighting this battle alone anymore."

"That's for damn sure." Johnny Mack entered the kitchen. "We're all in this together."

Will jerked around to face his father. A man he hadn't known before a few weeks ago. A man Kent Graham had tried to make him hate. But he didn't hate Johnny Mack now. Begrudgingly he was beginning to like his father, maybe even to trust him.

"Want some breakfast?" Lillie Mae asked.

"Yeah, a big breakfast," Johnny Mack said. "The works, with a couple of your delicious biscuits."

"Where's Lane?" Quinn asked.

"I imagine she's sleeping late," Johnny Mack replied as he exchanged a quick, conspiratorial glance with Lillie Mae. "She probably had a restless night."

"Mama doesn't usually sleep this late." It was after seven, and as a general rule his mother was in the kitchen by six-thirty every weekday morning. "Maybe I should go up and check on her. Make sure she's all right."

"I'm sure she's—" Johnny Mack said before he was interrupted.

"You do that," Lillie Mae told Will. "You go check and make sure she's okay. And if she's still sleeping, then don't disturb her. I can take her breakfast up on a tray later."

Will glanced around the room, noting the expression on each adult face. Something was up. He sensed the tension in Johnny Mack as well as Lillie Mae, not to mention the speculative look Quinn Cortez had in his eyes.

"Y'all want to talk about me, don't you?" Will looked directly at his grandmother. "You want to discuss what to do with me. How to handle the situation."

"You're too smart for your own good," Lillie Mae said. "How about scooting on upstairs for a few minutes. I'll put your breakfast in the oven to keep warm."

"Should I take Mama a cup of coffee?"

"Why not?" Lillie Mae lifted the glass pitcher, poured the coffee and handed the cup to Will.

As he headed upstairs, he heard Johnny Mack say, "We're not going to do anything unless Lane agrees to it. If it's all right with her, I'll bring in the best psychiatrist in the country to help Will."

Lane woke slowly, languidly, and stretched as she rose to a sitting position. The satin sheet dropped to her waist when she lifted her arms over her head. She couldn't remember ever feeling so wonderful, so alive, so much a woman. One passionate encounter with Johnny Mack had done all that for her—and more.

And for the first time since Kent's death, she truly believed that there was a solution to her problems, that there was a way to save both herself and Will. In her desire to protect Will, she had disregarded common sense and charged forward with a flawed plan to keep him safe. She should have realized that Will's conscience would plague him, that deep inside he longed to know the truth about what happened the day Kent died, even if that truth turned out to be unbearably horrible.

Johnny Mack was right about their trying to help Will remember. And she knew now that no matter what, she and Will could count on him to stand by them and see them through the bad times ahead.

Kicking back the sheet, Lane swung her legs off the side of the bed and slid her feet into her yellow terry cloth slippers. After a shower, she would dress in something feminine before she left her room to find Johnny Mack. Glancing at the clock, she wondered if everyone else was up. If so, she wouldn't have a chance to see Johnny Mack alone. They really needed to talk about what had happened between them. When they had returned to the house earlier this morning, they had both still been in a fog of sexual satiation and in a hurry to return to the house and their separate bedrooms before anyone discovered them together.

Lane got up, hugged herself tightly and twirled about the room. So, this was what it felt like to have been loved by Johnny Mack Cahill. Indescribable. Gloriously, marvelously indescribable. She sighed as she came to a halt in front of her cheval mirror. Did she look different now? Did what she had done with Johnny Mack show on her face? On her body? Surely she had changed outwardly as much as she had inwardly.

"Mama, are you all right?"

Lane whirled about to find her son standing in the doorway, a china cup and saucer in his hand. "Will, sweetie, what are you—"

"I brought you some coffee," he said. "It's past seven and I wanted to make sure you were all right."

"I'm fine." She motioned for him to come to her. "Bring me that coffee. I can sure use it. I'm a real sleepyhead this morning, aren't I?"

Will grinned, then met her halfway in the middle of the room. She took the coffee from him, then kissed his cheek. Suddenly the telephone rang. Once. Twice. Then silence.

"Lillie Mae probably got it," Lane said. "So, tell me how you're feeling this morning?"

"I'm okay."

"Do you want to talk?" she asked. "All you wanted to do last night was be left alone."

"Yeah, I know. I needed time to think. Time to make a decision about what I should do."

"And have you made a decision?"

"Yeah. I want Johnny Mack to bring in a psychiatrist. I want to remember what happened the day Kent died. If I killed him—"

"You didn't," Lane reassured him.

"I hope I didn't, but if I did, then you and I and Johnny Mack . . . and Lillie Mae, we'll deal with it together, won't we?"

Lane bit down on her bottom lip in an effort to stem the tears lodged in her throat. "You bet we will."

Lane started to set her coffee on the nightstand; then in her peripheral vision she caught a glimpse of movement in the hallway. Glancing over Will's shoulder, she took a better look and saw Johnny Mack and Lillie Mae walking down the hall toward her room. A nerve-wracking sense of foreboding overwhelmed her.

"What's wrong, Mama?" Will asked. "You've got an odd look in your eyes."

Johnny Mack entered her bedroom, standing only a couple of feet behind Will. Lillie Mae hovered in the doorway, a stricken expression on her face.

Will whirled around when he realized Lane was staring at someone behind him. "What is it?" he asked. "What's happened?"

"That phone call was from Miss Edith's housekeeper," Johnny Mack said. "There's no easy way to say this—"

"Just say it, dammit!" Lane set her cup on the nightstand and grabbed Will's trembling hands.

"Jackie Cummings is dead. The police . . . that is, Buddy Lawler is saying it looks like suicide."

"Aunt Mary Martha!" Will cried.

"She's in the hospital." Johnny Mack walked over to Will and Lane, stood behind them and wrapped his arms around their shoulders. "Somehow Mary Martha got hold of her sleeping pills and took an overdose. They aren't sure what happened. Maybe she woke, saw Jackie's body and panicked. They don't know."

"How is she?" Lane asked.

"Mrs. Russell said that Mary Martha was still alive when the ambulance took her away."

"I want to go to the hospital." Will broke free, heading for the door.

Lillie Mae blocked his path. "You aren't going by yourself. You'll wait for Lane and Johnny Mack. They'll take you to the hospital to see about Miss Mary Martha."

Lane's gaze met Lillie Mae's, and they exchanged a knowing glance. What would it do to Will if, when he went to the hospital, he found out that the aunt he adored had died?

Chapter 19

Johnny Mack hated the smell of a hospital, the medicinal and antiseptic odors that mixed with the stench of human waste and sickness. He disliked the clamoring nurses and technicians who went about their jobs like robots, some thinking less about their patients than about what they would eat for lunch. The sight of the old, the infirm and the helpless, their doors often open for the world to view their plight, created tension in his gut. And the sad, forlorn faces, the silent tears and the mournful cries of loved ones waiting for death to claim a husband, wife, child or parent unnerved him.

He had been in this hospital twice before. He'd been just a kid when Faith Cahill died, after being stabbed by her latest lover's jealous wife. Wiley had brought him to the emergency room, and they had stood by Faith's bed. She had opened her eyes, stared up at him and said, "Screw 'em before they can screw you, baby boy." Those had been her last words. He hadn't shed a tear at her funeral or afterward. He had learned long before Faith died that tears didn't help.

When Wiley Peters succumbed to years of alcoholic binges and emphysema caused by his chain-smoking habit, Johnny Mack had been sitting with him all night. He supposed he had loved Wiley as much as he'd ever loved anyone up to that point in his life. In an odd sort of way he had seen Wiley as a substitute father. God knew, the old drunk had been the only permanent male fixture in his life. He'd been eighteen when Wiley died. The government had taken care of the funeral, since Wiley had been a decorated Vietnam veteran. Johnny Mack had taken the hundred bucks he had saved up and bought flowers for the grave. The big spray of red roses had been the only floral arrangement at the funeral. Nobody else had given a damn that Noble's Crossing's war hero had been put to rest unappreciated and unmourned, except for the town bad boy.

The elevator doors opened, bringing Johnny Mack back to the present. He hurried along behind Lane, who rushed to keep up with Will. His son had been distraught on the ride to the hospital, so afraid that when he arrived he would find that his aunt had died.

Will didn't hesitate when they reached Room 310. He flung open the door and marched into the dimly lit interior. The window blinds were closed, and only the light over the bed shined softly, enough to illuminate all the bells and whistles that could summon help if necessary. An intravenous bag hung from a stand, like a silent sentinel, protecting the patient's body. Sitting beside the bed, Miss Edith held Mary Martha's limp hand. Buddy Lawler stood behind her, his fingers curled over her shoulder. James Ware leaned against the wall, his arms crisscrossing his chest.

"How's Aunt Mary Martha? Is she going to be all right?" Will asked.

Edith glanced at Will, then lifted her free hand to him. "Come here, dear." Tears flooded Edith's eyes.

She appeared haggard, her eyes red from tears. But her appearance was immaculate. Not a hair out of place and her makeup perfect. Not knowing, at the time, whether her daughter was going to live or die, had she actually taken time to apply lipstick before leaving the house this morning?

Johnny Mack surmised that Edith Graham Ware was capable of almost anything, including love for her only remaining child. But would the selfish, self-centered woman ever be able to put anyone else's needs above her own?

He glanced from mother to daughter. Mary Martha looked pale and fragile, her face void of color and her light strawberry blond hair tangled about her shoulders. Lying there so quietly, unmoving except for the barely noticeable undulation of her chest as she breathed, she still maintained that unique Mary Martha aura of delicate innocence.

Will walked over and knelt down beside Edith, who immediately leaned her head over and kissed his forehead.

"Will, sweet boy, how did you know?" Edith asked.

"Mrs. Russell called and told us what happened."

"It's been a nightmare," Edith said. "That awful Jackie Cummings killing herself right there in Mary Martha's room. And my poor baby waking up and finding her dead body or perhaps even seeing. . . . She wasn't supposed to awaken. She had been given a sleeping pill and—"

Johnny Mack couldn't help but notice the way Buddy's hand tightened on Miss Edith's shoulder and how she suddenly stopped talking.

"Is Aunt Mary Martha going to be all right?" Will repeated his question.

"The doctors pumped her stomach," Buddy said. "They think she'll be just fine." He released his tenacious hold on Edith's shoulder, then reached out and urged Will to stand. "Your grandmother . . . that is, Miss Edith is tired. Why don't you persuade her to take a break and get some coffee?"

"I don't want to leave my baby." Edith gripped her daughter's hand tightly.

"I'll stay here with her," Buddy said. "You've tired yourself out and you aren't thinking clearly. Why don't you go with Will?"

"Come on, Grandmother," Will said. "Buddy's right. You do need a break. You look exhausted."

When Will helped Miss Edith to stand and then walked her out of the room, Lane and Johnny Mack stepped aside to allow them into the corridor. James eased away from the wall and followed. When he passed Johnny Mack, he nodded, but didn't speak.

"Why don't you go with Will," Johnny Mack suggested to Lane. "I want to ask Buddy a few questions about what happened."

Lane gripped Johnny Mack's arm, her eyes questioning him, but all she said was, "We'll take Miss Edith to the lounge. Join us when you finish your conversation with Buddy."

"I'll be there shortly."

The minute he and Buddy were alone in Mary Martha's room, Buddy all but snarled at him. "What the hell do you want, Cahill?"

"The answers to a few questions."

"What makes you think I'll answer any questions you have?"

Johnny Mack sat down in the large chair that converted into a cot and was standard equipment in all the hospital rooms. He leaned back, crossed his right leg over his left knee and relaxed. "One suicide and one attempted suicide in the same house. Even in the same room. On the same night. Strange, don't you think?"

"Nothing strange about it. Jackie Cummings killed herself, and when Mary Martha saw her dead body, she went berserk and for reasons we'll never know took an overdose of her sleeping pills."

"Now, why would she do that?"

"Who knows why Mary Martha does what she does?" Buddy hovered over the peaceful, serene figure lying in the bed. "She hasn't been herself since Kent was murdered."

"She sure did take his death hard, didn't she?"

Buddy's angry gaze pierced Johnny Mack. "He was her brother. She loved him."

"Hmm . . . that she did. Loved him almost as much as she hated him."

Buddy clenched and unclenched his fists. "Whatever you think you know, leave it be. For everybody's sake."

"For Lane's sake?"

"There's no jury that'll find Lane guilty," Buddy said, his voice pleading. "She'll never be convicted."

"If you're so sure of that, then why do you suppose Wes Stevens took his evidence to a grand jury and was able to persuade them to hand down an indictment?"

"You'll have to ask Wes that question." Sweat popped out above Buddy's upper lip.

Aware of Buddy's nervousness, Johnny Mack rose from the chair and faced the police chief, then smiled at him. "I just might do that."

"Do whatever you want, you always did. But I'm

warning you that if you spread any dirty lies about Mary Martha, I'll—"

Johnny Mack nailed Buddy with a warning glare. "I've never hurt Mary Martha, and I can promise you that I'm not out to hurt her now. But then, I figure you already know that. Somewhere along the way, you found out that I wasn't the evil brother, didn't you?"

Buddy did not respond, but the look of sheer horror in his eyes told Johnny Mack all he needed to know. Buddy was privy to *the secret*, just as he was. Breaking eye contact, Johnny Mack turned and walked out, then stopped and glanced back into the room as Buddy sat beside Mary Martha's bed. The look of adoration and longing on Buddy's face almost stopped Johnny Mack from asking one last question. Almost.

"By the way, how did Jackie Cummings kill herself?"

"What?" Buddy's head snapped up, his eyes round with shock.

"How did—"

"Shot herself in the head."

"Strange that no one heard the shot."

"She used a silencer on the gun."

"Damn nice of her not to want to disturb the household, wasn't it?"

Before Buddy could reply, Johnny Mack headed down the hall. There was a great deal more to this situation than met the eye. He would bet his last million on it. Two women, a nurse and her patient, both attempt suicide on the same night. Why? And was there any connection between what happened and Kent's murder? Somewhere there were answers to his questions. All he had to do was find them.

* * *

Lane wished that James and Will would return with the coffee soon. She hated being alone with Edith, alone with Kent's mother, the woman who had condemned her for his murder.

"Thank you for allowing Will to come here this morning." Edith offered Lane a forced, closed-mouth smile. "I feel certain that he'll be the first person she wants to see when she awakens."

Edith sat perched on the edge of a green vinyl chair positioned in the corner of the waiting area. With her ankles crossed and her hands folded in her lap, she gave the appearance of being a genteel lady. Lane knew better. Edith Noble Graham Ware might have been born into a wealthy, blue-blooded old Southern family and reared as a lady of impeccable breeding, but in truth Kent's mother was a ruthless business woman, a power-hungry grand dame and a first-class bitch.

"Why would you think I'd try to keep Will away, knowing how much he and Mary Martha love each other?" Lane ceased her nervous pacing.

"Considering the circumstances . . . I couldn't have blamed you if you hated me enough to—"

"I think that for the time being, for Will's sake, we need to forget our personal differences."

For the first time since she had known Edith, and that had been since her infancy, Lane thought the woman was beginning to look old. Despite her surgically maintained smooth face, her slender, petite figure and her dyed hair, Miss Edith didn't appear youthful and vibrant anymore.

Of course, the woman had lost her son only weeks ago, and today she had come very close to losing her daughter. Grief and worry had a way of aging a person.

Whatever the reason, something had certainly taken the luster from Edith's time-has-stood-still image.

"Even though I'm quite grateful to you for allowing Will to come here today, I find it impossible to put aside our differences." Edith rose from the chair and, with a regal strut, crossed the room to confront Lane. "I blame you for what happened to Mary Martha. She's been distraught since Kent's death. If your actions hadn't taken her brother away from her, she wouldn't have been half out of her mind and swallowed that overdose of sleeping pills."

"I realize that you're terribly upset, but you can't honestly blame me for the actions of a woman who has been mentally unstable all her life!"

"I can and I do blame you! And until Kent's death, my daughter hadn't had a bad spell in quite some time. My children were very close to each other. Mary Martha loved Kent dearly, as he loved her."

Lane opened her mouth to speak, but from somewhere behind her, Johnny Mack growled a startling comment.

"Mary Martha hated Kent as much as she loved him, and you, Miss Edith, know that as well as I do!" Johnny Mack stood just inside the waiting room doorway.

"I have no idea what you're talking about." Edith hissed the words, then turned her back to Johnny Mack, dismissing him.

"You know exactly what I'm talking about."

He gave Lane no more than a glance as he zeroed in on Edith. When he came up behind her, she refused to face him.

"I know the secret," he whispered.

Lane eased closer, wanting to hear what he was saying to Miss Edith. Had he said that he knew the secret? What secret?

Edith shivered ever so slightly, but stood her ground, unmoving and unresponsive. Lane had seen Edith this way more than once—whenever she heard something she didn't want to hear, she did her best to ignore it, just as she was trying to do now.

"I know the dirty, ugly little secret," Johnny Mack said. "Mary Martha told me all about it years ago. That night Kent caught me with her when I'd taken her home. You know, after I'd found her wandering around not far from the country club. She was tipsy and talkative."

Edith's shoulders tensed. Lane waited, holding her breath, wondering what secret Johnny Mack was talking about.

"She begged me to make love to her that night, but I refused." Johnny Mack shot Lane a quick glance, a silent plea for understanding. "I told her that if the rumors were true, she might be my half sister."

"The rumors were true," Edith said, her voice deadly quiet. "You knew as well as I did that John was your father. Why do you think I—" She cut herself off abruptly, as if she had caught herself about to confess to some personal secret sin.

Surely, Johnny Mack's true parentage wasn't considered a well-kept secret. The whole town had heard those old rumors. No, whatever *the secret* was, Lane decided, it wasn't something that was common knowledge.

Johnny Mack persisted. "Do you know what Mary Martha said when I told her that I couldn't make love to her because we might be brother and sister?"

Edith whirled around, hands clenched in front of her, red nails bared to attack. "No one will believe you. Do you hear me? Whatever filthy lies you tell, no one will believe you."

"Won't they? Doesn't what I know explain why Mary Martha has been plagued with mental and emotional problems all her life?"

"She's simply delicate, the way my mother was delicate," Edith countered, tilting her nose in the air.

"That may be true, but—"

"I refuse to listen to whatever story you've dreamed up."

Johnny Mack pushed, refusing to be silenced. Lane held her breath, waiting, wondering, halfway afraid of what truth he was about to reveal.

"Mary Martha told me that it was all right if she and I had sex, that it didn't matter if I was her brother. That she and Kent had been—"

Edith screeched, then slapped her hands over her ears and keened loudly. Lane looked to Johnny Mack for help. My God! My God! Was he implying that . . . No! It couldn't be true. No matter how much she had hated Kent, no matter how badly he had treated her, had he actually been capable of. . . . No. Please, no.

"Do something for her!" Lane demanded.

Johnny Mack grabbed Edith and shook her soundly, then pried her hands from her ears and held her in place in front of him. "Kent had been sexually abusing Mary Martha since she was eleven years old."

"Nooooo . . ." Sobbing uncontrollably, Edith crumpled, falling helplessly against Johnny Mack's chest.

Lane gasped. Her knees gave way as her legs turned to rubber. She eased down into the nearest chair. Clasping her trembling hands together, she forced herself to breathe in and out slowly, calmly. And all the while Johnny Mack's words replayed inside her head. Over and over again, like a litany from some sordid TV movie of the week.

Kent had been sexually abusing Mary Martha since she was eleven years old.

Chapter 20

Buddy Lawler stormed out of his office. "What the hell's going on out here?"

Before any of his men could explain the ruckus, Buddy saw Glenn Manis being forcefully restrained by Sergeant T. C. Bedlow and Officer Mike Davis. This was a complication he had been expecting. After all, Glenn and Jackie had been an item for nearly a year now, so it was only natural that Glenn would be making some inquiries. But if he didn't handle this situation just right, Glenn could wind up being a major pain in the ass.

Buddy ambled over to Glenn and smiled. "What's the matter with you, boy? You done gone loco or something?"

"I ain't loco," Glenn said, struggling to free himself. "And neither was Jackie."

"Promise me that you'll calm down and act reasonable and I'll get T. C. and Mike to let you go," Buddy offered. "But I've got to have your word that you'll behave yourself."

"I'll behave myself." Glenn ceased his struggling, but his agitated breathing sounded like a snorting bull preparing to charge. "All I want is some answers to my questions."

Buddy motioned to the officers flanking Glenn. "Let him go."

They followed orders and released Glenn, who immediately dragged a handkerchief from his back pocket and wiped the sweat from his fat, red face. "Me and Jackie's uncle Ronnie are making funeral arrangements for her and I need to know when her body will be released."

Buddy sighed, undeniable relief spreading through him. The last thing he needed was to have to lock up Jackie's boyfriend. The sooner the Jackie Cummings situation was over and done with and the woman was buried, the better for everyone involved, especially for Mary Martha. That was the reason he had demanded an immediate autopsy. Get the death ruled a suicide and put an end to it.

"Why don't you come on into my office, Glenn." Buddy waved an invitation. He waited for his guest to precede him into his private quarters, before following him and closing the door behind them.

"Have a seat." Buddy indicated a wooden chair in the center of the room, then positioned his hip on the edge of his desk and crossed his arms over his chest. "I asked Doc Thompson, as a favor to me, to get the autopsy done today if possible. He finished up about thirty minutes ago and sent his report right on over. I've got it right here." Curving sideways, Buddy reached behind him on the sturdy metal desk and picked up a file folder. "You can call over to the funeral home and have them pick up Jackie's body in the morning.''

Tears pooled in Glenn's eyes. Poor bastard, Buddy thought. Apparently he really had loved Jackie, despite the fact that probably a fourth of the men in town had bonked her at least once. Hell, he could remember back in high school when Jackie had spread her legs for him and half the football team.

''Did Doc Thompson agree that Jackie shot herself?'' Glenn asked, then blew his nose loudly into his sweat-stained, white handkerchief.

Buddy lifted the folder, slapped it down on the open palm of his hand and sighed dramatically. ''I'm afraid so.''

Making a sound somewhere between a snort and groan, Glenn shook his head repeatedly. ''But it don't make no sense to me. She didn't have no reason to kill herself. We were talking about getting married, and she said that . . . well, that she was coming into some money soon.''

''I can let you read a copy of the suicide note, if you'd like,'' Buddy said. ''But Miss Edith has already taken a look and said the handwriting was Jackie's all right.''

''Not doubting Miss Edith's word or nothing, but I'd like to take a look at that note all the same.'' Glenn lifted his wide butt just a fraction and stuffed his handkerchief in the back pocket of his pants.

Buddy opened the folder and flipped through the pages, then lifted a sheet of copy paper and handed it to Glenn, whose hand quivered just a tad when he reached for the suicide note. As he scanned the message slowly, seeming to study each word, fresh tears formed in his eyes. He swallowed several times, apparently struggling to keep from boo-hooing like a baby.

Buddy knew the words by heart. He had read the damn thing at least a dozen times. *Please forgive me for taking the coward's way out. I've done some terrible things in my life, but I hope that God will take me on up to heaven despite all my sins. If there was any other way. But there's not. I am so very sorry. Jackie.*

The message said a whole lot, yet didn't really explain a damn thing. But he had seen suicide messages that said less. And he had worked numerous cases where the person hadn't even left a note.

"I'm telling you, Buddy, this note don't make no more sense than Jackie killing herself." Glenn's tight clutch wrinkled the paper. "Surely to goodness if something that bad was bothering her, she would've told me."

Buddy slid off the desk and walked over to Glenn, then placed his hand on the man's shoulder and gave him a comforting squeeze. "I'm awful sorry about this, and I know you've got questions that I can't answer. But they're questions nobody can answer except poor old Jackie. Something awful must have been bearing on her mind for her to have resorted to suicide."

"I just can't believe she did it." Glenn sniffed several times, sucking back tears. "She didn't own a gun. I don't think she even knew how to use one."

Buddy patted him on the back. "The evidence is clear. Doc Thompson and I agree that Jackie shot herself. We may never know why. And as far as the gun goes, well . . . she took it from Mr. John Graham's collection that was stored in the attic. Miss Edith distinctly remembers telling Jackie about the collection one day when they were discussing Miss Edith's collection of teapots."

Glenn stood. The letter fell from his hand and floated to the tiled floor. Buddy wrapped his arm

around Glenn's broad shoulders and walked him out
of his office, through the police station and outside
to where his old Chevy pickup was parked by the
curb. The sweltering sun hung low in the western
sky, preparing for sundown. Glancing up and down
the street, Buddy noted that there wasn't much traffic
and the sidewalks were nearly empty. Noble's Crossing rolled up the streets after dark, becoming a quiet,
sleepy little town. And that was the way he liked things.
Nothing wild and wooly going on, at least not out in
public. Nope, all the sex and sin in Noble's Crossing
went on behind closed doors. Mostly after dark.

"You take care now," Buddy said. "And let me
know about the arrangements for Jackie's funeral.
Miss Edith will want to attend. And of course, I'll be
there."

"That's mighty fine of Miss Edith. Jackie sure did
admire that woman. She was all excited when she got
the job as Mary Martha's nurse." Glenn choked up.
Pursing his lips, he strained to keep from crying.

Glenn got into the truck, looked point-blank at
Buddy and shook his head. Tears trickled down his
chubby cheeks.

When the truck disappeared up Third Street, Buddy
heaved a sigh of great relief. He had been dreading
the confrontation with Glenn, not knowing for sure if
he could convince Jackie's lover that she really had
committed suicide.

Once back in his office, Buddy removed his cellular
telephone from where it was clipped to his belt. Best
to use his private phone for this call. He punched in
the familiar number.

They sure as hell had themselves a mess with Mary
Martha. After all these years of emotional and mental
problems, why had she chosen now, of all times, to
try to take her own life? Was it because she simply

couldn't live without Kent? Or was it possible that waking and finding Jackie dead, she had just acted on impulse? Or had Mary Martha not been asleep and actually witnessed Jackie's death?

Edith answered on the third ring. "Hello."

He figured she had been waiting to hear from him. "Glenn Manis was just in to see me and I've dealt with that problem. He's confused and in a lot of pain; but we talked things over, and I think he'll accept the facts without stirring up a stink. After all, what else can he do?"

"I'm not concerned about that nitwit Manis," Edith snapped. "Johnny Mack Cahill is the man we need to be worried about."

"I don't think Johnny Mack would do anything to hurt Mary Martha."

"You idiot! No, he'd prefer not harming Mary Martha, but he will if he thinks it will help Lane. Haven't you got sense enough to know that if we don't find a way to get rid of him, he's going to repeat those vile things he said about Kent? And what happens if someone believes him?"

Buddy squinched his eyes and gritted his teeth as his face contorted with anger. Damn the woman! Was Kent's reputation all that concerned her? "Those vile things he said about Kent were true. Your precious son damaged Mary Martha beyond repair."

"Don't you think I know that. I have to live with that knowledge every day of my life . . . every time I look at Mary Martha." Edith cleared her throat. "We have to do something about Johnny Mack. And the sooner the better."

"What do you have in mind?"

"I'll come by your house tonight, late. And we'll discuss our options."

"Ten o'clock?"

"Eleven," she replied and then hung up.

Buddy clipped his cell phone on his belt and fell back into the swivel chair behind his desk. If he knew Miss Edith, and he did, discussing ways to deal with Johnny Mack wouldn't be her top priority tonight. Getting laid would.

Johnny Mack didn't want ten inches between them, let alone ten feet. But he simply sat there on the sofa in the den and watched Lane pace the floor. She had been nervous and edgy since their return from the hospital. At first he'd chalked it up to concern over Mary Martha. But Mary Martha had survived her suicide attempt and, after a few days in the hospital, would return home. And Will wasn't the cause of Lane's distress. Once the boy had seen for himself that his aunt was all right, he had calmed down. So that left only one thing—Lane's agitation was probably due to the little bomb he had exploded in Miss Edith's face. A truth bomb, that would no doubt leave more than one casualty in its wake.

"Want to talk about it?" he asked.

"Yes, I want to talk about it." Lane halted, planted her hands on her hips and confronted him. "Knowing the truth about what Kent did to Mary Martha, why didn't you do something? Why didn't you tell someone?"

"What should I have done?" he asked. "Who should I have told?"

"You could have gone to Mr. John or Miss Edith and told them. Or you could have gone to the police."

"And Mr. John and Miss Edith would have believed me, wouldn't they? And there was no reason the police wouldn't take the word of a trailer trash bastard over the word of the town's golden boy, was there?"

Johnny Mack got to his feet, reached out and grabbed Lane's hands. She resisted at first, but when he tugged her toward him, she went willingly. "When Mary Martha told me that Kent had been sexually abusing her since she was eleven, she was half-drunk and upset with me because I wouldn't . . . because I'd turned her down. Hell, a part of me didn't even believe her."

"But a part of you did."

"Yeah, but dammit, Lane, there was nobody in this town who would have believed me. And my guess is that in the cold, hard light of day, with Kent at her side, Mary Martha would have denied it and called me a liar to my face."

"You could have gone to my father. He—"

"He would have wanted to believe me, but he would have had a difficult time taking my word over Kent's." Johnny Mack slipped his arm around her waist. "Your father liked me, but we both know if he could have chosen a husband for you, it would have been Kent."

"Yes, it would have been. And Daddy would have been wrong in that choice." Lane laid her head on Johnny Mack's chest and wrapped her arms around him. "How could we have all been so blind to Kent's true nature? I knew that after he started drinking he turned into a vicious, vindictive monster, but I had no idea. . . . Poor Mary Martha."

"Kent Graham deserved to die the way he did— beaten to a pulp." Johnny Mack stroked Lane's back, caressing her tenderly. "Whoever killed him hated him, that's for sure."

"You don't think Mary Martha . . ." Lane groaned.

"Perhaps. Or maybe even Miss Edith. And I wouldn't rule out Buddy Lawler. He knew about Kent's relationship with Mary Martha, and I'd say that man would do just about anything for her."

"But Miss Edith and Mary Martha were together

when Kent was killed. And Buddy was downtown at his office.''

''Mmm-mmm.''

''What are you thinking?'' Lane lifted her head from his chest and gazed up into his eyes.

''I'm wondering if there's any connection between Jackie Cummings's so-called suicide and Kent's murder.''

''What do you mean so-called suicide?''

''Call me a male chauvinist pig if you want to, but it's my opinion that as a general rule, women don't use guns when they commit suicide.''

Lane grasped Johnny Mack's forearms, the act putting some space between them. ''What do you mean?''

''Honey, men blow their brains out. Women take pills.''

''The way Mary Martha did.''

''Yeah.''

''So that means you think Jackie didn't kill herself.''

''I think somebody went to an awful lot of trouble to make it look like suicide, even down to writing a phony suicide note. But the question is why?''

''And the answer is?'' Lane asked.

''The answer is that Jackie Cummings knew something she wasn't supposed to know and somebody killed her to keep her quiet.''

''But who?'' Lane sucked in a startled breath when realization dawned. ''You think whoever killed Kent killed Jackie, too.''

''That's my guess.''

''Oh, Johnny Mack.'' Lane sighed. ''Can life get any more complicated than it already is?''

He eased her back into his arms and kissed her softly, then lifted his head and grinned at her. ''What happened between us this morning is another complication, isn't it? I figure you're confused about us.

About the way you feel. About the way I feel. And about how Will might react if he knew you and I were . . . together."

"Are we together?"

He lowered his hands from her waist to her hips and shoved her up against his arousal. "We are most definitely *together*."

"We had sex, Johnny Mack, but that doesn't necessarily mean anything."

"It damn well means something to me. And you can't tell me that it doesn't mean a hell of a lot to you, too, lady. You don't give yourself to a man the way you gave yourself to me and that act be meaningless."

"You've had sex countless times, with numerous women," she said. "You can't tell me that most of those encounters were anything more than—"

He kissed her. Forcefully. Demandingly. Couldn't she get it through her pretty head that anyone who had come before her didn't matter? That every other woman he'd ever had didn't mean anything to him in comparison to her.

"We both know that I sowed more than my share of wild oats," he said. "But these days, I'm no horny kid who has to lay everything in a skirt. I'm a man who knows what he wants. And what I want is you, Lane Noble."

"Lane Noble Graham," she corrected. "Neither of us can forget that I was Kent's wife for ten years."

"Okay, so we can't forget your past or mine, but what we can do is put the past where it belongs. Behind us. All that matters is the here and now. Today. And what we can have together."

"No commitments? No plans for the future?" she asked. "We'll just take this relationship one day at a time?"

Yes, he wanted a commitment. Lane was his, and

he sure as hell would never give her up now. But maybe she wasn't ready for him to stake a permanent claim on her. After all, what had he ever done to deserve her? But he could be patient, especially when it came to getting something he wanted. He most definitely wanted Lane. And he meant to have her. Tonight. Tomorrow. For as long as there was breath in his body.

"We'll take it one day at a time," he lied. "Just as long as you let me keep on loving you. Once didn't even begin to satisfy me. I can't get enough of you, honey. Don't you know that?" Cupping the back of her head, he speared his fingers through her hair and brought her lips to his.

When he kissed her, she moaned quietly, surrendering herself to him. God, how he loved the sounds she made, those enticing, feminine sighs and gasps that told him, without words, the way his touch affected her.

"Johnny Mack—" Will came rushing into the library. "Hey, I'm sorry. I didn't know y'all were . . . I'm sorry." Will froze to the spot several feet over the threshold. Embarrassment colored his face.

Lane ended the kiss abruptly and shoved on Johnny Mack's chest, but he held her in place, refusing to relinquish his claim on her.

"Will, let me explain," Lane said.

"There's nothing to explain." Will shrugged.

Johnny Mack eased his hands upward, then draped his arm around Lane's shoulder. "Your mother and I care about each other. We haven't made any plans for the future, but I promise you that when the time comes to make some serious decisions, you'll be included in that decision making. Your mother would never do anything—"

"Look, save it, will you?" Will said. "If you and Mama have got something going on, then it's okay by me.'' Will puffed out his chest and stood straight and tall. ''But you just remember that if you hurt her, you'll have to answer to me.''

''I'll keep that in mind.'' Johnny Mack forced himself not to smile. He had one hell of a son there. Yes, he did.

''Will, honey, did you want something?'' Lane asked.

''Yeah. Quinn sent me to tell y'all that Mr. Foster, the PI guy Johnny Mack hired, is here. And he's got some information that might prove somebody besides Mama had a strong motive for killing Kent.''

Chapter 21

Johnny Mack exchanged a hardy handshake with Wyatt Foster and indicated for the man to take a seat, but the tall, rugged PI, shook his head.

"I'd rather stand," he said, his voice like sandpaper against metal.

Foster nodded an acknowledgment to Lane and then gave Will a quick glance. The man's aura of command probably intimidated a lot of people, Lane thought. But nothing and no one intimidated her these days. And that was good, considering she was in a room with three ultramacho guys. Her peripheral vision caught a glimpse of Will, standing at Johnny Mack's left, and she emended her count to four ultramacho guys. No doubt about it, Will was his father's son. Strong. Stubborn. Handsome. An alpha male in the making.

"I understand you've unearthed some information that might help us." Johnny Mack reached down and took Lane's hand in his.

"That's right. I think I've found y'all a new suspect. But it's just a hunch on my part, you understand."

"At this point, we'll take your hunch," Quinn said. "Remember, I know all about your hunches." He turned to the others and explained. "If Wyatt Foster's gut instincts tell him something, then that's the way it is. His hunches are practically foolproof."

Foster had come highly recommended by Quinn, who had used the former Dallas cop on numerous cases. If Quinn trusted the man's instincts, then why shouldn't she? After all, her new lawyer had never lost a case, and she had to believe that he could find a way to prove her innocence.

Foster's lips twitched, but he didn't smile. "Y'all want the kid in on this?" He glanced at Will.

"I can leave." Will headed for the door.

"No." Johnny Mack grabbed his son's arm. "Will's not a kid. He's a young man now. And he's as involved in this mess as any of us. He stays."

In that one moment, Lane knew why she loved Johnny Mack Cahill, why she had always loved him. Nothing he could have said or done would have won him more points with Will. If given the chance, he was going to be a really good father.

"Is that all right with you, Mama?" Will asked.

"Of course," she replied, suddenly realizing how important it was for a boy to have a father's understanding of the male psyche to counteract the feminine protectiveness of his mother.

"Get to it, Foster," Quinn said.

Wyatt Foster opened his brown leather briefcase and removed a folder. "I've documented all the information, and there's a few pictures in here, too."

"Give the folder to Quinn," Johnny Mack said. "Now, tell us what you've got."

"James Ware, Nobel's Crossing's mayor and Edith

Ware's husband, has been having an affair with a beautician named Arlene Dothan for quite some time now.'' Foster cut his eyes in Will's direction, cleared his throat and continued. "The man has no money of his own, so to speak. His wife holds the purse strings, and the two signed a prenup. So a good question is how did he pay for Ms. Dothan's new car? He purchased the new Buick in her name over in Huntsville six months ago. And there's a talkative jeweler over in Decatur who identified James Ware and Arlene Dothan from photos I showed him. Seems that over the past few years, Mr. Ware has bought his sweetie several pieces of expensive jewelry. A ruby ring. A diamond-studded wristwatch. A couple of gold necklaces and a diamond heart pendant.''

"Interesting," Quinn said. "How did a guy who is dependent on his wife for his income pay for a car and expensive jewelry?''

"There's more," Foster said. "Seems there's been several nice vacation trips. To Jamaica. To the Smoky Mountains. To Aspen. And even one to Disney World, when they took Ms. Dothan's two kids with them.''

Johnny Mack let out a long, low whistle. "James is getting his hands on some cash somewhere. Want to take a guess as to where?''

"From Edith," Lane said.

"Grandmother would never have given him that kind of money," Will told them. "And those trips James went on were supposed to be business trips, conventions where mayors from other towns got together.''

Johnny Mack grinned. "Miss Edith didn't give him the money. He stole it from her.''

"Of course!" Lane agreed enthusiastically. "James took over as Miss Edith's lawyer as well as my family's lawyer when his father died. He takes care of all of

Edith's holdings. It wouldn't be that difficult for him to skim a little off the top.''

"There's no telling how much money he has embezzled from her.'' Johnny Mack focused his attention on Wyatt Foster. "Have you found any hidden bank accounts?''

"If the man has a secret bank account, it's probably in Switzerland,'' Wyatt surmised.

"I know this information is damning,'' Lane said. "But I don't see what James's embezzling money from Miss Edith could possibly have to do with Kent's murder or how it can help me.''

Wyatt lifted his shaggy eyebrows in a but-what-if mannerism. "I'm just supposing here . . . but what if somebody else found out what we suspect James of doing? And what if that somebody confronted James and threatened to expose him? Now, what if that somebody was Kent Graham? I'd say that would give James Ware a damn good motive for murder.''

"My God!'' Lane covered her mouth with her hand. Was it possible that sweet, easy-going, hen-pecked James was capable of murder?

"But you don't have any proof that Kent knew what James was up to or that he confronted James.'' Will draped his arm around his mother's shoulder. "What good is this information if you can't prove your theory? Besides, I can't believe James would hurt a fly, let alone kill somebody.''

"I'm just the messenger,'' Wyatt said. "I don't know the players personally. But my knowledge of human nature tells me that anyone is capable of murder, given the right motivation.''

"Getting the truth out of James should be easy enough.'' Johnny Mack entwined his fingers, bringing his big hands together in a choking gesture.

"Don't do anything stupid,'' Quinn advised.

"All I'm going to do is pay the mayor a little visit first thing in the morning."

"I'll go with you," Lane said.

"No, honey, I'll handle this alone. Man to man, just James and me."

Arlene sighed with contentment as she lay on the cot in the back of her beauty shop and watched James Ware dressing. By most women's standards James wouldn't be considered all that good-looking. His hair was thinning and turning gray. He was of medium height and medium build with a thick middle and the beginnings of a beer belly. But to her, he was prince charming. She loved the guy something awful and lived for the day they could stop sneaking around to be together. All she wanted was for them to get married and start a new life somewhere outside of Noble's Crossing. But James kept saying that they needed more money. Didn't he realize that she would live with him in a tent if they could just be together?

"I've got to go." James leaned over and kissed her on the mouth. "God, I hate to leave you."

"Then, don't leave me. Stay the night."

"Now, sugar, you know I can't do that." He kissed her again, but when she tugged on his tie, he grabbed her hand. "I've got to go. I'm supposed to pick Edith up at the hospital and take her out for dinner."

Arlene jerked her hand from his grasp, crossed her arms over her naked breasts and puckered her lips in what she hoped was a sultry pout.

"Now, don't be angry with me. I'm doing what I have to do to secure our future. Yours and mine and the kids."

"I'm getting tired of waiting for that future you

keep promising me. We're not neither one getting any younger. Before I get too old, I'd like to give you a kid all your own."

That stopped him dead in his tracks, as she knew it would. James adored her two children, and she suspected he wanted one of his own. He cupped her face between his hands and stared directly into her eyes.

"I love you, Arlene. And I promise you that you're going to have everything you ever wanted, including that baby."

With downcast eyes, she sighed. "You'd better get going. Don't want to keep your wife waiting."

"Sugar, I'm sorry. Really I am."

"It's all right," she told him.

"No, it's not all right, but I can't do any better by you right now. But soon, Arlene. I promise."

She nodded. Then when he started to leave, she jumped up off the cot and ran after him, catching him before he opened the back door into the alley. She flung her arms around him and covered his face with kisses.

"You think about me tonight while you're dining out with Miss Edith."

She knew James was torn between wanting to screw her again and needing to meet his wife. Maybe she should feel bad about making things difficult for him, but dammit all, she didn't know how much longer she could stand it—thinking about James with another woman. Even though he swore to her that he hadn't shared a bed with Miss Edith in years, Arlene found it hard to believe that his wife didn't want him. Not when she wanted him so badly.

"Let me go, sugar," James pleaded.

Arlene released him, stepped back and put a false

smile on her face. "Call me, after you go to bed tonight."

James nodded, then exited in a hurry. Arlene slumped down on the cot. *That's it, run to Miss Edith like a good boy. Like a damn obedient little slave.*

Arlene repeatedly slammed her fists into the pillow, wishing the blows were connecting with Edith Ware's tight-as-dick's-hat-band face. After venting her frustration, she got up, put on her clothes and went out into the shop to clean up the place. She should be the one dining with James tonight, not Edith Ware. And she should be the one sleeping in his bed every night and sharing his last name.

Arlene couldn't remember a time when she hadn't loved James Ware, Jr. She had known from the very beginning, when they'd been in junior high, that they came from two different worlds. His old man had been a lawyer to all the rich folks on Magnolia Avenue, and his mama had been a former debutante from New Orleans whose family had more pedigree than money. But James had loved her, too, despite the fact that she lived across the Chickasaw River in a house not much bigger than his family's garage.

They had sneaked around to be together back then, too, when they were teenagers. James had been her first. For that much she was thankful. They had made plans for a future together, but the minute old man Ware had found out that James was serious about her, he'd sent James off to college and forbade him to ever see "that white trash gal" again. She had believed James would stand up to his father and refuse to turn his back on her, but in the end James had proved himself to be the obedient son.

She had up and married the first boy who asked her. And the only reason Wade Cash had proposed was because he'd discovered that Arlene didn't put out. Not for anybody. Except James. Only James. She had been a good girl, and nothing short of love had made her give up her virginity. She supposed folks would laugh at the idea that Arlene Vickery Cash Motes Dothan, a three-time divorcee, considered herself a moral woman. But she was. The only men, other than James, she'd ever had sex with had been her husbands. And James was practically her husband, wasn't he? In her heart, she felt as if she and James were already man and wife. If love united two people, then they were as joined together as any legal ceremony could ever make them.

She had to be patient. James had promised her that they would take her kids and leave Noble's Crossing soon. All he had to do was put away just a little bit more money.

When James Ware arrived at his office the next morning, he found an unexpected visitor waiting for him. Before his secretary, Penny Walsh, had a chance to speak, Johnny Mack Cahill rose from the wing chair by the fireplace and gave James a speculative look.

"It's nearly eleven," Johnny Mack said. "You're kind of late today, aren't you?"

"I stopped by the hospital to see Mary Martha."

"Ever the dutiful stepfather."

James cleared his throat, glanced over at Penny Walsh, who was hanging on every word of the conversation, and then hazarded a direct look at Johnny Mack. "I happen to be very fond of Mary Martha." James opened his office door, turned back to his guest and said, "What can I do for you this morning?"

"Well, it isn't so much what you can do for me, as what I can do for you."

"I'm afraid I don't catch your drift."

"Some information about you has recently come into my possession and I'm willing to—"

"Come with me," James said, then motioned to his secretary with a wave of his hand. "Penny, would you mind going over to the bakery and getting some fresh pastries and then fix us a pot of fresh coffee."

"Certainly, Mr. Mayor."

The minute Penny left, James closed the door to the outer office and confronted Johnny Mack. "I assume you've found out about my . . . my relationship with a certain lady."

"Your affair with Arlene Dothan."

"Yes, well. Yes."

"Let's get something straight from the get-go," Johnny Mack said. "I don't care who you're fucking. I'm not here to threaten you because you're cheating on Miss Edith."

"Then, what?" James broke out in a cold sweat. Surely Johnny Mack didn't know about the money. Of course not. How could he know?

"I have one of the best private investigators in the country poking his nose in everybody's business here in Noble's Crossing. As far as I'm concerned, anybody who had a connection to Kent Graham is under suspicion."

Stay calm, James cautioned himself. *Don't let Johnny Mack intimidate you. Don't give yourself away.* "I can understand your reasoning. You're doing everything you can for Lane. If there's anything I can do to—"

"There is. You can confess to killing Kent."

"What!" Was the man insane? There was no way anyone could connect him to Kent's murder. And even if there were, he had an alibi. Arlene would swear on a stack of Bibles as high as a mountain that she was with him, giving him a manicure. That had been his story to Buddy Lawler, who probably suspected Arlene had been giving him more than a manicure. But come what may, he planned to stick with that story.

"Did you kill Kent?" Johnny Mack asked.

Damn but Cahill scared the shit out of him. He always had. He was big, lean and mean. And with a killer stare that put the fear of God into a person.

"No, I didn't kill Kent. Why would I have killed my stepson? Kent and I had been friends all our lives. I was even his best man when he married Lane."

James noticed Johnny Mack flinch and surmised that Lane's marriage to Kent was a sore spot with him. Best to stay clear of anything that might make the situation more intense.

"Where did you get the money to buy Arlene a new car and expensive jewelry and to take her on several really nice vacations?" Johnny Mack narrowed his gaze, his eyes becoming mere slits, as he focused on James.

Tugging on his collar and inadvertently loosening his tie in the process, James swallowed several times before he even tried to reply. How the hell had he found out? Oh, yeah, the PI. But did he know about the embezzlement? Of course he did. Cahill was no fool. He would realize that there was only one way James could have afforded to splurge on Arlene and her kids—by stealing from Edith.

"You know, don't you?" James sank down into the oxblood leather chair behind his desk.

"I know you've been embezzling money from Miss Edith and that you're storing it away in a secret bank account." Johnny Mack grinned as he leaned over James's desk and looked him square in the eye. "And I know that Kent Graham found out what you were doing and confronted you about it."

James trembled from head to toe, but the worst quivers were in his hands. He laid them flat atop his desk in an effort to steady them. Johnny Mack was bluffing, wasn't he? He was just spouting off suspicions. There wasn't any way even the best private eye in the world could have unearthed that kind of information.

"You're playing a guessing game, Cahill." James prayed that his voice sounded stronger and more confident than he felt.

"Kent threatened to expose you, and you killed him to keep him quiet."

James jumped up, leaned across his desk and glowered at Johnny Mack. "You can't prove a word of what you're saying."

"You and I both know what the truth is, don't we? We know Lane didn't kill Kent, so that means that someone else did."

"I didn't. I swear I didn't."

"Then, you don't have anything to worry about, do you?"

"Are you . . . are you going to tell Edith about. . . . If you mention your suspicions to my wife, she'll destroy me."

"I came here today to give you a chance to help us prove Lane is innocent. Any information you have and share with us will be greatly appreciated."

"But I don't know anything that can help Lane." When he saw the disbelief in Johnny Mack's eyes, he realized he had to come up with something to temporarily satisfy the man who could ruin his future. "I know Edith has used all her influence to see that Lane was charged with Kent's murder. She's hell-bent on seeing Lane convicted. But I swear to you that I didn't kill Kent and I don't know who did."

Johnny Mack speared James with his deadly glare.

"If you're lying to me. . . . Well, let's just say that jail is preferable to what I'll do to you if I find out that you're letting Lane take the rap for something you did."

"I understand."

Without another word, Johnny Mack opened the door, but before he went any farther, James caught up with him and stopped him. "You aren't going to say anything to Edith about . . . about what we discussed, are you?"

Johnny Mack lowered his head and whispered close to James's ear, "Whatever Miss Edith gets, she deserves. If you didn't kill Kent and don't know who did, then you don't have to worry about me blowing the whistle on you. But if Lane's case goes to court and things don't look good for her, Quinn Cortez may call you as a witness. And if he thinks it'll help Lane, he just might have to point a finger at you."

Unable to move, incapable of speaking, James watched Johnny Mack smile pleasantly and tip his Stetson to Penny, who had just returned from the nearby bakery. Then Johnny Mack began humming as he walked outside, leaving the door open behind him. Penny quickly closed the door, then turned around and stared at James.

"Are you all right, Mr. Ware? You look sort of green."

James's head bobbed up and down several times. No, he wasn't all right. He was screwed, that's what he was. Screwed big time. What the hell was he going to do? Something like this couldn't be kept under wraps for long. Maybe the best thing for him to do was take Arlene and her kids and get out of town as soon as possible. He didn't have as much money as he had planned for, but they would just have to make do.

"Mayor, is something wrong?" Penny asked.

"No, nothing's wrong," he replied. "I—I have a phone call to make, Penny. Please see to it that I'm not disturbed."

"Of course."

James went inside his private office, closed and locked the door, then made his way to his desk and picked up the telephone. After dialing, he sat in his leather chair and waited.

"Kut & Kurl. This is Arlene Dothan. How can I help you?"

"Arlene."

"Well, hello, there." Her voice turned syrupy sweet.

"Listen very carefully. I want you to start making plans for us to leave town. As soon as possible."

"What's happened? Why all of a sudden—"

"Johnny Mack Cahill knows about us, about the things I've bought you and about the money I've been squirreling away. The man hired a private detective and now he knows everything."

"Everything?" Arlene lowered her voice to a mere whisper. "Even about Kent?"

"Yes, even about Kent. He doesn't have any proof, but he's got some mighty big suspicions. And if he tells what he suspects and there's an investigation, I'll wind up in the pen for sure."

"What are we going to do?"

"Be ready to leave when I say the word," James told her. "And you just let me take care of everything else."

"But what if Johnny Mack goes to Miss Edith or to Buddy Lawler?"

"Don't worry. I'll handle Johnny Mack."

Chapter 22

"You don't have to do this if you don't want to." Lane placed her arm around Will's shoulders.

"I want to," he said, despite the fear that ate away inside him. "If I saw someone murder Kent, I need to know, and if I'm the one"—Will looked straight at his mother—"who killed him, then I'll have to face the truth and . . ." Will gulped. "God, Mama, I'm scared."

"It's all right, sweetie."

When Lane gave him a reassuring hug, it was all he could do not to fall into her arms and cry like a baby. How could he live with himself if he discovered that he actually had bludgeoned Kent to death? Even though, in the end, Kent had been unfair and cruel, there had been a time when he and the man he had thought was his father had loved each other.

He owed it not only to his mother to remember, but he owed it to himself.

"What's she like?" Will asked, as he stood with his

mother in the middle of his bedroom. "I mean you've already met her and talked to her, so what do you think?"

"Dr. Agee seems like a very nice person. She told me that she has two sons of her own, so she's very understanding about my feelings as well as yours."

"Johnny Mack said that she's the best there is. She's got a Ph.D. and everything."

"That's right. She's a licensed professional counselor who is certified in clinical hypnosis."

"And it's all right with her that you and Johnny Mack be there in the room with me?"

"Yes, she has no problem with our being there."

"Then, come on." Will pulled away from Lane and headed toward the door. "Let's get this show on the road." He forced a smile, as much to shore up his own courage as to convince his mother that he could handle the situation.

Lane followed him out into the upstairs hallway, where Johnny Mack waited for them.

"Ready?" his father asked.

"Yeah, I'm ready."

But he wasn't ready. Not really. The frightened kid inside him wanted to bolt and run back into his room, lock the door and refuse to ever resurface. But he couldn't chicken out. Not when so much depended on him remembering what had happened the day Kent was murdered.

His parents stood side by side, each watching him intently. What were they expecting to happen? Did they think he would fall apart before their very eyes? Or were they just worried, as afraid for him as he was for himself?

"Hey, you two, stop acting as if it's the end of the world." He managed a couple of lame chuckles.

"If at any time during the session with Dr. Agee

you feel like you want to stop, just say so." Johnny Mack's big hand hovered above Will's shoulder. "Don't push yourself to remember if the memories aren't there."

Will knew his father wanted to touch him, to grip his shoulder and assure him that he was there, that he was going to be there for him from now on. Whatever Johnny Mack had done in the past, whatever sins he had committed, he wasn't the man Kent had described.

"He's right, Will. We"—Lane glanced at Johnny Mack—"don't want you to do anything you don't want to do."

"Listen, you two, I'm okay with this hypnosis thing. It's what I want . . . to remember everything about that day. This could be the only way we'll ever know the truth about what happened."

Johnny Mack nodded. Lane grasped Will's hand. Together, the three of them went downstairs and into the den where a petite brunette of about forty immediately rose from the sofa and came forward with a warm smile on her face. So, this was the famous Dr. Agee, Will thought. She looked more like somebody's mom dressed up for church in her pretty beige suit. Her brown hair was styled in a neat, short cut, and her blue eyes were bright and friendly.

She held out her hand. "Hello, Will, I'm Nola Agee."

"Hi." Will shook her hand.

"Before we begin, is there anything you'd like to ask me, anything you want to discuss?" Dr. Agee asked.

"I'm not sure," Will admitted. "Mama and Johnny Mack have pretty much filled me in on everything, except . . . well . . ."

"Whatever your concerns are, don't be afraid to bring them up."

"I guess I'm just wondering if . . . if you think this will work. Can you really hypnotize me and make me remember?"

"Why don't we sit down," the doctor suggested. "Then I'll explain what we're going to do and what we might expect. Okay?"

"Yeah, sure."

Nola Agee glanced at his parents, who both seemed pretty uptight. "Mr. Cahill, why don't you and Ms. Graham take the chairs over by the window; that way you can observe what's happening without being in the way."

He almost laughed when he saw how quickly his mother and Johnny Mack obeyed the doctor. Heck, they were scared, too, and wanted this mumbo-jumbo hypnosis to work as much as he did.

"Will, why don't you sit on the sofa?" Dr. Agee inclined her head in that direction. "You don't have to lie down unless you'd like to."

"I think I'll just sit."

Once everyone else was seated, the doctor placed herself in a straight-back chair directly in front of Will. "Hypnosis is a method of communication that induces a trance or trancelike state. Our goal is to narrow your focus to such an extent that your mind will be relatively free of any distractions. However, you should be able to hear my voice and possibly even the ringing of the telephone. I'll have you focus on an object, and then I'll ask you to relax as I guide you into the trance."

"All right." Sounded simple enough to him, but what if—"What happens if I don't go into a trance?"

Dr. Agee smiled. "Don't worry about it. Some patients can't be hypnotized, while others go into a deep trance. But for the most part, patients tend to simply go into a meditative state."

"Okay. I'm ready." As ready as he would ever be. His belly cramped, but he dismissed the pain, knowing it was just a symptom of his nervousness. "Go ahead and . . . well, do your thing."

"Try to relax," she said. "Try to free your mind of fear and worry and thoughts of any kind."

"Big order there, doc," Will joked.

She laughed. "I know this isn't easy for you, Will, but try."

He tried. God, how he tried. *Relax, you numbskull. Relax. How hard can it be?*

Dr. Agee rose from her chair, strolled across the wide plank floor and flipped the wall switches, shutting off the overhead light and turning on the large ceiling fan at low speed. Although a modicum of daylight peeked through the slats in the oak plantation blinds covering the windows, for the most part soft shadows enveloped the room.

"Listen to the gentle hum of the ceiling fan," the doctor told him. "Look up and concentrate on the rotation. Around and around."

Her voice was soft, calm and soothing. He lifted his gaze to stare at the revolving oak blades and listened to the barely discernible drone of the fan's motor.

"Keep looking at the fan," she told him. "Relax. Free your mind. You're warm. You're comfortable. You're safe. And you're getting just a little drowsy."

"Uh-huh." She was right. He felt everything she had mentioned. Warm. Comfortable. Safe. And drowsy.

He continued staring at the fan as it whirled around and around. His eyelids grew heavy. He felt as if he were floating on a soft, gray cloud. He closed his eyes.

"Breathe deeply. Feel yourself relaxing. Feel yourself drifting off to sleep."

*   *   *

Lane grabbed Johnny Mack's hand, and the two exchanged a concerned glance. Originally she had been opposed to doing anything that might help Will remember what had happened the day Kent was murdered. She had been so afraid that Will would recall having struck the fatal blows that ended Kent's life. But now that she understood how tormented Will had been not knowing the truth, she prayed that this trained professional Johnny Mack had flown in from Chicago would be able to help her son regain his memory.

"Will?" Dr. Agee asked.

"Yes?"

"Are you comfortable?"

"Yes."

"I'd like for you to think back a few weeks to the day that you and Lillie Mae were in the backyard. Do you remember that afternoon?"

"Yes."

"Tell me what's happening. What are you and Lillie Mae doing?"

Lane tightened her grip on Johnny Mack's hand. He scooted to the edge of his chair, close enough so that he could reach over and drape his arm around her shoulders. If ever she had needed him, she needed him now. *Whatever happens, he'll be here to help Will. Together, we'll take care of our son.*

"I was practicing," Will said. "Lillie Mae was pitching the ball to me so I could practice my hitting."

"That's right, you had your baseball bat with you in the yard, didn't you?"

"Yeah, I did."

"Were you and Lillie Mae alone?"

Will nodded. "Mama had gone down to the *Herald.*

Grandmother had fired a couple of reporters, and Mama wanted to talk to the managing editor and see what had happened, find out why those people had been let go."

"So your mother wasn't at home; she wasn't in the yard with you and Lillie Mae?"

"No, she wasn't here."

"While Lillie Mae was helping you practice that day, did someone stop by to see you? Did you have a visitor?"

"I don't know." Will began to squirm, obviously disturbed by the question. He inclined his head to the left and then to the right.

"Breathe deeply. Stay calm and relaxed," Dr. Agee coached. "You're comfortable and safe."

Will's agitation lifted, and once again he said, "I don't know if we had a visitor."

"Picture yourself and Lillie Mae in the backyard. See the grass and trees. Feel the sunshine."

Will sighed.

The doctor continued. "Maybe you and Lillie Mae were laughing and talking, and then someone came into the backyard and you stopped laughing and talking."

"Kent was drunk and angry." Will's shoulders lifted tensely. He knotted his hands into fists. A pained expression pinched his face. "Ever since he got that letter from Sharon Hickman, he's been mad and mean and"—Will gasped for air—"and Mama had forbidden him to come to the house. She'd told him to leave us alone."

"Relax, Will," Dr. Agee said. "You're safe. Lillie Mae is safe. Kent can't hurt you."

"He *can* hurt us," Will cried. "He hurt Lillie Mae. She . . . she told him to leave, that if he didn't go she'd call the police. But he wouldn't leave. He was so hateful. He called Mama all kinds of ugly names, and then he told me that Johnny Mack Cahill was a worthless, white trash bastard, that I was the spawn of the devil and he was sorry he'd ever thought I was his child. Sorry that he'd ever been good to me, that he wished I'd never been born! He just kept spouting off all this garbage about my real father.''

Lane moaned softly.

Johnny Mack tightened his embrace. *Keep on holding me*, she silently pleaded. *Whatever you do, don't let go of me. I can't make it without you. I need you. Will needs you.*

"You said that Kent hurt Lillie Mae," the doctor prompted. "How did he hurt her?"

"When he wouldn't leave, she told me to go in the house. But when we started toward the door, he tried to stop us. He hit Lillie Mae so hard that she fell to the ground. I had to stop him."

Lane's breathing halted for a split second. Waiting. Uncertain. Afraid. Praying silently.

Will groaned with anger. "I—I took my baseball bat and hit him across his back and knocked him down. While he was lying on the patio moaning and cursing, I helped Lillie Mae get up. Then I told Kent that I wanted him to leave us alone and if he didn't, I'd kill him."

Lane bit down on her bottom lip to stifle her cries. And Johnny Mack kept on holding her.

"Do you remember what you did next?" Dr. Agee asked.

"I helped Lillie Mae to her room," Will said. "I was afraid she'd broken an arm or leg when she fell. She told me to lock the doors and call the police."

"But you didn't call the police, did you, Will?"

"No, I didn't. I went back outside to see if Kent had left."

"And was he gone?"

"No, he was still there. On the ground, where I'd left him. But he wasn't moaning and cursing. He wasn't moving. There was blood all over the place. Lots of blood. Kent was . . . he was dead. Somebody had smashed in his head. God, it was awful!"

"That's enough," Lane cried as she jerked free of Johnny Mack's hold and jumped to her feet. "Please, that's enough."

Johnny Mack got up, grabbed her and pressed her face against his chest. She clung to him, shaking uncontrollably.

"There was somebody else in the yard," Will continued, apparently oblivious to Lane's outburst. "I saw the shrubbery shivering. Somebody was hiding in the shrubbery."

"What shrubbery?" Dr. Agee asked.

"The shrubbery between our yard and Grandmother's yard. Somebody was crying." Will began rubbing his hands together. "I think it was me. I was crying."

"It's all right, Will. It's all right to cry."

Tears pooled in Will's eyes, and several drops trickled down his cheek. "I hated him! I hated him so much because he was so mean to Mama and me. But I didn't want him dead. I didn't!"

Will shivered as tears streamed down his face. Dr. Agee stood and motioned to Lane and Johnny Mack to come forward. Then she spoke quietly to Will.

"You can stop now, Will. You don't have to remember anymore. Do you hear me? You can bring your mind back to the present where you're safe and what happened to Kent is in the past."

Will took a deep, cleansing breath and glowered at the doctor. "I didn't kill him. I didn't kill Kent."

Lane rushed to her son and took him into her

arms. Johnny Mack encompassed both of them in his embrace.

A hushed stillness settled over the old house. The clock in the foyer struck the half hour. Lane pushed back the jet black strands of Will's hair that had fallen across his forehead. Her baby boy. Almost a man and yet still so much a child. He was safe, here in his room, in the home that had housed generations of Nobles. Glancing around the room, lit only from the light coming through the door from the hallway, she smiled as she remembered how they had redecorated this room together shortly before Will's thirteenth birthday. Will had changed the theme from a boy's room, with a toy box still stationed beneath the windows, to a teenager's room, with posters on the walls and copies of *Playboy* magazine hidden under the bed.

Today's session with Dr. Agee had revealed little more new information, yet Will had remembered enough to bring two extremely important facts to light. One: he hadn't killed Kent. And two: he had seen someone hiding in the shrubbery. But if Will had seen the murderer, undoubtedly the murderer hadn't seen him. Otherwise, Will's life would be in danger.

A second session was inevitable. And even then, it was possible Will wouldn't remember, and more sessions would be required to help him regain his complete memory. But knowing Will hadn't bludgeoned Kent to death was enough for now.

After kissing Will's cheek and tucking the sheet around him, Lane tiptoed out of his room, but left the door slightly ajar.

"Is he finally asleep?" Johnny Mack asked.

"Yes, finally." Lane sighed. "I think everyone's asleep except you and me. Lillie Mae might still be awake, even though she usually goes to bed early and rises early. We've all been a bit on edge since Will's session with Dr. Agee."

"Quinn went to bed over an hour ago, right after he returned from his dinner date with Nola."

"They certainly did take a liking to each other, didn't they?"

"I've yet to meet a woman who could resist Quinn Cortez once he pours on the charm."

"Something you two have in common."

"If I'm so damn charming, why couldn't I persuade you to eat any dinner?" He caressed her cheek with the back of his hand. "You haven't had a bite since breakfast."

"I suppose I've been too keyed up to eat." She stood on tiptoe, stretched up and draped her arms around Johnny Mack's neck. How wonderful to have him here, within arm's reach, at her beck and call. "Knowing that Will didn't kill Kent—"

"I want to believe as much as you do that what Will remembered today is exactly what happened, but Dr. Agee explained that it's possible for a patient to have a false memory, that there's no guarantee that things remembered under hypnosis are a hundred percent accurate."

"Please, don't play devil's advocate," Lane said. "Not now. Not tonight. Not when I know in my heart that what Will remembered is true. He didn't kill Kent."

"I agree. I don't think he did. But that poses another problem. We all know that Will probably saw the killer, and sooner or later, he's going to remember who it is. For your sake, we need for it to be sooner. Before you go to trial. I think we should take

Dr. Agee's advice and try another session as soon as Will is willing to . . ."

"All right. As soon as Will is willing."

"Okay, now that we have that settled, young lady, I'm taking you downstairs, and you're going to eat." Johnny Mack placed his hands on either side of her waist. "Even if I have to force feed you."

Lane rubbed her body seductively against his. She had never thought of herself as the aggressive or brazen type, but this man—and only this man— brought out the hussy in her. Today had turned out to be a very good day, and she wanted to celebrate. Celebrate the beginning of a breakthrough for Will. Celebrate Johnny Mack's return. Celebrate her awakening as a woman. Hell, she just wanted to celebrate being alive and in love. "I'd rather feed another appetite, wouldn't you?"

Johnny Mack groaned. "Ah, honey, you don't play fair." He disengaged her arms from around his neck, clasped her shoulders and shoved her back a couple of feet. "As much as I want to indulge in some hanky-panky, I'm not going to take you to my room and make mad, passionate love to you all night."

"You're not?"

"No. Not until you've eaten."

"Good grief." Lane threw up her hands in exasperation. "I give in." She grabbed his wrist and tugged. "Come on. Let's raid the refrigerator."

Thirty minutes later, they cleaned off the kitchen table, dumped their glasses, plates and silverware into the sink and returned the leftover ham, potato salad and Lemon Ice Box pie to the refrigerator. Lane watched while Johnny Mack squirted detergent into the sink and sprayed water over the dirty utensils.

"That's what I like to see," Lane said. "A man who's handy around the house."

Glancing over his shoulder, Johnny Mack blessed her with one of his breath-robbing smiles. "Oh, honey, you have no idea just how handy I can be."

She giggled. An honest to goodness giggle. She couldn't remember the last time she had actually felt so lighthearted, even if the sensation lasted only a moment before her mind reminded her of her troubles. Kent's murder. Will's amnesia. The upcoming trial. Her uncertain relationship with Johnny Mack.

"Hey, I don't like that frown," he said as he stacked the last glass on the drain board. "This has been a good day. I put the fear of God into James Ware, and Will remembered that he didn't kill Kent. So you should be smiling."

"Yes, I know. And I'm grateful." She shrugged. "I suppose I was just wishing that I didn't have the trial facing me and Will didn't have more sessions with Dr. Agee to go through and that the relaxed, happy feelings I've enjoyed this past half hour could last."

Johnny Mack wiped his wet hands off on the floral-print dish towel, and with his wickedly devastating smile broadening, he came toward her, his steps deliberately slow. "I think I know how I can make you even happier." He grabbed her by the waist and hauled her up against him. "And I promise that I'll do my best to make those good feelings last as long as possible."

When he took her into his arms and nuzzled her neck with his nose, she giggled again, but quickly shoved against his chest. "We can't . . . can't do . . . *something* in the kitchen. What if Lillie Mae were to wake and—"

He ended her protest with a kiss. Possessive and demanding. An all-consuming urgency. She tried to think rationally, to make some show of protest, but the longer he kissed her, the less she cared whether or not someone walked in on them. When he cupped her buttocks, lifted her up and pressed her against his erection, she stopped thinking altogether.

She clung to him, returning his kiss with equal passion. He backed her up against the wall and forced his hands beneath the waistband of her slacks. And while he caressed her hips and butt, she grasped his shoulders to brace herself. Bringing his hands up and out, he hurriedly unzipped her gabardine pants and tugged them down her hips and thighs. When the garment caught around her ankles, she raised one foot and then the other, then kicked her slacks aside. Johnny Mack lifted her so that she could wrap her legs around his hips. And all the while he continued kissing her.

She had never experienced anything this wild and free and totally exhilarating. Desire so strong she thought it would burn her alive controlled her actions. Since they had made love yesterday morning, thoughts of having sex with Johnny Mack again kept creeping into her consciousness, no matter how hard she tried to keep them at bay.

When he came up for air, his breathing ragged, he mumbled against her lips, "Maybe we'd better not finish this here."

With her legs around him and his lips wetting a path from her mouth to the vee opening of her blouse, he carried her toward the pantry. Using her behind as a battering ram, he shoved open the partially open pantry door and made his way inside. He placed her on the counter top that ran parallel from one floor-to-ceiling shelf to an identical one on the other wall. Without a word exchanged, he removed her panties, unzipped his pants and freed his sex. Lifting her again, he positioned her so that when she wrapped her legs back around him, he thrust up and into her. She keened with pleasure and held on to him when he raised and lowered her hips, creating unbearable friction as he moved in and out of her. Bouncing lunges. Hard, unsteady, undulating rhythm. Mouths devouring. Body attacking body with fierce need. Lust dominating every action.

The moment Lane felt the first tight pressure that signaled the onslaught of an orgasm, she clamped her nails into Johnny Mack's shoulders and whimpered his name.

"That's it, baby, give me what I want. Come for me."

He increased the tempo, hammering into her until she cried out and fell apart in his arms. Her climax hit her like a tidal wave. While the aftershocks rippled through her body, Johnny Mack jetted into her. Groaning, trembling, he held her tightly to his sweat-dampened body, until he had drained every ounce of energy from his own climax.

She eased her legs from around his hips and settled her feet on the floor, but kept her arms around his neck. As he swooped down to take her lips in another kiss, she lifted her face to his.

When he ended the kiss, she refused to release him. He slapped her bottom playfully and said, "Let's take this upstairs to my bed."

She could think of nothing she wanted more. But they weren't the only ones in the house, and they had already taken an enormous risk having sex in the pantry. What if she shared Johnny Mack's bed tonight and didn't wake in the morning before Will got up? What if her son discovered that she had stayed the night? How would he react? What would he think of her?

"If Will were to know that I—"

Johnny Mack placed his index finger over her lips. "This isn't some illicit affair we're having. And eventually we're going to have to tell Will how we feel about each other. But if you want to be discreet for now, then I'll make sure you're back in your own bed before daylight."

We're going to have to tell Will how we feel about each other. Wasn't that what he'd said? *But how do we feel about each other?* she wanted to scream. *If you love me, why don't you just say so?*

"I want to be discreet," she replied.

He grinned as he straightened his pants and zipped them, then bent down, picked up her discarded panties and handed them to her. "Come on."

He tugged on her hand, and she followed him out of the pantry and back into the kitchen. He lifted her blue gabardine slacks off the floor by the bar stool and held them out to her. She grabbed her slacks and slipped into them hurriedly.

"You go on up, honey," he told her. "I'll turn off the lights down here and double check to make sure the doors are locked and the security system is on. When I come upstairs, we'll take a shower together and then we'll—"

"If you start telling me what we're going to do, I'll never leave and we'll wind up back in the pantry."

"Then, get out of here before it's too late," he kidded.

With a contented smile on her face, Lane left him in the kitchen and headed up the back stairs. Just as she reached the landing, she heard a loud bang. Then a second blast quickly followed.

Her mind registered the sounds, and she made a reasonable assumption that the noise had come from a nearby car backfiring.

But suddenly she realized that the sound had been

caused by something else. Gasping for breath, she clutched the stair rail as adrenaline pumped through her body. The sound had been a gunshot. Whirling around, she raced down the stairs and back into the kitchen.

"Johnny Mack?"

No reply.

"Johnny Mack!"

She found him by the bay windows, sprawled out, lying facedown on the floor. Blood oozed from a bullet wound in his back and from a second wound in his arm.

Chapter 23

Lane felt as if she were going to throw up. Her stomach was tied in knots, her nerves were frazzled and her head throbbed. She gazed through the solid glass wall in the waiting room for the surgical intensive care unit at the Samuel Noble Memorial Hospital. The medical facility had been renamed in honor of her great-grandfather, who had donated a sizeable amount of money in the late nineteen-thirties for a new wing added to the original building. In the almost empty parking lot below, the tall security lights spread a muted, cream blush over the dark pavement and the neatly manicured shrubs and flowers planted in narrow, rectangular-shaped beds. The traffic light at the end of the street in front of the hospital flashed caution yellow.

Strange, she thought, how life went right on, unchanged, as if nothing significant had happened. The sun would rise in the east shortly. The streets would fill with traffic. The floor nurses would change shifts at seven. People would eat breakfast, take their children to school and go to work. Phones would ring, radios would blare out the latest tunes and billions of e-mail messages would be exchanged.

How was all that possible? Didn't anyone realize that nothing was the same? That life had been drastically altered? She felt as if the end of the world was approaching and only one thing could halt her personal Armageddon—Johnny Mack Cahill coming out of surgery alive. She had lost him once, but after fifteen long years he had come back to her. She couldn't lose him a second time. If he died. . . .

Who could have done such a reprehensible thing? Who had lurked outside her house, waiting for an opportunity to shoot Johnny Mack in the back?

Lane shuddered involuntarily as she remembered hearing the shots and finding Johnny Mack's still body lying on the kitchen floor. She had screamed loud enough to wake everyone in the house. While she had remained huddled on the floor by Johnny Mack, Lillie Mae had called for an ambulance. Lane had come to the hospital in the ambulance with him, while Quinn followed, with Lillie Mae and Will, and arrived at the emergency room seconds behind the ambulance.

"Mama?" Will came up behind Lane and wrapped his arms around her. "He's going to be all right. He has to be."

She patted Will's arms where they crisscrossed her waist. "I love him. I've never loved anyone else."

"I think he loves you, too," Will told her. "He sure acts like he does."

As Lane turned in her son's arms, she grasped his hands and offered him a weak smile. "He loves you, Will. Of that I'm certain. He wants to be a father to you, if you'll let him."

"If he . . ." Will pulled away from Lane, turned his back on her and faced the glass wall. "Dammit, why doesn't somebody come out here and tell us what's happening? He's been in surgery for nearly five hours. What's taking them so long?"

Lane laid her hand on Will's back. "I keep telling myself that no news is good news. We have to hold on to the hope that the doctors can save Johnny Mack."

Will swerved around to face Lane. "Who could have shot him? And why?"

"I've been asking myself that same question, and I haven't come up with an answer yet." But a couple of suspects came to mind. James Ware for one. And Miss Edith for another. Each of them knew how to use a rifle. Miss Edith was an avid skeet shooter, and after he had married her, James had begun attending shooting events with her.

"I want you two to sit down and try to rest." Holding two canned colas, Lillie Mae came up beside them. "Here"—she held out one to Lane and the other to Will—"I got y'all a Coke a piece. Figured y'all could use a little caffeine and some sugar. I know how when you get nervous, Miss Lane, you have a problem with nausea. A Coke will settle your stomach."

Lane accepted the cola. "Thank you, Lillie Mae. I do feel a bit queasy." She popped the lid and put the can to her lips. The cold, syrupy drink tasted good, and after several sips, her agitated stomach began to settle down a bit.

Just as Will opened his canned drink, Lane heard Quinn Cortez's voice coming from outside in the hallway. She had been so absorbed in her own misery that she hadn't said more than two words to Quinn in several hours. She had almost forgotten that he was there. But sometime in the past few minutes, he had left his chair in the corner of the waiting room and stepped out into the corridor.

"Can't your interrogation wait?" Quinn asked. "Lane's in no shape to answer any questions."

"All I need is a statement," Buddy Lawler said. "I've got an attempted murder investigation going on here, maybe even a murder investigation if Johnny Mack doesn't pull through."

"Dammit man, will you please lower your voice," Quinn demanded. "There happens to be a woman and a kid in there"—Quinn hiked his thumb toward the waiting room—"who don't need to hear any speculation about Johnny Mack dying."

"Look, Cortez, I have no intention of upsetting Lane or Will. But I have to ask Lane a few questions. My people have conducted an investigation at the house and come away with pretty much nothing, except a good guess that somebody stood outside Lane's kitchen and used a rifle to shoot Johnny Mack."

Lane handed her cola to Lillie Mae. "Will, you stay here with your grandmother."

"Looks like Buddy could show some decency and wait about questioning you," Lillie Mae said.

"He's just doing his job." Lane patted Lillie Mae's arm as she passed her and walked straight out into the hall where the two men were still arguing. "What do you need to ask me?" She looked directly at Buddy.

"I'm sure sorry about this, Lane."

Buddy sounded sincere, but she knew better. Noble's Crossing's chief of police had as much reason to despise Johnny Mack as Miss Edith or James. Maybe more. After all, he had been the ringleader in the gang who had nearly beaten Johnny Mack to death fifteen years ago. And he had been the one who had dumped him into the river.

"Did I hear you right, that you didn't find any evidence outside my house?" Lane asked.

Buddy shook his head. "No, ma'am, we didn't find a thing, except a spot outside the kitchen windows that looked like somebody had stomped on the marigolds planted in the flower beds."

"Then, you have no idea who shot Johnny Mack . . . in the back?"

"Sure don't." Buddy looked everywhere but at Lane. His eyes darted to the floor, to the ceiling, past her shoulder and even at Quinn. "How is Johnny Mack? Any word on his condition?"

"He's been in surgery for right at five hours," Quinn said. "We haven't heard a thing in three hours. A nurse told us then that the bullet wound in his arm wasn't too serious, but the bullet that went into his back collapsed one of his lungs and did some other internal damage."

"Well, that's too bad. I promise y'all that I'll do whatever I can to find the person responsible." Buddy glanced at Lane, but avoided prolonged eye-to-eye contact by letting his gaze wander. "Tell me exactly what happened tonight?"

"I was walking up the back stairs when I heard two shots. I ran down the stairs and saw Johnny Mack lying on the kitchen floor. He'd been shot in the back and in the arm. He was bleeding . . . there was blood on his shirt and on the floor." She gasped for air. Quinn put his arm around her shoulders. She breathed deeply—in and out, in and out—until she calmed. "I must have screamed really loud. Lillie Mae came running out of her room, and when she saw what had happened, she called 911. Within a couple of minutes, Will and Quinn came into the kitchen."

"Did you see anyone outside?" Buddy asked. "Even a shadow?"

"No, I didn't see anyone, but then my main concern was Johnny Mack."

"Of course." Buddy nodded. "Do you have any idea who might have shot him? I mean, do you have a good reason to suspect someone in particular. I know that Johnny Mack made a lot of enemies before he left town fifteen years ago, so there's probably more than one pissed-off husband whose wife Johnny Mack fu—er . . . fooled around with back then."

"Fifteen years is a long time to hold a grudge, don't you think?" Quinn asked.

"And you and I both know the real reason why Johnny Mack left town, don't we, Buddy?" Lane raised her voice just a fraction. "And it wasn't because some woman's husband had threatened him."

Buddy's face flushed, and sweat popped out on his forehead. "I'll need for you to come down to the station . . . later on . . . and sign a sworn statement. With you already being accused . . . well, it sure does look bad, your being found with a second dead body."

Lane gasped. Quinn's narrowed gaze bored into Buddy Lawler.

"Johnny Mack is still alive!" Lane said.

"Well, yeah, I know, but five hours in an operating room doesn't bode well for his recovery, now does it?"

Lane wanted to hit Buddy Lawler. Hit him repeatedly. Smash the asshole's face in! He was a cocky little son of a bitch who couldn't hide the pleasure he seemed to feel over the possibility that Johnny Mack might die.

"Have you finished questioning Ms. Graham?" Quinn asked. "If so, I suggest you leave. You aren't wanted here, Chief."

"I'm finished. For now."

Quinn wheeled Lane around and walked her back

into the waiting room, then closed the door behind them. "Lawler's counting on Johnny Mack dying, but he's going to be disappointed. It would take more than a couple of slugs to kill him. No way would he die and give so many people in Noble's Crossing that much satisfaction."

Lane chuckled softly. "You know him well, don't you? You know he's a survivor."

Quinn squeezed Lane's shoulders. "Got that damn straight."

The minute Lane sat on the tan vinyl chair just inside the doorway, Lillie Mae came over and offered her the canned cola. "Are you all right?"

Lane nodded. "I'm okay. But if Buddy Lawler had stayed another minute, he wouldn't have been okay. I'd have strangled the son of a bitch."

"What did he say to you to upset you?" Will asked as he approached.

"Oh, sweetie, it doesn't matter what Buddy said. And I didn't mean to curse. But I'm so angry, I could. . . . I don't care what anyone thinks; Johnny Mack is going to live." Lane grabbed the cola Lillie Mae offered, took several hefty swigs and then set the can on the wood-veneer table beside her chair. "Why don't y'all sit down?"

"I think I'll go downstairs and find a coffee machine," Quinn said. "I'm not much of a cola drinker. Besides, I need to walk off some of this pent-up energy." He glanced at Will. "Want to go with me?"

"No, thanks. I'll stay with—" Will halted mid-sentence as he stared past Quinn.

"Ms. Graham?" A short, stout, blond nurse stood in the open doorway.

Lane shot to her feet. "I'm Mrs. Graham."

"Dr. Gordon will be in to talk to you in just a few minutes," the nurse said.

"How's Johnny Mack?" Lane asked.

"Mr. Cahill is out of surgery and holding his own."

A collective sigh of relief resonated throughout the room. Lane's stomach flip-flopped. When Quinn slapped Will on the back, the two grinned at each other.

Lillie Mae said, "Thank you, Lord."

A couple of minutes later, Dr. Gordon spoke to them briefly, updating them on Johnny Mack's condition and explaining, in layman's terms, the surgery and its aftermath. Once Lane heard the words, *There's every reason to believe Mr. Cahill will have a complete recovery,* the doctor's voice seemed to fade away as did the rest of the world. Nothing else mattered. The man she loved was going to live!

"The man has nine lives!" Edith Ware complained, as she clawed her nails up and down the arm of the Duncan Phyfe sofa on which she perched. "Obviously, he can't be killed."

"Seems you're right, my dear," James said. "The man is indestructible. You can't beat him to death. You can't drown him. And apparently he's impervious to bullets."

James had assumed that Johnny Mack would be dead by now, but instead he was recovering quite nicely in the local hospital's SICU ward. But even if Johnny Mack was still a threat to him, he could use the man's near-death experience to his advantage. While Edith and Buddy were so consumed with Johnny Mack, it was the perfect time to put his plan to leave town into action.

"If he'd died, it would have made all our lives

easier," Buddy said. "A dead man doesn't tell any tales."

"If he ever breathes a word about . . ." Edith lowered her voice. "About Kent having abused Mary Martha, I'll find a way to shut him up. When I think of the scandal . . . the shame . . . what people will think and say about Kent and Mary Martha. About me."

James guffawed, amazed that his dear wife could actually be concerned about scandal and shame, especially when her son's murder was front-page news. "The Graham family seems to have thrived on scandal. After all, Mr. John had a reputation as a womanizer and a hell-raiser. And you, my dear, are notorious for being a first-class bitch."

"The liquor has made you quite bold." Edith sneered at her husband. "But I warn you, be careful what you say."

James downed the last drops of whiskey from the glass he held, then crossed the room and poured himself another drink. Disregarding Edith's warning, he continued his assessment of the Graham family. "Of course, you've done a rather good job of keeping your . . . er . . . dalliances discreet. A few people may suspect that you have a penchant for younger men, especially after you married me, but they don't know the real truth, do they—that you've been whoring around for years with guys young enough to be your son."

"Shut the hell up!" Buddy lunged toward James.

"Stop it. Both of you." Edith stood, her head regal, her spine stiff. "Fighting among ourselves is stupid."

"My goodness, Buddy, you certainly did seem to take personal offense at my accusations. You aren't by any chance fucking my wife, are you?"

"You're drunk, James," Buddy said. "Why don't you just shut up before I knock you on your ass."

James found the situation ludicrous. But then his whole life had become a travesty. Sometimes he felt as if he were trapped inside an insane asylum. All he wanted, all he had wanted for several years now, was to escape, to run away with Arlene, before he succumbed to the lunacy that plagued this house.

"So that's the way it is," James said. "You can't screw Mary Martha, so you've settled for screwing her mama."

Buddy rammed his fist into James's face. James went flying backward, into the wall. As he slumped over, slid down the oak paneling and his butt hit the floor, he thought he heard Edith cursing.

"I didn't hurt him much," Buddy said. "But if he ever says anything about Mary Martha again, I'll kill him."

James wiped his mouth and felt something sticky. Blood. His lip was bleeding. And he would probably have a big bruise on his jaw. Damn, Buddy might be a small man, but he had a wicked right cross.

"Are you all right, James?" Edith asked.

"I'll be fine." Bracing himself by placing his hands behind him on the wall, James managed to stand. "I suppose I went a bit far, didn't I? And for that I apologize. Just the liquor talking, you know."

Get out of here, James told himself. *Leave the room before you spout off again and Buddy winds up knocking your lights out permanently.* The good police chief had a mean temper. And when it came to Mary Martha, he was totally unreasonable.

"Think I'll go out to the kitchen for an ice pack," James told them. "You will excuse me, won't you?"

Buddy glowered. Edith simply nodded. James breathed a sigh of relief and headed toward the kitchen. While he was rummaging in the freezer for ice cubes, his cellular phone rang. For just a minute, he thought about not answering, in case it was Penny inquiring why he hadn't come in to work today. Or had she already called? He couldn't remember. He had definitely consumed too much alcohol this morning.

After removing the phone from his shirt pocket, he flipped it open and placed it to his ear. "Mayor Ware," he said.

"Jamie?"

"Arlene?" He spoke her name in a hushed whisper.

"I just had to call you when I heard about Johnny Mack getting shot. Is it true?"

"Yes, it's true. Last night, someone shot him through the kitchen window at Lane's house. But the bastard's still alive, and I'm in as much hot water as ever, maybe more."

"Oh, Jamie, you—you didn't shoot him, did you?"

Chapter 24

Lane lay across her bed and listened to the rain dripping from the roof, a soft pitter-patter blending with the cadence of the slow, steady downpour. Outside her windows the sky was gray and gloomy. A September steaminess filled the air, heat and moisture combining as it does only in the South. This was languid, lazy weather that sapped a person's strength and induced sleepiness. Lane had promised herself that she would take a nap while Will was at school and Lillie Mae was at the grocery store. Quinn had taken a flight to Dallas three days ago to attend to some urgent business, and they didn't expect him back until the weekend. So she and Johnny Mack were alone in the house.

Lane hadn't been sleeping much at night, mostly tossing and turning as she thought about her upcoming trial. Less than two weeks away. And they were no closer to discovering Kent's real murderer than the police were to apprehending a suspect in Johnny

Mack's shooting. To hear Buddy Lawler tell it, the shooter might as well have been a ghost, for all the evidence he had left. Not one clue, except the bullets taken from Johnny Mack's body. Identified as .30 caliber, 180 grams, the bullets, according to ballistics tests, had been fired from a bolt-action Remington 700. An Alabama deer hunter's weapon of choice. T. C. Bedloe had commented that the shooter must have been an experienced gunman to have gotten off two shots so quickly. Of course, in a town where over half the men were avid hunters, that didn't narrow the field much.

During the two weeks since Johnny Mack's return home from the hospital, she had smothered him with tender, loving care, and Lillie Mae had pampered him like a baby. Trying to deal with a man accustomed to living an active life, who had suddenly been forced into inactivity, was like attempting to tame a wild beast. He growled and grumbled and often roared with rage. Lane understood that a great deal of his frustration centered on her—the fact that he had yet to accomplish his objective and save her from standing trial for a murder she hadn't committed.

Of course, they were all worried about Will and concerned about his determination to remember everything that had happened the day Kent died. He had undergone three hypnosis sessions the week when Johnny Mack was in the hospital, but when all three attempts failed to erase the last fragments of his amnesia, Dr. Agee had suggested taking a break. She had told them that Will was pushing himself too hard. And Lane knew why. Not only was her son desperate to save her, but he believed that if he could remember the person he'd seen hiding in the shrubbery the day of Kent's death, then they would discover not only Kent's murderer, but the identity of the man or woman who had shot Johnny Mack.

One good thing had come from the shooting— Will had been spending more time with his father, and the two were growing closer with each passing day. Only yesterday, she had walked past Johnny Mack's room, where father and son were playing chess, and she had overheard Will say, "I'm glad you're my father and not Kent." She had gone straight to the bathroom and cried.

To make matters worse, the sexual tension between Johnny Mack and her hadn't lessened any simply because he was recuperating from surgery. She suspected that his mood would improve if he could release some of his pent-up energy. She knew for a fact that if she could be with him, make love with him and fall asleep in his arms, she could finally get some much-needed rest.

"No time like the present," she mumbled to herself, as she hopped off the bed and rummaged around in her closet, looking for just the right thing to wear. Hmm-mm. What did a lady wear to a seduction? Ah-ha! She had found it—a lightweight, gold silk robe. She had bought the item on a whim, loving the look and the feel of it. But she'd never worn it. There hadn't been an appropriate occasion. Not until now.

Lane hurriedly stripped out of her cotton slacks and blouse, then removed her underwear and slipped into the robe. After belting it tightly, she left her room and walked down the hall. Although Johnny Mack was able to be up and about, the doctor insisted that he get plenty of rest, so he often stayed in his room until ten or after most mornings. She opened his door and peered inside. With the wooden window shutters closed, the room lay in semidarkness. Pinpricks of sunlight escaping from between the slats spotlighted tiny, dancing dust particles in the air.

Wearing only a pair of old, faded jeans, Johnny Mack lay sprawled across the half-canopy bed, atop the crumpled tan sheets and striped coverlet. He rested flat on his stomach, with his eyes closed and his breathing steady and even.

She crept inside, and with every step she took, she expected him to open his eyes. But he didn't. The closer she got to the bed, the more erratic her heart beat. She felt like a brazen hussy. Attempting a seduction was totally out of character for her. But that had been the old Lane, the sexually repressed Lane, the Lane who had buried her sexual desires years ago. But this was the new Lane, the Lane who was Johnny Mack Cahill's lover.

As she stood beside the bed, she gazed at this magnificent man, taking inventory from the top of his head to the heels of his big feet. Broad shoulders. Wide back, marred only by the healing scar left by the surgery to remove the bullet that had almost killed him. Large, muscular arms. Slim hips. Tight butt. And long, long legs. His skin was naturally dark, but recent days spent in the sun by the pool had burnished his flesh to a light copper shade.

He was a beautiful man.

There had been a time when he had been a beautiful boy, but back then his beauty had been, as the old saying goes, only skin deep. He had been a wild, untamed young man filled with anger and rage and a need to strike out at everyone around him. He'd done some *almost* unforgivable things in the past. But she had forgiven him—always. Because she had loved him with the foolish ardor of a teenager. The fact that he had been the town bad boy had simply added to his appeal. As an adult she had come to realize that women were usually drawn to the rascals, the rogues, the hell-raisers. The men who beat their chests and roared at the top of their lungs. As a general rule, such men made unforgettable lovers, but bad life mates.

Lane eased to the very edge of the bed and lifted her hand over his back. Dare she touch him and arouse the sleeping beast?

Johnny Mack was still Johnny Mack, and yet he was a very different man today. The outward beauty went beyond the surface. This wonderful man lying before her was as beautiful inside, in his heart and soul, as he was in physical appearance. He had matured into a fine man, into a decent human being. Although the untamed elements of his personality still existed, he was no longer unredeemable.

When she leaned closer, her hand within inches of caressing him, Johnny Mack flipped over, grabbed her and tumbled her onto the bed with him. Lane cried out, startled by his lightning-fast maneuver. Pinning her hands above her head, he straddled her hips.

"I thought you were asleep," she said breathlessly as she gazed up into his black eyes.

"And I was beginning to wonder just how long you were going to stand there before you made your move." He gazed down at her and smiled, that wicked, bone-melting grin that had been the ruin of many a good woman.

"What move?" She playfully twisted beneath him.

He laughed, a low, throaty chuckle. "Don't play innocent with me." Still gripping her wrists with one hand, he reached down with his other hand to loosen the belt of her silk robe.

Lane sucked in her breath when her robe slipped just a fraction, parting in the middle enough to reveal a line of flesh from chest to belly button. Johnny

Mack lowered his hips so that his erection pressed against her mound.

He groaned. "Where's Lillie Mae?"

"At the grocery store." Lane wiggled, and her robe opened another couple of inches, enough so that the material barely covered her nipples.

"Then, we're alone in the house?"

"All alone."

He chuckled again and bent his head to kiss her. Demanding. A release of barely constrained desire. An eruption of need too long denied. She squirmed and bucked and moaned, but he held her hands tightly, above her head, refusing to allow her to touch him. And she needed to touch him. Wanted to touch him. Had to touch him or she would lose her mind.

When he finally released her mouth, she sucked in air, as did he. They stared at each other, their eyes bright with passion.

"Let me go." She struggled, trying to free her bound wrists. "Please, Johnny Mack. I wanted to make love to you. I had planned to. . . . Since you're still recuperating, I thought I would give you pleasure without risking your getting hurt and reopening your incision. And then you grabbed me and—"

He silenced her with a maneuver that created shivers deep within her. His nose shoved aside her robe and revealed one pebble-hard nipple. "Look at you," he said, his voice thick with desire. "Your nipples are puckered and begging for my mouth."

"You have to be careful. You aren't completely recovered yet."

Using his index finger, he traced a line from her throat to her navel. She drew in a deep breath. Just the merest touch and she was lost. His finger slid farther, parting her robe as it went south and exposed, inch by inch, more and more of her flesh. When the robe parted completely and fell to either side of her body, his hand cupped her mound, and she lifted her hips to accommodate him.

In self-defense, before she lost complete control, she made a bold move. "You can't make love to me."

"What?" His gaze met hers, a startled expression on his face.

"I want to make love to you. I've never. . . . I need to do this," she told him. "I've dreamed of looking at and touching and tasting every inch of your body. You have no idea how much I want to—"

"Stop talking and start showing me."

With that devilish grin making him totally irresistible, Johnny Mack released her hands, then shoved himself up and off her. Before she could grab him, he rose to his feet and shucked off his jeans. The sight of him standing there in all his male glory took Lane's breath away. He was big, hard and dangerously male. When she reached out for him, he avoided her touch, then crawled into bed beside her and folded his arms behind his head. Pivoting around so that she faced him, Lane saw that he was spread out before her, waiting.

Now what? a nagging inner voice asked. *This is what you wanted, what you've dreamed of. He's yours to do with as you will.* A shudder of pure sexual energy surged through her. She sensed a heady feeling of power.

Reversing their former positions, Lane straddled his hips and lowered herself just enough to kiss him. She started with his forehead and soon covered his face with tiny pecks. Zeroing in on his mouth, she nibbled and sucked and finally invaded. He responded by engaging her tongue in a damp, frenzied duel. When she ended the kiss, she moved her lips down his chin, down his neck, over his chest and stopped when she reached one tiny male nipple. She laved first one nipple and then the other, while she laid her hand over one of his hairy thighs and began caressing him. Slowly, maddeningly, she touched him everywhere.

He lay beneath her, silent and barely moving, but she noted that he was gripping the bedspread with both hands. The more she kissed and touched, the hotter the fire within her grew. She ached unbearably as moisture collected between her legs, between the hot folds of her femininity. But she wouldn't give in, wouldn't seek her own pleasure. Not yet. Not when the pièce de résistance lay before her. Untouched. Unconquered. Begging for her attention.

She spread his legs and eased her open palms down his hips. Then she brought her hands together in the center of his body, threading her fingers through the black hair that surrounded his jutting sex. Touching his scrotum gently, she caressed his balls all over, then leisurely turned her attention to his penis, pumping him slowly, rhythmically. She wet her fingertips and petted the bulbous tip, then ran a moist streak from top to shaft.

By his hard, deep groans, she could tell that he was finding it difficult to remain in control. When she replaced her hand with her mouth, Johnny Mack's hips came up off the bed. To soothe him, she returned her attention to his upper body. After he settled back down, she eased slowly, attentively south again. Several times she repeated the back and forth, upper and lower torso torture until she felt heady with power.

As Lane licked his shaft, she circled the root and slipped her hand up and down, adding just the right amount of pressure. He grew bigger and harder. He moaned and shivered.

"Ah, babe, you're killing me!" He threaded his

fingers through her hair, then grasped her head and held her in place.

She licked and sucked, bringing him almost to the brink, then released him. Using his hand on her head, he urged her to return to her task. And she did. Only this time she slid her mouth from the tip to the base of his penis. With each undulating movement she tightened her mouth. As if he were afraid she would stop, he pushed her head back and forth, trying to take control, fucking her mouth. But her lips, her tongue, her adoration of his sex gave her complete power over him. And when he came, jetting his release, she savored the pleasure she had given him.

As she released him and licked her lips, his animalistic groans excited her. She crawled over him and snuggled to his side. He lifted her just enough to wrap his arm around her.

After kissing her forehead, he smoothed his hand down over one breast and then the other. She shuddered when he pinched her nipples.

"You're a wild woman," he said. "My wild woman."

Bracing himself on his elbow, he leaned over and suckled her breast. Tingles of pleasure radiated from her nipples to her core. While he continued laving her breasts, he maneuvered his hand down over her belly and between her thighs. Using his fingertips, he petted her, his strokes gradually becoming more intense. Tightly wound tension broke free, into orgasmic fragments as Lane climaxed. Quickly. With earth-shattering intensity. As sensation after sensation sizzled through Lane's body, Johnny Mack rose up and moved over her. While the aftershocks still rippled within her, he thrust deeply, to the hilt. Big. Hard. Hot.

He possessed her completely. Leaving no room for anything or anyone else. And Lane knew that this—

being Johnny Mack's woman—was what she had been born for.

Will watched his parents sitting together on the sofa and suspected they would like to be alone together. Although he had never actually been in love himself, he figured he was old enough to know the signs. His mama and Johnny Mack were mooning over each other, exchanging odd looks and quick little smiles. And he realized that they were trying awfully hard not to touch each other.

He could go up to his room and leave them alone. He doubted they would even know he was gone. But just as he started to get up, Johnny Mack spoke.

"I've got cabin fever this evening. How about since it's stopped raining, we take a walk down by the river?"

"Great idea," Lane replied. "After that big supper Lillie Mae cooked, I could use a walk."

Johnny Mack stood, held out his hand to Lane and pulled her up onto her feet. They gazed at each other for a brief moment; then Lane turned to Will.

"Want to go with us?" she asked.

"Nah, I think I'll watch TV. You two go ahead."

"If Lillie Mae gets home from her prayer meeting before we get back, tell her not to worry, that we'll be in the house by dark," Lane said.

"I'll tell her. Maybe she won't worry too much." Will shook his head. "She's convinced that whoever shot Johnny Mack is going to try again."

"Lillie Mae worries too much," Johnny Mack said. "But she has a point. Until we find out who killed Kent, we're all in danger. Somebody wants your mother convicted of a crime she didn't commit. They want me to stop nosing around and put an end to the private investigation. But I figure they know by now that even if I'm dead, they can't stop the truth from coming out. Eventually.''

"If the person who murdered Kent knows that I've gotten some of my memory back, that it's only a matter of time before I remember who was hiding in the shrubbery, then I guess that makes me a prime target, too, huh?''

"Oh, Will.'' Lane sighed. "No one outside the family knows about your sessions with Dr. Agee.''

"Maybe not, but whoever was hiding in the shrubbery that day knows I saw them. I'm surprised they haven't—''

"As long as no one else knows that your memory is returning, then you're safe,'' Johnny Mack said. "But I've been considering hiring private security for all of us, when Buddy pulls his officers off duty. I was surprised that he posted someone at the hospital and then here at the house for the past two weeks.''

"Do you think we need bodyguards?'' Lane asked.

Johnny Mack grabbed her hand and entwined their fingers. "Yes, I do. And to be honest, I've already contacted Wyatt Foster, and he's making arrangements to send some trained professionals for around-the-clock surveillance of the house. And I'd like someone close to Will at all times, to watch over him.'' Johnny Mack glanced at Will. "Is that going to be all right with you?''

"You really do think I'm in danger, don't you? You believe that whoever shot you might try to kill me.''

"I don't want to take any chances. We're dealing with a murderer. Someone beat Kent to death. And I'm fairly certain that someone killed Jackie and made it look like a suicide. If I hadn't pulled through, I would have been murder victim number three. Someone like that won't hesitate to kill again if they feel threatened."

"And my regaining my memory is a major threat if the killer finds out," Will said. "Are you sure it's safe for you and Mama to take a walk?"

"I think we're relatively safe in the daylight," Johnny Mack assured him. "Our killer probably isn't going to take any chances on giving himself away and being seen, especially not by the policeman out front. If and when he makes his next move, he'll probably do it at night."

"He killed Kent in broad daylight," Will reminded them.

"Yeah, but there wasn't a policeman keeping an eye on the house that day, was there?"

Will shrugged. "You two go take your walk. It'll be sundown in thirty minutes or so."

"Are you sure you don't want to go with us?" Lane smiled warmly.

"Nah. Y'all go on."

Will picked up the remote and switched on the television, then waved goodbye as his parents exited the room. Just as they walked through the door, Will noticed Johnny Mack slip his arm around Lane's waist.

Did he like seeing his mother and Johnny Mack together? Was he comfortable with the thought that something permanent might come out of their relationship? Yeah, he supposed he was okay with it. After all, he couldn't remember ever seeing his mother so totally alive, certainly not when she had been married to Kent. No matter how happy she had been at times, he'd known something was fundamentally wrong. Even as a kid he had sensed that something wasn't quite right with his mother. Now he knew what had been missing from her life all those years. Johnny

Mack Cahill. He doubted his mother could ever be truly happy without the man.

And it wasn't as if he.hated Johnny Mack anymore. Heck, he didn't even dislike him. Whatever he had done in the past, Johnny Mack was certainly trying his best to make amends now. You had to admire a guy who could own up to his mistakes and make a real effort to right the wrongs in his life.

The telephone ringing broke Will's concentration and released him from thoughts about his father and the man's relationship with him and his mother. He got up, leaned over and picked up the cordless phone from where it had been left on the coffee table.

"Hello," he said.

"Oh, thank goodness you answered the phone, Will."

"Aunt Mary Martha?"

"I need your help." His aunt's voice quivered with excitement. "Please, come over to the house. Meet me outside in the garden."

The last time he had seen his aunt in the hospital, after her suicide attempt, she'd been reticent and regretful, but now she was talking hurriedly, her words practically running togther. "Where's Grandmother? Does she know you're calling me? And don't you have a new nurse? Where is she?"

"Mother and James are having dinner," Mary Martha said. "I had mine on a tray in my room. And that cow of a nurse Mother hired ate with me, and after she stuffed herself, she fell asleep in her chair. I slipped down the back stairs and crept by Mrs. Russell into the living room. That's where I'm calling you from now. I must see you, Will. It's urgent."

"What's wrong? Why do you need to see me?"

"It's about your father . . . about Kent. He isn't dead, Will. Your father isn't dead."

"Now, Aunt Mary Martha, you know he is. You went to his funeral. Don't you remember?"

"That wasn't Kent in the casket. It was someone who just looked like him. I tell you, Will, your father is alive. And now the three of us can be together, the way we were supposed to be."

Will groaned silently. His poor aunt's mental condition seemed to seesaw from a theatrical high to an equally melodramatic low. Being delusional wasn't anything new for her. Ever since he was a small child, he had felt compelled to pacify her, something his father had encouraged him to do.

"You stay right where you are and I'll come over immediately," Will said.

"No, no. You must meet me in the garden. I don't want anyone to know you're here. And you must promise me that you won't tell Lane that you're coming to see me. This must be our little secret."

"All right. I'll meet you in the garden in a few minutes."

"Thank you, darling. I knew my baby boy would come to me if I needed him."

Manipulating Mary Martha had been easy. Planting a few seeds was all that had been necessary for them to take root in her fertile imagination. Just hinting that Kent was still alive and that he wanted to see Will achieved the sought-after goal. Will knew who murdered Kent, even if that memory was temporarily suppressed. They thought they were so smart. They believed that no one knew about the Chicago psychiatrist. But there were ways to find out whatever a person needed to know. Apparently Will had not regained his memory of that day—that hot, humid afternoon when a drunken Kent had finally met his fate.

Johnny Mack posed a threat, one that still existed. Trying to kill him had been an irrational, emotional decision. Acting on impulse had been stupid. Will posed the greatest danger. If at all possible, the boy had to be dealt with tonight. Killing Will would upset Mary Martha, but perhaps a way could be found to protect her. After all, there were times when she believed that Kent was still alive, so maybe she could be convinced that Will had simply been sent away and would one day return.

Ah, there they are now—Mary Martha and Will. In the garden. Talking.

You must play things by ear. Wait and watch. And when the opportunity arises, take it. Strike quickly and then hide the evidence.

They're on the move, going down the pathway that leads toward the river. Follow them. Stay a discreet distance behind.

Ah, that's it, Mary Martha, lead him away from the house. Get him close enough to the river and I can drown him.

Dammit, they're stopping by the tool shed! Hide and listen. Find a way to distract Mary Martha, then kill Will.

"I tell you, your father is alive." Mary Martha gripped Will's hands in hers. "He always liked to play games. Naughty little games. They were our secret. But I can tell you about them. You're my baby." She reached up and caressed his face. "Mine and Kent's baby."

"Aunt Mary Martha, think about what you're saying. Kent was your brother. I'm your nephew."

"You're not my nephew. That's what they wanted me to believe, but I knew better. They told me my baby was dead, but you're not dead, Will. You're alive."

Did she honestly believe that Will was her baby? Had she lived in that crazy, delusional world for so long that she would never return to reality? Maybe believing Will was the child that she had aborted fifteen years ago comforted her and allowed her moments of sanity. If that were the case, then how would she react to his death?

It can't be helped.

If only Will didn't have to die. But he did. There was no other choice. He couldn't be allowed to remember. The murders and attempted murders were adding up. Such a shame. But a person did what a person had to do. In the name of love.

"You must help me find your father," Mary Martha said. "Then the three of us can be together for ever and always."

"I'm going to take you back to the house," Will told her as he clasped her hand. "We'll find Grandmother and—"

She jerked away from him and ran toward the side door of the old brick building, which had once been a carriage house. "He may be hiding in the tool shed. We used to play down here when we were children. And later on, we came here to be alone. We'd play games and . . . I'll bet he's waiting inside for us."

Will chased Mary Martha and caught up with her just as she reached the door. "Let me go inside and see if Kent's here, and if he's not, then we'll go back to the house and talk to Grandmother."

"All right," she readily agreed. "But I'm sure he's in there. Waiting for us."

Now was the opportunity to strike. The carriage entrance was at the front of the shed. Just go in that way. While Mary Martha waits for Will at the side door.

Dark and dank and creepy. A ramshackle old building that should have been demolished years ago. The only illumination came from the two open doors. Will was making a great show of searching for Kent. Playing games with his aunt. Pacifying her. The boy had always been kind to Mary Martha. Such a pity he had to die.

Being prepared always paid off. The small iron rod picked up out of the garbage made a perfect weapon. Creeping slowly, quietly. Don't breathe. Don't make a sound. Strike. Now!

Ah, that had been easy. The boy lay on the ground, unconscious. Can't leave him here. Don't have time to bury the body. But they'll search for him. Can't leave him uncovered.

"Will, is he there? Is Kent in there with you?" Mary Martha called from outside the shed. "Does he want me to come in or are y'all coming out?"

How to hide the body? Glancing around, up and down and—that's it. Above. The old rowboat hanging from ancient ropes attached to the ceiling.

"Will, why don't you answer me?" Mary Martha asked.

Hurry. Can't waste time. She'll come in here and find him. Cut the ropes. Let the hull fall on top of him and cover his body.

Grabbing hold of Will brought a startling revelation. The boy wasn't dead!

"If you don't answer me right this minute, I'm coming in there. Do you hear me, Will?" Mary Martha warned.

Where was that damn iron rod? Dropped somewhere on the floor. But where? No time to find it.

Rags. Dirty rags in the wheelbarrow. Hog-tie and gag the boy. Hide him away and come back later to finish the job.

Quickly. Do it quickly. Take those rusty old hedge shears and cut through the ropes that hold the wooden boat to the ceiling. We're far enough away from the house that no one, except Mary Martha, will hear. Once it's done, then you can deal with her.

Chapter 25

"Will isn't here, Lane," Edith said. "What made you think he came over here tonight?"

"He left us a note saying that he was going to see Mary Martha."

"Why did he have to leave a note? Where were you?"

"Johnny Mack and I took a walk, and when we returned to the house, we found Will's note on the kitchen table." Lane glanced over her shoulder at Johnny Mack, who stood directly behind her. "We've been home over an hour and Lillie Mae's back from her prayer meeting. It's dark outside now and I'm worried. If he's not there with y'all, then where is he?"

"I have no idea, but I can assure you that I haven't seen him tonight, but . . ." Deep breath.

"But what? Dammit, Edith, if you know where Will is—"

"I don't know where he is, but it is possible that he was with Mary Martha tonight. You see . . . well, she got away from Mrs. Bryant, her new nurse. As soon as I can find a replacement, I'm firing that incompetent creature. She dozed off to sleep after supper and didn't realize Mary Martha was gone.''

''I assume you found Mary Martha. Is she all right?'' Lane asked.

''We found her in the backyard, several feet outside the garden. She was totally incoherent. She kept rambling about Kent. James helped me get her back into the house, and Mrs. Bryant gave her an injection.''

''Do you think Will could have been with her?''

''I don't know, but I suppose it's possible. However, I don't think he would have left her outside alone, do you?''

Lane bit down on her bottom lip. Of course not. Will would have taken care of Mary Martha. ''No, he wouldn't have left her.''

''Perhaps he changed his mind about coming over here and decided to take a walk himself. Have you checked the yard or—''

''Johnny Mack has covered the entire yard.''

''You're seriously worried about him, aren't you?''

''Yes, I am.'' Lane took a deep breath. ''If Will shows up at your house, would you please have him call me immediately.''

''Certainly. And when he comes home, let me know.'' Edith paused. ''I realize Will's not my grandson, but I still care deeply for him.''

''Yes. I know. Thank you.'' Lane replaced the receiver and turned into Johnny Mack's waiting arms. ''They haven't seen him.''

''What good is that policeman sitting out there in his car''—Lillie Mae inclined her head toward the front of the house—''if Will can just up and disappear like that?'' She snapped her fingers.

''The man's probably asleep, just the way Mary Mar-

tha's new nurse was when she sneaked away from
her.'' Lane left Johnny Mack's arms and began pacing
the floor. Where was Will? Had something happened
to him? Had the killer somehow discovered that Will's
memory was returning?

"We know that someone from Miss Edith's house
phoned Will.'' Johnny Mack pointed to the caller ID
on the telephone. "My guess is that Mary Martha
called him.''

"He never refuses her when she asks for him.''
Lane stopped pacing. "If he didn't go to see Mary
Martha, where is he? What could have happened to
him?''

"I think we should get that policeman in here and
he can call for help,'' Lillie Mae said.

"I agree,'' Johnny Mack said. "I'd like the idea of
involving the police better if Buddy Lawler wasn't the
chief, but we need help searching for Will. And we
need it now.''

"Go get him,'' Lane said. "Please. We have to do
something. I'm slowly going out of my mind.''

When Johnny Mack headed for the front door,
Lillie Mae grabbed Lane's hand and squeezed.

No way to finish the job. Not with Johnny Mack
and Lane snooping around along the row of shrubbery that separated the Graham and Noble estates.
Don't fret. Nobody's going to find Will. Mary Martha's
in no condition to tell anyone that she saw him
tonight. And when she comes to herself, she probably
won't remember anything. Even if she does, you can
always chalk her accusations up to her mental condition. Just say she had to be imagining things. But if
she tells them that Will is in the old carriage house,
they might look. You must return and get Will before

morning. Kill him and toss him into the river. And if you're lucky, his body won't ever be found.

Dawn spread across the eastern horizon in a glorious pink light. People milled around on the grounds of the adjoining Noble and Graham estates. Police officers. Sheriff's deputies. Neighbors. Everyone taking part in the search for Will. Lane hugged her arms around her waist as the cool morning breeze wafted up from the river. Johnny Mack glanced at her, and it was all he could do not to rush to her and take her into his arms. They had spent endless hours scouring the neighborhood together, neither of them concerned about their own welfare, caring only about their son. If anything had happened to Will, he didn't think Lane could bear it. Her whole world had revolved around her son for the past fourteen years. She had sacrificed so much for Will. It wouldn't be fair to her or to him or to Will, if—No, dammit! He couldn't think that way. He couldn't allow himself to believe the worst.

Will is alive, he kept telling himself. *He cannot be dead!*

"We're bringing in the bloodhounds," Sheriff Larry Carroll said. "I offered to bring 'em in earlier, but Buddy thought we could locate the boy without using 'em." Larry removed his cap and scratched his glistening bald head. "Sure does have me stumped. We found footprints in the mud all over the place, and we've searched the grounds here at the Grahams' and over at the Noble place, too; but we haven't found a clue to help us find Will. It's as if he just up and disappeared. Poof."

"If we don't find him by morning, we'll call in some

divers and search the river behind Magnolia Avenue,''
Sergeant T. C. Bedlow interrupted.

"Will you keep your voice down," Johnny Mack
said. "Will's mother is right over there, and the last
thing she needs is to hear speculation that Will's body
might be in the river."

"Sorry, Mr. Cahill." T. C. looked downright embarrassed. "I sure don't want to upset Miss Lane. We
all think highly of her, you know, despite her being
accused of Kent Graham's murder."

Before Johnny Mack could respond, he heard a
series of mournful howls, the low, throaty yelping of
hunting dogs. One of the sheriff's deputies handled
the leashed pack with expert ease.

"There's them dogs now," Larry Carroll said.
"That bunch is the best trackers around. They belong
to Old Man Farlan. If Will is anywhere around these
parts, they'll sniff him out."

"We'll need something that belongs to the boy,"
T. C. said. "How about I ask Lillie Mae to fetch us a
piece of Will's clothing. We don't need to bother
Miss Lane."

"Fine," Johnny Mack agreed.

When he noticed Buddy Lawler talking to Lane,
he excused himself and hurried over to her. Buddy
had been on the scene all night, issuing orders and
sending out groups who had gone from door to door
throughout the areas closest to Magnolia Avenue.

"I'm sorry that Mary Martha hasn't been any help
to us," Buddy said. "She got so hysterical when Miss
Edith questioned her about Will a little while ago
that her nurse had to give her another sedative."

"Poor Mary Martha." Lane glanced up when she
saw Johnny Mack approaching, then held out her
hand to him.

"Buddy, Sheriff Carroll tells me that you asked him

to wait about bringing in the bloodhounds. Why did you want to wait?'' Johnny Mack grasped Lane's hand and pulled her to his side.

"I felt certain we could find Will without using those damn yapping dogs. And''—he glanced meaningfully at Lane—"I was concerned that Lane would believe we thought Will was dead if we brought in the hounds.'' Buddy removed a handkerchief from his back pocket and wiped the sweat from his face. "Damn hot for a September morning.''

Ignoring Buddy altogether, Lane leaned against Johnny Mack. "I don't know how much more of this waiting I can stand. Something terrible has happened to Will or we would have found him by now.''

Johnny Mack hugged her close, then bent to kiss her cheek. "Don't you give up hope. We're going to find Will . . . find him alive. And when I discover who's responsible for whatever's happened to him, there's going to be hell to pay.''

If only he had hired bodyguards for Will, Lane and himself immediately upon his release from the hospital. Yeah, if only. But then hindsight was always twenty-twenty. Why he ever thought that the police in a Podunk hick town like Noble's Crossing could offer substantial protection, he didn't know. If Will was dead, if the killer had murdered again, Johnny Mack knew he would never forgive himself.

Suddenly the tracking hounds bayed as if they had trapped their quarry. Deep, prolonged wailing. The kind of howling that chilled the blood. Lane clutched the front of Johnny Mack's shirt. He soothed her with strokes across her back.

"Do you think they've found Will?'' Her anxious gaze met Johnny Mack's, hope and fear warring within each of them.

"Maybe.''

"Let's go see what they've found." She grabbed his hand and pulled him with her as she broke into a run.

The howls came from the far side of the Graham estate. Lane and Johnny Mack, along with most of the searchers, both lawmen and civilians, rushed toward the sound. Within minutes, they reached the old carriage house, used as nothing more than a tool and storage shed for the past fifty-some-odd years. The pack of hounds strained on their leashes at the carriage entrance of the dilapidated building.

"The boy must be in there," Larry Carroll proclaimed. "Them dogs aren't ever wrong."

"But the carriage house has been searched," Buddy Lawler said. "I checked it myself and there's nobody in there."

"You must have missed a spot," Larry said. "If Old Man Farlan's dogs have tracked Will Graham here from the scent off that shirt Lillie Mae gave us, then you can bet your next week's paycheck that the boy's in there somewhere."

Buried in the carriage house? The unthinkable went through Johnny Mack's mind. *God, please! Not for my sake, but for Lane's. Don't let our son be dead.*

"Open the doors," Larry shouted. "Take the dogs inside. They'll pinpoint the spot for us."

Johnny Mack restrained Lane. "Why don't you stay out here with Lillie Mae and let me go inside and see—"

"No! I'm going with you."

"Lane, honey . . ."

"Please, don't try to stop me."

As he wrapped his arm around Lane's shoulders, he caught a glimpse of Miss Edith standing beneath a nearby oak tree, a look of sincere concern on her face. Despite herself, the old bitch actually cared about Will.

"There, under that rowboat," T. C. Bedlow said. "The dogs have stopped right by it."

After surrounding the boat, several men lifted the mildewed, rotting hull, while the sheriff's deputy held tightly to the dogs' leashes. Lane gripped Johnny Mack's hand so tightly that her nails bit into his flesh. Swallowing hard, he prayed, prayed harder and more fervently than he ever had. He pleaded with God for his son's life, instead of cursing the Lord the way he had when Buddy Lawler had dumped him in the Chickasaw River fifteen years ago.

"Look there!" T. C. cried.

"Good God Almighty." Sheriff Carroll shoved aside several onlookers. "Miss Lane, come here. We've found your boy, and by the way he's squirming around, I'd say he's alive."

"I've told you a hundred times, Buddy, that I didn't see who hit me over the head." Will sat on the edge of the examining table in the Samuel Noble Memorial Hospital emergency room.

"I don't mean to upset you, son, but somebody tried their best to kill you last night and it's my job to find out just who that was." Buddy puffed out his chest. "Already looks bad that my department hasn't found out who shot Johnny Mack. How's it going to look if we can't find the person who tried to kill you?"

"I'd say if you find one, you'll find the other," Johnny Mack commented.

"Yeah, well, that could be and then again, might not be," Buddy said.

"Look, Will's told you all he knows." Lane moved between Buddy and her son. "Just leave him alone.

If you need to ask him more questions, you'll have to wait until tomorrow. After the doctor stitches up the cut on Will's head, he's being admitted for twenty-four hours of observation. Not only does he have a nasty slash on his head, but he has a mild concussion, too.''

"Why don't you talk to Mary Martha again?" Johnny Mack said. "Maybe she's more at herself this morning, and it's just possible she'll actually remember something."

"It's possible, but highly unlikely." Buddy nodded. "Nothing would please me more than if Mary Martha had one lucid day. Back before Kent was murdered, she had a good day now and then."

"I promise you that if Will remembers anything else, we'll call you immediately." Johnny Mack clutched Buddy's shoulder. "Come on, let me walk you out."

Lane breathed a sigh of relief as the two men exited the ER cubicle. If Buddy had stayed one minute longer, if he had asked one more question, she would have screamed. Considering what she had just survived, she certainly didn't want to go berserk *after the fact*. Will was alive, and except for the cut and the concussion, he was fine.

So what exactly did that mean? Had the person who had attacked her son only meant to hurt him, not kill him? Or had the attempt on Will's life somehow gone awry and he had survived by mere chance?

"May I come in?" Edith Ware asked as she hovered outside the open door.

"Will, do you want to see Miss Edith?" Lane asked.

"Sure." He glanced past Lane and smiled at the woman who had been his grandmother all his life. "Come on in." He motioned to her with a welcoming wave.

"How are you, Will?" Edith walked past Lane and went straight to the side of the examining table.

"They say I'll be fine. Comes from having such a hard noggin." He pecked himself on the side of his head. "I just need a few stitches."

"He has a minor concussion," Lane said. "They're keeping him twenty-four hours for observation."

"Was Mary Martha with you when it happened?" Edith asked.

"She was outside the old carriage house when I went inside," Will explained. "She was convinced that Kent was in there waiting on us."

Gasping, Edith clutched the strand of pearls that rested atop her bosom. "Dear Lord. You don't think . . . I mean it's not possible that she would have . . ." Tears glistened in Edith's eyes.

"Ah, Grandmother, don't cry." Will slid off the table and onto his feet; then he patted Edith on the back. "Aunt Mary Martha would never hurt me. She couldn't hurt a fly. You know she's the most gentle person in the world."

Edith's lips trembled. She swiped away the teardrops as they escaped from the corners of her eyes. "I'm so glad you're going to be all right. We were all so very worried about you. Your mother and Johnny Mack. James and I. And Buddy, too. He was determined to find you."

"I'm sure glad Sheriff Carroll brought in Old Man Farlan's hounds," Will said. "If he hadn't, who knows how long I'd have stayed under that old rowboat."

Until the killer came back for you. The horrific thought flashed through Lane's mind. She barely stifled a gasp as the realization of how close Will had come to dying hit her full force.

Dr. Lewis entered the room, followed closely by Johnny Mack. The young resident frowned when he

saw how many people were crowded into the ER
cubicle.

"Would everyone step outside, please," the doctor
said.

"Do you want me to stay?" Lane asked Will.

"Mama, your baby's a big boy now," Dr. Lewis told
her. "I don't think he needs you to hold his hand
while I put in a few stitches. Isn't that right, Will?"

"Yeah, Mama, you go on outside. I'll be fine."

Lane hated to leave, wanted to stay. But she forced
her legs to move. It wasn't as if Will were in any danger
here in the emergency room. But a mother's fears
could often be irrational. Especially when her only
child had recently come close to dying.

Johnny Mack hadn't felt as powerless as he did right
now—not in many years. He didn't like not being
in control. In Houston, he had become one of the
moneyed elite, the materialization of his every whim
only a snap of his fingers away. Anything his bank
account could pay for was his. Beautiful women pursued him. Businessmen either called him friend or
feared him. He was a man to be reckoned with, and
he liked the person he was today, who was a far cry
from that white trash *poor boy* who had fled from
Noble's Crossing years ago.

But despite his wealth, power and sophisticated
veneer, here in his hometown he would always be
Faith Cahill's bastard. In Noble's Crossing he wore
his heritage like a badge of dishonor and couldn't
escape the past. Here he had come face-to-face with
that past. Here he had to pay for his sins. And it was
here he had to make atonement to the innocents he
had wronged, no matter how inadvertent his actions
had been. The last two people on earth he would

have harmed had been harmed the most—the child he had never known existed and the woman he had never been able to forget. But he could protect them now, keep them out of harm's way. By suppertime today, three top-notch body guards, hand picked by Wyatt Foster would arrive at the Noble home.

Johnny Mack looked in the mirror, then scooped up a handful of water from the sink and washed the shave creme from his cheeks and chin. After towel drying his face, he reached for his shirt hanging on the wooden peg on the door. Just as he finished buttoning and started to stuff the shirt into the waistband of his jeans, a soft rap sounded on the outer bedroom door.

Lane entered the room, but halted a few steps over the threshold. "She's here, and Will is already downstairs talking to her, while Lillie Mae serves coffee." Wringing her hands together, Lane walked toward Johnny Mack. "I don't understand why Will is insisting on doing this now, so soon. We just brought him home from the hospital."

Leaving his shirt half in and half out of his jeans, Johnny Mack came forward and clasped Lane's nervous hands in his steady ones. "We have to let Will do this, honey. It's what he wants."

"I know." Lane clenched her teeth together and frowned.

Johnny Mack hugged her, encompassing her with all the strength he had to give. He had never realized how much a man could care for a woman, how vital her existence could become to him. He couldn't explain it, could hardly believe it, but somehow, someway, Lane had become as essential to him as the air he breathed.

"Let me finish dressing and we'll go downstairs." He hugged her again, then cupped her face with his hands and looked deeply into her beautiful blue eyes. "Whatever Will remembers . . . if he remembers anything else . . . we'll face it together. You and me and Will. A family."

Lane drew in a deep breath and released it slowly. "Thank God Lillie Mae sent for you." Tears misted her eyes. "I thought I had become a strong woman who didn't need anyone to lean on, least of all some man. But I realize that I do need someone. I need you, Johnny Mack." A lone tear trickled down her cheek.

Johnny Mack kissed her. Half comfort and half passion. Part love and part lust. A combination of all the varied emotions Lane brought to life within him. She sighed when he ended the kiss.

He pulled away and hurriedly shoved his shirttail inside his jeans, then buttoned them and snapped his belt buckle. "Let's go."

They found Will with Dr. Agee in the den, the two talking quietly. The minute he saw his parents, Will stood and went to Lane.

"Mama, stop worrying," Will said. "I can tell by the look on your face that you're scared for me. Don't be. I'll be okay. I promise."

"But what if . . ."

Standing directly behind her, Johnny Mack clutched her shoulders and gave her an encouraging squeeze. "We'll be here with him the entire time. And Dr. Agee isn't going to do anything she thinks is bad for Will."

Nola Agee came forward and smiled cordially at Lane. "Will and I have been talking, and I believe that he's ready for another session. I think his not knowing what happened that day is far more harmful to him than whatever he'll have to face when he remembers everything."

Lane and Johnny Mack took their seats, while Dr. Agee prepared first the room and then Will. Slowly, progressively, she led him into a state of relaxation, in a similar manner to the other times that she had helped him reach a deep level of meditation. She began by asking him simple questions, ones designed not to upset him; then when Will was fully prepared, she led him back to the fatal day—the last day of Kent Graham's life.

"You helped Lillie Mae to her room; then you went back outside," Dr. Agee said, mentally returning him to the moment he had encountered Kent's body. "What did you see when you walked back into the garden?"

"Kent was there. On his knees. He was moaning. And holding up his hands. God, no. Don't! Stop! Please, stop!"

"Will, calm down and tell me what's happening."

"Don't hit him again. Please. You're killing him."

"Who is hitting Kent?"

Lane gripped Johnny Mack's hand, leaned toward him and whispered, "He's never remembered this before. He's always remembered finding Kent's body. Oh, dear Lord, could he have actually seen Kent being murdered?"

"Will, who is hitting Kent?" Dr. Agee repeated.

"I grabbed my baseball bat away from her, and when I did, she ran away, crying. I saw her. Standing there near the shrubbery. I bent over to check on Kent. He was dead. And she just kept crying and crying."

Johnny Mack held his breath. *So close,* he thought. *Come on, Will. Tell us who you saw. Who killed Kent?*

"Will, who was crying? Who did you see standing near the shrubbery?" The doctor's voice remained steady and confident.

"She came through the shrubbery. I heard her voice. She said, 'What have you done?' But I couldn't say anything. I wanted to scream, 'You know I didn't kill him. You know I didn't do it.' "

"Who was there with you, Will? Who did you see? Who spoke to you?"

"You know it wasn't me!" Will cried as tears poured down his cheeks. "Oh, Grandmother, you know I didn't do it."

Chapter 26

"Ma'am, there's a phone call for Chief Lawler." Mrs. Russell, ever the humble servant, stood outside the double French doors that opened up into the living room. "It's Sergeant Bedlow."

"Take it in here," Edith told Buddy, then dismissed the housekeeper with a wave of her hand.

Buddy rose from the chair in which he had been reclining while he reassured Miss Edith that he'd had absolutely nothing to do with the near tragedy that had befallen Will Graham. He didn't think she believed him, and he simply couldn't understand her reasoning. She knew Will wasn't her grandson, knew he was the offspring of two trailer trash lowlifes, and yet she seemed to still love the boy. She shouldn't care what happened to Johnny Mack's kid, but she did. Was her affection for Will somehow connected to the fact that he was John Graham's grandson? Buddy suspected that despite their turbulent marriage, Edith had probably never loved any other man.

Buddy lifted the receiver of the fancy crystal and gold telephone resting on the cherry commode. "Chief Lawler here."

"Buddy, this here's T. C. I thought you should know that I just got the oddest call from Lane Graham."

"What kind of odd call?"

When Edith widened her eyes and stared straight at him, Buddy shook his head, indicating to her that he didn't have all the information yet.

"Well, she asked to speak to me and no one else," T. C. explained. "Then she told me that since you were so close to Kent's family, it would be better if I handled the situation. She seemed real concerned about sparing you the ordeal. But I figured since you were already there at the Graham place, there wasn't no need for me to come over and take care of something I know you're going to want to handle yourself."

"What situation? Hell, man, get to the point." When Buddy experienced a sudden choking sensation, he slipped two fingers beneath his collar to loosen it.

"You're not going to like this if it turns out to be true. It's going to be damn hard on you if you have to arrest Miss Edith."

Buddy's heartbeat accelerated at an alarming rate. "What the hell are you talking about? What did Lane tell you?"

Edith sprang off the sofa, her eyes wild with concern. Buddy pumped his hand up and down, warning her to sit down and keep quiet.

"Well, it seems that Will's got his memory back," T. C. said. "At least he remembers seeing Kent murdered. He told his therapist that he saw his grandmother hiding in the shrubbery, after she had beaten Kent to death with Will's baseball bat."

"This is ridiculous," Buddy said. "The boy's been

duped into believing some cockamamie story Lane and Johnny Mack have cooked up to try to place the blame on someone other than Lane.''

"Could be, but you sure got yourself an open can of worms here, Chief. Can you imagine what's going to happen when everybody in town hears about this new development? It'll be the boy's word against his grandmother's.''

"No one who knows Miss Edith would believe that she'd kill her own son. She adored Kent. She's been devastated by his—''

"I know all the arguments,'' T. C. said. "But right now, you've got an immediate problem. Miss Lane asked me to meet her and Johnny Mack over at the Graham house. They're on their way there now.''

"Damn!''

"And there's one other thing you should know— they've already called Wes Stevens and told him exactly what they told me. So, you'd better get Miss Edith ready for some tough questioning.''

Buddy gripped the receiver which quivered in his shaky hand. "I appreciate your letting me know.''

"Do you want me to come on over there? If somebody has to arrest Miss Edith—''

"No, I can take care of things here. And please, call Wes and tell him that I'm conducting an investigation and will report to him as soon as we sort through this mess.'' Buddy replaced the receiver and turned to Edith. "Will's memory is returning. He remembers seeing you hiding behind the shrubbery the day Kent was killed. He's told his therapist that you beat Kent to death.''

Edith closed her eyes momentarily and took a deep breath. Her slender shoulders lifted and fell slowly. Suddenly the woman looked every day of her sixty

years. The strain of these past few weeks had taken
its toll.

"Will is confused at the moment," she said. "But
if he has remembered seeing me, it's only a matter
of time before he recalls exactly what happened."

"There will have to be an investigation. There's no
way to avoid it. But you can say that yes, you were
there that day. But you can deny killing Kent. You
can say that you saw Will kill Kent and you've kept
quiet to protect the boy you've loved like a grandson
all his life." Buddy grabbed Edith by the shoulders
and shook her. "It can be your word against his. And
in this town, who are people going to believe?"

"You idiot! Framing Lane for Kent's murder was
one thing, but blaming Will is another matter altogether. I will not accuse that child of something he
didn't do." Edith jerked free of Buddy's tight grip.
"Don't you see that once Will remembers everything
and if Johnny Mack tells what he knows about Mary
Martha and Kent, people are going to believe the
truth. The vile, ugly truth."

"You're not going to involve her in this," Buddy
warned. "I will not allow her to suffer anymore."

The only reason he had become embroiled in Miss
Edith's schemes was to help protect Mary Martha. He
would do anything for her. Go to any lengths to keep
her safe. Guilt and regret had been eating away at
him for some time now, ever since he had learned
the truth about what Kent had done to Mary Martha.
If only he had known years ago. If only he had suspected the truth. He would have killed Kent. He
would have happily beaten the man to death himself.

Miss Edith had called him minutes after Kent's
murder, and together they had concocted a believ-
able story, one they hoped would protect both Edith
and Mary Martha. But before they could speak to Will

and persuade him to back up their fabricated story, Lane had arrived and phoned the police, saying that she had discovered the body. The shock of Kent's death—luckily—had traumatized Will so badly that he had suffered from partial amnesia.

"I don't see any way to keep Mary Martha out of it. We took a chance, counting on Will's amnesia being permanent," Edith said. "I had hoped Will wouldn't remember, that we could get Lane convicted and put an end to it. But that damn Johnny Mack had to come back to Noble's Crossing and stir things up."

"Well, you'd better prepare yourself to meet the devil," Buddy told her. "Lane and Johnny Mack are on their way over here right now. They've already phoned Wes Stevens and told him that you killed Kent. Thank God, T. C. called me instead of coming over here himself the way Lane had asked him to do."

Buddy knew what he had to do, what he probably should have done weeks ago. They shoot horses to put them out of their misery, but they allow people to suffer the torment of the damned. But no more. No more suffering. No more pain. Peace. The peace of eternity.

Buddy walked out of the living room, prepared to handle this situation the only way that he could—in order to protect the woman he loved. Edith ran out into the foyer and followed him to the foot of the staircase.

"Buddy, where are you going? Lane and Johnny Mack will probably be here any minute now. We need to plan our strategy."

"You plan your strategy, Miss Edith," he replied. "I'm going upstairs to see Mary Martha."

"It won't do any good to talk to her. She won't

understand what's happening." Edith wrung her hands together. "Whatever happens to me, I can survive. But if they take Mary Martha away and put her in an institution—"

"No one is ever going to put Mary Martha in a mental institution," Buddy said softly as he continued climbing the stairs.

Lane rang the doorbell several times before she gave up and tried the front door. Unlocked. How strange.

"T. C. hasn't arrived, yet," Johnny Mack said. "I think we should wait on him."

"I don't. I want to speak to Miss Edith right now! I want her to look me in the eye and deny that she killed Kent."

"She very well could deny it," Johnny Mack said. "I don't see her willingly admitting that she murdered her own son."

Johnny Mack followed Lane into the large foyer and almost ran into her when she skidded to an abrupt halt in the middle of the entranceway. She stood perfectly still. There was an unnatural quiet about the house. No activity whatsoever. Where was Mrs. Russell? For that matter, where was Edith?

"Listen," Lane said.

"I don't hear anything," Johnny Mack replied.

"Neither do I. Something isn't right. This house is never deadly quiet. And the front door is never unlocked."

Johnny Mack grabbed her shoulders and whirled her around to face him. "I want you to go outside and wait on T. C."

"And what are you going to do while I'm waiting?"

"I'll search the house. Somebody has to be here.

Since Edith fired Mrs. Bryant, she would make sure someone was with Mary Martha.''

"I'll help you look.''

Johnny Mack tightened his grasp on Lane's shoulders. "In case something goes wrong, I don't want you in harm's way. Stay here.''

"Wait!'' Lane cried, when he released her and turned to leave. "What if . . . maybe we shouldn't have trusted T. C. Maybe he notified Buddy and Buddy told Miss Edith and she's already left town.''

"I don't think Miss Edith has had time to escape. Besides, she's the type who'd stay and put up a fight, not run. She's confident enough to think she could beat a murder rap in this town.''

"If she's here, I'm not leaving this house without talking to her. I will not let her maneuver her way out of this. She's going to confess what she did, even if I have to beat the truth out of her.''

A piercing scream chilled Lane to the bone. She and Johnny Mack exchanged a quick, startled look, then immediately turned their heads in the direction of the ear-splitting yell. It had come from the second story of the house.

"Stay here,'' Johnny Mack ordered, then headed toward the staircase.

"You're not going without me.''

When he paused to issue her a warning glare, she shook her head in a refusal to obey his command and caught up with him on the fifth step. He nodded and grunted, obviously realizing that she had no intention of being left behind. Whatever was happening in this house, she wasn't going to wait and hear about it secondhand.

Together, they raced up the stairs, flung open door after door and searched for the screamer. After coming out of the third room they had checked, Lane spotted the open doorway at the end of the hall. Standing there, her mouth agape, her shoulders trembling, Mrs. Russell wandered into the hall. When she saw Lane, she reached out toward her, and even though her lips moved, she said nothing.

"That's Mary Martha's room," Lane told Johnny Mack.

Together they rushed up the hall where the house-keeper, as if in slow motion, headed toward them. Although she continued working her mouth, no words came out.

Lane grabbed the woman's shaky hands. "What's wrong, Mrs. Russell? What's happened? Are you the one who screamed?"

She nodded, then grasped Lane's hands tightly. "Help ... help them. Please." Mrs. Russell folded over, grabbed herself around the waist and began rocking back and forth as she cried.

"Come on over here and sit down." Lane led the woman to a settee nestled within a small alcove in the hallway, then knelt down in front of her. "Will you be all right here while we check on Mary Martha?"

"I'll be all right," Mrs. Russell said. "But she's not ... she's not ... she ... please, go help Miss Edith."

Lane didn't know what to expect, had no idea what they would face when they entered Mary Martha's bedroom. The room seemed unchanged in any way. A little girl's fantasy room. Bright and beautiful and filled with light. No blood. No gore. No stench. Nothing the least bit frightening.

Miss Edith sat on the side of the bed, her arms draped around Mary Martha, who lay quietly, her head in her mother's lap. A serene scene of maternal affection. Edith repeatedly smoothed Mary Martha's hair away from her face.

"Miss Edith?" Lane approached the bed, Johnny Mack following directly behind her.

Edith glanced up, her eyes slightly dazed, her expression mournfully sad. "She won't ever suffer again. She's at peace for the first time since she was a little girl."

Lane's breath caught in her throat. Lord, no! Had Edith actually killed her daughter? Had she murdered both of her children? As Lane drew closer to the bed, she noticed that Mary Martha lay unnervingly still. She wasn't breathing!

Johnny Mack placed a hand on Lane's shoulder. "Find a phone and call T. C. Tell him to get his ass over here as fast as possible and send an ambulance."

Just as Lane nodded agreement, Edith spoke, halting Lane's exit.

"I had no idea what was happening between Kent and Mary Martha. I knew they were very close, that they loved each other dearly, but it never once entered my mind that Kent would have . . . that he could have. . . . I should never have married. I should never have had children."

"Miss Edith, do you know what you've done?" Johnny Mack asked as he approached the bed.

"Yes, I know," she replied, and when Johnny Mack knelt beside the bed, she reached out and stroked his face. "So like John. In every way. He loved me once. When we first married. He wanted a son. Even knowing the risk I took in giving him a child, I. . . . It was wrong of me to bring babies into this world when I knew that my own dear mother had been sick. So sick. And her father before her. I knew and yet I took the chance, and my children paid the price."

"What are trying to tell us?" Johnny Mack took her hands in his.

"If I hadn't been so involved with social events and

elicit love affairs . . . if I'd paid more attention to Kent and Mary Martha, I might have realized what was happening. I thought Kent was normal. If I'd spent more time with him, I could have put a stop to what he was doing and gotten him the help he needed. And maybe Mary Martha could have been helped, too.

"But my children were never my top priority. I had them because John wanted them. My life was too full . . . I was too busy to be bothered with them. And look what happened."

Lane eased closer to the bed, her heartbeat humming inside her head. How was it possible that she could actually feel sorry for Miss Edith, even knowing that she had murdered both of her children?

"What happened?" Johnny Mack prodded. "Tell us what you did the day Kent died and what you did today."

Edith pulled her hands from Johnny Mack's and gazed down at her daughter. "Look at her. So beautiful. So sweet and gentle and loving. But so damaged. And it's all my fault. If I'd been a better mother, I could have spared her from so much. All these years, I didn't understand. I didn't know. Not until the truth came out about Will's true paternity. That morning Kent had come by the house, and Mary Martha overheard us talking. I've never seen her react in such a violent way."

Edith covered her face with her hands and wept. Johnny Mack glanced at Lane, and she realized that he was as confused as she. Confused by their odd sympathy for a woman they both disliked intensely. And confused as to why she had felt compelled to murder her own children.

Edith continued speaking, her voice eerily soft and completely controlled. "Mary Martha ran toward

Kent and began hitting him with her little fists, and all the while she kept screaming, 'You made me kill my baby, but you let her baby live. You didn't want my baby, but you wanted hers.' I didn't understand. But I listened when Kent began talking to Mary Martha, telling her that Will *was* her baby, that her baby hadn't died.''

Lane gasped. Was it possible that Mary Martha had been pregnant and the child had been Kent's? Yes, of course it was possible.

Kent had gotten his sister pregnant!

''Miss Edith, are you saying that Mary Martha had at one time been pregnant with Kent's child?'' Johnny Mack asked.

''Yes,'' Edith replied. ''That summer, fifteen years ago, only a few months before Sharon Hickman discovered she was carrying your child, Kent had taken Mary Martha to a private clinic in Birmingham for an abortion.''

Lane thought she might vomit. Sour bile rose in her throat and left a bitterness on her tongue. Poor, pitiful Mary Martha. And that bastard Kent had encouraged her to believe that Will was her baby, the child he had forced her to abort. No wonder that all these years, Mary Martha had thought Will was her son.

''You see, Mary Martha's memories of that abortion had been buried deep in her subconscious until the truth came out about Will,'' Edith said. ''Then suddenly she began remembering . . . remembering what Kent had done to her. And remembering that he had made her abort their child.

''That day, the day Kent died, I'd left her in the garden to go into the kitchen and ask Mrs. Russell to prepare us some iced tea, but when I returned Mary Martha had disappeared. At first, I was fright-

ened when I couldn't find her, but then as I neared
the row of shrubs that separate our property from
the Nobles', I heard her talking to Kent. I walked
through the wooden arbor in the middle of the
hedge, and that's when I saw—'' Edith sucked in a
deep breath. ''Kent was on his knees, obviously drunk,
and Mary Martha had Will's baseball bat in her hands.
She was striking him with it, and before I could reach
her, she hit him in the head repeatedly.''

Edith gulped down tears. ''She kept saying, 'You
made me kill my baby. You made me kill my baby.' ''

''And Will saw what happened, too,'' Lane said.
''He just doesn't remember it all. Not yet. That's why
he. . . . You weren't asking him what he'd done; you
were asking Mary Martha. She's the one he heard
crying.'' Lane shook her head sadly as the truth
became crystal clear. ''Why did you put us all through
this nightmare when you could have admitted the
truth? Mary Martha wasn't responsible for what she
did. She wouldn't have gone to prison.''

''She would have spent the rest of her life in a
mental institution,'' Edith said. ''I couldn't allow that
to happen.''

Johnny Mack rose to his feet and faced Lane. ''Call
T. C. Now. I'll stay with Miss Edith. And while you're
at it, call James. She's going to need a lawyer.''

''Right. I'll check on Mrs. Russell and see if I can
get her to go downstairs. T. C. must have been delayed
by something. He should have gotten here by now.''

When Lane found the housekeeper just where she
had left her, she asked her if she wanted to go downstairs, to her own room, but the woman refused to
budge.

''I should go back in there and see to Miss Edith.
That poor woman.'' Mrs. Russell sobbed quietly.
''Miss Mary Martha dead. Sweet, pitiful child.''

"Yes, Miss Mary Martha is dead."

"I suppose she's better off, but it's such a shock. When I first saw her, I thought she was just sleeping, but then Miss Edith told me she was dead. . . . I shouldn't have screamed, but I couldn't help it. I was so shocked."

"It's all right." Lane patted Mrs. Russell on the back. "I'm sure Johnny Mack could use some help seeing to Miss Edith. He's going to stay with her while I make some phone calls."

Lane helped the housekeeper to her feet, then gave her a pat on the back before she went in search of a telephone in one of the bedrooms. Just as she started to enter the nearest room, she heard something downstairs. Footsteps on the marble floor in the foyer? Maybe T. C. had finally arrived.

Lane flew down the stairs, but came to an abrupt halt when she saw Buddy Lawler waiting for her at the bottom. *He's the chief of police,* she reminded herself. *Even if he doesn't want to arrest Miss Edith, he'll have no choice. And once he learns that she has killed Mary Martha—Buddy will go crazy when he finds out that the girl he's loved since they were kids has been murdered by her own mother.*

"What are you doing here?" Buddy asked.

Lane took several tentative steps farther down the stairs. "I could ask you the same question."

"T. C. told me about your telephone call," he said. "I told him that I'd handle the situation."

"Then, T. C. isn't coming?"

"Whatever police business there is here, I'll be the one to handle it."

"All right." A peculiar uneasiness settled in Lane's stomach. "But I'd think it would be easier if you let T. C. arrest Miss Edith."

Why was Buddy so pale? Why was he sweating so

profusely when the temperature was only in the low eighties today? And why were his hands trembling?

Lane stopped at the foot of the stairs, instinct warning her that she couldn't trust Buddy, that even if he was a policeman, his first loyalty was and always had been to the Graham family and not to upholding the law.

"Get Miss Edith a glass of water," Johnny Mack instructed the housekeeper.

Mrs. Russell nodded, hurried into the adjoining bathroom and returned with a glass, which she handed to her employer. Then she glanced at Johnny Mack. "I can't believe that Miss Mary Martha's really dead. But she is, isn't she?"

"Yes," he replied.

Mrs. Russell clasped her hands together and shook her head sadly. "She was fine earlier today. But this afternoon when I brought her a nice bowl of ice cream, she was . . ." Mrs. Russell nodded to the bowl which lay in the middle of the floor, its melted chocolate contents staining the area rug. "She enjoyed a little treat in the afternoons." The housekeeper continued shaking her head. "I panicked when Miss Edith told me that Miss Mary Martha was dead. I didn't mean to scream. I just don't understand what happened. How did she die?"

"She was smothered," Edith said quite calmly, then lifted a satin pillow from the floor. "With this."

"Oh, Lord have mercy!" Mrs. Russell said.

"Why did you do it?" Johnny Mack asked. "How could you have killed her?"

"I—I. . . . You think I smothered Mary Martha?" Edith gazed at him, an expression of surprised disbelief on her face. "I didn't kill my daughter. He did."

"Who did?" Johnny Mack asked, fear clawing at his throat.

"Buddy did. He said that he killed her because he loved her. He did it to protect her, to keep her from spending the rest of her life locked up in a mental hospital."

"Buddy did this?"

"Yes, he did it because he loves her so dearly. Everything he's done, he's done to protect her, just as I have. He killed Jackie when she overheard a conversation between Buddy and me and she tried to blackmail us. And he shot you. And he tried to kill Will."

"And you knew what he was doing and didn't do a thing to stop him."

"By the time I realized just what lengths he'd go to in order to keep the truth from coming to light, it was too late for me to do anything. Buddy and I were in this together. I couldn't turn him in without revealing that Mary Martha had killed Kent.

"I had no idea that he'd actually . . . that he would take her pillow and smother her. I followed him upstairs and found him doing it. I tried to stop him, tried to pull the pillow off her face, but—" Edith broke down and flung herself across her daughter's lifeless body.

"Stay here with Miss Edith," Johnny Mack told a stunned Mrs. Russell.

The police had to be alerted that their chief was a murderer. Buddy Lawler was a dangerous man, one whose actions were unpredictable. Lane was alone downstairs. Lillie Mae and Will were alone next door. And no local policeman would question the chief if he showed up at either house. Johnny Mack's guts tightened, and he sensed danger close by. He had to get to Lane. Now.

When he reached the landing, he heard voices.

Lane was talking to someone. A man. He stopped at the head of the stairs and looked down into the foyer. Buddy Lawler glanced up at him, and their gazes locked for a split second.

"Johnny Mack is upstairs with Miss Edith." Lane lifted her foot and eased backward, up one step. "Let me tell him that you're here."

Buddy rushed Lane before Johnny Mack could reach her. He clamped his hand over her mouth, twisted her arm behind her back and dragged her off the stairs and into the foyer.

"Don't hurt her!" Gut-wrenching fear dampened Johnny Mack's face with perspiration as he ran down the stairs.

"You stop right where you are, Cahill," Buddy warned.

Johnny Mack froze to the spot, halfway down the stairs, halfway to Lane. "Let her go. You don't want to add another murder to the list, do you? Lane's never done a thing to you."

Buddy unsnapped his holster. Johnny Mack realized he could never make it to Lane in time. He was too far away. He watched helplessly as Buddy withdrew his Magnum and aimed the weapon at Lane's head.

Buddy eased his hand away from Lane's mouth and down to her throat. "Tell your lover goodbye."

"Buddy, please, you don't want to hurt me." Lane spoke to her abductor, but her gaze settled on Johnny Mack's face.

"You're right, I don't want to hurt you," Buddy said. "But I didn't want to hurt Mary Martha either. I had no choice. I did what I had to do. She was too sweet, too fragile to endure years in a mental hospital. I knew she'd rather be dead than to go through that."

"You killed Mary Martha?" Lane gasped.

Trembling from head to toe, Buddy tightened his

hold on Lane and dragged her backward, toward the partially open front door. Johnny Mack waited until Buddy had taken Lane outside before he ran the rest of the way down the stairs. He had to find a way to stop Buddy. The man wasn't thinking straight; he was acting irrationally. There was no telling what he would do next. Where the hell was T. C.? He should have been here by now. A blood-chilling thought crossed Johnny Mack's mind—what if T. C. had told Buddy about Lane's call and that was why he had shown up? What if T. C. wasn't on his way to the Graham house?

If only he had a weapon of some sort, a way to stop Buddy. If he rushed Buddy, the man was liable to kill Lane.

"Here, take this."

Johnny Mack whirled around at the sound of the familiar female voice. Miss Edith stood a few feet away, a rifle in her hand. She held it out to him.

"It's one of your daddy's rifles," she said. "I went up to the attic and got it and loaded it for you. Take it and do what you have to do to save Lane. There's been too much killing. It's got to stop. For Will's sake."

His mind jumbled with confusing thoughts and mixed emotions. He grabbed the rifle and ran. Outside, in the driveway, Buddy tried to force Lane into his car, but she struggled with him. Where the hell did Buddy think he was going? Had the man completely lost his mind?

Johnny Mack knew that he had one chance. One shot to save Lane. If he missed, Buddy would kill her. And if that happened, nothing else mattered. In that one split second he understood how Miss Edith must feel. With both of her children dead, what did she have to live for?

He had handled a gun all his life. Wiley Peters had

taken him hunting every year during deer season. And Judge Brown, who had been an avid hunter, had trained him to be a sportsman. But this was the first time someone's life depended upon his marksmanship.

Johnny Mack prepared quickly. No time for anything except action. Getting his quarry in his sights, he drew in and held a deep breath, then aimed and fired.

Chapter 27

Lane had been opposed to Will visiting Miss Edith at the jail, but her son had insisted that he wanted to see his grandmother. She supposed Will would always think of Kent's mother that way. Even knowing the part she had played in the recent events that had resulted in death and tragedy for so many, Will's kind heart urged him to comfort a woman whom he had once loved so dearly. Perhaps in her own way, Miss Edith still loved Will, too.

Johnny Mack waited with Lane, he a tower of strength in comparison to her being little more than a bundle of nerves. In the past twenty-four hours since Miss Edith had confessed to helping cover up the truth concerning Kent's murder and the subsequent actions Buddy Lawler had taken to shield Mary Martha, James Ware had, despite Edith's icy cold attitude, stood staunchly at her side. He had hired his wife a high-priced lawyer out of Atlanta, made funeral arrangements for his stepdaughter and found time to plead with Johnny Mack and Lane not to turn him in to the police.

"Give me a chance to return the money I stole from Edith," James had said. "All I want, all I've ever wanted was to be with Arlene. We can find a way to make it just fine without Edith's money."

But even now, Miss Edith kept the deepest, darkest family secret. The sordid little tale of incest and a child conceived in that sinful act. Neither she nor Johnny Mack saw any need to reveal that truth, not when it could serve no purpose.

Lane would never forget how close she had come to dying, how easily Buddy Lawler could have pulled the trigger. She owed her life to Johnny Mack. He had killed a man to protect her. And in an odd way, she had Miss Edith to thank. After all, her former mother-in-law had provided Johnny Mack with the weapon.

T. C. Bedlow walked alongside Will, bringing him out from the holding cells in the back of the building into the heart of the police station. The apologetic sergeant had bowed and scraped and said I'm sorry a dozen times over, and they had assured him that they didn't hold him responsible. After all, he'd had no way of knowing that Buddy had snapped and become a danger to those around him. No one had even suspected.

"I'm ready to leave now," Will said as he approached his parents.

"How did it go with Miss Edith?" Lane asked.

"Okay, I guess." Will shrugged. "She's got herself a lawyer coming in from Atlanta. A guy named Steve Whitaker. He's supposed to be every bit as good as Quinn Cortez."

"Yes, we know," Lane said. "I spoke with James

this morning. He's the one who arranged for Mr. Whitaker to defend Miss Edith.''

"She's sure the judge will set bail this afternoon and she'll be home by tonight," Will said. "She asked me if I could ever forgive her."

Johnny Mack laid his hand on Will's shoulder. "What did you say?"

"I told her I didn't honestly know."

"Lane, why don't you and Will go on home," Johnny Mack suggested. "I have a little unfinished business here that I need to take care of before I leave."

"Will it take long?" Lane asked.

"No, not long."

She clutched his arm. "We could just wait for you in the car."

"No, don't wait. After I finish up here, I plan to drop by the mayor's office. Then I want to take a walk around Noble's Crossing. I have some decisions to make and I need some time alone."

"All right. We'll see you at the house later." She kissed his cheek. He offered her a half-hearted smile.

Lane hurried Will out the door and onto the sidewalk. He didn't question why she was rushing, but once they were seated inside the car, he reached over and hugged her.

"It's not about you, Mama," Will said. "Johnny Mack killed a man yesterday. That's what's wrong with him. Even though he did what he had to do to save your life, he's the kind of man who'd regret taking any human being's life."

Lane ruffled her son's hair. "When did you grow up and become so smart?"

* * *

Johnny Mack took a good hard look at Edith Ware. Not even dealing with her daughter's death and spending the night behind bars made the woman appear any less regal. She had been born Noble's Crossing royalty, and she would no doubt die the same.

"Come to gloat?" she asked.

"Nope. Came to make a deal with you. It's a win-win situation."

"What sort of deal?" In a giveaway gesture of nervousness, she ran the tips of her red nails over the legs of her black slacks.

"Lane and I know the truth about Kent. That he sexually abused Mary Martha for years and that he forced her to abort his child."

"Y'all know too much. If I'd been thinking straight, I wouldn't have shared so much information with you two. I should have just told you and Lane what I told the police, that my daughter's mental problems reached a severe point and she didn't know what she was doing when she killed her brother."

"We wouldn't have bought that explanation and you know it."

Edith nodded, the weak smile on her lips quivering ever so slightly. "I realize you don't owe me anything, and I'm not asking for myself, but for—"

"Lane and I don't intend to mention anything about Kent and Mary Martha's incestuous relationship. Not to the press. Not even to the police."

"Thank you."

"Don't thank me yet," he said. "Our silence will cost you."

"What do you mean it'll cost me?" Edith's sharply defined eyebrows rose as her eyes widened with curiosity.

"Well, it seems your husband has been embezzling

money from your accounts for the past few years and—"

"What!"

"I'd say he's got at least a hundred thousand stashed away, if not more."

"Why, that weasel, that boot-licking, cowardly little bastard!"

"Here's the deal, Miss Edith"—he couldn't help grinning when she ceased her tirade and glared at him—"you give James an uncontested divorce, pay him a hundred-thousand-dollar settlement and swear you won't have him prosecuted for embezzling. If you do all that, then your family's dirty little secret is safe. Lane and I will take it to our graves. Of course, I can't swear Mrs. Russell won't—"

"Nelda Russell is a loyal, trusted servant."

"All the same, I'd give her a really good Christmas bonus this year."

"Why do you care about James? The two of you were never friends." Edith's mouth twitched in an almost smile. "You do realize that James knew exactly what Buddy and Kent did to you fifteen years ago. He didn't do a thing to try to save you."

"I'm well aware of James's past sins."

"Then, why help him?"

"Let's just say that I know what it's like to make some bad mistakes and then to finally get a second chance with the only woman you've ever loved."

"James has a woman on the side?" Edith's expression hardened. "Is that what you're saying? I should have known. He certainly wasn't warming my bed."

"Do we or do we not have a deal?" Johnny Mack asked.

"We have a deal." Edith smiled. A wicked, powerful-people-never-lose smile. "Tell James that once the divorce is final, he'd better take his money and his whore and leave Noble's Crossing for good. Because I'll soon be back home and I never want to see his lying, cheating, thieving face again.

"I don't intend to serve any prison time. Steve Whitaker should be able to easily prove that Buddy was the villian in all this, that I was afraid to cross him. You see, he loved my daughter to the point of madness, and what I did, I did out of fear he would harm her, which in the end, he did. I was so traumatized by seeing Mary Martha kill Kent that I can't be held responsible for my actions."

Edith laughed. A cold, vicious sound that scraped up Johnny Mack's spine like a dull-bladed knife.

Where was the sad, regretful, pitiful mother who had held her dead daughter in her lap and had taken full responsibility for her children's ruined lives? Eaten alive and swallowed by the real Edith Noble Graham Ware, the self-centered, self-serving bitch who would survive at any cost. He didn't doubt for a minute that she would come out of this ordeal with little or no jail time. Using her wealth and the power she wielded in this county and state, she knew the odds were in her favor.

And the strange thing was, he didn't care. He didn't give a damn if Miss Edith got off scot-free. Actually, he didn't give a damn what happened in Noble's Crossing once he was gone. He could never stay here in the town that had scorned him, belittled him and in the end disposed of him like yesterday's trash. The sooner he got back to Texas, the better.

"I'll let James know that you want a divorce," Johnny Mack said.

"You do that."

When he turned to leave, she called after him. "You're not planning on staying in Noble's Crossing, are you?"

Without giving her even a backward glance, he replied. "No, ma'am. I'll be leaving soon, and this time it's for good. I won't be back."

Lane removed her navy blue straw hat and laid it on top of the dresser, then kicked off her navy heels and stretched her toes. Without removing her suit, she lay down on the bed, flat on her back, and stared up at the ten-foot ceiling.

Mary Martha's funeral had been bittersweet, much like the woman herself. Sunshine had flooded through the stained-glass windows. The choir had sung several hymns that brought tears to everyone's eyes. Flowers had filled the sanctuary to overflowing. And a black-clad Edith Ware had sat beside James on the front bench, her head held regally high as she had cried silently.

A rap on her bedroom door ended Lane's musings. She sat up, ran her fingers through her hair and scooted to the edge of the bed.

"May I speak to you?" Johnny Mack asked through the closed door.

"Yes, of course. Please come in."

He entered just as she stood to meet him. The sadness that had prevailed at the chapel seemed to have followed them home. Standing there in his gray, pinstriped suit, Johnny Mack looked at her, a somber expression on his face.

"I've been putting off talking to you about this." He bowed his head a fraction and gazed down at the floor.

Lane's heart stopped momentarily. She held her breath. "You're leaving," she said.

He nodded. "Yeah. I've done what I came here to do. I've met my son and gotten to know him. And we found Kent's real murderer. Mary Martha's been laid to rest, and Miss Edith's trial is slated to begin in a couple of months." He lifted his gaze to Lane's face. "I can't stay in Noble's Crossing. I don't belong here. My life is in Texas."

"Your life is in Texas and my life is here. Is that what you're saying?"

"Not exactly. I'm just trying to explain that I can't live here in Noble's Crossing."

"So, you're going to leave me . . . leave us. Again." *Don't cry. Don't you dare cry. If he can leave you so easily, then he doesn't love you. He never has.*

"That's just it," he said. "I don't want to leave you and Will. I love you, Lane. I think I always have. And I love my son."

"Then, how can you talk about leaving?" She took a tentative step toward him, her heart filling with hope.

"I can't stay here, but you and Will could come with me. And Lillie Mae, too."

"You want us to come with you?" Fifteen years ago she had begged him to take her with him. Fifteen years ago, she would have gone without a second thought. But how could she just pack a bag and go? She had responsibilities. She still owned forty-nine percent of the *Herald*. She had her family's home entrusted to her. And Will. What would Will think about moving to Texas? She wasn't sure he would want to live with his father.

"You're taking way too long to answer me. I remember a time when you wouldn't have thought about it; you'd have just said yes."

"Things were more simple then. My life is complicated now. Back then I was a teenage girl, not a woman with commitments and responsibilities and—"

"The decision isn't complicated, Lane. It's very

simple. Either you love me enough to go with me to Texas and become my wife or you don't.''

Johnny Mack's wife. The dream of a lifetime. To be the one woman on earth he truly loved.

''I love you,'' she said, holding out her hands beseechingly. ''I've never loved anyone else. But you're asking me to make an instant decision, to uproot Will, to change my entire life, to leave the home that's been in my family for generations. You could stay here with us. We could build a good life together. You and Will and I.''

''You don't know me as well as I thought you did if you think I can stay in Noble's Crossing. I love you and I want to spend the rest of my life with you, but it can't be here. I'll live with you anywhere else on earth, but not here.''

''I love you, too, but—''

''I'm leaving tonight,'' he said. ''I've neglected my business in Houston long enough. If you change your mind . . .''

He left her standing there in the middle of her bedroom. Stunned. Hurt. Angry. He expected her to give up her life to go with him, but he wasn't willing to do the same for her.

You're a fool if you don't go with him, an inner voice told her. *If you give up this chance for happiness, you'll never get another.*

''Mama?''

Lane glanced up and saw Will standing in the doorway. ''Will, sweetie, what is it?''

''I'm afraid I was eavesdropping,'' he admitted. ''I heard Johnny Mack ask you to marry him and go to Texas to live.''

''How would you feel about leaving Noble's Crossing? About my marrying Johnny Mack?'' she asked. ''Could you live in Texas with your father?''

"I could live in Texas," he said. "I could live anywhere as long as I'm with you, Mama. Don't you know that? And if you love Johnny Mack and want to marry him, it's okay with me. I'd say it's high time you two got together permanently, wouldn't you?"

"Do you mean it? You really could live in Texas with Johnny Mack?"

"Sure. Why not? What kid doesn't want to live with both of his parents?"

"Oh, Will." She grabbed him and hugged him fiercely.

"Don't you think you'd better go tell Johnny Mack the good news and put the man out of his misery?"

Lane laughed. "You're right. You're so right."

She found him in his bedroom, placing clothes in his suitcase, which lay open on the bed.

"May I come in?" she asked.

"Sure." He didn't look up from the task at hand, just continued fitting socks and underwear alongside his shirts and jeans.

"I'm not going to sell this house," she said. "And I'm keeping my forty-nine percent of the *Herald*. I'd like to give both to Will one day or to Will and whatever other children we might have. Is that all right with you?"

He looked up, and the corners of his mouth lifted gradually into a smile.

"I want a small, intimate wedding, performed by a minister. I want Will and Lillie Mae to be our witnesses. And I want a honeymoon. Nothing fancy. Just a few days alone with you."

"How does a week at my ranch in the Texas Hill Country sound?"

"It sounds wonderful."

Johnny Mack opened his arms, and Lane flew into his embrace. He lifted her off her feet and twirled her around and around until he fell over on the bed and took her with him.

"I promise that you'll never regret—"

She laid her index finger over his lips. "The only thing I regret is that we've lost so many years when we could have been together."

"We'll make up for lost time," he told her, then covered her mouth with his.

Epilogue

Lane rested in the big wooden rocker on the porch, two-year-old Cathy Sue Cahill sleeping peacefully in her lap. Four-year-old Michael Cahill wrestled on the floor with the family's black lab, Bailey. A cool autumn breeze floated across the wide ranch house porch. She had loved Johnny Mack's Hill Country home the moment she laid eyes on it, five years ago when he had brought her here for their honeymoon. Since then they had spent more and more time here, until finally last year when Will had left to attend the University of Alabama, her father's old alma mater, Johnny Mack had sold their house in Houston and moved the family to the ranch permanently.

"Got them chocolate chip cookies ready." Lillie Mae came outside and peered into the distance. "I thought Will and Johnny Mack would be home by now."

"I think Will is having girl trouble," Lane said. "He's asking his father for advice."

"Lord help us all if he's asking that rascal for advice on his love life."

Lane laughed. "Johnny Mack may be a rascal, but he's my rascal. And who better to give Will sound advice than a man who made more than his share of mistakes and knows it."

"Here they come!" Michael jumped up and down. "I see their horses."

"Quiet down before you wake your sister."

Lane shushed her exuberant son. He always got excited when his big brother came home for a weekend visit. Will adored his younger siblings and they him.

"Michael's right," Lillie Mae said. "I can make out Johnny Mack's big Appaloosa." She reached down and lifted Cathy Sue out of Lane's lap. "I'll go put her down for her nap before I start supper."

Lane stood, stretched and grabbed Michael's hand. Together they raced toward the stables. The minute Johnny Mack dismounted, he dragged Lane into his arms and gave her a passionate kiss. Will reached down and lifted Michael up on his shoulders.

"They're always kissing," Michael said. "If they're not kissing each other, they're kissing me and Cathy Sue."

"Don't you like to be kissed?" Will asked teasingly, then pulled Michael off his neck. Swooping his little brother down to the ground, he goosed him in the ribs. "Maybe you like tickling better than kissing."

Michael giggled as he squirmed away from Will, who immediately began chasing his little brother. As the boys ran toward the house, Johnny Mack grabbed Lane around the waist and pulled her back into his arms.

"Mrs. Cahill, have I thanked you lately?"

"Thanked me for what?" she asked, her tone ever so innocent.

"For making me the happiest man in the world."

"Oh, that." She lifted her arms, draped them around his neck and nuzzled his nose with hers. "Words are nice, but I prefer action. Tonight when the kids are all tucked in, how about showing me your appreciation."

"There's nothing I'd like better."

Arm-in-arm, smiling happily, Lane and Johnny Mack headed for home. Although the past would be a part of them always, they lived in the present, within the security of their love, united forever by the bonds of the family they had created together.

NOWHERE TO RUN

The crime scenes are horrifying: the victims arranged
with deliberate care, posed to appear alive despite
their agonized last moments and the shocking
nature of their deaths.

NO PLACE TO HIDE

Chattanooga grief counselor Audrey Sherrod moon-
lights for the local police. It's clear to her, and to
Special Agent J.D. Cass, that the murders are the
work of a deranged serial killer. At first, the only link
is the victims' similar physical appearance. But then
another connection emerges, tying them to a long-ago
series of horrifying crimes Audrey hoped would never
resurface—crimes that hit all too close to home.

NO TIME TO CRY

Each grisly new discovery proves the past has not been
forgotten, and the worst is yet to come. Audrey went
looking for the truth and she's about to find it . . .
and it will be more twisted and more terrifying
than she ever imagined . . .

**Please read on for an exciting sneak peek of
Beverly Barton's
DON'T CRY,
coming in September 2010!**

J.D. Cass listened to his breakfast date's end of the telephone conversation and knew it was bad news. In his profession, bad news was the norm, as it was in Holly's, so he wasn't surprised. When a guy was dating, even in an on-again/off-again relationship, an assistant district attorney, he became accustomed to their dates being interrupted by business. Of course, it worked both ways. How many times had one of Holly's meticulously planned romantic evenings ended abruptly when he'd gotten an urgent call?

They hadn't managed to get together for the past three weeks, and J.D. was way past horny. So, yeah, his invitation for them to share an early breakfast today was his selfish way of wooing her back into his bed, and the sooner the better. Since he and Holly were both early risers, a 6:30 A.M. breakfast date had seemed the perfect chance to see each other and the least likely time that their professional lives would intrude. So much for great ideas.

"My God!" Holly Johnston's big blue eyes widened and her full lips parted in a silent gasp. "Who found her? Hmm . . . When? Is the press already there?"

Curious about the identity of the person who had been found and eager to hear the details, J.D. frowned when his own cell phone rang. He checked caller ID and grunted.

He hit the On button. "Cass here. What's up?"

"They found Jill Scott." His boss, SAC Phil Hayes, had a deep baritone voice made even rougher and throaty from a lifetime of smoking.

"Alive?"

"No."

"Where?"

"How close are you to Lookout Valley?"

"Why?" J.D. got a sinking feeling in the pit of his stomach.

"Because we're fixing to get dragged into this mess, so I want you to head on over to the crime scene pronto."

"Shit! Why is the TBI getting involved?"

"Because the DA wants us to be on standby. It turns out that there is a second missing woman. Debra Gregory, the mayor's wife's cousin, disappeared sometime late last night."

"Doesn't the mayor think his own police force can handle the investigation? This isn't our—"

"His Honor wants to use every resource available to him," Phil said. "And that includes us, buddy boy. The mayor called the DA and then Everett Harrelson called me personally fifteen minutes ago. Last night, the Chattanooga PD had two missing persons cases. This morning they have a murder case and a suspected kidnapping case. Since both women fit the same profile, there's a chance the same guy kidnapped Jill and Debra."

"When I show up at the crime scene, just how official am I?"

"You're unofficial for the time being. We'll ease into this gradually. Tell the investigators you're there in an advisory capacity. Assure them that the TBI isn't taking over their case."

"Yeah, sure. Like they're going to believe that."

After J.D. returned his phone to the belt holder, he looked across the table at Holly. She slid her phone into an outer pocket on her shoulder bag and shrugged.

"Bad news?" he asked.

She nodded. "What about you?"

"Yeah. That was Phil. They believe they've found Jill Scott, the woman who's been missing for the past two weeks."

Scott, a local middle school teacher, beloved by students and parents alike, had mysteriously disappeared two weeks earlier. Her parents, her fiancé, and her friends assured police that Jill would never leave without a word to anyone. They were convinced that she'd been abducted. Thanks to local media coverage, there probably wasn't a man, woman, or child in Hamilton County who didn't know the teacher's name.

"It seems our calls were about the same case," Holly told him. "Of course, I'm not actually involved with the case, not yet, but—"

"But your nephew was in Jill Scott's seventh-grade class and her murder is semipersonal for you, right?"

Holly nodded. "So, did the TBI get drafted to—?"

"Unofficially at this point," J.D. said. "But that status can change at any time." He offered Holly a life-sucks-sometimes frown. "I have to head over to the crime scene." He stood, pulled out his wallet, and laid down a couple of twenties to pay for their meal, plus a generous tip.

"Mind if I go with you?" she asked.

When he gave her an inquisitive stare, she said, "I'll stay out of the way. I know that I'm nothing more than a concerned citizen." She smiled. "Okay, a nosy concerned citizen."

"And I'm a TBI agent sticking my nose in where I may not be wanted and probably won't be welcomed."